EMBODIMENTS OF THE IDEAL

Shingrayu pulled himself out to his full length, an impressive eighteen feet, and drew his scales in tight so that he seemed to blaze green in the murk. "We see prey and we eat. We see invaders and we defend. We see insult and we take offense. We see Svayyah's ambition and we protect ourselves and our ways. There will be no serpent queen here."

The other nagas raced through the water at the sound of those words, whirling faster and faster around the bubble Devorast floated in until it began to turn in the water. He held out his hands—those freakish appendages of the *dista'ssara*—and steadied himself. Svayyah waited for him to speak, but he said nothing. He met her eyes finally and she fell into his gaze in a way she couldn't understand—in a way that almost made her believe that Shingrayu had been right all along.

The Sea of Fallen Stars and the Shining Sea,
two of Faerûn's greatest trade routes,
forever separated by a few dozen miles of land.

One man dares to accomplish his vision,
to build a canal joining these two great seas.

The only things standing in his way
are the rulers of Innarlith,
the Red Wizards of Thay,
a faction of bloodthirsty nagas,
and the haunted passions of the most beautiful
woman in all of Faerûn.

FORGOTTEN REALMS®

The **Watercourse** Trilogy

Book 1
WHISPER OF WAVES

Book 2
LIES OF LIGHT

Book 3
SCREAM OF STONE
JUNE 2007

FORGOTTEN REALMS®

PHILIP ATHANS
LIES OF LIGHT

The Watercourse Trilogy BOOK II

LIES OF LIGHT
The Watercourse Trilogy, Book II

Cover art by Carl Critchlow
Map by Rob Lazzaretti
First Printing: September 2006
Library of Congress Catalog Card Number: 2005935521

9 8 7 6 5 4 3 2 1

ISBN-10: 0-7869-4019-0
ISBN-13: 978-0-7869-4019-6
620-95547740-001-EN

U.S., CANADA,	EUROPEAN HEADQUARTERS
ASIA, PACIFIC, & LATIN AMERICA	Hasbro UK Ltd
Wizards of the Coast, Inc.	Caswell Way
P.O. Box 707	Newport, Gwent NP9 0YH
Renton, WA 98057-0707	GREAT BRITAIN
+1-800-324-6496	Save this address for your records.

Visit our web site at www.wizards.com

For Peter Archer
My boss, my editor, and my friend.

ACKNOWLEDGMENTS

Marek Rymüt's speech to the Guild of Stevedores was paraphrased from the article *The Rise of a New Labor Movement* by Henk Canne Meijer, first published in German in *Rätekorrespondenz*, numbers 8-9 (April 1935), and translated in *International Council Correspondence*, number 10 (August 1935). The complete text can be found at: http://www.geocities.com/~johngray/canne.htm.

Inspiration continues to be drawn from *The Fountainhead* and other writings of Ayn Rand.

Other sources cited include *Faiths & Pantheons* by Eric L. Boyd and Erik Mona; *Complete Adventurer* by Jesse Decker; *Serpent Kingdoms* by Ed Greenwood, Eric L. Boyd, and Darrin Drader; *Cormyr* by Eric Haddock; *Volo's Guide to Cormyr* by Ed Greenwood; *Player's Guide to Faerûn* by Richard Baker, Travis Stout, and James Wyatt; of course, the *Forgotten Realms Campaign Setting* by Ed Greenwood, Sean K Reynolds, Skip Williams, and Rob Heinsoo; and the core DUNGEONS & DRAGONS® rule books. I couldn't even have started without them.

And thanks to Mark Sehestedt, who stepped in last minute, and stepped up admirably.

Innarlith

Lake
of
Steam

1st Quarter
2nd Quarter
3rd Quarter
4th Quarter

Ransar's Ride

THE STORY THUS FAR

The city-state of Innarlith sits on the far eastern shore of the Lake of Steam, all but ignored by the wider Realms. There, the poor suffer in the crime-ridden streets of the Fourth Quarter, craftsmen ply their trades in the Third Quarter, the privileged few live in luxury in the Second Quarter, and ships come and go from the docks of the First Quarter.

Pristoleph was born into the day-to-day horrors of the Fourth Quarter slums, but even as a boy he dreamed of greater things. As a man he's become one of the city's most powerful men.

Marek Rymüt, son of a wealthy Thayan merchant, was indoctrinated into the ranks of the mysterious Red Wizards. Decades later he's sent to Innarlith where he quickly insinuates himself into the city-state's inner circles.

Ivar Devorast and Willem Korvan, students from Cormyr, both find their way to Innarlith as well. There, Devorast learns shipbuilding, while Willem pursues power and influence.

Phyrea, daughter of the city's influential master builder, is the perfect young lady by day—and a cunning thief by night. When she spends the summer at her family's country estate, she meets Devorast and is changed forever, encounters the ghosts of the haunted manor, and is slowly driven mad.

As Willem's star rises in Innarlan society, Devorast sinks into poverty, but only one of them feels the icy chill of desperation. Willem sees all his dreams come true, but satisfaction eludes him. Devorast is inspired to build a canal to link the Lake of Steam with the Sea of Fallen Stars. When completed, it will change the face of Faerûn forever. But for everyone who wants to see that day come, there's at least one who would kill to prevent it.

PART I

1

Phyrea watched it eating, and it was the most horrifying thing she'd ever seen.

After only the first few bites the mystery of what had been killing the workers at her father's vineyard had been explained. They'd blamed one animal after another; hunted for wolves, then bears, then giant boars. The remains had always been found in the morning—bones with a few strips of bloody flesh or tendon hanging from them like threads off the edge of an old blanket. They never found the skulls.

At first, Phyrea didn't pay any attention. She didn't even know anything was wrong at the camp until a tenday and a half and six murders had passed. It had been more than three months since she'd left Berrywilde for Innarlith, and she wasn't happy about having to go back.

The ghosts had come with her, but at least in the city she didn't feel so alone with them, so much like them.

But when her father told her about the murders, complained that the workers were beginning to desert the site and the winery construction was woefully behind schedule, something nudged at her. She wanted to call it guilt, but wasn't sure what the feeling was. It wasn't as though she had killed and eaten those men herself. She'd been miles away when it happened, but the voices that spoke to her when no one was there seemed to relish the news of the murders. They took some kind of spiteful glee in the fact that something was eating those innocent men. It was the feeling that they knew something she didn't that brought her back to the country estate. Her own instincts, and her sense of smell, brought her to the ghast.

It didn't see her, hear her, or smell her. At least it hadn't yet. Phyrea wanted to look away from it, but couldn't. In the dim starlight it was difficult at first to tell that it wasn't human—or at least was no longer human. She had heard of things like it before—ghouls—undead creatures that feasted on the flesh of humans, but what was killing the workers was something similar, but stronger, more dangerous.

Phyrea sighed.

The ghast took another bite, a huge mouthful of bloody skin from the dead man's thigh. It came away with a tearing sound, duller than fabric. Thick blood pattered on the wet grass. The thing's jagged fangs ripped the skin and meat into strips that it gulped down with undisguised relish. Its burning red eyes rolled back slightly in its misshapen skull, and its shoulders twitched. The ghast's purple flesh was the color of a bruise, but a single bruise that covered its entire bony, naked form. Even from a distance Phyrea could smell rotting flesh, decaying meat, blood both old and new . . . the odor of a crypt.

You made that, a voice—one she had come to associate with the old woman who'd lost the skin from the side of her face in what must have been a terrible fire—echoed in Phyrea's mind.

Pretty, pretty thing, a little girl's voice added.

Phyrea tried to answer with a feeling of impatience. She tried to tell them to be quiet without words, and for the moment at least it seemed to have worked.

They were well outside the perimeter torches of the work camp—far enough that no one could hear the ghast feed. The workers who remained, and the guards her father had hired to protect them, slept as soundly as they could knowing that the murders were still going on. Phyrea couldn't see in the dark any better than any other human girl her age, but the starlight would just have to be enough.

You don't want to see it any better anyway, a man's voice told her.

She smiled, nodded, and took a step closer to the still-feeding ghast. It didn't hear her first step, and went on chewing with the same calm abandon. She had the gentle winter breeze in her face, so had reason to hope that the undead cannibal couldn't smell her either.

As she moved closer still, one silent footstep at a time, she wrapped the fingers of her right hand around the pommel of her sword. The grip tingled at her touch, almost as though the beautiful blade were trying to communicate with her. She'd been getting that feeling more and more from the sword she'd found in the hidden tomb beneath her family's country manor. Like before, she ignored it. The weapon felt good when she used it, so she let it nettle her when she wasn't.

Though the blade didn't make the faintest whisper of a sound when it left the scabbard, the ghast looked up when she drew it. Perhaps the finely crafted, wave-shaped blade had caught a bit of the starlight. Maybe the creature finally smelled her despite the cool breeze. It could have heard the toe of her boot sink into the rain-soaked, muddy grass.

It can taste you already, the burned old crone told her. *It remembers you.*

Remembers me? she thought, and was answered with the feeling of morbid amusement.

The ghast growled and lunged at her. She stepped back, skipping on the tips of her toes, and brought her sword up in front of her. She stopped, and froze for half a heartbeat, for two reasons. First, she was hit by the stench like she'd fallen from a tree onto her head. And second, she recognized the thing.

Closer, a break in the gathering clouds letting through just enough starlight to reveal it's violet-hued features, she could see its face. Skin stretched taut over its skull, it appeared to be a man who hadn't eaten in weeks. Stretched back over teeth that would have been even more horrifying to the man it had once been, its cracked lips drew back into something that might have been a smile.

"You," the ghast said, its voice a desiccated mockery of its living counterpart. "I know you."

"Yes," Phyrea replied. "Yes."

"It's you," the thing hissed.

Phyrea tried to speak again but gagged instead. The smell of the thing was thick in the air. She could taste it as much as smell it. The damp night around her had a greasy quality to it. Bile rose in her throat, and she found herself fighting just to breathe. Her lungs at once lusted for air and rejected the putrescence, and they had no choice but to inhale.

"Why?" the ghast asked, and Phyrea thought it was going to cry.

She shook her head and coughed. The ghast took that as an opportunity to lunge at her, its yellowed talons out in front of it to rake her flesh from her bones. Its fang-lined mouth opened wide. If she could have breathed, she would have screamed, but instead she acted.

Was it her arm that reacted or the sword itself? She didn't know, but in the moment, she didn't care. All she knew was that the blade took one of the ghast's hands off at the wrist before the claws could touch her.

The undead thing scrambled back, screeching so loudly that Phyrea's eyes closed against the sound. The cry was one part pain, one part anger, and it was the second part that snapped Phyrea's eyes open as fast as they'd shut. It was going to come at her again.

The sword once again moved her arm, pulling at her. She stabbed at the ghast, letting the enchanted blade do the work for her. The wavy steel sank deep into the thing's chest, releasing black blood that fell in clumps to the ground. The smell made her stomach twist and her eyes water. She was too close to the thing and tried to back away, tried to pull the sword out of it, but the blade only went deeper.

"What now?" the ghost rattled, it's voice like the last gasp of a drowning man.

A chorus of voices, none of them her own, echoed in Phyrea's head: *Obliteration.*

"Obliteration," she whispered to the man she'd killed three months before.

"No," the ghost whimpered.

Dissolution, the voices cried out.

"I'm sorry," Phyrea breathed.

The second time, one of the voices told her, *is forever.*

"The foreman," Phyrea whispered, and the ghost, with the last bit of strength left to it, nodded. "I killed you."

The ghost froze, every muscle tense, and only then did Phyrea realize it was on its knees. She coughed, and the face she recognized blew away, the purple-bruised skin turned to dust. A white skull glowed in the meager starlight, then more bones as the rest of the undead flesh drifted away on the damp winter breeze. It fell apart, clattering to her feet, a pile of bleached white bones.

The smell was gone.

Phyrea took a step back and looked at the sword. It tingled in her hand, and more than ever, she was afraid of it.

Yes, the voice of the man—the man with the scar on his cheek in the shape of a **Z**—whispered into her consciousness, *it was the sword. It was the sword that killed him.*

"And the sword that brought him back," Phyrea whispered in reply.

2

7 Hammer, the Year of the Sword (1365 DR)
THE CANAL SITE

As far as Hrothgar could tell, no one in the camp worked harder than Ivar Devorast. And by all rights, Devorast was the one who should have been working the least. It was his project after all, his brainchild, his life's work.

Or was it?

"There are times, Ivar," Hrothgar told him that cool, gray morning in the first month of the year, "that I think this mad delusion of yours is more whim than obsession."

Devorast heard him, though he gave no outward sign. The human read from a list of provisions that had recently been delivered to the work site by one of the ransar's supply caravans.

"That half-elf ... what's his name?" the dwarf prodded.

"Enril," Devorast replied.

"For the sake of Moradin's sweatin' danglies, Ivar, do you really know the name of every swingin' hammer at work here?" That drew the slightest trace of a smile from Devorast, and Hrothgar pressed on. "Can't Enril see to that? It's his job, isn't it?"

"He has," Devorast said.

Hrothgar was about to heave a dramatic, world-weary sigh, but stopped himself, knowing full well it would be lost on that peculiar human he'd come to call a friend.

"There's a difference, you know, between a dwarf and a pick-axe," Hrothgar said.

A warm breeze blew in from the south, bringing the sulfur-tinged breath of the Lake of Steam with it, rattling the wood shutters that closed the window from the morning's damp. Devorast got to the end of the list, folded the parchment once in half, then stuffed it into the wood stove that warmed the little cabin that was Devorast's home, office, command post, and ...

"Temple," Hrothgar mumbled. It felt like a temple of sorts, but devoted to no god but Devorast himself. A god who asked for and accepted no worshipers, no prayers, no mercy, no pity, but enormous responsibility.

"I'm going to understand you one day," the dwarf said. "I may have to live as long as a withered old elf, but I'm going to figure your mind out if it's the death of me."

Devorast ignored him, moving on from the list of

provisions to a written report from one of the foremen. Hrothgar didn't bother trying to read over the human's shoulder. He didn't really care what the foreman had to say, and by the look on his face neither did Devorast. Still, Hrothgar could see by the way his eyes moved that Devorast read every word before stuffing it, too, into the fire.

"It's an old saying from the Great Rift," Hrothgar went on. "Wisdom from home, right? 'There's a difference between a dwarf and a pick-axe.'"

Devorast looked at him, and Hrothgar was momentarily taken aback by the sudden shift in his friend's attention. The dwarf swallowed.

"It means," Hrothgar said after clearing his throat, "that a good king doesn't use his people like tools."

"I'm no one's king," Devorast said.

"Close enough, out here," the dwarf said.

"I've read the complaints."

"I'm not talking about complaints. A man signs up to dig he should shut up and dig; he signs up to cut trees he should get to sawin'. What I mean is how you use your own self, my friend. Doin' the work of a thousand men is only necessary when you don't have a thousand men to do as you say. You don't have to do everything. You don't have to wield every tool, read every supply list. Trust yer people for the Gray Protector's sake."

"You know I don't mean any disrespect at all when I remind you that I don't do anything for the Gray Protector's sake," said Devorast. "I trust the people here to do what they do, but I hold myself to a certain standard and so I hold this canal to that standard, which means I have to hold everyone who touches it to the same standard. You never struck me as the sort who would find that unreasonable. I've seen the standards you set for your own work."

Hrothgar took a breath with the intent to argue, but he couldn't find the words. He wasn't quite sure what to say. If Devorast noticed his discomfiture he made no sign.

The dwarf let his breath out in a sigh and let his gaze

roam around the single room as Devorast sifted through a bowl of loose soil with his fingers. The room was a clutter of sheets of parchment, some as big square as Hrothgar was tall. Drawings had been tacked to the walls, clothes lay in rumpled piles on the floor, and a meager collection of dishes sat clean—perhaps never used—on a little shelf by the stove. Devorast looked much like his quarters. His red hair was clean but in a fashion Hrothgar thought atypical of humans and elves, it was long and uncombed. His skin was weathered from their time in the damp and rain of a winter north of the Lake of Steam. His clothing was simple and practical, sturdy and unadorned. He wore not a single piece of jewelry. His fingertips were stained with the charcoal he used to write and draw, and the dirt he was in some ways moving himself, handful by handful, to form his straight-line river to connect sea to sea.

"If you find a worm in there, save it for me," Hrothgar said, nodding at the bowl of dirt Devorast still sifted through, deep in thought. "I've been meaning to take up this 'fishing' I've heard tell of."

Devorast didn't look up from the bowl when he said, "You won't like fishing."

"Oh, and why not?"

"It depends too much on the whim of the fish."

3

15 Hammer, the Year of the Sword (1365 DR)
SECOND QUARTER, INNARLITH

It's cold outside," Phyrea said, staring out the window, her back to Marek Rymüt. "I hate it when it gets cold like this."

Marek didn't feel cold. There was a bit of a chill in the air, but it never really got too cold in Innarlith. The stinking warm waters of the volcanic Lake of Steam kept the air warm and damp most of the year.

But it wasn't the weather that Marek found interesting just then. It was Phyrea herself.

"It's positively freezing, my dear," he said to her back.

She didn't turn around, but seemed to relax a bit. Her shoulders sagged, but didn't hunch. Marek couldn't shake the feeling that she wanted to turn and face him but was afraid to. He couldn't imagine that she feared him for any reason. She'd never shown any sign of that before, and they had known each other at least in passing for some time.

"There's something different about you," he said, keeping his voice light, though what he began to feel emanating from her was increasingly disturbing. "You've been away."

"I've been at Berrywilde," she all but whispered.

He knew it well. He'd been to one or another social engagement there—her father's country estate. The first time he walked into the main house he knew it was haunted, but no one else seemed to sense it, so he'd kept quiet.

"Lovely," he said. "I've been dabbling myself with a little place ... outside the city."

And he would never tell Phyrea just how far outside the city the Land of One Hundred and Thirteen was.

"It's cold," she said again, hugging herself, wrapping her slim fingers around her upper arms. She shivered just enough for Marek to notice.

"Has something scared you?" he said. It was a risk to ask, but Marek couldn't think of a reason not to.

Phyrea stiffened.

"Do you want to tell me about it?" he asked. "Is that why you came here today? To tell me about what—?"

"We don't know each other that well, Master Rymüt."

There was a long silence before Marek finally said, "Of course that's true, isn't it? One could say we're really little more than distant social acquaintances. I'll admit that when I received word that you wanted to come see me in my home I was as surprised as I was intrigued. What is it I can do for you, my dear?"

Still not turning to show him her face, she said, "I have a certain item that I . . . found."

Marek smiled. He'd heard rumors about her but had never believed them. Could they be true? Could the master builder's beautiful little debutante really be the leather-clad sneak thief that had stolen from the finest families in the city-state? If she was, Marek puzzled over why. Her father was wealthy and well-placed, and she his only family. She couldn't want for anything.

Just like me, he thought, before the zulkir came to take me away.

"Tell me all about it," he prompted, then swept his robes up behind him and sat on a divan of pastel lavender rothéhide that had cost him exactly twice the annual income of the average citizen of Innarlith. Marek always liked reminding himself of that otherwise trivial fact.

Phyrea sighed in a way that almost felt to Marek as though she was condemning his musing over the divan, then she said, "It's a sword."

"Is it?" he said around a half-stifled yawn.

"I think it's called a falchion."

"A falchion, then."

"Is that what you call it?" she asked. "The blade is wavy, like water." And as she said that she moved one finger in a series of slow, undulating arcs that almost anyone else in Faerûn would surely have found sensual. "Is that a falchion?"

"Flambergé," he corrected. "But surely that's not all you'd like to know."

"I've been assured that you know how to . . ." She paused and he could tell she was searching for the right word, but it also appeared as though she listened intently to something or someone, though the Thayan wizard heard no sound. "You can read, or sense the magic in things. You can tell me what this sword can do."

"So," he replied, "you came across an enchanted blade at your daddy's country retreat and you'd like me to identify its properties for you?"

She nodded, still not looking at him.

He took a deep breath and said, "Well, you certainly have come to the right place. I won't pretend that I'm not at least a little disappointed that this visit isn't entirely social. I was so hoping we could get to know one another just a little bit better."

"I'll pay you," she said.

"You insult me," he shot back fast, his voice cold.

She stiffened again, and still appeared to be listening at the same time.

"But never mind that," he said. "Do you have the weapon with you?"

She shook her head.

"Well, of course I'll have to not only see it but handle it in order to give you any relevant information. We can work out a mutually beneficial arrangement as far as payment or exchange of services is concerned. But I get the feeling you have one particular question you'd like me to answer."

"The sword kills people," she said.

Marek laughed and said, "Well, then, it's fulfilled its one true destiny, hasn't it?"

"No," Phyrea replied, "that's not what I mean."

She turned to face him, and Marek was taken aback by the cold and terrified gaze she leveled on him. Her eyes shook, though her face remained perfectly calm, almost dead.

"Tell me, girl," he whispered.

"I used it to kill a man," she said, "and he came back."

Marek flinched a little, raised an eyebrow, and asked, "He came back . . . ?"

Phyrea shuddered, hugged herself again, turned back to face the window though her head tipped down to look at the floor, and said, "A ghoul."

"A sword that makes ghouls, is it?"

"No," she said. "It was a ghast."

"Have you heard about the canal?" he asked, changing the subject as fast as possible in hopes of snapping her out of what seemed almost a hypnotic state.

She turned and faced him again. The terror in her eyes replaced with annoyed curiosity, she asked, "What?"

"This mad man has convinced our dear ransar to give him all the gold in the city in order to dig a trench all the way from the Lake of Steam to the Nagaflow and fill it up with water. I understand it will take a hundred thousand men a hundred thousand years to dig it, but they've begun in earnest."

She didn't seem to believe him, and not just because he'd so greatly exaggerated the number of men and the length of time the project would require. She'd been back in the city long enough that surely she'd have heard of Ivar Devorast and his fool's errand. But she hadn't.

"Does my father know about this?" she asked.

"Of course," Marek replied. "He doesn't like it one bit, of course. A sensible man, your father, his loyalties are with the city-state."

"A canal," she said, her voice a breathy, barely audible whisper. "If they can connect the Sea of Fallen Stars to . . ."

He watched her stare at the floor, thinking about it. She seemed impressed, and Marek hated that. He hated people who were impressed with that dangerous idea, that mad errand.

"You will bring me the flambergé?" he asked.

Phyrea nodded, but her eyes gave no indication that she'd actually heard him. Again, she listened to something or someone Marek couldn't hear.

So, he thought, the country house isn't the only thing of the master builder's that's haunted.

4

3 Alturiak, the Year of the Sword (1365 DR)
Second Quarter, Innarlith

What is so special," Surero whispered into the cold, damp air of his cell, "about one hundred and twenty-five?"

When they first locked him up, he'd been told that they would feed him once a day. Assuming they had been as good as their word, he'd been in the cell for one hundred and twenty-five days, since the first day of Marpenoth in the Year of the Wave.

"The third," he told himself. "It's the third day of Alturiak."

"That's right," the voice from beyond the door replied.

The sound of the first human voice he'd heard in four months tickled Surero's ears. Much as he'd tried to engage his jailers in conversation, none of them had ever answered. All they did was take the bucket of urine and feces, replace it with an empty bucket, then slide in the moldy, hard bread and the tin cup of water. Sometimes they gave him a strip of pork fat or a fish head.

"Why?" he asked the door. "Why today?"

There was no answer right away, and Surero's heart raced. He stood on legs that had been too weak to support him for most of the last month. They held him, though, even if they were a bit shaky. He'd taken to spending his days sitting against the cool, rough stone of the subterranean cell. He had no window, and after he'd eaten the first two he came across, eventually even the spiders stopped wandering in.

A sound came from behind the door—the clank of keys on a ring.

"Hello?" Surero called out, his own voice hurting his ears, which had grown so accustomed to the utter silence of the tomb.

"Stand away from the door," the man's deep voice rumbled, and Surero imagined it made the heavy, iron-bound oak door quiver as if in fright.

He slid one foot back, then the second foot to meet it, and almost fell. He put a hand against the wall, scraping some skin from his palm, but he held himself up. His eyes burned, and if he'd had enough water in his body, he'd have begun to cry. Instead he just stood there and quivered.

"We're going to let you go," the voice said. "Do you understand?"

Surero's voice caught in his throat. He nodded, but the man wouldn't be able to see him. He stood and waited, and it seemed as though an awfully long time had passed. The door didn't open.

"Rymüt?" he whispered.

Then his throat closed again, and his knees were going to collapse under him, so he sat. He ended up leaning half against the rough stone, his cheek pressed against the wall, his nose filled with the spice of mold.

He's taunting me, Surero thought. They aren't going to let me go. It's Rymüt. He's playing a trick on me.

"He's playing a trick on me," Surero whispered.

Then his teeth closed as tightly as his throat, and his wasted, filthy, clammy body trembled with impotent rage. He boiled inside his six by six cell, and tried to close his ears to the sound of men moving on the other side of the door.

They aren't there, he told himself. Give up. Give up hope.

Surero hadn't had a word of news from the outside world for a hundred and twenty-five days. For all he knew, the hated Marek Rymüt was dead. But he doubted that. Surely the Thayan scum had only further ingratiated himself into the petty aristocracy of Innarlith. Surero had no doubt that Rymüt had taken from more and more people like him. The Thayan had taken his customers, had stolen his formulae, had robbed him of his reputation. Surero, who had lived every moment of his miserable existence in the pursuit of excellence in the alchemical arts, had been reduced to a ragged, homeless, desperate husk of a man, no more substantial a creature than the wretch four months in the ransar's dungeon had made him. When he'd done the only thing fitting, the only thing a man in his position could do, he had failed. Something had gone wrong. The mixture itself had worked and the explosion was powerful, but Marek Rymüt had lived.

And Surero had gone to the dungeon to rot. Forever.

A key turned in the lock. The sound was unmistakable.

Surero looked up at the door, his eyes locked on the very edge so he could perceive any minute crack that might actually open.

Fear washed away his hatred, but the source was the same. Was it Marek Rymüt behind that door? Was it the Thayan robber come to kill him once and for all?

"Rymüt?' he asked, his voice squeaking past his constricted vocal chords.

The door swung open to a flash of blinding light and a deafening squeak of hinges that hadn't been used, much less oiled, in four months. Surero's eyes locked shut against the brilliant illumination of the single torch, and he could only listen as the man stepped into the room, his steps heavy and confident, shaking the stained flagstones beneath them.

"Stand up," the voice commanded, closer and clearer with no door between it and Surero.

"Kill me," Surero croaked, his hands pressed hard against his burning eyes. "Go ahead and kill me, Thayan bastard."

A hand that seemed the size of a god's grabbed a fistful of the soiled linen gown that had been his only clothing since the previous Marpenoth, and took a few dozen chest hairs along with it. Surero winced and shook as he was pulled to his feet.

Hot breath that smelled almost as bad as his cell washed over his face, and the man said, "Who in the Nine perspirin' Hells are you calling a Thayan?"

Surero chanced it. He opened one eye.

"You . . ." he mumbled. "You're not . . . Rymüt."

"I'm the jailer, wretch," the man said. "I'm the bloke what's been feeding you these months. How's about a little gratitude here, eh?"

Surero swallowed, forgetting how much his throat hurt, and replied, "Yes. Sorry. Thanks."

That made the jailer laugh, and Surero was just relived

enough that it wasn't Rymüt who'd come to claim him that he laughed a little too.

"Are you really . . . ?" the prisoner stuttered. "A-are . . . are y-you going to . . . ?"

"You're all done, mate," the jailer said, setting Surero down and letting go his clothes. "The 'Thayan bastard' said you'd had enough so the ransar's springin' ya. You're free."

"Free?" Surero asked. It was not possible—not for the reasons the jailer gave. "I've had enough?"

"Well, kid, you didn't kill him after all."

"But I tried."

There was a short silence while Surero just looked at the man. He was hardly less filthy that his prisoner, but bigger, better fed, and capable of smiling.

"Maybe," said the jailer, "you'll want to keep that bit to yourself, son."

5

9 Alturiak, the Year of the Sword (1365 DR)
SECOND QUARTER, INNARLITH

Everybody who would eventually be somebody was there. Willem Korvan made an effort to talk to each and every one of them, but didn't bother listening. He watched their mouths move. He nodded and smiled. From time to time he tipped his head a bit to one side as if really concentrating on what they had to say then he would nod again and smile. Nodding and smiling, he might make a meaningless comment on what they were wearing. Then he would smile and nod. Each and every one of them smiled back, and nodded.

What Willem was most concerned with at the time was the smell. Marek Rymüt's fashionable Second Quarter home had all the right furniture and fixtures, everything predictable and acceptable, but the smell could not be ignored.

Oranges? he thought. No. Nothing so simple.

Willem wondered if it could be a combination of things. Oranges after all, maybe, but mixed with . . . lamp oil?

No.

The mortar they'd used on the city wall project combined with a Fourth Quarter beggar's sick and the porridge his mother used to make when he was a boy?

Closer.

"The current state of things," another young senator said to Willem's blank, smiling face, "guarantees naught but that the wealthy grow only wealthier while the poor become increasingly desperate over time. Really, it's up to us, isn't it, Korvan, to set things aright once and for all, just as Master Rymüt suggests?"

Willem smiled and nodded, and the young senator appeared pleased. They wandered away from each other and into the same conversations with different people.

"It did seem radical to me at first," a young woman trolling for a husband said behind too much Shou-inspired makeup. "After all, my family has sold horses for generations and hardly worked as hard as they have in order to see our estates divided among the tradesmen. That idea in particular . . . but, well, if Master Rymüt thinks it's best. . . ."

Willem nodded but didn't smile. He caught the woman's eye and detected just enough desperation in her gaze that he fled her presence as quickly as he could.

Looking for Rymüt in the crowded sitting room, Willem began to formulate his excuse for leaving so early. Before he could find his host, though, he was stopped by an apparition.

It had been some time since he'd seen her, but there she stood. She'd just stepped into the room, and all at once the smell was gone, as though the air had refreshed itself in her honor.

"Phyrea," he whispered.

She either heard him or sensed his eyes on her, and she

looked right at him. Willem took a step back and smiled. She stared at him, but didn't smile back. When she stepped into the room the guests parted for her, and it was as if the air itself gave way before her. They weren't afraid to touch her, just unworthy.

Willem stepped forward to meet her and almost stumbled to a stop when Marek Rymüt slid between them. Focused only on Phyrea's jaw-dropping beauty, he hadn't seen the pudgy Thayan.

"Ah, Phyrea," Marek said. "Did I invite you?"

Phyrea smiled at him, and the sight of it made Willem's mouth go dry.

"Ah, Marek," Phyrea replied. "I came anyway."

They shared a conspiratorial smile that made Willem feel as though he should get out of that house as fast he could, then they both noticed him at the same time.

"You've met Willem Korvan," Marek said.

Phyrea nodded but didn't smile, and Willem smiled but didn't nod. The other guests around them seemed to quiver.

"So these are the young masters?" Phyrea asked Marek.

"The heirs apparent, yes," he answered with a grin.

Phyrea, unimpressed, said, "This canal-builder I've heard about . . ." She turned to Willem. "It's not you."

"No," Willem said. He wanted to elaborate, but the words failed him. Phyrea wasn't listening anyway.

"Is he here?" she asked Marek.

"No, he isn't," said the Thayan, with a hint of fire in his eyes.

"I'm not surprised," Willem ventured, "that you and he wouldn't see eye to eye, Master Rymüt."

Phyrea scanned the room, bored, even exhausted. She wasn't listening.

"The young fool our unfortunate ransar has trusted with this exercise in endless ditch digging?" Marek replied.

"You don't know him?" Willem asked Phyrea.

She shrugged the question off. How could she know Ivar Devorast, after all?

"The last time we spoke, you inquired about a certain item," Marek said to Phyrea. "Tell me you brought it along."

"Hardly," she said, looking around the room so she didn't register Marek's annoyed look.

Their host's expression changed back to its placid, friendly mien and he muttered, "Enjoy my little caucus."

With a bow Phyrea didn't return but Willem did, he was gone.

"Phyrea," Willem said when he saw her begin to take a step away from him.

She turned, impatient, and folded her arms in front of her.

"Come with me," he said, reaching out to take her by the elbow.

She flinched away from him as if his touch would scald her, and Willem's heart leaped.

"Please," he said.

She wouldn't look at him, but turned and let him follow her to Marek's veranda. They had to wave their way through huge clay pots that someone told him Marek had gotten from as far as Maztica. The plants were local, but appeared unhealthy.

"Phyrea," he said when he hoped they were alone. He tried to touch her again and she flinched. She made no effort to mask her contempt for him.

"Hate me if you want to," he told her. "It doesn't make me want you any less."

"I don't hate you," she said.

Relieved, Willem sighed.

"I would have to think about you at all to hate you."

She isn't ignoring me, he told himself, then shook his head to try to rid himself of not only the words but the feeling of relief that washed over him.

"I don't care if you hate me, or think of me at all, or love me, or think of me as a brother," he said, the words spilling out of him. "I will serve you. I will be your slave, if that's what you wish. I will do anything to have you. And I may be the only man in this wretched city who understands you—the only one willing to give you everything and ask for nothing in return."

She allowed him the briefest, unconvinced glare.

"I understand that you're the kind of woman that the world has got to come to a screeching halt for," he went on. "You have to be the center not only of attention but of infinity itself."

"If you tell me you love me, I'll kill you where you stand," she said, and he could tell she meant it.

"And if I told you I thought that might be worth dying for?" he asked.

"Then all you'd be telling me is that you're a fool," she shot back. "A boy."

"If—" he started.

"When I was away from the city last summer," she interrupted, "at my father's estate in the country, there was a man. He had me in a way you'll never have me."

Willem could swear at that moment that his heart turned to glass.

"You're pretty," Phyrea said. "You serve well. You make friends easily. You have position and potential, and all of that meaningless stupidity I couldn't possibly find less interesting."

Willem closed his eyes against her words, but they kept coming.

"That man, last summer," she went on, "was a stone mason. He was nothing ... no one. He was a brute, but he was more than you'll ever be, and no matter what happens between us for the rest of our lives, Willem, you will never be a tenth the man he is. I'm not even sure it's because he's so great a man or you're so insignificant, but likely a bit of both. And not only did he fail to offer me his mortal soul, when he left, he didn't even say good-bye."

Willem couldn't quite breathe.

"There," she said. "Still want me?"

He moved his lips, but no sound came out.

"You're pathetic," she whispered as she brushed past him and disappeared behind the dying potted plants.

A drop of cold rain hit the bridge of Willem's nose and made him flinch. He took a breath and sighed.

"Yes," he said to the cool night air, to the rooftops of Innarlith, "I still want you."

6

12 Alturiak, the Year of the Sword (1365 DR)
FIRST QUARTER, INNARLITH

The brutish man came at her with a hook, but it was his smell that Ran Ai Yu found most disturbing. They all smelled bad, as though they were rotting from within—and they looked it too. She'd fought animated corpses that didn't stink so bad.

She slit the dockworker's wrist, and the hook clattered onto the pier. She didn't recognize any of the words that spewed at her from his mostly toothless mouth, but his intent was clear.

"You will stop this," she said to the wounded dockworker while she kept him at bay with her sword. "I will pay you fairly."

Another string of unintelligible curses followed, and the man made the mistake of reaching for the hook. She cut him again, and he backed away.

"I don't want to kill you," she said.

Another dockworker fell at her feet, pushing the man she'd cut even farther back from her. That man held some kind of crude club and had been kicked in the face hard enough to flatten his nose and soak his face with his own blood.

Ran Ai Yu glanced back in the direction the bloody man had come from. Lau Cheung Fen stood with the great porcelain ship *Jié Zuò* behind him. He stood on one foot, the other hanging in front of him, his knee at waist level. The morning sun shone from his shaved head, which sat atop his unusually large neck in a loose, comfortable way, as if suspended from above by a wire.

The little hairs on the back of her neck stood on end.

Something hit her on the side of the face. Her teeth rattled, and her vision flared white, but she was still able to get her blade up fast enough to slap away the second blow. The man she'd cut had been joined by two more, as ragged and reeking as he. Though it was barely past dawn, they were drunk. Ran Ai Yu heard her passenger kick two more men. She could only hope that he could take down enough of them to get to her before the two dockworkers that fast approached her joined the three she did her best to fend off. They were drunk, slow, and brutish, but five was too many for her.

"I will pay you," she said.

Her face felt hot. The horrible men leered at her like hungry dogs.

"You'll pay all right," the man she'd cut growled at her—perhaps he was a dog. "But not with coin."

Ran Ai Yu shifted her weight back onto her rear foot and set her sword blade parallel with the pier. She looked the lead thug in the eyes, sensed he was going to shift right, and that's what he did. She let him step into the sword tip, but didn't stab him. The blade only went in the barest fraction of an inch. She didn't want to kill him. If she killed him, she'd have to kill the rest of them.

His two friends lunged at her, and Ran Ai Yu stepped back a few fast steps. Then one of the men fell flat on his face. She watched a stone roll along the wood planks, and blinked at it.

When the second man fell she relaxed her stance, and let her sword arm fall to her side, the blade crossed in front of her legs. She stood like that and watched Ivar Devorast knock the other man to the ground with his fist. He smiled at her over the man's limp form, and she smiled back. A thud from behind her turned her attention back to her passenger. Lau Cheung Fen, like Devorast, stood over the unconscious bodies of drunken dockhands.

"Miss Ran," Devorast said.

She turned back to face him, sheathed her sword, and said, "Master Devorast, is good to see you once again." Lau Cheung Fen stepped up behind her, and she added, "May I present my passenger, the honorable Lau Cheung Fen of Liaopei."

"Mister Lau," he said. "Are you injured? Do you need any further assistance?"

"Your manner ..." Lau said. "So like Shou."

Devorast just looked at him.

"We will require a crew to unload our cargo," Ran Ai Yu answered. "These men tried to ..." She paused, searching for the word.

"Who is this man?" Lau asked her in Kao te Shou, their native tongue.

She looked at Devorast, but detected no outward trace that he was offended by Lau's speaking in front of him in a language he did not understand.

"Master Ivar Devorast is the man who created the great *Jié Zuò,"* she answered in the Common Tongue of Faerûn.

"Ah," Lau responded, and his head bent low on that strange long neck of his. His eyes glittered black in the sunshine. "You are the great genius. It is truly an honor to meet you, Master Devorast."

"Master Lau is a most important dignitary from my province," Ran said in hopes that she could help Devorast frame his response properly.

"Thank you, Master Lau," Devorast said, but his eyes stayed on Ran Ai Yu.

"You have built many such ships, then," Lau said. "I should purchase a number of them. Though my home is far from the sea, many in Shou Lung have commented on the strange and wonderful ship of Ran Ai Yu, and would pay much for one of her kind."

"There are no more of her kind," Devorast said before Ran could say the same thing.

"You have sport of me," said her passenger.

"No," Ran Ai Yu cut in. "He has built only this one, and will build no more like her."

"This is true?" he asked Devorast.

"It is," was the Faerûnian's only reply.

"Is this some secret the white men seek to keep from us?" Lau asked in Kao te Shou.

"With apologies, Master Devorast," she said, then turned to Lau. *"It is no secret. He is a very unusual man, and that is all. He will likely find it rude, however, if we continue to speak in a language he does not understand. With respect, Master Lau, he is a friend and important trade contact."*

"Indeed," Lau replied, then bowed to Devorast. "Please accept my most humble apologies for my rudeness, Master Devorast. Perhaps you would be so kind . . . if you no longer build your tile ships, what is it that occupies you? Perhaps if it is one of a kind as well, I might have it instead."

"It's a canal," Devorast replied.

The two Shou merchants exchanged a glance.

"Pardon me," Lau said. He asked Ran Ai Yu, *"Kuh-nahl?"* She gave him the word in their language, and he nodded. "Well, then I will not be able to take it with me. Pray, where is this canal?"

"Northwest of here," he replied.

"To connect the Lake of Steam with your great Inner Sea," Ran Ai Yu said.

Devorast nodded.

"This will be a mighty boon to trade," said Lau.

"For me," said Devorast, "it's a canal."

"I should like to see it," Ran Ai Yu said. A memory tickled the edge of her consciousness—a similar conversation that she had had with Devorast when she'd last seen him.

"I should like to show it to you," he said. "But in the meantime, we should see to a dock crew for you."

"Is this the way trade is always conducted here? With such violence?" asked the tall merchant—a man Ran Ai Yu had her suspicions was no human at all. He gestured to the fallen dockhands, some of them beginning to rise.

"It was not so when I was last here, two years and three months ago," said Ran.

"They made a mistake," Devorast said.

Ran Ai Yu smiled.

7

20 Alturiak, the Year of the Sword (1365 DR)
THE CANAL SITE

When she first saw the work site Ran Ai Yu thought it was some kind of military drill. The sight of it gave the immediate impression of rigid organization that she had only experienced at the edge of a parade ground. But then details presented themselves, pieces took shape out of the whole, and that impression disappeared. She was left with chaos—madness, even—a barrage of colors and dizzying movement that erased any sense of organization at all, until she once again let those details melt into the beautiful whole.

"These men are all at your command?" she asked Devorast, who stood beside her on a low hill.

The sound of the men working deafened her, but then Devorast didn't answer anyway. Picks chipped stone, shovels moved dirt and clay, and carts trundled past full of rocks, earth, wood, and more men. Oxen grunted, foremen shouted orders, and it was like music for a great dance.

"This is as it should be," she said, unconcerned with whether or not Devorast could hear her. "You will find your destiny here. Your spirit will fill itself with this work."

The heavy, damp air carried the smell of the Lake of Steam, but only faintly under the stench of turned earth and sweating bodies. It smelled like hard work.

"I hope you live to see its completion," she said.

Devorast shrugged—a response that would have been considered rude in Shou Lung—but she took no offense.

Ran Ai Yu crouched and touched the dirt at her feet. It was damp but not muddy, and she was able to scoop up a handful, testing the weight of it in her hand. She tried to imagine the weight of the dirt and rock, the trees and weeds, that Devorast meant to move to make the trench for his canal. Then she tried to imagine the weight of the water that would fill it, and though she'd plied the waters of a far greater canal in her far-off homeland, still the weight felt unbearable.

"You will not require that I tell you how many people there must be . . . powerful people even . . . who will wish for you to fail," she told him.

He waited for her to look up at him before he shrugged again.

She let the dirt pour out through her fingers, and something made her touch the tip of her tongue. She didn't try to understand the impulse to taste it any more than she wanted to stop it. She just wanted to taste it—wanted to experience it with every one of her senses. It tasted like life, but not the same way food or water tasted; not physical life, but a deeper need within each human, the drive to build, the imperative to leave something behind, to make some mark. It tasted like the vital necessity to say, "I was here."

"Yes," he said, "you are."

Ran Ai Yu felt her cheeks redden and her ears burn. She stood, avoiding his eyes.

"I had not meant to . . . to speak that," she stammered, her Common almost deserting her.

Devorast said, "I've tasted it too."

She smiled at that, and smiled wider than she felt

proper in front of a man she had not—

The Shou merchant pushed that thought away before it was completed.

"This is supported by your leader," she asked, "your ransar?"

"I don't consider him my ransar," Devorast replied, "but yes, it is."

"Both with the gold to pay these men and to buy their tools and materials, and so on," she said then had to pause to again search her memory for the correct word. "Politically?"

Devorast nodded. He didn't look at her. Instead, his eyes darted from one part of the realization of his genius to another.

"It is my understanding, having traveled to Innarlith on more than one occasion," she went on, "and over more than a few years, that their ransar is a temporary post. Is this not true?"

He glanced at her with a mischievous grin that further embarrassed her, and said, "Any job that is answerable to others could be called temporary."

"Ah, and is that not true of master builder?"

"I'm not the ransar's master builder," he said.

"Even worse for you, I should think."

He looked at her again, but for a longer time, and she finally met his gaze.

"If it is the ransar's gold and the ransar's men," she said, "then you work for him, whether either of you admit it or not. If . . . pardon me, *when* there is a new ransar, will that ransar be as generous? Will he be as taken with this canal as is Osorkon?"

Devorast replied, "Perhaps, but perhaps not. Of course, I've considered that."

"And you have a plan?"

Devorast was silent.

"Meykhati," she said. "You've heard this name? You know this man?"

"I've heard the name."

"There is a reception at his home in six days' time," Ran Ai Yu said. "I have been invited, and you should come with me there."

"I have no time for social—"

"Do you have time to bury your garbage to keep the seagulls away?" she asked, glancing up at the sky but gesturing with one open hand at a refuse pit.

He didn't follow her gaze. He knew there were no gulls.

"Of course you do," she said. "You make time for what is important for the completion of your canal, even if it is not pleasant to consider or to do."

Again, silence.

"Meykhati will likely be the next ransar," she said.

"How do you know that?"

"I do not know that," Ran Ai Yu replied. "I have heard it said by people who I have reason to believe have reason to believe it. That is enough, for me, to begin to acquaint myself with this man so that he knows my name and my face, knows my trade, in the event that these people are correct."

"And I should do the same," he said. "I should ingratiate myself to this pointless, mumbling busybody so that on the off chance that he succeeds Osorkon he will continue to support the canal?"

"Master Lau Cheung Fen will be there," she added, "at this gathering of Meykhati's friends and associates."

"And sycophants."

"And those who think ahead."

He shook his head.

"Perhaps," she said, "if Meykhati feels well toward you and your efforts here, with Meykhati as ransar, you will be his master builder, even if you are not Osorkon's."

"I have no interest in titles and offices," Devorast told her. "I build to build, not to advance myself in the Second Quarter."

"I understand that the master builder of the moment

may have decided to keep hold of that title and office anyway, should Meykhati advance. He will be there with his daughter."

Devorast stiffened—not much, barely enough for Ran Ai Yu to notice. Could it be that Devorast sought the post of master builder after all? Or was it something else she'd said?

"Perhaps," he said. "Yes. Fine."

8

26 Alturiak, the Year of the Sword (1365 DR)
SECOND QUARTER, INNARLITH

Marek watched the dancers for a few heartbeats, then watched one of the partygoers watching the dancers, then the dancers again, then another guest, on and on. He hadn't come to Meykhati's ridiculous affair for the pleasure of it, after all, but to do what he always did.

The dancers had been brought by the exotic merchant Lau Cheung Fen, and the guests were dazzled by their otherworldly beauty and alien gestures. Seven women dressed in silk gowns covered in tiny brass bells and what appeared to be miniature cymbals, twitched and jerked to the strains of a Shou "musician" who made the most horrendous, atonal bleats on some kind of unwieldy string instrument. Marek's head began to pound, and he found he had to use a spell to make the "music" fade from his hearing, to be replaced by the private, often whispered conversations of Meykhati's other guests.

"Miss Phyrea," the Shou woman Ran Ai Yu, who Marek found almost as fascinating as he did frustrating said with a shallow bow. "I have not had the pleasure to see your father this evening."

"He's not here," Phyrea choked out.

The beautiful, haunted daughter of the inept master builder couldn't even look at the Shou woman. Her eyes had fastened themselves to the red-headed man who stood at Ran Ai Yu's side. Marek had never been formally introduced to the man, but he knew who Ivar Devorast was. So too, it would seem, did Phyrea. Devorast, if he recognized the master builder's daughter at all, gave no outward sign of it. For all that, the man gave no outward sign of anything. Phyrea squirmed under his ambivalent glances.

Yes, Marek Rymüt thought, much more interesting than dancing girls.

"May I introduce you to Ivar Devorast of Cormyr," Ran Ai Yu said.

Marek found the look on Phyrea's face so priceless he just had to smile and clap his hands. The other guests around him clapped as well, apparently thinking he was applauding the performance.

"Aren't they just?" a shrill voice invaded from his side. The effect of the spell made it painfully loud, and Marek couldn't stifle a grunt and body-racking twitch. "Goodness, Master Rymüt. Are you well?"

Meykhati's awful wife.

He forced a smile and nodded. "Yes, quite," he whispered, his own voice rattling his ears. "I would hate to further interrupt the music."

The woman smiled and made a childlike motion as though she were locking her lips closed. A spell that would actually do that came to Marek's mind, but he suppressed the nearly overwhelming urge to cast it, and a second incantation that would make the lock permanent. Instead, he kept his ears on the Shou merchant and her odd little couple, while his eyes made a great show of adoring the dancers from beyond the Utter East.

"No," Phyrea said, her voice so thick with the lie that Marek wished he could at least glance at Ran Ai Yu's face to be sure she detected it as well, but alas Meykhati's hideous wife still stood at his elbow, believing him to be every inch the dilettante her husband was. "No, we haven't met."

"I would have remembered, I'm sure." Devorast must have lied too, but there was no hint of that in his steady, uninterested voice.

"Of course, though," Phyrea said, "I have heard of your great . . . your great undertaking."

Two of the dancers swayed their hips to the jarring rhythm while the other five stood as still as statues. Marek found their utter lack of motion interesting, but only passingly so. The two lead dancers jangled their bells and otherwise made rhythmic hissing and pinging noises. They waved their hands in a way that Marek thought looked a bit like they might be casting spells, but he detected no fluctuation in the Weave.

"It keeps me occupied," Devorast replied. "I am away from the city for prolonged periods."

"Are you?" Phyrea accused. Marek raised an eyebrow. "Perhaps that explains why our paths have never even once crossed, though we seem to know many of the same people."

"Not too many," Devorast assured her.

"Meykhati, at least," she said.

Devorast shook his head, but it was Ran Ai Yu who said, "I asked Master Devorast to come with me tonight so that he might make the acquaintance of the senator."

"And have you?" Phyrea asked Devorast.

"We have been introduced," he replied.

The two lead dancers wiggled back to the line behind them, and looking for all the world like water foul plucking food from a still pond, pecked one each of their companions and froze. Those so pecked began to sway and slipped out of line to take over the incomprehensible series of motions. The music changed too, going from one set of atonal pings to a series of bursts of grinding metal. Marek resisted the urge to flee.

"It can be a burden, can't it?" asked Phyrea.

"Ma'am?" Devorast prompted.

"Having too many friends."

"I wouldn't know."

"Wouldn't you?" she asked, and Marek got the feeling she thought she might be toying with Devorast. Silly girl. "You seem like a man who would have unusual friends. Like Miss Yu, here."

"Miss Ran," Devorast corrected, and Marek so wanted to see Phyrea squirm. But instead, he watched the dancers sway around each other like two snakes reluctant to mate. "I have friends, yes. I don't feel burdened by them."

"Sometimes I feel so burdened I can hardly stand," Phyrea said, and again Marek lifted an eyebrow.

"Perhaps you don't have enough to occupy your mind," Devorast said.

"Should I build a canal then?"

"No," he told her, still without a trace of emotion. "But you can do anything else."

"I wish that were so."

"It is," he assured her, and Marek felt bile rise in his throat.

"Oh, yes, my darling," Meykhati's pinch-faced wife whispered at Marek's elbow. Her hissing voice was so loud to him that Marek had to close his eyes. "Straight away."

With that, at least she was gone.

As the new lead pair of dancers worked their way back to the line behind them, Marek turned to glance at Phyrea and Devorast. Ran Ai Yu had wandered off to be replaced by Lau Cheung Fen, who took Devorast by the arm.

The Shou gentleman had no trouble pulling Devorast away from Phyrea, who all but ran to the farthest corner of the large room, disappearing into a crowd of her father's friends and political associates. Devorast didn't watch her go, but a twitch of his eye betrayed him to one as observant as Marek Rymüt.

This, the Red Wizard thought, is a relationship I will need to follow as closely as possible.

Two new dancers began to quiver so quickly they appeared in the throws of some sort of catalepsy. The jangle of their various bells and cymbals began to intrude on Marek's spell, and he noted a few in the crowded room place hands to their ears to fend off the foreign cacophony.

"I will leave it to you to determine the advantages to you and your trade," Devorast told Lau Cheung Fen.

"And there is nothing you wish to add?" the Shou asked. "I should think that to have the endorsement of the merchant fleets of Shou Lung would be for you a very ... ah, but help with the word ... ?"

"Advantageous?" Devorast provided.

Sharp, Marek thought. Very sharp of mind indeed, this shipwright turned canal builder.

Lau sketched a shallow bow and said, "To have this *advantageous* support from afar would give you greater support at home, is that not true?"

"I have all the support I need," Devorast replied, and Marek cringed at the supreme self-confidence of that, the bold naïveté. "I will build the canal, who uses it and why makes no difference to me."

"Ivar," Willem Korvan said, appearing from the crowd holding a half-full tallglass of Inthelph's upstart local vintage. He took Devorast by the arm and bowed to the Shou. "If I may."

Lau Cheung Fen appeared reluctant to release him, but apparently felt he had no choice and returned Willem's bow.

All seven of the dancers began to move in a slow, fluid motion that Marek assumed most men would find alluring. For him, though, there was Willem Korvan. The young senator's immaculate dress complimented his perfect features. Next to the disheveled, weather-beaten, ill-dressed Devorast, Willem appeared soft, still in the full flower of youth. Though Marek had heard the two were of an age, he would have thought Ivar Devorast at least a decade Willem Korvan's senior.

"Is that the best you can do?" Willem said to Devorast, the contempt soaking each word in bile.

"Hello, Willem," Devorast said.

"Is that the best you can do?"

"Is there something you need from me?" asked Devorast.

Willem's handsome face went flat, his jaw tight and his lips twisted.

"Do you realize that that one man could—" Willem started to say, and just then Marek's spell faded out, and the clashing harmonics of the exotic music once more assaulted his ears.

He started moving in the direction of the two Cormyreans before he even made up his mind as to which of the several reasons for doing so drove him over there. Did he want to break up what might become and unseemly brawl? Other than the fact that it would be a shame should something happen to damage Willem's face, why on spinning Toril would he care if the two men came to blows? Of course, he wanted to hear their conversation but knew that as soon as he was close enough to hear them without the aid of a spell they'd stop talking in front of him.

Whatever the reason, he arrived at their side in a shot, but refused to look at Devorast.

"Ah, Senator Korvan," he gushed, "there you are."

"Master Rymüt," Willem mumbled, his face red, his eyes darting around as though he were a rabbit caught in a snare. "May I present—"

Marek didn't want to be introduced to Ivar Devorast just then. Not yet, he thought. So he clamped his hand on Willem's arm and squeezed.

"Master Rymüt. . . ." Willem almost protested, but let himself be led away at a pace that drew alarmed glances from the mingling aristocrats around them.

When they were out of earshot of Ivar Devorast, Rymüt said, "Really, Senator, you should take care with whom you're seen conversing."

"But—" the pretty weakling started to protest.

"Go tell our host how much you enjoy this hideous

clanging and stomping about," he said, pushing Willem away, but releasing his grip only slowly, and with some reluctance.

Willem looked down at his hand with vague discomfort, but Marek was quickly distracted by Phyrea. The girl stood on her tiptoes, peering as best she could above the heads of the other guests. The crowd erupted in insincere applause for the imported entertainment, and Marek stopped to make a show of it. His eyes never left Phyrea though, and he took some interest in her crestfallen mien.

As the applause died down, he made his way to her side. She looked up at him as if he were the last man in Faerûn she wanted to see, and maybe he was.

"Master Rymüt," she said, "hello again."

"Hello again to you too, my dear. I couldn't help but notice ... were you looking for someone?"

She sighed, her shoulders slumped, and she looked off to her right at nothing.

"Phyrea?"

"Yes," she answered fast. "No. I mean ... that man. Devorast is his name."

"The savior of merchant captains across Toril, yes," Marek mumbled. "What of him?"

"He's ..."

"Gone, yes," Marek said. "I'm sure Senator Korvan told me he was just leaving. Surely you don't have anything to do with that beastly man."

She nodded and shook her head at the same time, and Marek risked a playful laugh at her confusion.

"The ransar—" she started.

"Is not immune to the occasional ill-considered decisions, my dear," he finished for her. "I assure you that Ivar Devorast is just that."

"Still, there's something about him, don't you think?"

"No," he lied. "There's nothing about him at all but a man in deep water who hasn't sorted out that he's already drowned."

Phyrea wasn't listening. Marek could tell. She listened to someone else, and nodded ever so slightly in response.

What do you hear? Marek Rymüt wondered. What do you know?

9

27 Alturiak, the Year of the Sword (1365 DR)
THE CANAL SITE

The stout wooden planks that braced the sides of the trench shattered. They crumbled to sawdust all at once; an explosion of brown dust that followed a loud sizzling sound that must have been a million softer cracks all intermingled.

Hrothgar looked up at the sound. He'd heard a lot of new, strange sounds in his time among humans, under the limitless sky and so near the unforgiving sea, but he'd been at the canal site long enough to grow accustomed to its noises, and that one—those millions at once—didn't belong. Because of the sound, though, he saw the planks shatter, and the dried-mud walls begin to crumble. He saw the men inside paw at their dust-blinded eyes, and their screams tore up from the depths of the trench. As tall as the humans were, the lip of the trench towered over their heads, twice again as tall as the tallest of the diggers.

"By the unhewn rock of Deepshaft Hall," the dwarf cursed. "They'll be—"

Devorast pushed past him at a run, but it took some time for Hrothgar to realize they were being attacked. At first the trench collapse was just another accident—not that there had been many. In fact, Hrothgar had commented to Devorast and to his cousin Vrengarl on many occasions already how surprised he was that so few men had been injured, and how incomprehensible it was that no one had yet died for the cause of the canal. What they were building was so big, there were so many men, and so many things that could go wrong.

A trench could cave in, but what made the planks explode into dust?

The wind had been light all day, the clouds gray but thin and dry. Though Hrothgar could hardly be called an expert on the ways of wind and storm, the wind that blew the dirt onto those poor diggers didn't just blow in on its own from the Lake of Steam.

He ran after Devorast, not bothering to consider how many times he'd done just that in only the past few years. Devorast reached the crumbling edge of the trench long before the dwarf. He skidded to a stop, sending dust swirling around his toes only to be whipped into a series of tiny little tornadoes around his feet.

Then the wind changed again, and lifted Devorast off the ground. The human hurtled backward through the air, his arms pinwheeling at his sides in a vain attempt to either stop or control his sudden flight. He slammed hard into Hrothgar. The dwarf tried to wrap his arms around the human's waist, made every effort to catch him, but was rewarded with a broken nose, a poked eye, and an impact on his chest hard enough to drain his lungs of air.

They ended up on the ground in an undignified sprawl, their hair and clothing still whipping around them in the sourceless gust of hurricane-force wind.

"The men!" Devorast barked.

His eyes were closed, and blood trickled from under the line of his shaggy red hair. Hrothgar blinked back unwelcome tears and shot blood and snot out of his nose in a painful exhalation that at least let him start to breathe again. The two of them stood at the same time, neither helping the other to his feet.

By the time Hrothgar reoriented himself, the trench was gone. Wind whipped the dirt so thoroughly that anyone passing by who had not seen it only moments before, would never have suspected that there had been a hole there at all.

"Five men," Hrothgar growled to himself.

He looked to Devorast, who stood tall but still. His head moved to one side, then the other.

"What is it?" the dwarf asked casting about for a weapon. Where's my gods bedamned hammer? he thought. "Is it some mage? Some wind wizard?"

Devorast stopped—he saw something. Hrothgar moved back and his foot kicked something heavy. Without looking, he reached down and grabbed it—just an old tree limb the clean-up crew had missed.

It'll do, he thought, then followed Devorast's gaze.

"Sweet Haela's bum," the dwarf oathed.

"Naga," Devorast said.

The human relaxed. Hrothgar couldn't believe it. He hefted the makeshift club and stepped forward, but Devorast didn't move. He faced the creature as if they were old friends, and Hrothgar realized that perhaps they were.

"What do you want here, *naja'ssara?*" Devorast called out.

The creature hissed at him. For all the world it was a giant snake, but with a human's face. That face held all the hate, anger, and violent rage Hrothgar had ever associated with humans, and more. The dwarf could only guess that the thing was a male.

"Ivar," he said, "you told us that you—"

"Speak," Devorast called to the naga, ignoring the dwarf.

"This false river will not be realized," the thing said. Hrothgar didn't like its voice, not one bit. "Go from here, *dista'ssara*. Go now, or more will die."

Devorast crouched and picked up a rock. The action elicited from the naga a sound that Hrothgar assumed to be a laugh. He liked that sound even less than its speaking voice.

"What of Svayyah?" Devorast demanded. "She and I—"

"Svayyah?" the naga shrieked, hurling the name at Devorast as if it were a spear. What it said next had no meaning Hrothgar could fathom. Devorast threw the rock at the same time it spoke.

As the rock arced through the air, four slivers of red-orange light appeared perhaps a yard in front of the naga and arrowed through the intervening space, unerringly for Devorast. When they hit him, the human staggered back with a grunt. His face twisted in what Hrothgar perceived to be frustration, not pain—certainly not fear—but he kept on his feet.

The rock Devorast had thrown went wide—but then, it shouldn't have.

Hrothgar blinked and shook his head. The naga was there, then it was just a step or two to the side of there. The rock was supposed to hit the thing but . . .

But you've seen it use foul magic, the dwarf told himself. Now here's more.

"All right then," he said aloud so Devorast could, perhaps, benefit from his wisdom, "aim a yard or so to the snake's left."

As if they'd planned it that way, a work gang bearing all sorts of nasty implements—shovels, awls, picks, and hammers—came up over a rise, attracted by the wind and commotion. They'd seen Devorast staggered by the naga's magic, and though Devorast had assured them all that he'd garnered the snake-people's support, even those simple men could add two and two. They rushed at the naga.

"Careful, boys," Hrothgar tried to warn them, "it's—"

The thing let loose another string of nonsense words, and light flashed in the air. There was no getting a sense of the source of it and there were so many colors it was impossible for the eye to pick one from the next. Devorast turned his face away.

"Don't look at it!" Devorast shouted, but only Hrothgar was able to heed his words.

The on-rushing gang stopped dead in their tracks, eyes wide, moths agape, fixed in their places and thoroughly mesmerized by the naga's incandescent display.

"Damn their eyes," Hrothgar muttered.

He charged, trying not to consider what bizarre and horrendous fate the snake monster with the human face had in store for him.

One hit, he thought, slapping the tree limb against his palm as he ran. Just one.

Devorast threw another rock, and the naga started to rattle off another one of its spells. Hrothgar sent a silent thanks to Clangeddin Silverbeard that the rock not only beat the incantation from its mouth, but actually struck the creature a glancing blow. Surprised more than hurt, the thing stumbled over its words then growled in frustration. Sparks of blue and green light played in the air around its head, but that was all, and Hrothgar was there.

He swung hard and spun a full circle when the club missed its target. All his warrior's instincts—by the Nine Hells, all his stonecutter's instincts—told him he should have hit the thing, but it simply wasn't where it appeared to be.

"Fool!" the naga hissed at him, then said something else in either the language of the wizards or the language of the nagas. The dwarf hoped it was the latter.

Hrothgar swung again with the tree limb, but at what appeared to him to be thin air just to the creature's left. He felt the branch scrape something, but couldn't see anything. The naga twitched its tail and though it appeared as if the tip of it was a full armslength from Hrothgar's side, it slapped him hard enough to crack a rib—but that was the least of it.

The dwarf's body spasmed and shook, and his teeth clamped down hard.

He'd lost his club and tried to find it. There it was—in Devorast's hands.

The human swung the club hard from right to left across his body, and it hit something more or less near the naga, who reacted as though it had taken the full force of the blow. Devorast lost his grip on the club, and it went whirling past Hrothgar's face.

"It pays!" the naga shrieked. "It pays or more of its stinking kind dies!"

Hrothgar looked up at the sound of another muttered incantation—a short one—and watched the naga slither away at such a speed....

"Look at it ... go," he huffed out.

Devorast dropped the club on the ground at his feet. Hrothgar stood, his whole body still tingling from whatever the naga had done to him.

"You hurt it bad, my friend," the dwarf said, bending to retrieve the makeshift weapon. "But you can bet it'll be back."

Devorast didn't even bother to shrug that off. He ran for the spot where the trench had collapsed. Hrothgar followed, grunting with pain the whole way. They dug as fast as they could, brought in as many men as would fit around the trench, but not one of the five diggers were pulled out alive.

10

5 Ches, the Year of the Sword (1365 DR)
THIRD QUARTER, INNARLITH

She hadn't done any of the things she would have expected herself to do.

She had taken no one's advice. She'd used none of her father's—her family's—gold. The rented flat wasn't in the worst part of Innarlith, but it wasn't in the best either. Deep in the Third Quarter, it was a tradesman's flat above a vacant storefront that used to sell cheese. She hated the smell that was left behind and under any other circumstances never would have put up with it. It was the kind of building she'd have burned down just because she didn't like it. She spent not a single silver on furniture or decorations, and even promised herself—and any disembodied spirits that might be listening in—that she would sleep on the stained mattress, sit on the flea-ridden chair, and keep her clothes in the cupboard with the rat skeleton and the hardened undergarment the previous tenant—perhaps the cheesemonger's wife—had left behind. She didn't bring the flambergé, and had not even a slim dagger or kitchen knife with which she might cut herself.

Phyrea sat on the floor. She had a candle, but had forgotten to bring anything with which to light it, so she sat in the dark.

She folded her arms in front of her and doubled over. Her stomach hurt almost as much as her head throbbed. She wanted to cut herself so badly she wanted to scream. But she wouldn't let herself do either of those things.

The ghosts screamed louder and louder as the room grew darker and darker.

Cut yourself.

You long for it, came a shrieking wail. *We know you crave the cold bite of steel. That thin chill of the blade passing through your own flesh, and the delicious quiver of your hand as you force it to draw your own blood.*

The sword.

That blade bites the best.

Use the flambergé, they screamed at her in a chorus of disembodied howls. *Let it drink you in. Let it bring you to us.*

One of them said, *Take me home. I don't like it here. Take me back to Berrywilde. Berrywilde....*

It sounded like a little girl, but Phyrea could feel its soul sometimes, and it was the cold, bitter, mean spirit of a devil.

"No," she whimpered into the deathly quiet of the merchant quarter at night. "Get out of me."

A man screamed into her ear in inarticulate rage, but no real sound disturbed the silence. The voices didn't speak into her ear, but rather from it.

"Tell me what you want," she asked, though they'd told her before. She wanted a different answer.

Cut yourself.

Use the sword—the sword I gave you.

Don't give it to him. Don't give it to the Thayan.

Go home.

Take us back to our pretty home and stay with us there forever.

Kill for me.

Give us your life.

Spill your blood.

Phyrea shook her head.

She'd gone there—rented the flat, broken from her life in whatever ways she could—in the hope of gaining some clearer understanding. Perhaps, she'd thought, in the silence of a strange place, away from the people and the places that kept the ghosts rooted in her, she might find some answers.

Did you hope to catch us off guard? one of them—a little boy by the sound of his voice, but a monster by the cold dread that followed his words—asked. *What did you hope? That we would just rot in the ground, or that we would be frightened by the stench of rotten cheese? Have you ever smelled the inside of your own moldering casket?*

Phyrea shook her head.

Of course you haven't, a woman whispered at the edge of a sob. *But you will.*

Phyrea opened her eyes, wondering how long she'd had them closed, and saw them gathered all around her. They loomed over her, each one drawn in the air from violet light. They existed as a glow, as a sourceless luminescence, and as voices.

Free us, a little boy with one arm demanded through stern, gritted teeth.

Free yourself, the man with the scar on his cheek said.

Phyrea shook her head, pressed her hands to her temples.

Cut yourself, a woman whispered in her ear so close it made her jump. The desperation plain in the woman's voice made tears well up in Phyrea's eyes. *Maybe it will make it go away.*

Phyrea began to sob so hard she feared her ribs would crack, and that fear only made her cry some more.

Feel that little pain, the woman—the ghost—went on. *Just a little pain of the body makes all the pain of the mind go away. At least for a little while, yes? Just a little? Isn't that good? Doesn't that make it go away? Can't you just make it go away?*

Still crying, Phyrea nodded.

Trust us, said the man with the z-shaped scar—some long-dead relative she'd never known. *We love you. Will you listen while we tell you some things you need to do?*

Phyrea wiped the tears from her eyes only to feel her cheeks soaked with tears again a scant heartbeat later.

Trust us, the old woman insisted.

Phyrea started to nod, and the ghosts started to laugh.

11

7 Ches, the Year of the Sword (1365 DR)
THE CANAL SITE

This is disgraceful," Phyrea said.

She glanced to her left to make sure the strange man was looking at her—he was.

She folded her arms in front of her and let a breath hiss out through her nose. The man didn't speak, but Phyrea knew he'd heard and understood her.

A very short man—no taller than a halfling, but he looked human—rushed up to the stranger and spoke to him in a language Phyrea didn't recognize, though she assumed it was the language of Shou Lung, from whence they'd come.

Lau Cheung Fen answered the little man in clipped

tones that sent the servant scurrying away as fast as he'd approached.

"You object, Miss, to the viewing station or to the endeavor itself?" the Shou merchant asked.

Phyrea paused to consider her response carefully. She'd learned from Meykhati's dreary wife that Shou would only respect slow speech and careful responses.

"Please accept my assurance, Master Lau," she said, "that this is a subject that I have given considerable study. I object to both."

The merchant nodded.

"This canal is a fool's errand," she added.

"I have heard quite differently of this Ivar Devorast," Lau replied.

"There are some who mistake madness . . ." she began, but stopped to think. Then she continued, "Thank you, Master Lau, for letting me reconsider what I was . . . for letting me think."

"One should do precisely that," he said, "before one speaks. But in fact there is more of interest to me in what your first response might have been than in what you might believe I wish to have you say."

Phyrea let one side of her mouth turn up in a smile. Though he was alien to her in so many ways, she could feel him respond to her beauty the same as any Innarlan.

"I hope," she said, "that those who have given you reason to believe that this canal will be of use to your trade will think again. This Devorast has ideas and passions, but he has no true skill."

"He will not be able to finish this?" the Shou asked.

Phyrea looked down at the toes of her boots and sighed. She scraped a line of dried mud from her boot across the wood planks.

"I think this . . . station, as you called it," Phyrea said, "is all one needs to see to understand the nature of this canal." She put as much sarcasm as she could into that last word—and feared it might have been a bit too much. "This is for show. It's a performance. A master manipulator is at work here, not a master builder."

Lau Cheung Fen nodded, and looked out over the men scurrying this way and that, going about the complicated business of digging a miles-long trench from the Lake of Steam to the Nagaflow.

"Soon," Phyrea went on, "this will all stop. This will all be closed down, and all these men will go back to Innarlith."

"I was to understand that he had the support of your ransar," Lau said.

"And he does, for the time being. That will surely change once the gold has run out."

"The ransar's gold?" Lau asked.

"The gold he's already given Devorast," Phyrea told him. "It's all the gold he's going to get—all the gold the ransar will give him. And from what I have been told, there might be enough coin left for a tenday's work. No more."

Lau Cheung Fen nodded again, and she thought it appeared as though he was considering her words. At least she hoped he was.

You're hurting him, the sad woman's voice asked her. *Why?*

She felt her cheek begin to twitch and so she turned away from the Shou merchant.

"To begin, and not to end. . . ." Lau Cheung Fen said, trailing off with a shake of his head.

"It might still be finished," Phyrea offered, "but not by Devorast."

Why? the woman asked again.

But it was the old man, his voice a hoarse croak, who answered, *Because she can.*

Phyrea smiled and Lau asked, "By someone else then?"

"The master builder of Innarlith," she said, "has an apprentice who by all accounts has surpassed him in skill if not position. This man is a senator in Innarlith, well liked and with all the right friends. He will be master builder himself soon, and this canal, should the ransar decide it's indeed something that should be finished, will be—should be—completed by him."

Phyrea swallowed. Her mouth and throat had gone entirely dry. Her chest felt tight, and she drew in a breath only with some difficulty.

"For me," said Lau Cheung Fen, "it matters only that there is a canal. If Ivar Devorast or . . . ?"

"Willem Korvan," she said.

"Or Willem Korvan builds it, it will mean nothing to my ships. If there is water between here and there, they will float."

Phyrea bobbed down in a small bow and grinned. Her upper lip stuck for half a heartbeat on her sand-dry teeth.

"Then I won't belabor the point," she said.

"I did expect to see him here," said Lau, "but I'm told he is away."

"He's gone to beg peace from the nagas," Phyrea replied. She had been at the canal site for less than a day, but had heard things. "They agreed to let him build the canal at first—or so he told the ransar—but came recently and killed some of the workers. I fear that if the canal is completed it might succeed only in spilling ships out into hostile waters, controlled by those monstrous snake things."

She saw the very real concern that prospect elicited on the Shou's face, and turned away.

12

7 Ches, the Year of the Sword (1365 DR)
THE NAGAFLOW

We feel anger," Svayyah said for all the assembled *naja'ssara* to hear. "We feel great, grave, crippling anger, and that anger is directed not toward this *dista'ssara* before you, but for one of our own."

The source of her frustration glowered back at her from where he hung suspended, almost motionless in the cool, murky water. Six more of their kind swirled around them, their attentions struggling between the accused—Shingrayu—and the human, Ivar Devorast. Their tension began to heat the water, and Svayyah's red-orange spines grew redder still.

"Anger?" Shingrayu replied, literally dripping venom from his fangs into the water with each sneered syllable. "What does Svayyah know of anger? Let us tell our tribemates of anger."

Svayyah brought to mind a spell that would heat the water around Shingrayu to so scalding a temperature that his scales would slough from his body. But rather than cast it, she said to the other water nagas, "This *dista'ssara,* this human, is known to us. We have given it our word. We have made an agreement with it."

She looked at Devorast, who floated in the bubble of air she'd made for him with his arms folded across his chest. She could read nothing in his face, but his irritation came off him in waves that nettled at her sea-green scales.

"We care nothing for an agreement with this low monkey of the dry cities," Shingrayu spat. His serpentine body twitched, and he moved forward—only a foot or two—but Svayyah reacted to the threat by enveloping herself in a protective shield of magic. It lit around her with a pearlescent glow, reflecting off the particles of dirt that floated in the water. *"You* made this agreement, Svayyah."

The other half dozen water nagas writhed at the sound of that word: you.

"We close upon the place where words fail," Svayyah warned him.

"Discussions were had," Zaeliira cut in. Her blue-green scales looked dull and old in the meager light from the surface and the glow of Svayyah's shield.

"Zaeliira has been swimming the Nagaflow for eight centuries," said Shuryall, "and however weakened by age, Zaeliira may be, all *naja'ssara* heed the counsel of Zaeliira."

"We make our own way," Shingrayu hissed. "We are *Ssa'Naja.*"

"Shingrayu went above the waves and brought violent magic to the *naja'ssara* in the employ of Ivar Devorast," Svayyah accused. "Does Shingrayu deny this?"

"Is there denial?" asked Zaeliira, who appeared to smart from Shingrayu's comment.

Shingrayu pulled himself out to his full length, an impressive eighteen feet, and drew his scales in tight so that he seemed to blaze green in the murk. "We see prey and we eat. We see invaders and we defend. We see insult and we take offense. We see Svayyah's ambition and we protect ourselves and our ways. There will be no serpent queen here."

The other nagas raced through the water at the sound of those words, whirling faster and faster around the bubble Devorast floated in until it began to turn in the water. He held out his hands—those freakish appendages of the *dista'ssara*—and steadied himself. Svayyah waited for him to speak, but he said nothing. He met her eyes finally, and she fell into his gaze in a way she couldn't understand—in a way that almost made her believe that Shingrayu had been right all along.

"What this *dista'ssara* works will be of great benefit to all the *naja'ssara* of the Nagaflow and the Nagawater," she said, shouting into the tempestuous waters.

The other nagas began to calm, but Shingrayu remained just as rigid.

"Ivar Devorast comes here of his own will," Svayyah went on, "and entirely at our mercy. Should we but wish it, the water would rush in to fill his human lungs and take him to whatever afterlife awaits him. He braves this, for a work."

"A work?" Shuryall asked.

"We have heard of this thing the *dista'ssara* seeks to build," said the young and impetuous Flayanna. "It will bring human after human, ship after ship to our waters.

Human filth. Shingrayu speaks and acts true. We should also like to go to these *dista'ssara* and kill."

"If Flayanna wishes to kill Svayyah first to do so, then we stand at the ready," Svayyah challenged, knowing the younger naga would back down.

Flayanna wouldn't look at her, and only swam more slowly in a circle around Devorast.

"If this human wishes it," Shingrayu said, "let it ask us all, not only Svayyah, who is no queen here."

"Again, that word," Svayyah growled. She twitched her tail to bring herself closer to Shingrayu. "Speak it once more, and it will be the last word to pass Shingrayu's poison tongue."

The other nagas swam then, not too fast, but with a purpose. They gave the two combatants room. They knew what was going to happen. And Svayyah knew that the future of the canal would rest with her. If Shingrayu killed her, Devorast would never live to see the surface again. He likely wouldn't outlive the last dying spasm of Svayyah's own heart.

"There will be no canal to bring human excrement into our home waters, Svayyah," Shingrayu said, his voice heavy with challenge. "There will be no Queen of the Nagaflow."

Svayyah opened her mouth wide, showed her fangs, let her forked tongue taste the familiar waters, and shrieked her challenge at the damnable Shingrayu. The sound, amplified by magic, sent visible ripples through the water. The other nagas pulled even farther back. When the wave front hit Shingrayu, he closed his eyes and withstood the battering force. The side of his face he'd turned into the shockwave burned red, and a welt rose fast to mar his smooth skin. Though his eyes were closed tightly, his tongue slipped through a fast incantation.

Shingrayu opened his eyes to watch three jagged bolts of lime green light slice through the water, leaving not a bubble in their wakes. They crashed into Svayyah's spell shield with force enough only to sting her, but the shield unraveled fast, drifting away into the water like a cloud of luminescent sediment.

Svayyah closed the distance between them with a single lash of her muscular body. In the brief moment that passed before their bodies met, Shingrayu rattled off another spell.

Svayyah wrapped her serpentine body around Shingrayu's, and the first touch sent a nettling ripple through her veins. The touch of the other naga was painful to her. Scales stood out from her flesh, and the ridge of long spines on her back leaped to attention. A painful cramp raced up the entire length of her body and slammed into her jaw.

But she felt it coming, and before it got there, she opened her mouth wide again. Perhaps confident that his shocking grasp would fend her off, Shingrayu left his all too vulnerable neck open. Svayyah's fangs pressed down, and the lightning touch of his spell clamped her jaws closed like a vise. She bit so deeply into Shingrayu's neck that she felt her teeth come together. She couldn't swallow, and couldn't release the hot mouthful of flesh. The blood in the water, like black-red smoke in the air of the surface world, burned her eyes and filled her nose so she could neither see nor smell. The sound of her own blood whooshing through veins and arteries as clamped tight as her jaw drowned out all other sounds.

Holding her breath, Svayyah writhed against Shingrayu as though they were mating. The series of cramps that wrapped her ever tighter around her adversary threatened to snap every bone in her body, and Svayyah steeled herself against that certainty. A loud *snap*, then the second and third, came to her not through her ears but through her scales. She thought at first that her bones had begun to break under Shingrayu's magic, but there was no pain.

It wasn't her bones that were breaking.

The effect of Shingrayu's spell fled all at once. Svayyah

uncoiled, out of control, like a string from around a child's toy. She floated away from Shingrayu and spat the mouthful of his throat out into the water between them. She coughed and shuddered, just trying to breathe.

Shingrayu drifted limp, but his eyes were open. He blinked and opened his mouth to speak. He had something to say, but couldn't get the words out. His lips twitched. Intelligence and intent left his eyes first, then the life itself fled.

Svayyah continued to gasp for a breath as the other water nagas circled closer.

"Svayyah says that this is a great work this *dista'ssara* does," Zaeliira said. "Does that make this human a great being? Does it make it *senthissa'ssa?*"

Does it? Svayyah thought.

She turned to Devorast, who's expression had not changed at all. She felt a sense of inevitability from him. It wasn't that he knew she would kill Shingrayu, but something else—something that depended in no way on what she did, what Shingrayu did, or what any of the *naja'ssara* did.

"Are you, Ivar Devorast?" she managed to whisper through a throat still struggling open. "Is Ivar Devorast a teacher worthy of emulating?"

"Well?" Zaeliira pressed.

Svayyah turned to her kin and said, "If he builds it."

She had spoken like a human, and had done it on purpose. The phrasing was not lost on Zaeliira at least.

"Very well," said the aged water naga. "Let this *dista'ssara* build its great work. If it succeeds, it will have proven itself *senthissa'ssa*. Do the *naja'ssara* of the Nagaflow and Nagawater agree? All of like mind on this?"

Each of the other five nagas signaled their agreement and one by one swam off to their own business. Zaeliira and Svayyah shared a look, then she too swam off at her own slow pace.

Svayyah looked at Devorast in his bubble and shook her head. He had done precisely what he should have, and Svayyah found herself wholly unable to believe it.

He hadn't said a thing the whole time.

13

10 Ches, the Year of the Sword (1365 DR)
THIRD QUARTER, INNARLITH

How did you—" Phyrea began, then quickly chose from two possible endings to that question—"find me?"

Devorast stepped closer to her, but stopped more than her arm's length away. He'd been sitting in one of the uncomfortable old chairs that came with the rented flat, waiting for her in the dark. In the light of the candle she'd lit before she knew he was sitting there, his skin looked softer than she knew it to be, but his eyes were no less guarded, no more forthcoming.

"Osorkon," he said. His voice sounded different, softer too, but that couldn't have been the candlelight.

"The ransar?" she asked. She didn't really care how he'd found her, but a chill ran down her spine at the revelation that the ransar knew of what she thought of as her hiding place. Of all the conversations, of all the things she hoped would pass between them that night, the wheres and whys and hows of the things Osorkon knew about her was of the least interest. "How did he—?"

Phyrea stopped when Devorast moved even closer to her. He smelled of the dry earth, the poison sea, and the bitter wind.

"Is that it?" she asked, her voice below even a whisper, but she knew he heard her. "Is that how you can do this to me? Is that your secret? Are you an elemental? Some creature of all the forces of nature—earth, air, fire, water . . . the Astral ether itself?"

He reached out a hand and though her mind wanted her

body to flinch away, she found herself leaning forward. When the tip of his finger found the lace of her bodice she fell half a step closer to him.

"What are you?" she asked.

He raised his other hand and began to unlace her bodice. Phyrea's knees shook, then her hips, then her shoulders. Her hands had been shaking already. She found it difficult to breathe in, but exhaled in throaty gasps.

"I'm all I ever needed to be, and all you ever need from me," Devorast said. "A man."

"No," she said, even while wishing it was true. "That can't be. That can't be all."

The stiff leather bodice fell away.

"I've said things about you," Phyrea told him as he put his hand to the side of her face. His palm was warm and rough. "I've hurt you."

He kissed her on the cheek, and she leaned against him. She put her hands on his forearms. The thin tunic he wore was made of rough material, cheap peasant clothes.

"I poison people against you," she told him as his tongue played on her ear. Her body quivered at his touch. She couldn't quite breathe. "I hurt you on purpose."

"No, you don't," he whispered, then kissed her on the mouth.

She tried to melt into him, tried her best to disappear into his embrace, but couldn't.

"If you tell me to stop, I'll stop," she said when their lips finally parted. "If you demand my obedience, you'll have it. If you want me as your wife, your harlot, your slave, or your mistress, you will have me. I will remake myself to whatever standards you impose. I will erase myself if that's what you wish. I'll cut myself. I'll kill myself. I'll—"

"Do none of those things," he said into the skin of her neck. "You don't need to do anything to satisfy me, the same way I'll never do anything simply to satisfy you."

Tears streamed from her eyes.

"I can't have you, can I?" she asked.

"Not the way you mean," was his answer.

She cried while he held her for a little while, and she only stopped when she realized that in that time, she hadn't heard one of the voices, or seen a single apparition. She hadn't wanted to hurt herself, though she'd offered to.

"I have to destroy you," she told him even as she let him carry her to her bed. "This world is too small for you."

He moved to kiss her again, but she stopped him.

"There are people who are trying to stop you," she told him, though he must have already known. "They'll succeed, too, because it's easy to do what they do. It's the easiest thing in the world to tear a man down, to pick at his flesh till there's nothing left of him but bones. I can't watch that happen. Do you understand me?"

He smiled in a way that made Phyrea's heart seem to stop in her chest.

"I won't let you live to be so degraded," she whispered as he finished undressing her. "Not by them."

Those were the last words either of them spoke that night, and the ghosts didn't come back until Devorast finally left.

14

5 Kythorn, the Year of the Sword (1365 DR)
SECOND QUARTER, INNARLITH

Marek Rymüt couldn't see the ghosts that haunted Phyrea, but he knew they were there. Though he was no necromancer—enchantments were more his cup of tea—he knew enough of the ways of the undead. He knew their power and their sharply delineated limitations. Over the past few tendays he'd learned more and more about the spirits that had taken up residence in that poor little rich girl, that tortured daughter of a wealthy idiot, and he found himself inventing more and more excuses to see her.

"My apologies, gentlesir," Phyrea said to Marek's oldest friend, "please help me to pronounce your name."

"In-*sith*-rill-ax," the black dragon said, enunciating each syllable with great care. In the guise of a human, he smiled at her without the barest sliver of interest.

"Insithryllax," the girl repeated. "It's an imposing name. To look at you I would have to say you are Chondathan, but that doesn't sound like a Chondathan name."

"I suppose," the disguised dragon replied, "that I'm more Mulhorandi than Chondathan, but the name is ... a very old one."

Marek caught the twinkle in Phyrea's eyes that told him she might have been close to figuring out that Insithryllax was no more Mulhorandi than Marek was a field mouse.

"How are you enjoying the tea, my love?" Marek asked her, returning the twinkle.

She did her best not to look him in the eye when she answered, "I've never been one for tea, Master Rymüt, but I'm sure it's wonderful."

"The leaves are harvested on Midsummer's eve from the slopes of one particular mountain high in the Spine of the World," he told her, inventing every word of the preposterous tale as he went along. "Orc slaves carry them whole to a shop in the heart of fair Silverymoon, where they are purified with spells granted by the grace of Chauntea. One must have a signed writ from the Lady Alustriel herself to buy it."

Phyrea laughed and said, "Somehow I doubt you possess such a writ, Master Rymüt."

"You wound me with the truth, my darling girl," he responded with an entirely false chuckle. "The owner of the tea shop knows someone who knows someone who knows someone."

Phyrea nodded, making it plain she'd lost interest in stories about tea she didn't even drink. Instead she looked at Insithryllax.

"The way your eyes dart around the room," she said to

the dragon, "constantly on the lookout for—what? Another mad alchemist? A rival wizard determined to resist the inevitable? I was under the impression that no such attacks have come for some time."

So, Marek thought, you've been studying me, too. Well done, girl. But tread lightly.

"I am happy to report," Marek said before the even more wary black dragon could assume the worst from her playful question, "that my efforts to civilize the trade in enchanted items and spellcraft in Innarlith has met with some success of late. It is a credit to the city of your birth."

Phyrea forced a smile and said, "Any foreigner can have his way with Innarlith. It's to your credit only that you have tamed the other foreigners."

Marek laughed that off and said, "You hold so low a regard for your own city, I wonder why you stay here."

That elicited a look so grave Marek was momentarily taken aback.

"Please, Marek," Insithryllax said, "you'll offend the girl."

When the Red Wizard regarded his old friend, he was happy to see no trace of real concern on his face.

"Please do accept my—" Marek started.

"No," Phyrea cut in. "Don't bother. Of course I hold this cesspool in low regard." She paused to listen to something, but the tea room was characteristically quiet. "Of course I do."

Marek put the cup to his lips and whispered a spell, hiding the gestures as a momentary indecision over which of the little pastries to sample.

... him the sword, a voice whispered from nowhere. It was a strange sensation. Marek had heard voices in his head before, had often communicated in that way, but it was something else entirely to hear a voice in someone else's head. *It's for you.*

Then a woman: *We meant it for you.*

And a little boy: *If you give it to him, we will be cross with you.*

Marek resisted the urge to shudder. Instead he took a sip of tea and studied Phyrea's face.

She was beautiful, of that there was no doubt, but she looked older than he knew her to be. She'd seen only twenty summers, but to look at her eyes he'd say she was fifty.

"You're not well," he ventured.

She shook her head, but told him, "I'm fine."

"You've been busy."

"What do you mean?"

"I've heard the things you've been saying about that horrid man," Marek said. "You know, that ditch digger?"

"Devorast," she whispered, then cleared her throat and said more loudly, "Ivar Devorast."

Use the sword on him, a man all but screamed at Phyrea and Marek brought to mind a spell that he hoped could save his life if she followed that order.

Devorast, the little boy whined. *I hate him. You need to kill him with the flam ... the flam ..."*

"The flambergé," Marek said aloud, risking that the ghosts would realize he could hear them.

Phyrea looked him in the eye for the first time that day, but before Marek could do so much as smile she looked down at the tightly-wrapped bundle at her feet—a sheet of soft linen precisely the dimensions of a sheathed long sword, tied together with twine.

No! one of the spirits screamed.

Wait, breathed another.

"You'll be able to tell me ..." she started, but was interrupted by the boy.

I'll hate you if you give it to him. He'll kill you with it. He wants to kill you.

She shook her head.

"I will make a study of it," he promised her. "And I won't give it back."

We'll shred your mind if you let him take it away, said

the voice of an old woman.

It was for you, another ghost whimpered.

"I can't hand it to you," she said and took a sip of her tea. She grimaced.

"Leave it on the floor then," Marek told her. "I'll take it with me when I go."

Don't let him, a woman moaned. *Plea—*

His spell had run its course, but Marek had heard all he needed to hear of the voices in Phyrea's head.

"I hate to keep bringing him up, as he seems to upset you so," Marek said. "But I wish you would tell me why you're so opposed to the Cormyrean and his ludicrous mission. After all, isn't he, like me, a foreigner manipulating the weaknesses of the city you hate so? Why, one would think you'd have invited him to tea with us."

"I hope you two will never meet again," she said. "And anyway I don't care about the canal. I hope it is finished ... anyway it makes no difference to me if it is or isn't, as long as Devorast—" and only someone as astute as Marek Rymüt could have detected the pause in her voice just then—"doesn't get to see it through."

"Well, then ..." Marek chuckled. "Still, I wonder why Willem Korvan."

"What?"

"I know you've mentioned his name to a number of people," he pressed.

With a shrug Phyrea answered, "My father thinks highly of him. And he's a foreigner. Why not him?"

"Why not Devorast?" Marek continued to press.

Phyrea paused, almost froze in place. It appeared to Marek as though she searched deep within herself for an answer.

Or is she listening to the ghosts again? he thought.

"Because," she finally answered, "I hate him."

Marek took a breath to speak, but stopped himself when he realized he didn't know who she was talking about. Did she hate Devorast or Korvan? Or both?

15

Under any other circumstances, Marek would have demanded complete silence. He would have roared that order in a magically-enhanced voice loud enough to burst the eardrums of the offending parties, and he would have followed the order with threats so cruel the sound of them could peel the paint from a wall.

But he didn't do that. He unwrapped the sword to the accompaniment of saws and shovels, shouted orders and pained grunts, and stone grating against stone and hammers clanging on hot metal. As anxious as he'd been to examine that fascinating flambergé of Phyrea's there was still work to be done on his keep, after all.

The huge black dragon alit several paces away, scattering some of the black firedrakes that had been bent to their work beneath him. They scampered out of his way as he moved to the unfinished wall and craned his massive, serpentine neck down to regard Marek.

"Ah," said the dragon, "there you are."

The linen sheet came away from the scabbarded sword, and Marek stifled a giggle.

"Lovely, isn't it?" the Red Wizard said. "Such craftsmanship."

"Elven," Insithryllax said, betraying a dragon's appreciation for the finer things.

"I believe so, yes," Marek agreed. "And do you feel it?"

"How could I not?"

"Such a powerful enchantment," the wizard said.

The dragon made a show of sniffing the air in front of him and said, "Necromancy."

"Yes," Marek replied.

"What do you want with it?"

Marek looked up at the wyrm and smiled. Behind him, ringing the flat-topped hill upon which his keep was being built, was the sprawling camp of his army of black firedrakes.

"They're almost ready, aren't they?" Marek said, ham-handedly changing the subject.

The dragon snorted, releasing a puff of gray-black mist that made Marek's eyes itch even from a distance.

"Sorry," the dragon said when Marek blinked and rubbed his eyes.

"Part of the joys of your friendship," the Red Wizard quipped. "But be that as it may"—he pulled the wavy-bladed sword from its scabbard—"how could I not want a weapon such as this?"

"But you?" asked the dragon. "A wizard?"

"Phyrea thinks that anyone who is killed by this blade is reanimated in some state of undeath," Marek said.

"Is she right?"

Marek shrugged and replied, "Care to try? Haven't you always secretly wished to be a dracolich?"

The wyrm's nostrils flared, but he held his acidic mist in.

"A jest, I assure you, my friend," the wizard covered. With some difficulty—he almost cut himself twice—Marek sheathed the sword. "I will study this in great detail."

"Tell me in no uncertain terms, Marek, that you have no plans for that blade that involve me," the dragon insisted. "Unless you mean to give it to me."

Marek locked eyes with the dragon—not an easy thing to do—and said, "I would do nothing of the kind without your consent. My thoughts run toward . . . someone else."

Marek hoped the dragon would accept that. He was nowhere near ready to reveal any plans he had for that blade, especially since it could be some time, years even, before he set those plans in motion.

"Good," the black dragon said.

"I will offer yet another apology, my friend," said the

Red Wizard. "I have not been back here as much as I would have liked. Matters in the city have kept me occupied, but the progress here is a credit to your efforts, and you have my thanks."

The dragon twisted his neck in what Marek had come to know as one variation on a shrug, and said, "The black firedrakes are learning more quickly every day. They act almost entirely on their own now."

Marek placed the sword on a table crowded with other items of varying power and went to the edge of the incomplete wall. He looked out over the finite confines of his tiny little universe and sighed. The air tasted stale, and he realized that every breath he took felt less satisfying than the last. He could feel Insithryllax eyeing him.

"We can't last much longer here," the dragon said.

Marek shook his head and replied, "No, not with so many lungs to fill."

The black firedrakes, some in human form, others resembling small dragons, walked or flew in a constant flurry of activity. They'd built what could best be described as a small village on the rocky plain of the Land of One Hundred and Thirteen.

"Could be they sense it, too," Insithryllax said. With his eyes, and his great long neck he drew Marek's gaze up into the always-cloudy sky.

Two black firedrakes wheeled in the air, swooping in fast at each other to spray jets of hissing black acid. They dodged and weaved in the dead air, clawing and snapping their jaws. Another dozen or so of their kind circled the pair, watching their every move and sometimes spinning in the air in reaction to some surprise bite or well-placed spray of acid.

"They'll always do that, I think," Marek mused, watching the circling drakes.

One of the creatures managed to get under the other and bit down hard on its opponent's right foot. Though he was too far away to hear it, Marek could imagine the mighty crunch of the black firedrake's talon shattering under its sister's fangs.

"There are ways to replenish the air. Spells. . . ." Marek began.

The black firedrake that had been bitten snapped its head down and spat a mist of corrosive fluid at the drake that still had it's broken foot in its mouth. The acid poured over its wing like syrup, and pieces of the thin membrane tore off and wafted to the ground, sizzling on the edges.

"Still," Insithryllax said, "at least some of the fire-drakes will have to be taken out."

The burned firedrake opened its mouth to scream, and it fell away from its opponent's shattered foot. With one wing burned almost entirely away, it spun in the air like the seed from a maple tree, shrieking in agony the whole way down.

"Higharvestide, I think," Marek said, pausing only when the burned firedrake hit the ground and seemed to collapse in on itself.

Others of its kind dived in to tear chunks of flesh from its still twitching corpse and Insithryllax asked, "Why Higharvestide?"

"I don't know," Marek answered with a shrug. "I just have a feeling everything will be aligned properly by then."

Four black firedrakes went after the one with the shattered foot and brought it down in pieces.

"That's less than four months away," sighed the dragon. "We should survive until then."

16

9 Kythorn, the Year of the Sword (1365 DR)
ABOARD JIÉ ZUÒ, IN INNARLITH HARBOR

The air was so warm she didn't mind being wet, even so late at night. The thin material of her undergarments clung to her, and Phyrea was reminded of her leathers, which she hadn't worn in a very long time.

You have as much right to it as she does, the old woman with the terrible burn scars on her face and neck whispered, *maybe more so. It should be yours.*

Phyrea shook her head and looked at the woman. She stood only a few paces down the rail from her, though "stood" might not have been the right word. Her feet didn't quite touch the deck. Phyrea could easily make out the outlines of the sterncastle through her incorporeal form, and when she spoke her lips didn't move.

"No," Phyrea answered aloud, shaking her head.

You could have killed that man, the little boy said from behind her. Phyrea didn't turn to look but she could feel him there. *No one will do anything to you if you do it. You won't get in trouble. They're not from here. They're not like us.*

"I don't want to kill anyone," Phyrea said. "Not these people."

She looked out over the still water to the lights of the city. The moon was bright in the clear, star-speckled sky, trailing her glittering tears behind her. Phyrea felt a sudden urge to offer a prayer to Selûne—a prayer of forgiveness, perhaps.

You have nothing to be ashamed of, the voice of the man murmured in her head. He sounded bored, old, and tired. *Except for relinquishing the sword.*

Yes, said the old woman, *you should be ashamed of giving away that sword.*

"No," Phyrea sighed.

Yes, the woman repeated as she drifted closer. *The Thayan will destroy you and everything you've ever loved with that sword.*

And it was meant for you, the man said.

And we want it back, said the boy.

"You're wrong," Phyrea said, not looking at the ghosts. She ran a finger along the cool, smooth tiles on the railing. The glazed ceramic shone in the moonlight. "No, you're lying. He can't destroy everything I've ever loved, because I've never loved anything, except—"

"Who are you?" a strange, heavily-accented voice interrupted. Phyrea dismissed it as another ghost, until she heard a footstep. "Answer me, woman, or your head and your body will go separately into the next world."

Phyrea turned her head. The woman that had been there before, the one that had taken up residence in Phyrea's head, was gone. The silhouette of a woman stood at the hatch to the sterncastle. Phyrea couldn't see her face, but the straight-bladed long sword she held in her right hand reflected Selûne's brilliance.

"Speak," the woman demanded.

Phyrea sighed, and made a point to leave both her hands on the railing in front of her where they could be clearly seen.

Another hatch opened, and a man's voice rattled through a sentence's worth of words in some incomprehensible tongue. He was answered by a single word from the woman.

"I am master of this vessel," the woman said, "and I command you to explain yourself."

"I just wanted to see it," Phyrea said, her voice quiet and small, weak even, but carrying well enough in the still night air. "No . . . I mean, I wanted to touch it. I wanted to feel it."

The woman and the man kept quiet and still while Phyrea fought back tears.

"My man," the woman—Ran Ai Yu—said, "did you kill him?"

Phyrea shook her head.

The woman stepped closer, and Phyrea could feel her eyes on her. Phyrea was unarmed. She was practically naked. There were more footsteps, more men, more of Ran Ai Yu's crew.

"I might have hurt him," Phyrea said. "I'm sorry."

"I know you," Ran Ai Yu said. "You are the daughter of the master builder."

She wants him too, you know, the old woman's voice whispered inside her.

"Why wouldn't she?" Phyrea answered aloud.

Ran Ai Yu stepped closer still.

"Are you drunk?" the Shou woman asked. "Are you mad?"

Phyrea laughed and sobbed at the same time.

"He built this," Phyrea said. "He made it with his own hands, but more than that, he formed it in his mind from nothing. He conjured it, you know, but not the way a wizard would. It was an act of pure creation, the invention of something from nothing."

"Ivar Devorast," Ran Ai Yu said, "yes."

Phyrea cringed, almost seized when the woman of purple light shrieked, *You see?*

"Stop it," Phyrea demanded of the ghost. "You don't know."

"I do," the Shou answered.

Phyrea shook her head, her tears mingling with the harbor water that still dampened her face.

"What haunts you, girl?" Ran Ai Yu asked.

Phyrea looked up into the black sky, purposefully turning her head away from dazzling Selûne, and said, "Him, more than anything."

We are your blood, Phyrea, the voice of the little girl who walked through walls sighed, *and we love you. We love you more than he ever will, no matter how much you smile at him, or whatever presents you bring.*

"You lie," Phyrea whispered.

"You must find someone to help you," Ran Ai Yu said. "But not here. You are not welcome here."

One of the men spoke to his mistress in their native tongue, and again Ran Ai Yu answered with but a single word.

Then in Common she said, "No, I can not let her swim back at night. There will be *tonrongs*. I will have my men lower a boat and row you back to the city. I hope you will never again be so foolish as to do this, and if my man here is dead, or dies as a result of your attack upon him, there will be a debt owed."

Phyrea couldn't move, even just to shrug, nod, or hake her head. Her hands warmed the tiles on the railing, and her feet caressed the deck. Her heart seemed to swell in her chest and she stood there, her hair beginning to dry and swirl in a sudden breeze, while they lowered a boat.

Before she climbed down into it, she looked at the Shou sailor sprawled on the deck, and in the quiet she could hear him breathing.

You should have killed that slant-eyed foreign bastard, the little boy told her.

Phyrea saw him standing there, the outline of Ran Ai Yu visible through the violet luminescence, and she was all but overcome with sadness.

"Perhaps," the Shou woman said, "if you too had something of his ..."

Not wanting her to continue, Phyrea turned and followed a wary sailor into the waiting boat.

17

10 Kythorn, the Year of the Sword (1365 DR)
THE PALACE OF MANY SPIRES, INNARLITH

Though his skin was pale, verging on pink, and his features were typically brutish, the Ransar of Innarlith reminded Ran Ai Yu of the monks of her homeland. His head was shaved clean, and his dress was simple, functional, and devoid of ornamentation. Though in the strictly confined limits of the city-state he was a sort of king, it would have been impossible to draw any such conclusion merely by looking at him. When he walked, his arms swung at his side in an undisciplined, even boyish manner. He smelled faintly of garlic and the rough tallow soap the Innarlans too rarely used. His feet were clad in simple leather sandals that exposed his long, crooked toes.

"Her name is Phyrea," Ran Ai Yu said. "She is the daughter of your master builder."

Osorkon nodded as they strolled, and replied, "Of course. Everyone knows Phyrea, at least, as much as she allows us to know her. No small number of men would like to take her as a mistress if not a wife. There are rumors of a dark side to her, too—some accusations of thievery, even. What interest can she be to Shou Lung?"

"She is of interest to me, Ransar," Ran Ai Yu said. She didn't bother to once again correct him, to tell him that she was a merchant—mistress of a sailing vessel of her own—and not an official, ambassador, or other sort of representative of her homeland. "Only just before middark last night did I find her standing by the rail of my ship. She had swim . . . swum . . . I don't . . . but she swam there in the dark of the night at great risk, and with motives I am having trouble understanding."

"She can't have been trying to steal from you," Osorkon said.

"I do not have reason to believe that."

Ran Ai Yu let her fingertips brush a blooming rose as she strolled past a particularly healthy bush. The ransar's garden was impressive for a private residence, though the palaces of Shou Lung had gardens far larger. She'd noted the ransar's gaze darting from bloom to bloom as they walked and could see that he appreciated the foliage and the peacefulness of the place. Somehow, it didn't match the man.

"She is haunted," the Shou merchant said.

"Phyrea?"

"Spirits have attached themselves to her," she explained. "One of my men is sensitive to such things. Even without his counsel, I would have seen it in her myself. She speaks to people who can not be seen."

The ransar shrugged and said, "Maybe she didn't swim to your ship alone."

Ran Ai Yu skipped a step. Her hesitation elicited a

scant smile from the ransar. She hadn't considered that possibility—that Phyrea might have been accompanied by some number of compatriots cloaked in spells of invisibility—but somehow it simply didn't ring true.

"Nothing was missing of my cargo or personal items," she said. "I am sure she was alone."

"And you have a sensitive man. . . ."

Ran Ai Yu let that pass.

"Would you like me to inform the master builder?" he asked.

"If you feel that would be proper."

Ran Ai Yu let her gaze drift up from the flowers to the towering ramparts of the Palace of Many Spires. One tower in particular struck her eye. It was newer than the others and possessed of an ethereal beauty that was out of place in the otherwise underwhelming city of Innarlith.

"I find it difficult, sometimes," the ransar said, "to determine precisely what is and what isn't proper. It can plague one, don't you agree?"

"With all honor and respect, Ransar, but I do not. I have come to know many of the ways of Innarlith, so to me I am not surprised by what you have been so kind to confide in me, but in my realm we are schooled from our youngest age—from before we can even speak—in the ways of polite and civilized society. We are taught always to know what is proper in any situation. It is the blood and sinew of our very culture."

What she'd said seemed to please him, and he replied, "Well then I guess I will have to rely on you to tell me if it would be proper for a man like me to ask to see a woman like you in a social setting."

Ran Ai Yu was struck momentarily dumb. She wasn't even entirely certain what the ransar was asking.

"I am certain we will encounter each other again at receptions and such," she said. "My business demands that I—"

"Tell me if you are uncomfortable with my advances,

Ran Ai Yu," he said, his voice sending a chill down the Shou woman's spine.

"I am uncomfortable only because I have been here so long, and have been unable to unload precious cargo for trade in Innarlith," she said.

He sighed at the change in subject and said, "There are men in this city who are inflaming the passions of the working class, though I have no idea of the purpose behind it. I strive diligently, I assure you, to take matters in hand. You will unload your cargo when limited resources make it possible."

"It is warm today," she said.

Ransar Osorkon grunted in the affirmative.

"I arrived on the twelfth day of Alturiak," she said. "Though I greatly enjoy your city and its people, now it is four months gone by, the warm winds of summer blow, and still my ship is at anchor in the harbor."

"Take your complaints to the harbor master," the ransar replied.

Ran Ai Yu nodded and changed the subject. "I have been to visit the site of the canal that Ivar Devorast constructs in your name. It is of great interest to me, to one day be able to sail into the Sea of Fallen Stars, which I have long heard tell of, but have never seen."

"Devorast didn't tell you that he was building it in my name, did he?"

"I only assumed."

The ransar sighed, and Ran Ai Yu risked a glance at his face. His pinkish skin had turned a deeper red, and she could feel that he was embarrassed by her rebuff.

"It honors you, nonetheless," she told him.

"Devorast...." said the ransar. "Now that one is haunted."

"But not in the same way as the master builder's unfortunate daughter?"

"No," Osorkon replied. "Devorast is haunted by his own greatness. If the son of a whore had an once of political ambition I would have had to have him killed a long time ago."

It was Ran Ai Yu's turn to be embarrassed. She said, "She knows Ivar Devorast, yes?"

"Phyrea?"

Ran Ai Yu nodded, and the ransar shrugged and said, "I suppose so."

"I think she came to my ship because he built it."

"Devorast built your ship?"

"He did, yes," said the Shou merchant, "some three years ago."

"That's right," the ransar said. "He did build ships."

They went a few slow steps in silence, and Ran Ai Yu could no longer ignore the feeling that he wanted her to leave.

"I will allow you to proceed with your day, Ransar," she said. "Please accept my most humble thanks for the honor of your time, and your garden."

He stopped walking and turned to look at her. Though she didn't want to, etiquette demanded she do the same.

"I will try to convey to the master builder that his daughter is haunted," he said with a trace of a bow, "by Ivar Devorast, and other ghosts."

She didn't believe him, because it was obvious then that he didn't believe her. Still, she bowed, thanked him, and went back to her ship.

18

11 Kythorn, the Year of the Sword (1365 DR)
THE CHAMBER OF LAW AND CIVILITY, INNARLITH

Willem Korvan wasn't drunk, but he had been drinking. He'd come straight from the inn where he'd been with Halina. He still smelled of her—or at least he feared he did, but it was the smell of the wine he feared most. The air inside the giant chamber that served as a meeting room—a sort of temple—for the senate of Innarlith was dry and hot. Though it was many dozens of times the size of the room in the inn, he felt more closed in by the senate chamber. He found it more difficult to breathe there.

"Do you think it a waste of your time, my boy," the master builder said, "if I tell you again how proud I am of you?"

Willem couldn't answer, so he shook his head.

But I can't believe this, he told himself. She can't be the one I end up with. My mother is right. Marek Rymüt is right. They're all right. Halina is wrong.

"You've done well these past months, Willem," Inthelph droned on. "We are all very happy with you—all your generous patrons."

He thought of a dozen sycophantic replies to that but spoke none of them. He couldn't muster the energy to push that much air out of his lungs.

"But you should also know that I expect more of you than a vote in these chambers," Inthelph went on.

His voice made Willem's skin crawl. The master builder spoke to him in paternal tones, and Willem wanted nothing more than to strike out. He couldn't gather the strength to speak to him, but he felt sure he could snap the old man's neck in the blink of an eye. They were alone in the chamber, after all. It would be a simple enough thing to concoct a story—a tragic fall, almost silly really, that such a great man might trip on a stair and fall just so as to break his neck. No one would question, would they? Would they take the master builder's still corpse to a priest and inquire of his departed soul? Would Inthelph accuse Willem from beyond the grave? It was the sort of thing one had to consider, though they never did that with Khonsu....

"Though you're a senator now you're still a very talented young man, and the city needs your talents, perhaps now more than ever."

But then the old man was wrong, wasn't he? Willem had no talent—none at all—save the talent for impressing easily impressed old men and shy, bookish foreign women. He couldn't build anything. He couldn't leave a legacy, or a mark on the world. But he could kiss withered old arse with the best of them. Willem desperately craved more wine, or something stronger.

"I just simply deplore the notion that any serious program of public works should proceed without your involvement. It's a disservice to the city, the ransar, and the people of Innarlith—a grave disservice indeed."

Willem tried to sigh, but had no strength to do it, so he just sat there trying to keep a picture of Devorast's canal from forming in his head. They both knew that that was what the master builder was talking about. But apparently only Willem knew that there was no way in all Nine screaming bloody Hells that he would be able to build it. Willem couldn't even really imagine the thing. He understood the basic concept of course: Build a trench from the shore of the Lake of Steam to the bank of the Nagaflow and somehow fill it with water to form a man-made river. But it was such a long way, and would have to be so deep.

"I'm sure you know that the ransar will soon enough discover the sort of man your old friend Ivar Devorast is, after all. That fool—it's Tymora's most fickle whimsy that the man has avoided his unfortunate patron's wrath this long. I mean, honestly...."

Maybe, Willem thought, this ransar is not as stupid as you or I. Maybe he understands that though Devorast was no one's idea of a sparkling conversationalist, he was perhaps the only human being on the whole of spinning Toril that might ever have even conceived of the thing, let alone was in possession of the skills necessary to see it done. If the master builder insisted that Willem finish the canal, he would have to do it, and he would have to fail.

"But that's all just fancy now, isn't it? We'll let it be as it may, yes?"

Yes, yes, yes, Willem thought. Let it be. Let it be damned with the both of them to the endless Abyss. Willem rubbed his face, and an image of Halina came unbidden to his mind's eye. She lay naked on the bed in the inn where he'd left her. She smiled at him in that way she had of smiling at him that made him not want to kill himself.

"Really, Willem, I worry about you. You don't look all together well. Please tell me you've been sleeping. It's sleep that is the finest tonic for any man's body and soul. You've earned some rest, at least until you are called upon to finish some endeavor or another for your dear adopted home."

Rest? Sleep? With Halina, yes, two or three days out of every ten. The rest of the time he couldn't sleep. No half dozen bottles of wine could make him pass out, even. All he did was sit at home in the dark and think, the sound of his mother's snoring wafting through the strangely unfamiliar halls of his townhouse. That sound reminded him of his childhood, and was just barely enough to keep him from opening his veins in the wee hours before dawn, but the house he'd bought was no home for him.

"Perhaps you need a diversion, or better yet, a family. You know my feelings on this, Willem, and I think Phyrea's coming around. In fact, I know for a fact she is. By the Merchantfriend's jingling purse, my boy, I've long considered you a son—a part of the family already. Marry Phyrea, Willem, and let's make that truly the case, eh?"

Marry Phyrea? The thought made his head spin more than the wine or the memory of the softness of Halina's skin. Phyrea had shown him nothing but scathing contempt, and her mouth-breathing old imbecile of a father thought that she was "coming around?" Her disdain was something Willem carried around with him like other men carried knives. It had become a comfortable part of him. Marry Phyrea? He had a better chance of wedding Chauntea herself in a grand ceremony in the Great Mother's Garden.

"I suppose you've heard the things she's been saying about you. My daughter has become quite the devotee of

Senator Willem Korvan. She's mentioned you to the ransar himself—to all the finest people. She's sung your praises to Marek Rymüt, and even to some visiting celestial from Shou Lung ... you've met him, haven't you? The tall, willowy one that looks even more like an elf than the rest of his kind. She's made you something of a cause. All the wives are gossiping. They've sussed out her motives and I swear the wives of half the senators in Innarlith have already bought their dresses for the wedding."

The master builder was too stupid to have invented that. It must be true. But how? Why? How cold it possibly serve Phyrea to turn her opinion of him so sharply that she would even bother to criticize him in the higher social circles, let alone praise him. But the master builder couldn't be making it up. And what of Halina?

"Oh, gods ..." Willem muttered, his gorge rising in his throat.

"Goodness gracious, Willem," Inthelph cooed, putting a dry, bony hand on his back. "You aren't well, are you?"

"I'm fine," he managed to say. "I'm just ..."

The master builder laughed—a cackling, old man's laugh—and said, "My daughter can have that effect on men, can't she?"

Willem nodded once then emptied his stomach onto the floor of the senate chamber.

19

12 Kythorn, the Year of the Sword (1365 DR)
THE LAND OF ONE HUNDRED AND THIRTEEN

While Salatis stood in slack-jawed amazement, Marek Rymüt stood behind him and wove a spell that would, as he'd heard the Zulkir of Enchantment once say, "soften the ground a bit." It hadn't taken trust for Marek to bring Salatis to his pocket dimension. He would either be able to depend on the man, or he'd be able to kill him. But what he wanted more than the man's trust was his word.

"Where are we?" the senator asked, the words sounding hollow because he couldn't seem to get his lips to come together. "Beshaba protect us from her own ill will."

"Beshaba now, is it?" Marek asked.

He leaned in closer to the tall, angular man. Marek had to reach up a little to take the senator's pendant in his hand. Finely crafted of red enamel over silver, the antlers depicted there had been carved from a single thin shard of ebony. Though he'd expected Salatis to move away at his advance, the senator stood stock still, gazing out over the abrupt confines of the Land of One Hundred and Thirteen. Marek took the opportunity to study the man a little more closely.

He stood fully nine inches over six feet, but surely weighed less—by dozens of pounds even—than did Marek. Where Marek was bald, his head adorned with the tattoos of a Red Wizard, Salatis sported a full, healthy head of hair. A Chondathan, his hair was dark, but age and other difficulties had traced it with gray.

"What in the name of the Maid of Misfortune are those things?" Salatis asked.

"They are black firedrakes," Marek answered. "Do you like them?"

Insithryllax wheeled in the sky overhead, a cadre of firedrakes surrounding him in close formation. Salatis looked up, and his breath caught in his throat.

"M-Master Rymüt ..."

"Never fear," said Marek.

Salatis tried to run when Insithryllax reeled down to land on the hill next to them. Marek took the senator by the arm and held him. He could feel the tall man shake, and his skin was clammy and cold. The dirt shuddered under the dragon's considerable weight when it came to ground, and Salatis almost fell to his knees.

"Stand," Marek commanded. "This is Insithryllax. Though he will never be your subject, I would like for him to consider you an equal in the months and years ahead of us. Isn't that as we discussed, Insithryllax?"

Marek knew that the sound the black dragon made just then was a laugh, but Salatis surely assumed it was a growl.

"Insithryllax," the senator said, his voice shaking only a little less than his body.

"Ransar," the wyrm rumbled.

Salatis gasped and Marek sighed.

"Well, the cat's out of the bag now, isn't it," said the Red Wizard.

"What do you mean?" Salatis asked. "Lady Doom has held me in the embrace of the barbs of her Ill Fortune. I am not the ransar."

"You haven't told him?" the black dragon asked.

"Not yet," said the Red Wizard. "I wanted him to see first. After all, I'm not giving him the Palace of Many Spires, only the means to gain it for himself."

"You're giving me . . . ?" Salatis began.

"Really, Salatis," Marek said, "if you're going to be the ransar you'll eventually have to complete a thought. I know it's a lot to take in, my friend, but it's happening, I assure you. You're here, on a plane of existence of my own creation, and what you see before you are creatures made by my hand, with the indispensable assistance of my dear friend the black wyrm Insithryllax. They are the black firedrakes, and I give them to you."

Salatis shook his head and muttered, "I fear the Maid of Misfortune. I beg her to ignore me."

"Oh, please, Senator. Your mistress may have her way with us from time to time, but I assure you we petty mortals make our own luck. And it was neither Beshaba nor her sister who brought me to you."

"What can I do with these things?" the senator asked.

"The black firedrakes? Well, if you insist on getting ahead of ourselves, let's discuss precisely that. They were created, by me, from the cross-breading of ordinary firedrakes captured from the northern shores of the Lake of

Steam with my boon companion Insithryllax. He proved to be a hearty source of fatherly essence"—the dragon took a bow—"and the black firedrakes were born. After some months of nurturing, some half dozen or so began to exhibit unusually high functionality. I have put them in command of units of various sizes, though I admit that military organization is of little interest to me, so you may want to reorganize them to fit your own needs. You will be able to do so at your whim."

"My whim. . . ." Salatis said, perhaps just trying to get used to the idea.

"Indeed," Marek said. "My gift to you."

"An army of dragon-men?" asked the senator. "To invade Innarlith?"

"Well ..." Marek replied. "Not to put too fine a point on it."

The senator watched the firedrakes move around each other in silence. Some were in human form, some in the their natural shapes. He seemed equally interested in both, which Marek took as a good sign.

"Why me?" Salatis asked.

"I could give you any number of false answers, Senator," Marek said, "but I shan't. Suffice it to say that you have been recruited."

The black dragon's laugh rumbled through the stale air and was met with shrieks and calls from the surrounding firedrakes. Marek could see Salatis's skin crawl, but the hint of a smile played at the edges of the tall man's lips.

"You will command the firedrakes," Marek explained. "I will continue to control the tradesmen."

"The tradesmen?" said the senator, turning finally to look at Marek. "It's you, then? No one even suspects that."

Marek sketched a sarcastic bow and equally insincere smile, and said, "The comfort of the aristocracy has always been in the hands of the common man, Senator. Control their comforts, and you control them. Control them, and you control the city."

"And *you* control the city?"

Marek laughed at that and said, "Only the parts of it that interest me, Senator. For the rest, I will depend on you."

"What of Osorkon?"

Again, the black dragon laughed. Marek caught the senator glancing at the wyrm, fear heavy in his gaze.

"I suspect that you'll have one of the black firedrakes kill and eat him," Marek answered. "Anyway, that's what I would do. But first things first. I will give you the black firedrakes so that you can be ransar, and in return I will expect what favors from you I might choose to request. You will deny not a single one of those requests, nor shall you pause before seeing to their completion. Otherwise, the city-state is yours to do with as you wish."

"What favors—?"

"What he wishes," the dragon grumbled. "When he wishes it."

Salatis swallowed hard, almost choked.

"I will require from you only a single word answer, Senator Salatis," Marek said.

Without pause Salatis asked, "And if I refuse? I will never leave this strange little world of yours alive, will I?"

Marek took a deep breath, locked his eyes on Salatis's, and said, "Since time is a luxury that neither of us can squander on trivialities, we'll let that be as it may for now. I will have your answer."

Salatis swallowed again, looked out over the army of transformed monsters, and said, "Beshaba guide me."

Marek smiled, and studied the tall man. Salatis was afraid, but that passed in a few breaths to be replaced by a look Marek had seen too often in men like Salatis. It was a lust for power that transcended all sense of proportion. It was the drive that made empires rise and fall, and rise and fall, over and over and over again for millennium after millennium.

"This business with religion," Marek said. "It could be of use in controlling the people, of course, but from henceforth you will set it aside when you speak with me. You will hold sway over the black firedrakes for as long as I have your loyalty. The moment I feel I no longer have that—whether you've given it over to another man, or some god or goddess—you will no longer hold sway over the beating of your heart or the breath in your lungs, much less the firedrakes. Remember this gift and who gave it to you, or I will send Insithryllax to see you, and he will send you to the embrace of whatever Power is forgiving enough to take your disloyal soul into its embrace.

"Are you, or are you not, my ransar?"

Marek listened for one word, and heard it.

"Yes, I am your ransar," Salatis answered with an almost drunken grin.

My ransar, Marek thought. The ficklest daughter of Tyche will have to look elsewhere for hers.

20

16 Kythorn, the Year of the Sword (1365 DR)
THIRD QUARTER, INNARLITH

Willem watched Phyrea wander through the merchants' stalls for most of the afternoon. He was able to breathe, after a time, only to the rhythm of her footsteps and the graceful sway of her narrow hips. She wore a cloak of shimmering silk and carried a parasol of black lace. He hadn't recognized her at first because of the parasol. It was an aristocratic lady's affectation that was beneath her, especially with the thin, high overcast tempering the direct rays of the sun.

"How much?" she asked a vendor.

The man studied the boot she held up to him, glanced at her foot, and seemed at a loss for words. Willem slid past a woman who had stopped to admire a spray of cheap pewter jewelry laid out on a blanket on the street so that he could get a better look. He ignored the look of impatience the woman shot his way, even when her face softened and she smiled at him, trying to catch his eye.

"For the lady's husband?" the cobbler asked Phyrea.

She shook her head. The boot was easily twice the size of her own delicate foot, and cut for a man. The craftsmanship was exceptional. Willem could see that even from a distance.

Someone bumped him, and Willem looked down to see his purse stolen by a boy no older than ten. They looked each other in the eye for half a breath, the boy's dirty face frozen in fear, his mouth open to show yellow teeth—an old man's teeth. He ran into the crowd, pushing past a man carrying a crate of live chickens. The chicken farmer shouted some obscenity at the boy, and the chickens put up a fuss of their own. The boy didn't run too fast, and Willem could have caught him easily enough and got his coins back, but he didn't bother.

When he looked back at the cobbler's stall, Phyrea was gone.

His heart stuttered in his chest, and he whispered, "Oh, no."

He turned his head, unaware that his shoulders twisted at the same time, and he nudged the man with the chickens. One of the crates clattered to the cobblestones, eliciting a loud chorus of complaints from the chickens, and a louder burst of profanity from the man selling the cheap pewter jewelry.

"Oh," Willem breathed. "My apologies—"

But the man had already picked up his chickens and ignored him.

"Wait," Phyrea said, and Willem gasped. She put a hand on the chicken farmer's arm, and the man looked first at her hand, then only briefly at her face, before letting his eyes pour over her like warm, but stagnant water. "I'd like one of those."

"Phyrea," Willem said, not sure if he should, or even could, smile. "I—"

"A chicken, miss?" the farmer asked, obviously not sure he'd heard her correctly.

She dropped the boots she was carrying and dug in a pocket of her cloak for a coin. She handed him a gold piece—too much for a single chicken—and looked at Willem while the man pulled a squawking bird from the crude wooden box.

"It's a surprise to see you here," Willem lied, and by her face she didn't believe it.

"I may not be able to make change, miss," the chicken monger said, pocketing the coin at the same time he held out the bird to her.

"Keep it," she told him.

With some difficulty she took the squealing foul from the man, holding it as he had by the legs, at arm's length to avoid the furious flapping of wings. On the ground beneath them, the pewter merchant gathered up his jewelry, cursing under a shower of chicken feathers. The farmer arrowed off into the crowd before she changed her mind about the gold piece.

"Why are you following me?" she demanded.

"I'm not—" Willem started, but stopped himself before she could interrupt. "I wanted to ask you something."

"They're for you," she said, her eyes darting down to the cobblestones at her feet.

Willem looked down and saw the boots.

"Thank you," he said by reflex alone.

"You don't want to know why I bought them for you?" she asked from behind the still-panicked chicken. People on the street began to give the two of them a wide berth.

A smile came to him, and pleased with himself, he said, "I was actually more curious about the chicken."

Without the slightest change in her stony demeanor, she dropped the black lace parasol to the ground, and squinted in the dim light. Her hand free, she grabbed the struggling bird by the neck and twisted once, hard and fast. It sounded like a twig snapping underfoot. The chicken flapped its wings only faster, but not for long.

"The chicken is for dinner," she said.

Willem stepped back from her, and that elicited a smile. She dropped the chicken to the cobblestones next to the boots and retrieved her parasol.

"They are fine boots," he said, and found that his mouth was dry, his tongue heavy and sticking to his teeth. Sweat tickled his hair line. "Why are you helping me?"

"I abhor your taste in footwear," she said, and Willem blinked at the fire in her eyes.

Her jaw set tight, Phyrea stared him down. Willem blinked.

"You know what I mean," he risked, unable to put as much strength into his voice as he'd hoped to. "You have been talking to people on my behalf."

Her lips twisted with undisguised contempt, and she said, "Because they don't deserve it any more than you do."

"I won't pretend I have any idea what you mean," he said.

Something distracted her, and she looked off to one side, listening. Willem could pick out nothing from the background drone of the market.

"Thank me," she said, finally turning back to look at him.

He didn't speak, but studied her as best he could. Her perfect beauty was undiminished, even by the palpable madness that radiated from her burning gaze.

"You can keep the chicken, too," she told him.

Should I kill her? Willem thought. I should kill her.

"You are the most beautiful woman I've ever seen," he said.

Phyrea put a hand to her lips and gagged. The skin of her long neck twisted and rippled. Willem looked away, and watched a peasant woman carry a basket of lemons on her head.

When he looked back, Phyrea was gone. He stood there

for a long time, and if passersby noticed him at all they would have assumed he was deep in thought, but he didn't think at all. He just stood there.

Eventually he bent and picked up the boots, but left the chicken in the street for the beggars.

21

19 Kythorn, the Year of the Sword (1365 DR)
First Quarter, Innarlith

The rich and decadent masters of Innarlith have never been in greater danger than through the direct action of our brotherhood of the many, we who do the work of the city-state, but see so little, if any, of the gold that passes through this port."

Marek Rymüt paused to let the assembled dock workers cheer in their unruly fashion. Disguised by the simplest of illusions, to them he was but an ordinary worker, a burly, grimy, near-toothless hulk of a man. His magic had made him one of them, and because he was one of them, they listened.

"And so here we are, not because we are strong or because we are many; for we continue to struggle with tradition even as we remove ourselves inch by inch from the ten-copper words of the Third Quarter tradesmen. For that reason the aristocrats will find it fairly easy for a time to keep us and our confused, confusing brothers in the Third Quarter down."

He'd heard from many that his speeches to the tradesmen of the Third Quarter had been too confusing—complex words and concepts directed at simple men. If the skilled tradesmen were simple men, then what were the brutes who loaded and unloaded ships, plying a trade that barely required sentience, let alone skill or craft?

Whatever they are, Marek thought, as long as they're disrupting the flow of trade in Innarlith, as long as they're slitting their own throats by not laboring for at least the pittance they once made, they serve me.

"The danger to the senate is not that their power is directly menaced, but in the fact that we can not possibly form the guilds we've formed without overstepping the false limits placed on us by those thieves in their Chamber of so-called Law and Civility. The Guild of Stevedores is bound only by its own laws—laws that guarantee that we, the men who deserve it most, who have paid the highest price of sweat and blood and poverty, can once and for all take charge of this port and gather for ourselves our fair portion of the coin that trade with Innarlith—our city as much as theirs—brings here."

Most of the men were listening, a few jabbered to each other, but Marek could tell that his ideas, if not the finer points of his words, were getting through to them. One man shouted some incoherent muddle of drunken syllables at him and was answered by loud cheers from a small group around him. The rest of the dockhands ignored them, though, so Marek went on.

"Our guild shows that the simple folk—when we finally exhibit to those doddering dandies the true extent of our power—can seize control of the docks and the storehouses. Because the mastery of the senate depends on the control of the way everything is made and traded in Innarlith—for this reason the senate and its bullies have no choice. They must beat us down, and beat down our Third Quarter brothers, too, with the sharpest means at their command."

A thunderous barrage of boos rumbled up from the crowd of workers, and some began to wave torches in the air. Marek worried that someone would be burned, or the long wooden pier might be set ablaze, but Tymora favored the simpleminded once again. He let them revel in the idea that they had threatened the senate to the degree that the senate had no choice but to threaten them.

Of course, the disguised Red Wizard had no intention

of warning them that the senate and their bullies could, should they finally chose to do so, replace them all with summoned and undead servants provided, for a modest fee of course, by a Thayan Enclave of Marek's creation. And those automatons would never stop to eat, drink, sleep, or do any of the other things that plagued the living. They would work all day and all night, every day, without pause for rest and without the briefest whisper of complaint. Beyond the price of their creation they would require no stipend or upkeep, or even the merest morsel of food.

"As soon as we let a day go by without unloading their precious cargoes, the aristocrats will answer at once with martial law. Our guild, our long-awaited fraternity of sweat and toil, will be outlawed. Even now they argue over this in the Chamber of Law and Civility. But when a guild like ours comes finally to pass, it stands tall against the laws of the rich and weak-hearted. We will go on whether they like it or not. That, if nothing else, I can promise you!"

As Marek stood soaking in the cheers of the stinking mob of ungrateful brutes, he noted a disturbance at the far edge of the crowd. Perhaps a thousand of the dirty, sweat-soaked hulks had gathered to hear his words, and the speeches of a few of their comrades who had been duped early on by Marek's rabble-rousing. Though Marek couldn't see their faces, the tops of their rusted and dented helms, and the tips of their spears, rose above the heads of the men at the foot of the pier. The crowd began to compress toward Marek.

"But you will have to help me keep that promise, brothers, by taking up the struggle against the senate. Only if we draw back before them will the aristocrats be able to defeat us. But if we resist with the same strength of arm and heart with which we've unloaded their riches for them, the guild will become subject to its own inner law. On the quay, where we have something to say about it, a different law will prevail than what the senators try to make for us in their Chamber of Crime and Oppression."

The tenor of the cheer that followed sounded different. In it Marek could hear both the misguided revelry of the powerless empowered, and the growing desperation of men who were beginning to fear the consequences of their actions. The former sound came from the men closest to Marek's makeshift stage—cobbled together from crates that had been waiting for a tenday to be loaded onto a coaster from Athkatla—and the latter from the men closer to the foot of the pier who had become aware through the press of their fellow workers of the presence of the watchmen who had effectively cut them off from the city.

For all Toril as though he'd never noticed the helms and spears, Marek went on, letting his false face flush red with insincere passion.

"Our new law will show itself in our utter contempt of private property. And not because we seek poverty for ourselves—I think we've all had enough of that, eh?"

And there Marek paused, and folded his arms across his barrel-chest. His eyes closed, he couldn't see if the watchmen pressed the assembly further, but so what if they did?

"Our new Law of the Quayside will protect us the same way the laws of the senate protect the aristocracy, because the struggle itself makes it necessary. And what we start here today on the very edge of the city, will soon rise in the whole of Innarlith. It is revealed in our Laws of the Quayside that we can do nothing with our power unless we bend the senate to our will the same way they have bent us to theirs for so very, very long now. When our law becomes the only law, our struggle will end."

Marek scanned the edge of the crowd and had to struggle not to let his disappointment show through his illusory features. The watchmen stood their ground and after a time only the first few rows of dockworkers continued to send fearful glances their way. The rest of the laborers seemed to have fallen for Marek's Laws of the Quayside—a concept he had arrived upon the afternoon before and that had given him acute cases of the giggles off and on in the hours before bedtime.

"So long as our fraternity remains small, and separate from the guilds of our Third Quarter brothers, the tendency toward our mastery of all Innarlith does not come so clearly to light. But if we gather more men into our fold, and come together finally with the trade guilds, then more and more thunder gathers in the storm cloud fists of the working men. The Law of the Quayside must meet the Law of the Third Quarter. From that struggling mass there then comes about a fresh bridge between the common man and the forces by which we've been—until now—blown like the wind churns the water. A new era will come to pass. We will raise our voices in victory, even as the senate shrieks in horror!"

The frightful cheers that rose up from those words once again made Marek struggle not to laugh. It was as though they already celebrated the impossible eventuality he'd just promised them.

The zombies, he thought, will be quieter, too.

22

23 Kythorn, the Year of the Sword (1365 DR)
THE CHAMBER OF LAW AND CIVILITY, INNARLITH

Senators," the clerk called out in his clear, practiced baritone, "and all those having business with this distinguished body, please be upstanding for the Ransar of Innarlith."

Osorkon watched from the doorway, making mental note of those who stood the fastest and those who stood the slowest. Everyone in between were his true enemies.

He took the podium and said, "Be seated, honored colleagues."

He paused for a deep, dramatic breath during the ruckus that followed.

"I thank you all for allowing me to humble myself before you," he said, speaking the traditional opening line of a ransar's address to the senate without a trace of the contempt he held for the majority of that body. "I have come here today to speak once more of a great work."

The murmur that swept through the senate chamber was as forced as it was predictable.

"The near-continuous efforts of a small army of craftsmen has done honor to the city of their birth, to their ransar, their senate, and the man who so capably leads them in their historic endeavor. Of course, that man of whom I speak is Ivar Devorast."

The name sent a shockwave of affected outrage through the senate, and the ransar smiled.

"Oh, I know how you feel about Devorast," Osorkon continued, his tone conversational, as though the whole of the assembled senators was but one man. "Believe me, he can be"—a well-placed pause—"frustrating, at times. But does the city-state benefit from his genius or his charisma? Considering Master Devorast's considerable—"

"*Master* Devorast?" Salatis shouted from the floor of the senate. He stood, turning once to each side to indicate that he addressed his fellow senators. There were a few hisses, but most if not all of the men in that room expected someone to interrupt eventually. "Surely the ransar errs in the use of that title. For the city of Innarlith has but one master builder, and his name is Inthelph."

Osorkon looked to Inthelph's chair, and a few of the senators patted him on the shoulders, then urged him to stand. The master builder stood, bowed, then sat again, not once looking the ransar in the eye.

"You all know of my deep respect and affection for the master builder," Osorkon said. "Was it not I who appointed him, after all? No, when I used that appellation it was to honor a foreign dignitary."

"He is no dignitary, this man," Salatis broke in. "He is a commoner in the realm of his birth, not important enough, loved or respected enough, to be kept close by his king's side. If Cormyr recognized his so-called genius, why would Ivar Devorast be here?"

"In that, my dear old friend," Osorkon said to Salatis, "I will simply be happy that King Azoun's loss is Innarlith's gain."

"Need I remind you that you are no king, sir?" Salatis said.

A hush fell over the assembly then, all eyes darting back and forth between Osorkon on the podium, and Salatis alone standing among the seated senators.

"No," replied the ransar. "You need not remind me of that, Senator. I meant only that the kingdom of Cormyr has lost a good man to the city-state of Innarlith. Their loss, is our gain."

"Your gain, you mean," Salatis pressed.

"The canal benefits me, yes," Osorkon said. "There is no secret that my ships ply the waters of the Lake of Steam, and trade as far north as the Sword Coast. Should the Vilhon Reach be open to them at last, and the Sea of Fallen Stars beyond, Cormyrean coin, Sembian coin ... gold from the Moonsea to the Old Empires will find its way into my purse, but don't think for a moment—not for a moment—that it will fill my purse alone. Riches enough for us all will pass through that waterway. Of that I have not the slightest doubt."

Osorkon paused, and in some small way he still hoped someone would speak up then in support of the canal, with loyalty to their ransar, but he knew no one would.

Salatis looked around the room, his hands palms up at his sides, making a great show of waiting for the same thing. Finally he said, "Ransar, please believe me when I say that all of us realize that trade eventually will flow through this canal of yours, but—"

"This canal of *ours*, Senator," the ransar interrupted.

Salatis continued without missing a beat, "—how much and how soon? If it costs forty pieces of gold to build a wagon, and one sells it for thirty-five only after taking a decade to build the damned thing, what kind of trade is that? This insanity that takes place to the northwest will drain more gold from our coffers while it's being built than it will drain water from the Lake of Steam when it's completed. And will any one of us even live to see that day?"

Osorkon smiled through the round of applause and cheers that followed. When the senate quieted enough for him to be heard, he said, "Is there any guarantee, Senator, that any of us will live to see the morrow?"

The two men stared at each other across a stretch of air as heavy as it was silent.

"Perhaps," said Meykhati, rising with his hands at his side as though he was surrendering to someone, "we can agree that trade will flow once the canal is done, and that many in this body will profit from it either directly or indirectly—but is that the most pressing question?" Meykhati paused for effect, but Osorkon knew what was coming. "Perhaps it is the man who builds it, not the watercourse itself, that offends. Perhaps there is another man better suited to oversee this project so that it can be completed in a timely fashion . . . so that we will indeed all live to profit from that trade."

Once again the senators who sat around the master builder patted Inthelph on the back and whispered in his ear, all grins and chuckles. Osorkon's skin crawled, and his eyes met Salatis's.

"That," the ransar said, "is not an eventuality I am prepared to consider."

Salatis smiled, and spoke for a majority of the senate when he said, "Then perhaps it's time we find someone more prepared."

"Is that a challenge?" Osorkon asked, and again the chamber fell into perfect silence. The ransar imagined he could hear every one of their heartbeats. "Senator Salatis?"

"That's not a question the ransar should ask lightly," Salatis replied. "Let us say, for the nonce, that I respect the great traditions of this body and reserve, as do all senators, the right to petition for the office of first among equals. But on this day ... on this day that is not an eventuality I am prepared to consider."

23

10 Eleasias, the Year of the Sword (1365 DR)
SOMEWHERE ON THE NAGA PLAINS

Did you hear that?" Dharmun whispered, looking up into the warm rain. "Something ... up there."

Hrothgar sighed, and didn't look up. Even at night, even when it was raining, he didn't like to look up into the open, endless sky. He tightened his grip on his heavy hammer and listened.

"I can't hear anything," the dwarf said. "Rain ... the torch flame ..."

He resisted the urge to look at the torch that Devorast held over his head. The guttering orange light would dampen his darkvision.

"It's above us," Devorast said.

Hrothgar cursed silently and looked up. The rain made him blink, and he couldn't see anything.

"Should we go back for more men?" Dharmun said, his voice quivering a little. He might have been cold, with no shirt on late at night, but the air was still muggy with late summer heat, despite the rain. "I mean, we could go back and return with—"

At the same moment Devorast shushed Dharmun, something pushed Hrothgar to the ground. Pain skipped up his back in a series of rippling cramps, and he almost dropped his hammer. He slid face first in the mud, getting a little in his mouth, but thankfully none in his eyes.

Dharmun grunted and as Hrothgar rolled to his feet, pain in his back making it harder for him to breathe than to stand, the dwarf saw him swing his heavy wood axe at a shape made of deeper blackness than the already inky, moonless night.

"Damn it," Hrothgar breathed. "It's big."

Devorast swung at it with his torch, and Hrothgar caught a glimpse of it in silhouette. The light shone through one membranous patch that must have been a wing. Hrothgar could sense a serpent's wedge-shaped head, and there was a flash of long, curved talons. Sparks flew, but the thing didn't even flinch.

"Ivar," Hrothgar warned, "watch—"

A cloud of thick, oily black mist benched from the creature, dimming the torchlight like a black lace curtain. Dharmun screamed.

Hrothgar stomped forward with his hammer out in front of him. Devorast's torch was on the ground. He saw a booted foot, didn't know if it was Devorast's or Dharmun's, but before he could investigate further he was hit in the back again—harder.

The hammer flew from his grip and went cartwheeling through the air, and once again his face pressed into the slick mud. Claws raked at his back, digging into the leather tunic he wore. He was bruised, but not cut.

"Where's my axe?" Dharmun called out. "What is that thing?"

Hrothgar tried to answer him but coughed instead. He patted the ground around him for his hammer and found something like it. He staggered to his feet and was almost fully upright when he realized he'd picked up Devorast's torch instead.

"I have your axe," Devorast said—and it took a moment to realize that he was answering Dharmun's question from before.

The black creature screamed—a combination of some

kind of bird of prey and a blare of trumpets—and skipped along the ground between Hrothgar and Devorast. The dwarf saw it lift something in its claws as it swooped back up into the night sky—Hrothgar's hammer.

"Trove Lord take you, whatever you are," the dwarf roared into the night, spinning with Devorast's torch in a vain attempt to find the thing in the darkness. "That's my lucky hammer!"

"There it is!" Dharmun screamed.

"Where?" Devorast demanded.

Hrothgar looked at Dharmun, and the human met his eye, then looked up again, then looked back at the dwarf and shrugged.

"Is that a rock you have there?" Hrothgar asked.

Dharmun looked at the first-sized stone in his hand as if noticing it for the first time, shrugged, and said, "Master Devorast has my—"

Something hit Dharmun in the head, and the woodcutter fell like a sack of flour dropped from a third-story window. Hrothgar could hear the air punched from the human's lungs.

"What in the name of Dumathoin's hairy—"

"It dropped your hammer on him," Devorast said.

Hrothgar grimaced. He didn't like that at all. The dwarf didn't know Dharmun all that well. He was a woodcutter, who kept with the other woodcutters, and Hrothgar was a stonecutter who kept with the other stonecutters. But when Dharmun ran from his tent screaming that something had come in and snatched his tentmate away, Hrothgar was up and out almost as fast as Devorast. Together the three of them had pursued the beast out into the darkness and had gone too far from camp for Hrothgar's liking. Other groups of three, four, or five men had gone off in other directions, and just when they were no longer able to hear the other groups calling out the missing man's name, the thing had attacked.

"Is he dead?" Hrothgar asked, turning all the way

around once with the torch held high, waiting for the inevitable next attack.

"I don't—"

It was Devorast's turn to be pushed into the mud, and the sight of it only made Hrothgar angrier. He got a better look at the thing, though. It's scales as black as the middark sky, it looked for all the world like a miniature dragon.

Hrothgar threw the torch at it and shouted, "Eat this, lizard!"

The monster took the torch in midair and bit it cleanly in half. The lighted end skipped across the rain-soaked mud and sputtered out barely an inch from Dharmun's head. That seemed to rouse the woodcutter, who rolled to a seated position and grunted in pain.

"Where's my . . . ?" Dharmun gasped, feeling around on the ground with one hand while he held the other pressed tight against his chest. Hrothgar couldn't see any blood, but he could smell it. "I need my axe."

Dharmun found something on the ground next to him and picked it up—it was just a stick.

A loud thump brought Hrothgar's attention back to the creature. Devorast stood next to it, dwarfed by it, but pounded away at it with the rock Dharmun had found. The beast seemed more surprised than anything else.

Hrothgar charged it, having no idea what he was actually going to do when he got to it—he didn't even have a rock.

The creature hissed at Devorast and flapped its huge, leathery wings. Hrothgar turned so fast he almost twisted his ankle, but avoided the wing. He tripped again when he kicked something heavy. Stumbling to a stop, the dwarf almost fell but managed to pick up Dharmun's axe. The weapon felt good in his hand—it was just a hammer with a sharp edge, after all.

Devorast threw the stone, but the thing dodged it. The dodge brought it closer to Hrothgar, though, who swung the axe. The axe head caught in the monster's wing, fetching up on one of the bony spurs. The thing reacted with

violence and an ear-splitting scream. Its wing bashed
Hrothgar in the face, cracking the bridge of his nose and
sending him flying three feet off the ground, and four
times that backward through the air.

He rolled to a bruising stop and with some difficulty
sat up so at least he could see the thing coming to kill him.
But the creature hadn't moved. It flailed both wings and
hopped about trying to dislodge the axe that still hung in
its right wing.

"Hrothgar?" Devorast called.

The dwarf couldn't see his friend. He took a deep breath
to answer that he was all right, but couldn't get enough air
in his lungs. He coughed, hoping that sound would be good
enough to tell Devorast that he still lived.

"Dharmun," Devorast shouted, "no!"

"What—?" Hrothgar gasped.

Dharmun stood and waved his twisted, ridiculous stick
at the creature, which reared back, startled by the human
that it apparently thought it had killed.

"This isn't . . ." the woodcutter said.

"Don't—" Hrothgar wheezed.

The creature took a deep breath, it's scaly chest expanding like a bellows. When it exhaled, Hrothgar winced at
the stench of the fluid that rushed from its mouth. The
greasy black cloud descended over the woodcutter, but
Hrothgar could still see the outline of Dharmun's body,
which stood rigid but quivering.

The cloud dissipated, sizzling in the pouring rain, and
Hrothgar blinked away a sudden sting. He heard the woodcutter fall and knew he was dead. Living people didn't fall
like that.

"Hrothgar," Devorast said, startling the dwarf.

"How did you . . . ?" Hrothgar started to ask, but finished
with another fit of coughing. There was pain in at least
three parts of his body that was bad enough to actually
worry the dwarf. "Where . . . ?"

Devorast had obviously run around behind the dragon-thing as it burned Dharmun to death with some sort of liquid.

"Can you stand?" Devorast asked.

Hrothgar shook his head, but tried to stand anyway. The creature beat its wings hard again and rolled on the ground.

"What's it—?" the dwarf started.

"The axe," Devorast finished for him.

The axe came free of the beast's wing finally, and slid along the wet mud. The monster turned to watch the weapon's progress, its eyes burning red in the night like hot coals. Black mist puffed from its nostrils and it ran, dragging it's ruined wing behind it, for the axe.

Devorast jumped over Hrothgar, making the dwarf grimace and groan with pain. Sprawling out face-first in the mud, Devorast got his fingers around the axe handl and rolled. The dragon-thing came down right next to him and snapped at him with jaws like a crocodile's.

Hrothgar cast about for something—anything—he could use as a weapon. All he found was a rock, no bigger or more threatening than the one poor Dharmun had come up with, but then Devorast had used it to distract the thing, hadn't he?

Devorast swung the axe and cut the creature deep at the base of its neck. It growled and backed up, and black acid sprayed form its nose.

It whirled back at Devorast, it's jaws wide, and Hrothgar threw the rock as hard as he could.

As a child, back in his home mines of the Great Rift, Hrothgar had thrown a lot of rocks. They'd set up elaborate games of skill and chance around the act of throwing a rock. He hadn't done it in a long time—adult dwarves don't throw rocks—but his body remembered.

The rock went down its throat.

The creature backed up again, twisting its neck, and made a terrible strangling sound that Hrothgar knew he would hear again in his happiest nightmares. Smoke billowed out from the corners of its mouth.

Devorast scrambled away from it, the axe still in his hands. Hrothgar set his jaw, closed his eyes, and got at least to his knees. Not sure what he could do in his current condition, he crawled forward—and his palm came down on the familiar handle of his hammer.

"Ah," he breathed, then gasped, "there you are."

Using the hammer to support himself, the dwarf stood. Devorast stood next to him. They looked at each other and smiled though they both panted like dogs. Hrothgar hefted his hammer, and Devorast put the axe up on his shoulder.

The choking, struggling dragon-thing seemed to have forgotten all about them. They strode in with care, but killed it with relish.

24

9 Eleint, the Year of the Sword (1365 DR)
THE NAGAFLOW KEEP

I didn't expect to have to wait," the tall Cormyrean Ayesunder Truesilver said with obvious impatience. "I don't suppose you have some idea when he'll be back?"

Hrothgar shrugged, and thought fast. He looked south, in the direction Devorast had gone and said, "I don't want to give the warden false hopes. Devorast could be away another day or so. It'll depend on how far afield the blasted creature fled."

The Cormyrean sighed and followed the dwarf's gaze out to the flat southern horizon. Hrothgar watched him, and saw his eyes pick up and follow the line of stakes with the thin red ribbons tied to them. The parade of tiny flags stretched in two parallel, perfectly straight lines, as far south as the eye could see—past the horizon.

"How often does this happen?" asked the Cormyrean.

The dwarf turned to face the man. Behind him rose the Nagaflow Keep, standing strong in the hot summer air. Hrothgar had to push back the flood of memories that struck him every time he laid eyes on the keep.

"These are still wild lands," Hrothgar said.

Truesilver glanced behind him at the fortress and said with a smile, "It's an impressive fortification. Quite new by the look of it."

"Being a part of its construction is one of the great joys—one of the great honors of my life."

"And it, too, was built by Devorast?"

"It's his genius behind it, aye," the dwarf said. "But there was some politics around it ... it was finished by someone else, but to Devorast's specifications."

Truesilver nodded and narrowed his eyes. Hrothgar had to look away—he didn't like the way the human examined him.

"Can it really be done?" asked the Cormyrean.

"The canal?" Hrothgar asked. When the human nodded, he continued, "By Moradin's sparking hammer, yes."

"You have considerable confidence in this man."

"When he sets out to do something, he does it," the dwarf replied.

"High praise from any dwarf," the Cormyrean observed. "Your accent is strange to me. You aren't from the North."

"The Great Rift," Hrothgar said, looking the human in the eye again. "Can I ask you, sir, why you're here?"

The human had come with a letter of introduction from Ransar Osorkon and half a dozen armed guards in leather armor and steel breastplates emblazoned with a stylized dragon. His guards wore bowl-shaped helms and carried odd hook-shaped polearms Hrothgar couldn't place a name to. Truesilver had a well-crafted long sword at his belt. He had the air and manner of someone important, and Hrothgar knew they needed all the friends they could get, even friends from as far away as the Forest Kingdom.

"I have been sent by His Majesty King Azoun the Fourth to assess the feasibility of this canal and report back to the Cormyrean nobility," he explained. "As you can imagine, a watercourse to connect the Sea of Fallen Stars to the Great Sea, the Sword Coast, and all points west, would be quite a boon to the shipping trade out of my home city of Marsember."

Hrothgar nodded and said, "Indeed. That's one of the things that drives us to complete the damned thing."

Truesilver chuckled, and though Hrothgar didn't usually like it when humans laughed at him, he found himself smiling back at the man.

"Tell me, though," Truesilver asked, his manner shifting quickly from jovial to earnest, "why did he go out there himself? Surely your—or, well, *the* ransar has sent soldiers to protect the workers and the work site. Why would the master builder himself go chasing off after some wandering monster?"

"Well, first off Ivar Devorast is surely *a* master builder, but he's not *the* Master Builder of Innarlith," Hrothgar corrected. He tried to resist a sneer at the mention of the idiot Inthelph's title, and once again his eyes were drawn to the great keep—great in spite of Inthelph's efforts to the contrary. "But the only answer I have to your question is I haven't the foggiest idea in boisterous Dwarfhome why Devorast thinks he's got to fight off every giant frog or baby dragon that happens by us, but he does. It's kinda the way he is. I've heard humans call it 'hands on.'"

Ayesunder Truesilver laughed, and Hrothgar felt compelled to join him.

"A man after my own heart," the Cormyrean said. "I've been accused of the same sin myself."

They laughed a bit more, then there was a pause in the conversation that made Hrothgar shuffle his feet. He didn't know what or whom to look at.

"I don't want to take any more of your time than necessary," Truesilver said, "but one more question: I was told that Devorast had something to do with a ship built in Innarlith that was meant for the Royal Navy of Cormyr."

"Aye," was all the dwarf wanted to say.

"The ship was called *Everwind,* and she broke apart in the portal that was to deliver her to the Vilhon Reach."

"Aye, it did at that."

"Not to press you on a subject that seems uncomfortable for you, but it was explained to me that the ship was built too large for the portal," said the Cormyrean. "If that's the case, and Ivar Devorast was at least in part responsible for that disaster, how can I give my king any assurance that a similar fate won't befall this much grander, more complex undertaking?"

Hrothgar let a breath hiss out through his nose and steadied his temper before answering, "I heard it told a different way, sir."

"Do tell."

"The ship wasn't too big for the magical portal, or whatever you call it. The portal was made too small for the ship, and made that way on purpose, by someone who didn't want that ship to get to the Vilhon Reach in one piece. The ship itself was sound, and I have no doubt it would have pleased your king, and yourself. Men like Devorast have enemies, Warden."

Hrothgar made himself stop there, but he held the man's eyes for a long moment. He got the feeling soon enough that the Cormyrean understood the gravity of what he was trying to say.

"Well, then ..." the man started, but trailed off when his attention was drawn away to the southwest. "Is that him?"

Hrothgar turned and saw a man crest the top of a low hill some hundred yards or so away. Long red hair blew in the hot summer wind, and Hrothgar knew the walk well.

"Aye," the dwarf said with a long, relieved sigh, "that'll be Ivar Devorast."

Truesilver set off to meet Devorast, and Hrothgar scurried to keep up with him, wincing a little at the lingering pain from the injuries that had slowed him down for a long and trying month. His muscles loosened up as he went, though, and soon they stood face to face with Devorast, who dragged behind him, lashed with ropes, the carcass of another of the strange black dragon-creatures. Two of the ransar's men who'd gone with him followed behind, each dragging a makeshift litter on which two more of their comrades lay. One of the soldiers on the litters was dead, melted beyond recognition. The other was burned badly and quivered in unrelenting agony. The men who bore their litters bled from cuts Hrothgar could tell came from both tooth and claw. Devorast appeared dirty, soaked with sweat and spattered with blood, but otherwise uninjured.

Truesilver motioned his men forward and though the Innarlan soldiers were confused by the presence of a troop of Cormyrean Purple Dragon regulars, they were grateful for the help. When the dead and wounded were on their way to the keep, Hrothgar made his introductions.

"Ivar Devorast," he said, "this here's Ayesunder Truesilver, Warden of the Port of ... what city was it, sir?"

"Marsember," Truesilver answered, holding out a hand.

Devorast took the Cormyrean's hand in the human manner—briefly—and said, "Warden, welcome to the Naga Plains."

The Cormyrean nodded at the dead monster and asked, "What is that thing? I've never seen the like."

Devorast dropped the rope from around his shoulders and stepped away from the carcass. "I don't know," he said, "but it's not the first one we've had to kill."

"Dangerous work," Hrothgar added.

"Any work worth doing generally is," said Truesilver. "So I understand that you're Cormyrean yourself."

"I was born and raised in Marsember," Devorast replied.

"Ah, well, then greetings from home," the warden said with a smile that Devorast failed to return.

"The warden was telling me that he was sent by the

king of Cormyr himself to report on the canal," Hrothgar cut in, hoping to forestall any uncomfortable exchange between the two men. Devorast wasn't one to pine for home, but Hrothgar was smart enough to have identified Ayesunder Truesilver as an important ally, and sometimes Devorast's manner....

"That's correct," the warden of the port said. "His majesty has taken a personal interest in your endeavor."

Devorast had no reaction to that. Some more of the ransar's soldiers had approached and Devorast waved them forward. "Take this to the keep. We should have it examined. I'd like to know what it is and where it came from."

Hrothgar watched Truesilver watch the ransar's men take charge of the dead dragon-thing. A smile threatened the edges of the Cormyrean's mouth.

"Maybe we should go back to the keep, too, eh?" the dwarf suggested. "Talk over this canal business over an ale or two, so the warden can report back to his king that he'll have a sea route to Waterdeep in his lifetime."

Devorast nodded, and Ayesunder Truesilver grinned and said, "Yes, let's. I'll drink to that."

When the two humans started walking to the keep, Hrothgar breathed a sigh of relief.

25

Higharvestide, the Year of the Sword (1365 DR)
THE PALACE OF MANY SPIRES, INNARLITH

" '...due to increasing civil unrest.' " Ransar Osorkon read from his own decree.

"Really, Ransar," one of the last of his hangers-on sighed, "there's no use in reading it over and over again."

"Indeed, my lord," said Kolviss, another of Osorkon's dwindling supply of toadies. "Thensumkon is right. You did the right thing."

They stared at him with their wet, dull, puppy eyes,

and Osorkon had to look away. He sat at his desk behind a bigger than normal stack of unsigned parchment with his head in his hands.

"Well, Tlaet?" the ransar asked when he thought the silence had dragged on long enough.

"Oh, Ransar, of course I agree!" Tlaet beamed, probably concurring with a point from the day before.

"And then there were three," Osorkon whispered.

"Ransar?" Thensumkon prompted.

Osorkon didn't answer, didn't even look at the bloated, sweaty advisor. Instead he looked at the wide double doors that were the only way in or out of his office. He'd contemplated having a secret door installed, but then none of the other ransars before him had done that—at least if they had it remained a secret. He'd never found one, and he'd looked. There was only one way into the ransar's office, and only one way out.

"That's fitting," he whispered to himself.

"Fitting, Ransar?" Kolviss asked. He smiled and revealed a silver tooth. His hair was greasy, and Osorkon could smell him even from six paces away—and he didn't smell good. "Do tell us what's on your mind."

Osorkon sighed and said, "I was just thinking that I used to have six bodyguards."

All three of his dim-witted "advisors" turned to look at the doors. On either side of the stout oaken portal, barred with a steel pole it took three men to lift, was a single guard. They stood stiff and at attention, and they were good men who'd been with Osorkon for a long time. For more than a tenday they'd been the only ones to report for duty.

"Did you order a reduction in your personal staff, my lord?" asked Tlaet.

"No, Tlaet, I didn't," he said.

"Well, then, who did?" the idiot Tlaet asked.

"Well, you piercer-brained spore-farm, if I had to hazard a guess I'd say it was Marek Rymüt."

"Ransar?" Thensumkon asked.

"Oh," Tlaet interjected, "there he is now."

Osorkon, confused, looked up and followed his boot-lick's empty gaze to one of the twenty crystal balls that still adorned his private sanctum. Over the past two months they'd one by one gone black until only two still glowed with the image of a distant locale. It had been about that long since he'd seen or heard from one of his staff of mages, so there was no one to tell him why they'd stopped working, and no one to make them work again.

One of the crystal balls was locked on a top-down view of Senator Salatis's seat in the senate chambers. The second showed Osorkon's outer office, empty since he'd sent his secretary home to hide in her house while dockworkers and tradesmen clashed in the street, drunkenly beating each other up in lieu of organized holiday festivities.

Osorkon looked into the first crystal sphere. Marek Rymüt sat in Salatis's blue-and-white upholstered armchair with its bright red cherry wood accents. On the top of the back of the chair was a cherry wood emblem of three lightning bolts converging on a single spot. The symbol was a clear indication that Salatis had recently converted to the worship of Talos, the Bully of Fury's Heart.

"Rymüt," Osorkon whispered, confident that the Thayan couldn't hear him anyway, "what are you doing there?"

Marek looked up, and Osorkon could swear they made eye contact. A cold chill ran down his spine, and he could feel his face go white.

"Ransar?" Kolviss said, his voice shaking. "Ransar, what's that?"

He pointed at the other functioning crystal ball. Displayed therein was the empty outer office—or at least it was supposed to be empty. Something pulsed in the center of the room. It looked like a cloud of black and purple smoke, formed in a tall oval shape.

"It looks like a door," Tlaet remarked with a childlike lilt in his voice.

"Ransar?" one of the bodyguards called from the door.

"Be ready," Osorkon told the two guards. "It's happening."

"What's happening?" asked Thensumkon. He didn't even sound curious.

Osorkon glanced at the crystal ball that revealed the senate chamber and saw Marek recline in Salatis's chair and put his sandaled feet up on the desk in front of him. Again, Osorkon could swear he made eye contact, and the Thayan wizard smiled.

"There's someone," Kolviss said.

Osorkon's eyes snapped back to the view of his outer office, and he stood. A man of medium height but sturdy build stepped out of the cloud of black and purple smoke just as if it was indeed a doorway. He held a finely-crafted longaxe in both hands and was dressed for battle in black leather ring mail.

Osorkon watched as five more followed the first man. All of them looked enough alike to be brothers. They appeared of mulan descent with dusky brown skin and eyes that appeared black in the crystal ball. All six of them went to the doors to the ransar's office. None of them spoke, no orders were given. They all held identical weapons.

"Stand alert, men," Osorkon told his bodyguards. "They have axes, so they'll get in, but it should take a while."

The ransar opened a cabinet behind him and drew out a carved mahogany box that he set on a stack of parchment on his desk.

"Ooh," Thensumkon said, "what's that?"

Osorkon looked at him, but didn't answer. The fool had no idea they were all about to be killed.

Well, he thought, ignorance is bliss.

While he dug in a desk drawer for the key to the box Osorkon kept his eyes fixed on what transpired in his outer office, though the temptation to look back at Marek Rymüt—who continued to stare directly at him from the Chamber of Law and Civility—nettled at his nerves. Two of the six assassins stood close to the double doors, opened their mouths, and for all appearances vomited on them. A stream of black fluid gushed up from deep in their throats and flowed over the smooth-polished oak. The wood began to dissolve like a sugar cube in a hot cup of tea ... actually a little faster than that.

"All right, men," he warned the guards, "they'll be through the doors a bit sooner."

He found the key and blinked sweat out of his eyes as he struggled with the lock on the mahogany box. He didn't remember feeling so warm before the assassins stepped out of a cloud in the next room.

"Should we be leaving?" asked Kolviss.

Osorkon had to smile at that one, but withheld his reply when he finally got the box unlocked. He opened it with a faint squeak of long-neglected hinges. Inside, nestled in rich green velvet, sat a mace. The weapon, which had been enchanted to contain the concentrated essence of lightning, had been in his family for generations and as a boy he'd been schooled in its use.

He drew it out and looked at the door. The sizzling sound of whatever caustic substance the strange men had vomited onto it grew louder and louder, then a wisp of brown-gray smoke twisted up from a spot a finger's length from the crack where the two doors met.

"There is another way out of here, isn't there, Ransar?" asked Kolviss.

"Where are we going?" Tlaet replied.

"Where are we going?" Osorkon asked. "That depends on what god you prayed to last."

"I always pray to Waukeen," Thensumkon said. "Don't we all pray to Waukeen, for gold and whatnot?"

Osorkon shook his head, hefted his heirloom mace, and stepped around his desk to stand in front of it, facing the door. He refused to look at Marek, so instead he let his gaze linger on his map. Painted onto one wall, the huge representation showed everything from the middle of the Nagaflow south to Firesteap Citadel in excellent detail. Ten months before, on the Ninth day of Nightal in the Year of the Wave, Osorkon had had a thin, straight blue line, running north-to-south, painted in the space between the Nagaflow River and the Lake of Steam.

The door sizzled so loudly his ears began to ring. Palm-sized chunks of wood fell off only to dissolve away to nothing but black blisters on the wood floor. Movement to the side caught Osorkon's attention and he watched as another figure stepped through the hovering black cloud into the room beyond the disintegrating doors.

"Salatis," Osorkon whispered.

"Who, Ransar?" one of the bodyguards asked as they both backed into the room with their halberds out in front of them.

"It's Senator Salatis," Osorkon said.

"Well," Thensumkon huffed with sincere disapproval, "he won't have that title for long."

"No," Osorkon said with a wry smile, "he'll have mine if we don't fight well."

"And get damned lucky," one of the bodyguards grumbled as he watched two more of the six assassins douse the failing doors with caustic secretions.

With a final sizzling, shattering cacophony they were in the room. The two bodyguards dropped back to defend their ransar, stepping past a startled, immobile Thensumkon.

"Well, now," the advisor started to say, but the words became a gurgle then were lost entirely to the *thump* of his severed head hitting the floor.

"Goodness!" Tlaet exclaimed.

"Really, now," Kolviss said, scurrying back in the direction of the ransar and his guards on legs shaking so badly he was obviously on the verge of collapsing, if not shattering, to the floor. "there is a back door out of here, now, isn't there? A secret door or a trapdoor . . . a concealed door, maybe? Some of kind of—"

Kolviss stopped talking when one of the bodyguards dropped him with the butt end of his halberd and said, "Sorry, Master Kolviss, but don't crowd us or—"

And it was the bodyguard's turn to stop in mid-sentence. Kolviss's hair, then scalp, dissolved away in front of their eyes, in just the blink of an eye revealing a dome of brilliant white skull. The advisor put a hand to his head, felt the bone, and fainted.

Osorkon decided that was a good thing—Kolviss wouldn't be able to feel his eyes melt, then his face. No one should have to be awake while his head was liquefied.

Tlaet squealed like a girl and ran so fast and so suddenly he accidentally avoided a swipe from one of the assassins' longaxes. Two of the assassins stepped right past him to engage the bodyguards. Osorkon stepped back behind his desk, holding his mace in front of him, his feet wide apart and his knees bent. The reach of the assassins' longaxes almost matched the bodyguards' halberds, and the four of them parried and struck, parried and struck.

One of the assassins grunted loudly and stepped back. Angry, bleeding from a huge wound in his chest, the strange man opened his mouth, but before he could launch a stream of black acid at the bodyguard who'd sliced him, his eyes rolled up in his head and he fell backward. The black fluid oozed out from the sides of his mouth and began to dissolve the wood floor under his still head.

Another stepped up in his place, and they were back at it again.

The second bodyguard fell to a disemboweling, low slash of a longaxe. He was at least alive enough to cry out for his mother before the assassin stomped on his neck and cut his plea short with an ear-assaulting *crack*.

"Ransar," Kolviss squealed, "let us away!"

"For the last time, Kolviss," Osorkon said stepping back fast to avoid a stream of black fluid that arced through the air at his face, "there is nowhere to go."

The acid started working at his desk chair, and Osorkon kicked it away and jumped up onto his desk—kicking the stacks of parchment to the floor. Kolviss, in a blind panic, leaped at him, grabbing at his legs, his face red and tears streaming from his eyes. One of the assassins stepped up behind Kolviss and brought his longaxe down in a smooth arc to imbed the blade into the top of the man's head. The blade sank down to the tip of his nose, and there was surprisingly little blood. Kolviss's eyes still moved, following Osorkon's, and his lips twitched silently a few times before he managed to say, "Osorkon?" in a voice made both wet and nasal by the bloody ruin his sinuses had become. The assassin twisted the handle of his long axe, choking up on it as he did so, and broke Kolviss's head open like an egg. Kolviss's legs collapsed, and he fell in a gory heap.

Two of the assassins crowded the last bodyguard, who bled from half a dozen wounds. The guard growled through gritted teeth and jabbed then swung, jabbed then swung, with his heavy halberd. When he spun the polearm up to parry a downward slash from one longaxe, the other assassin brought his weapon in low and took both of the guard's legs off at the knees with that one swipe.

"Surrender, Osorkon!" Salatis shouted over the bodyguard's agonized shriek.

The scream was silenced when one of the assassins took the guard's head off.

"Surrender!" Salatis called again from the doorway. "It's over."

Knowing the new ransar was right, Osorkon let loose an incoherent battle cry and charged the nearest assassin. He managed by pure luck to get inside the longaxe's reach and he smashed down on the dark man's shoulder. The carved steel head of the mace crunched the assassin's shoulder blade and sent a spiderweb of blue-white sparks crisscrossing over his twitching torso. The assassin's face screwed up in a spasm of agony, and he stood there, quivering under the mace's enchanted lightning for a heartbeat, then another, Osorkon shouting in defiance the whole time—which was long enough for another of the intruders to step in and take one of his arms off.

The lightning disappeared, and the assassin dropped

to the floor, still twitching, but otherwise dead. Osorkon staggered back, the mace still in the one hand he had left, and watched the blood pump from his open veins.

It doesn't hurt, he thought. Isn't that strange?

A dark-skinned assassin charged in, and Osorkon managed to beat his longaxe away with the mace, but he didn't register the other one standing right next to him.

The fluid was cold on his skin at first, and thick. It felt heavy, and that along with the weight of the mace made him drop his guard. He took a boot to the chest and fell. He tried to take a deep breath from on his back but couldn't.

Just as well, he thought. Now I can't give Salatis the satisfaction of a scream.

The acid took his skin and that hurt. Osorkon had never imagined pain like that.

Kill me, he thought, in some way desperate to communicate with the pain itself. Make me pass out, by Loviatar's bloody scourge.

His eyes slammed shut and his teeth chattered as the acid began to work on the meat of his arm. If he even had a hand anymore, he was no longer holding the mace. He watched it roll across the floor, the haft getting smaller and smaller as acid dissolved even the enchanted weapon.

"What—" he gasped. "What's that . . . smell?"

He caught a glance of the bone of his forearm. It was even whiter than Thensumkon's skull, if that was possible.

He looked up, blinking, the pain making all the muscles left in his body quiver so that he felt for all the world as if his blood had reached a rolling boil. Above him stood Salatis, dressed in a fine blue silk robe with a clean white sash, and one of the dark assassins. Osorkon was lost in the assassin's eyes. He'd never seen eyes so black—at least not on anything but a shark.

He tried to speak again but couldn't.

"The Storm Lord be praised," Salatis said, then glanced at the assassin. "Well done, Captain Olin."

Osorkon coughed. He couldn't breathe. The pain was

starting to go away. That didn't seem like a good sign.

"Well, Osorkon, my old friend," Salatis said. "By the grace of the Destroyer, by the will of Talos, I must inform you that your services to the city-state of Innarlith are no longer required." Salatis giggled in a way that made him appear, especially from below, like a drooling idiot. "May Talos eat your wretched soul to break his fast on the morrow."

Osorkon still couldn't breathe, and couldn't get any part of his body except his neck to move, but he could move his neck, and he did, tilting his head away from the gloating, laughing Salatis and his stoic, unamused, silent assassin. He looked at the map, tried to keep his eyes open and on the straight blue line.

Finish it anyway, he thought. Finish it, Devorast. It was never really mine, after all.

And those were the words Osorkon took with him to eternity.

PART II

26

Really, Willem, what in the diamond battlements of Trueheart do you have to be afraid of?" Marek Rymüt asked with a sibilant hiss to his accented voice—he pronounced Willem's name as if it started with a V and not a W. The rotund wizard blinked, almost as though he was batting his eyelashes. "I mean, really. You are well and truly blessed."

Willem swallowed and nodded, looking around the high-ceilinged room. Scattered about sat a number of crates. Hay had been piled in the corners, and canvas tarps had been spread over the scuffed wood floor.

"Willem?" the Thayan prompted.

"Yes," Willem replied, still not looking Marek in the eye. "I am well and truly ..." He paused to think, then risked: "... cared for."

Marek laughed, and the sound was so light and so sincere that Willem was forced to smile.

"You know, of course, that I can help you," Marek said as he crossed the room to one of the crates. "Please excuse the mess. We've only just begun to move in. Do you like it?"

Willem nodded, lying. The building was garish and overly large for one man, and he'd heard that Marek didn't even intend to live there.

"I understand you'll be keeping the house, too," Willem

said, as much just to make conversation to cover his nervousness than to verify the rumors.

"Of course," the wizard replied as he dug through first one crate then another. "This is a place of business. From this compound, the finest in magical items will be made available to the fine people of Innarlith."

Willem nodded, watching the man search apparently at random for the promised item, and asked, "It will be an embassy, too, I understand."

Marek stopped and turned to regard him with a gaze that made Willem's skin crawl.

Marek turned back to the next crate and continued his search, but just a little more slowly than before.

"It might one day serve a similar function," said the Red Wizard. "I suppose it's safe to consider this Thayan ground. But it's not so much an embassy as an ... an enclave. I am here not to influence, but to serve."

"You influence anyway," Willem said.

Marek chuckled and stopped rooting around in the crate. When he turned he held a small box of polished maple and wore a warm grin.

"When I am asked a question," the wizard said, "I answer. When my opinion is sought out, I oblige. If I influence, it is because I have made every effort to help, and always in the best interests of my adopted home."

Willem smiled and nodded, but couldn't help staring at the box. "Is that it?" he asked.

Marek glanced down at the box in his hand but said, "I understand you've had some success recently that has brought considerable coin to your personal coffers."

Willem nodded.

"An apple orchard, of all things," said the Thayan. "Really, Willem, my lad, I can't possibly be asked to imagine you a farmer."

"I'm no farmer," he said. "There are tenants to tend the trees. I just ..."

"Own it?" the Thayan prompted.

"I've been told that a senator must have an income," Willem said. "I was encouraged to acquire land."

"But at so meager a price," Marek replied, "and for so rich a harvest."

Willem shrugged, still staring at the box.

"You can afford more," the wizard said with a wink. "This is . . . a trifle."

"But it will do what I asked?" Willem asked. "It'll do what I need it to do?"

The Thayan nodded and stepped forward, holding the box out. Willem took it, flinching when Marek touched the back of his hand with a cool, clammy fingertip. Willem fumbled the box a little, and almost dropped it. Marek placed it in his hand, and Willem snatched it away a bit too quickly for decorum's sake. A brief glow passed through Marek's eyes that made Willem's breath catch in his throat.

They both released a breath together, and Willem opened the box.

"You have but to wear it," Marek said.

Inside the box was a simple brooch of fine gold fashioned in the likeness of a heart held in the palm of a hand. Willem had seen better workmanship. There was nothing about the thing that seemed particularly special.

"And if I do?" Willem asked.

"You will bear up under the strain," the Thayan explained with a smirk. "It will embolden you. You will not be so easily intimidated."

Willem looked up at him, his jaw tense. Marek was surprised but showed it only for the briefest fraction of a heartbeat before smiling once more.

"It may even have some benefit where the fairer sex is concerned," said Marek.

"What do you mean?" Willem asked, closing the box. "May I?"

Marek nodded and Willem put the box in the deep pocket of his weathercloak. From the same pocket he withdrew a purse heavy with coins.

"I mean that perhaps with its subtle influence you will finally be able to leave my niece in your wake," the wizard explained.

Willem shivered. He looked at his hand, which held the purse out to Marek, and saw it shake.

Marek wrapped his sausage fingers around the bag of coins and said, "A thousand?"

"As we agreed," Willem replied, letting his arm fall to his side. "So, with that I'll—"

"Oh, bother," Marek cut in, dropping the coin purse into one of the open crates. "Don't be like that, my lad. You know of my fondness for Halina, and certainly your perpetually-impending nuptials would be a rare social event among the least imaginative of Innarlan society, but honestly, is she the best choice?"

"The only times I can remember feeling even the slightest bit happy have been in her presence," Willem said. Sweat gathered at his hairline and under his arms. He hadn't meant to reveal so much, especially to the Thayan. "But my mother is of similar mind to you."

"Ah, yes," Marek replied. "And how fares the lovely Thurene?"

"She is well."

"Just 'well'?"

Willem shrugged. He didn't know what else to say.

"She whispers a name in your ear, I'll wager," Marek said. "I know that the master builder has been, too, and for some time."

Willem shook his head, hoping against hope that Marek wouldn't say the name.

"I'm happy with Halina," Willem said.

"And what of that?" asked the wizard. "Who are you to be happy?"

Willem looked him in the eye and shook his head. Had he heard the man correctly?

"I'm . . ." Willem started.

"All men are equal," the Thayan said. "We all have our roles to play in the gods' great theater. Who are you to expect to be happy when so many suffer? So what if you love Halina? You should marry Phyrea. Her father wishes it, and so do many others in this city—many others who have been watching over you and will continue to watch over you both."

"But..." Willem grunted. He didn't know what to say. He didn't want to have the conversation Marek seemed intent on bullying him into.

"I'm sure you find the fair Phyrea pleasing to the eye," said Marek.

Willem nodded, but said, "Will you forbid me from marrying your niece? Will you prevent me from seeing her?"

Willem had tried to keep that last from sounding like a plea, but he couldn't help it. Anyway, Marek Rymüt was too intelligent and astute a listener not to have sensed it. Willem could see it written plainly in the Thayan's sparkling eyes and uneven smile.

"I will do no such thing," said Marek. "If you are dead set on embarking on a path pointed away from the goals you've worked so diligently to achieve, how could I presume to stop you?"

"Phyrea hates me," Willem said.

"Wives hate their husbands, lad," Marek replied.

"Before they're even married?"

"Well...."

There was a heavy silence while Willem hoped he looked like he was thinking long and hard.

"Phyrea...." Willem said, his voice barely more than a whisper.

Marek smiled and said, "Wear the pin, son. It will help."

27

30 Nightal, the Year of the Sword (1365 DR)
THE PALACE OF MANY SPIRES, INNARLITH

The evening had begun with a lengthy and confusing prayer of appeasement to Malar, given by the newly confirmed ransar himself. Salatis had insisted that his guests attend the festivities in the guise of an animal, and Willem Korvan had chosen for himself the weasel.

"It's a creature with its own nobility, wouldn't you say, Meykhati?" Willem said. "Or should I say, 'Sir Crane'?"

The elder senator indulged him with a largely uninterested laugh from behind his avian mask of fine Shou porcelain and said, "If you say so, Will—Senator Weasel."

The laughs that sizzled up from the circle of guests Willem had merged with mocked him. He put a hand lightly to the brooch that held his cloak around his shoulders. A palpable sensation of warmth flooded his chest when he touched it.

"Tell us more, Senator Weasel," requested the woman with purple hair, a mask in the likeness of an eagle, and the familiar accent of Willem's homeland.

"You're Cormyrean," he said.

The woman, stout and heavy, immaculately dressed in a gown that included actual eagle feathers, bowed slightly and introduced herself as Tia Harriman, the newly-appointed ambassador from Cormyr.

The others—Meykhati behind his crane mask; the master builder with an elephant's ghastly trunk; Rymüt's man Insithryllax, wearing a frightening black dragon's head; Kurtsson with the face of a bear; and his mother, who pressed close to him, her eyes as cold and hard as the tigress whose features she'd borrowed—heaped niceties on the woman.

"I'm surprised," Willem said, marveling at the sound of

his own voice—so clear and strong.

"Whatever do you mean, my dear?" his mother inquired. He could feel her nervousness, and perhaps for the first time in his life he didn't care.

"Why does Azoun suddenly feel that Innarlith, of all places, requires the presence of an embassy?"

Willem stood in the center of the ensuing silence feeling like Talos in the eye of a hurricane of his own creation. Thurene squeezed his arm, but he ignored her.

"His Majesty," the ambassador replied, correcting his protocol, "has taken an interest in the canal."

"Well, you get right to the point, don't you, Ambassador?" Willem replied. He felt cheerful, and let his voice convey that. Everyone relaxed, at least a little. "I suppose I can see why Cormyr might benefit from it. Too bad it will never come to pass."

"Won't it?" asked the ambassador.

"No, madam," Inthelph answered before Willem could, "I don't think it will. The only two people in Innarlith who might make a go of it"—he nodded to Willem—"are standing before you right now. And neither of us have any interest in that fool's errand."

"No?" asked the ambassador. "And why not?"

"It's not necessary," Inthelph said.

"There are already means to travel from here to the Vilhon Reach," Kurtsson cut in, the voice from behind the bear mask had an exotic accent. "I could take you there myself right now, and back again, in but the blink of the eye. And I can do the same with an entire ship. Why, then, all the digging?"

The contempt he put into that last word stuck in Willem's ear a bit. An answer to Kurtsson's question occurred to him, but he didn't speak it. The idea for a canal was brilliant, and he knew full well that if anyone in Faerûn might have a chance to make it work it was Ivar Devorast, but that was the last thing he'd tell the people around him just then.

"My friend the bear is correct," said the strange man behind the black dragon mask. Even under the influence of the brooch's magic, Willem recoiled a little from the man, as did all of them. "But perhaps a more cheerful subject is in order."

"Indeed, Sir Dragon," the ambassador said. "I do have a question for our friend the weasel."

"Of course," said Willem. "We hunt birds, rabbits, rats, frogs, and various small rodents by the hundreds."

There was a pause while they all struggled in their own ways with his answer, then a few reluctant, almost frightened giggles.

"Oh, Willem, my dear, don't be silly," Thurene said as she dug her fingernails into his arm.

Willem endured the pain and said, "Interesting thing about us weasels: the young are born almost exclusively in the month of Tarsakh—as few as two, and as many as ten in a litter—in a nest lined with the fur of the mother's kills. Like humans, the female weasel has a strong instinct to protect her young. It takes three and a half tendays for their eyes to open, but they're hunting by the end of their second month of life."

"It must be difficult for the mother weasel to see them leave," the ambassador played along.

"Oh, my," Meykhati interjected. "Were we to have been prepared to discuss the behavior and mating habits of our animals? Isn't the dreadful mask enough?"

"Fear not, Senator," Willem reassured him. "For me, the weasel has always been of interest—its habits and its upbringing. I chose the mask for that reason, not the other way around. A similar devotion on the part of any other guest to their totems is hardly required. But in any event, I hope the ambassador is entertained."

"I am," she replied. "But I hadn't intended to inquire into the secret mating rituals of the weasel. I remain curious as to why one of His Majesty's subjects sits on the governing body of an independent city-state so far from home? Surely a young man of your accomplishments could have found a suitable position at home?"

"One would think," Willem answered, letting all the bile, all the old animosity he could muster weigh heavily on his words. Meykhati actually took a step back, Insithryllax tensed as if expecting a fight to break out, and Thurene gasped. "But, alas, I was wooed away. Once again, I'm reminded of the weasel. Their fur-lined dens are stolen from the burrowing animals they've killed and eaten."

"Have you killed and eaten us then?" Meykhati asked.

"Not quite eaten yet, no," replied Willem.

A waiter passed by, his naked body painted to resemble the colorful feathers of a native bird Willem didn't know the name of. He took a tallglass of wine from the proffered tray and drained half of it in a single swallow. The mask made that difficult, but he managed it without spilling any, even with his mother pulling on his arm.

The master builder cleared his throat and said, "So, Willem, do tell. Have you given any further thought to Phyrea?"

"Phyrea?" the ambassador asked.

"The master builder's lovely and charming daughter," Thurene answered. "Senator Inthelph and I have hopes for them."

"Our humble take on the royal marriage," Meykhati joked.

Willem took a deep breath and almost spilled the wine on his silk tunic when he went to touch the brooch again. It steeled his nerves, but did nothing to help him organize his thoughts. The mention of that name was enough to send him almost into a swoon. Phyrea—beautiful and disturbed, with her bizarre convictions and mysterious agendas—and Halina—soft and insubstantial, but comfortable—the two women in his life.

"Really, my dear," Thurene said, "what could possibly cause you to hesitate? She's such a lovely girl."

Three women, Willem corrected himself.

"Gracious as always, Madam Korvan," the master builder gushed.

But Willem knew all too well why Inthelph wanted him to marry his daughter. He thought Willem could rein her in, settler her, control her, and make her something she wasn't. He couldn't even do that for himself without the aid of Thayan magic. He touched the brooch again and felt just a little less warmth.

"In the winter," he said, "the weasel's fur turns white." He gestured with his tallglass to indicate the white mask he wore. "If this was the Midsummer revel, I'd have had it painted brown. Phyrea is the most beautiful woman I've ever seen."

There was another heavy silence, but Willem felt less inclined to revel in it. Insithryllax and Kurtsson traded a look. Thurene moved her hand up his arm and found fresh skin to mar with her expensively-manicured talons. The ambassador studied him from behind her eagle mask as though he'd just crawled up out of the sea. Meykhati chuckled, and the master builder nodded in a confused, dull way.

"If you will excuse us," Insithryllax said, and with a bow of his dragon head, he and Kurtsson moved away.

Willem caught a glimpse of a woman with a mouse mask standing behind them and got the distinct impression that she had been eavesdropping. Before he could study her in any detail, though, the master builder stole his attention.

"What do you say, Willem?"

"Yes, my dear," Thurene pressed. "Wouldn't the ransar's New Year's Masque be the perfect place for such lovely news?"

"Phyrea?" Willem asked, and they all nodded, even the woman from Cormyr. "The weasel is a night hunter that kills by biting into the back of its victim's neck."

"You mean its prey," said the ambassador.

"Yes, my dear," Thurene said with another painful

squeeze, "do say what you mean."

"Not everyone is fond of the weasel," he said, "though its poor reputation is hardly deserved. So it takes a chicken or two here and there. It also eats rats and mice, so even a chicken farmer can appreciate it. It's as noble a creature as any, the weasel, and deserves a chance to survive."

"I'm sure we would all do our best to preserve the noble weasel," Meykhati said, his voice making it plain what he wanted from Willem.

Willem touched the brooch and studied at the people who looked at him through their masks. Their eyes pulled at him.

"Even weasels must come together for the good of their kind," Willem said.

"Indeed," said Meykhati. "Even weasels."

"Master Builder," Willem said, turning to address Inthelph. Thurene's hand fell away from his arm, and he heard her breath catch. "In the spirit of the noble weasel, in the home of our ransar, in the presence of my mother, and because her beauty is unparalleled in all the world, I humbly seek your permission to ask your daughter to become my wife."

Willem ignored the ensuing gaggle of congratulations. He didn't really even hear the master builder give him his blessing, but he of course did—and with great enthusiasm. Instead, his attention was drawn to the woman with the mouse mask, who stood several paces away, staring at him. He blinked, but couldn't quite see her eyes. Still, there was something familiar about her.

"Oh, it will be a grand affair!" Thurene all but shrieked.

He glanced at her, but then movement drew his eye back to the mouse. She took her mask off with a shaking hand.

"Halina," Willem whispered.

Tears welled up in her eyes as she stared at him.

Willem touched the brooch, but it wasn't courage he needed just then.

"Willem, dear," his mother all but shouted at him. She grabbed his arm, again and he flinched.

Meykhati clapped him on the shoulder and said, "Well done, Senator. Well done, indeed."

Willem forced his gaze away from Halina, but he could see her turn and run into the crowd of revelers from the corner of his eye. He spent the rest of the last night of the Year of the Sword talking about weasels and marriage.

28

30 Nightal, the Year of the Sword (1365 DR)
THE CANAL SITE

He moved on top of her, inside her, to a rhythm that had started out as his own, but had become a perfect fusion of two heartbeats. Phyrea let herself gasp, let a tear trickle from the corner of one eye, and let her body take his and be taken by his. She gave herself to Ivar Devorast as best she could when he wanted so little of her. He made no sounds, but his body told her that he wanted her, wanted nothing more at that moment than to be there with her. She had from him the best he could give, and more than she could ever truly have hoped for: his undivided attention.

When finally he slipped off her, Phyrea had to gasp for air. Though it was cold in his odd little cabin, a sheen of sweat covered her. She lay there until she began to shiver before she drew the blanket over herself. He looked down at her, and she wanted him to see her. The air could have been drawn from the room, the blood drained from her heart, but as long as his eyes were on her she would be sustained.

He smiled at her in that way he had that made it appear as though he knew everything, and she shivered again.

Outside, the whistle of the winter wind mixed with the sound of men drinking and laughing, shouting and singing. Even in the remote work camp, it the New Year's Revel, after all.

"If you tell me not to speak," she whispered, "I won't. If you tell me to go, I'll go."

"I don't want to tell you what to do," he said. His voice was more relaxed than she'd ever heard it. "You don't have to await my command. I would like you to stay."

"Then I'll stay," she whispered, and put her hand on his chest. He took it in his, and her thin fingers were swallowed up in his grasp. He drew her hand to his lips and kissed her palm. When the tip of his tongue drew a circle there, her body alit once again. "I'll stay forever."

He smiled, his teeth white in the dark space of the cabin. "Surely you have something of interest waiting for you in Innarlith. I thought you said you were going to destroy me. That, at least, will—"

"Shut up," she said. Phyrea sat, letting the blanket fall away. She wrapped her arms around him for warmth. "Don't say . . ."

But he was right. She had been working hard to poison people against him and his canal. She'd gone so far as to let her father know that she would be willing to marry Willem Korvan. Far all she knew, he was arranging the ceremony at that very moment.

"I'm here now, with you," she whispered in Devorast's ear.

He returned her embrace, and another tear rolled down her cheek. The embrace was so tender, she was nearly overwhelmed.

"I suppose you could stay," he said. "Your work against me is done."

"Please, don't—"

"The new ransar could stop everything simply by drawing closed the purse strings," he said. "I've been told that he is less than enthusiastic about the canal."

"He listens to the mages," she told him. "But I don't want to have this conversation. I can't talk about any possibility of you failing."

"I thought you wanted me to fail," he said, "so that I would stop before I was beaten by lesser men."

The sarcasm was plain in his voice.

"Don't have fun with me," she said, and though she'd hoped to sound threatening all she heard in her voice was a little girl's pleading.

He turned to her and kissed her cheek, then her lips.

"Marek Rymüt," she whispered.

"The Thayan."

"He won't let you build it."

"Because he makes his living by selling the magic necessary to teleport, or to open portals. I know that."

Phyrea sighed and said, "Osorkon is dead. Who will protect you from him?"

"The Thayan has Salatis's ear?"

"People tell me he made Salatis ransar," she said.

"Then I'll have to accelerate the work."

She shook her head and told him, "By all accounts you've stretched your men too far as it is. How fast can one man dig? And I doubt you'll get our new ransar to send you any more strong backs. That uprising on the docks is over, and Innarlith is back to work. Peasant men don't need to come out here and risk monsters and trench collapses to earn a day's wage."

He smiled at her again, and the feeling it elicited in her was so intense, she nestled her face in his neck so he couldn't see it.

"You have it all sorted," he joked.

Phyrea stopped herself from crying by sheer force of will.

"Have you heard he word 'smokepowder'?" he asked.

She cleared her throat and pulled away just far enough that she could look at him again. "Some kind of alchemy that causes things to explode?" He nodded and she continued, "But what would you want with magic? I thought you were determined not to use magic."

"I use some form of magic every day, here and there,"

he said. "I have no aversion to the right tool for the right job, but anyway smokepowder is not magical in nature. It's a mixture of rare earth elements that together are quite volatile."

"And?"

"With the proper application of enough force, I can move more earth than any man could shovel."

"So, you want to dig with—" Phyrea said. She stopped when something occurred to her all at once. "The Thayan ... he ..."

"I won't accept it from Marek Rymüt, if that's what—"

"No, no," she interrupted. "Someone used smokepowder to try to kill Rymüt. You never heard of it? It caused quite a row. Innocent bystanders were injured, but the Thayan survived unscathed. The would-be assassin was just let out of the ransar's dungeon."

"Who is he?"

"An alchemist," she said, only then remembering the rest of the story. "He used to be quite in demand in the city, until Rymüt came along. They said he was bitter about the loss of trade to the Thayan, so he used his skills to try to blow him to bits."

"But failed."

"The smokepowder exploded, though," she said. Her heartbeat quickened, and she thought she could feel his race as well. "It worked, but Marek was able to get out of harm's way. The ground won't be so difficult a target."

Devorast nodded.

"Do you think it could work?" she asked, and he nodded again. "If you can dig faster, if you can show indisputable progress, Salatis may not be able to—may not even want to stop you, especially if you can bring in gold and workers from other realms, as you planned."

"Who is this alchemist?"

"I don't remember his name," she said. "I could find out. I could ask, in the city."

"Be careful," Devorast said. "If the wrong people know

what I intend, it could end everything."

"Trust me," she whispered and began to kiss his shoulder.

"Does that mean you no longer want to destroy me?" he said. "This would be the perfect chance. Tell Marek Rymüt that I want smokepowder to use as a digging tool, and tell him I want to hire the man who tried to kill him to make it for me. He'll finally just come up here and kill me himself."

Phyrea froze. And why hadn't Master Rymüt done just that? What was he waiting for?

"Trust me," she told him again.

29

17 Hammer, the Year of the Staff (1366 DR)
THE CITY OF SAELMUR, ON THE SHORE OF THE LAKE OF STEAM

Your name is Surero," the man said as he sat in the chair across the table for all the world as though he'd been invited to do so.

"Who in the infinite Abyss are you?" Surero asked, his eyes narrowing, his fingers tensing around the heavy earthenware mug he was a heartbeat from smashing over the man's red-haired head.

"Ivar Devorast," the man said. "If you're finished hiding out and drinking, I have a job for you to do."

Surero swallowed and nodded, looking around the low-ceilinged room. The tavern was crowded with people who drank and spoke, but rarely if ever laughed. The dank air was filled with pipeweed smoke and sweat, and the ale was bitter but still overpriced.

"You are Surero," Devorast prompted.

"Yes," Surero replied, not quite looking the stranger in the eye. "I am . . ." He paused to think, then finished, "I used to be."

Devorast laughed, and the sound was so light and so sincere that Surero was forced to smile.

"I understand that you are accomplished in the creation and use of smokepowder," Devorast said. "I have a challenge for you, closer to Innarlith, if you're interested."

Surero froze at the sound of that city's name, and had to force himself to speak. "I told myself I would never go back to that pit of foreign deceit. And why should I? So I can be robbed blind again? Go back and tell your Red Wizard master that I have nothing left for him to take."

"I don't work for any Red Wizard," Devorast said. "You've heard of the canal?"

Surero nodded, then took a sip of the bitter ale to try to hide the confusion and excitement that gripped him. His face flushed, and he began to sweat.

He waited a bit for Devorast to go on, but finally asked, "What of it? What do you want from me?"

"I need to move a great deal of earth in a very short time," Devorast explained. "I have the idea that with a sufficient quantity of smokepowder, set in just the right places, that could be accomplished. I know why you were sent to the ransar's dungeon, and I honestly don't care. I have no affection for Marek Rymüt, but nor do I waste any time hating him. He isn't involved in my project, and he won't be. You don't have to go back to the city. You can live and work at the site, as I do."

"I need to know who's coin will pay me," Surero said.

"Mine," Devorast said. "Where I get it from doesn't have to concern you."

With a sigh, Surero looked around the room again. "You see all these people, Devorast? Look at them. These are sad, desperate people. And do you know why?"

"No," Devorast replied.

Surero stopped himself from answering right away and looked Devorast in the eye. He could see the unspoken words in the man's steely gaze: *And I don't care.*

"Tell me, have you spoken with Rymüt about this canal

of yours? Has he made his opinion of it known to you?"

"I have reason to believe he's sent monsters to kill me on at least two occasions," Devorast said.

Surero found it difficult to breathe. He downed the rest of his ale and almost choked on it. Devorast held up a hand and got the attention of the serving wench. He held up two fingers, and she nodded and waddled to the bar.

"What are you doing here?" asked Devorast. "I've asked about you, and by all accounts you're an alchemist of considerable skill."

"I used to be," he said. "Then the Thayan . . ."

"He took your customers from you, and otherwise made it difficult to practice your craft," Devorast finished for him. "If you're ready to leave off crying about that, come with me and help do something that no one in Faerûn has ever done."

"I can't place your accent," Surero said.

"I was born in Cormyr."

Surero shrugged, and sat quietly while the serving wench set two more ales on the table, collected his empty and the Cormyrean's coin, and shuffled off.

"I need to know if this canal . . . when it's done, will Marek Rymüt hate it? Will he despise anyone who helped? Will he stop at nothing to destroy it?" Surero asked. "Answer me—and tell the truth. I have ways of knowing if you're lying."

There was a potion that would help him discern the truth, but he hadn't mixed one in years. Surero just needed to hear the man say it.

"I will build it, because I want it to be built," Devorast said. "I have no intention of seeking permission from Marek Rymüt."

Surero sighed again and met Devorast's firm gaze.

"It's a good idea," Surero said. "Smokepowder for digging . . . I hadn't ever thought of it, but it'll work. I'm sure it'll work. This canal, basically it's a trench that'll eventually be filled with water?" Devorast nodded, and Surero went on, "I can do that. I'd be the first to do it ... at least that I know of ... and I can do it."

Devorast took a sip of his ale and didn't seem to react at all to its bitterness. He looked Surero in the eye and waited.

The alchemist sighed again and said, "I came here with the intention of gathering what few coins I could before moving on farther west. I'd thought, maybe, Athkatla. I've heard that some of the port cities are experimenting with weapons powered by smokepowder that could hurl heavy objects long distances to crash into ships and whatnot."

Devorast nodded as if he'd heard that too, and as if he thought the idea was perfectly sound, but he said, "What I mean to build is more worthy of your talents."

Surero laughed and drank more of his ale, wincing at the bite of it on his tongue.

"Why me?" he asked.

"Because I think you can do it."

"To be the first ..." Surero said.

Devorast nodded and Surero pushed the flagon of ale away from himself with a grimace.

"What's it like?" the alchemist asked. "Your work site. Is it like this?" He gestured to the room full of desperate men.

"Yes," Devorast replied, "but the air is a little fresher."

Surero laughed and felt relief wash over him like a waterfall. It had been so long since he'd had anything to do, he nearly cried.

Nodding, he said, "All right then."

They finished their ales and Surero talked. He told Devorast everything—every last detail of his attempt to kill Marek Rymüt. He told him of his training in the alchemical arts, his workshop and business before the Red Wizard came to Innarlith. He talked and talked, and everything inside him spilled out into the ears of the red-headed Cormyrean who sat almost perfectly still, almost perfectly silent, and listened.

30

The sound of the explosion was muffled by eight feet of dirt, but much louder was the shower of loose soil that drummed through the air and back onto the ground in a hard rain of brown and gray. The crowd of workers that had gathered—at a safe distance determined by Surero—cheered and hooted.

"I think they like it," Surero said, smiling at the cloud of dust and smoke, slow to dissipate in the calm air. The dust began to mix with the incessant drizzle to form a dirty rain that followed the shower of dirt.

"They enjoy the spectacle," said Devorast, who stood beside him on the low hill to the side of the canal's path.

"Aren't they happy not to have to dig all that out by hand?" Surero asked with a shrug.

Devorast didn't answer. Instead, he walked down the hill to the wide, deep crater. He carried a measuring stick, and by the time Surero followed him to the edge of the pit, he had already climbed into the crater and begun to measure it.

"Careful of the loose dirt," the alchemist warned, watching Devorast's boot slip and sink half to his ankle in dusty soil. "What do you think?"

"It's definitely bigger," Devorast replied. "When the rest of the loose dirt is dug out, it'll be deeper still."

"I prefer to think of my creation as a pick more than a shovel," Surero said.

His measurements completed, Devorast led him back up the hill. Surero blinked in the drizzle and ran a hand through his wet hair. They climbed the low hill and stepped into the little hut they'd built to store the smokepowder.

Inside, lined up on half a dozen shelves, were cheap burlap sacks of various sizes, from barely the size of a small coin purse, to sacks made for forty pounds of grain. The sacks were filled with his latest masterpiece.

"The new ratio is better," Devorast said.

Surero smiled and replied, "I'm happy with it. the trick was increasing the amount of sulfur in the mix—convenient that it washes up on shore by the barrels-full every day. We don't even have to buy it, just scrape it off the beaches and let it dry."

"And the charcoal?" Devorast asked as he searched the sacks for just the right size.

"Willow," Surero replied. "From now on, I'll only use willow." Devorast glanced at him with one eyebrow raised, so Surero explained, "You can use almost anything. Zalantar isn't bad, but it can be expensive. Elder or laurel is pretty good. I've heard of people using grapevine. I could make it with pinecones, even."

Devorast lifted a sack from a low shelf and hefted it. He gave no indication that he'd heard a word the alchemist had said.

"You know what you are, Ivar?" he asked, not expecting a response and not getting one. "You're fearless."

Devorast glanced at him as he walked past with the sack of smokepowder, and Surero could see the trace of a grimace on his lips.

"See?" the alchemist continued, following him out of the shack. "That's ten pounds you have there. I measured it myself. If that went off now there wouldn't be enough left of you to use as fertilizer, but to look at you, anyone would think it was a sack of potatoes."

Devorast kept walking, down the hill.

"I know, I know ..." Surero went on. "It's not going to go off. You know it won't, because you know how to handle it. That's your secret, isn't it? Self-confidence. You just believe in yourself completely."

"Don't you?" Devorast asked.

Surero laughed and said, "Don't I? I still lie awake at night wondering why Marek Rymüt had me released from the dungeon. I experiment with smokepowder and every second of it my hands are shaking and sweating and I'm sure the next turn of the mortar and pestle and will be my last."

Devorast ignored him as, having set the sack of smokepowder on the ground next to him, he crouched to inspect the hole. Ten yards away from the crater they'd just made, and still a safe distance from the onlooking workers, Devorast had had another shaft dug. The hole was no more than a foot in diameter.

"That's ten feet," Surero said. "Ten pounds at ten feet? That's easy to remember."

Devorast tied the end of the smokepowder-infused twine onto the top of the sack, then lowered it down the hole. Surero watched Devorast count the depth from knots that had been tied in the rope every foot. When the sack finally rested on the bottom, and Devorast had counted nine knots, he stood and walked back up the hill, trailing the twine as he went.

"Aren't you paying me to do that?" the alchemist asked.

"I'm paying you for the powder," Devorast replied.

Once they were a safe distance away, up the hill, Devorast struck a flint and steel and a spark leaped to the twine. It sizzled and popped its way down the length of the fuse. Surero watched its progress with a self-satisfied smile.

"You'll want to cover your ears this time," the alchemist warned, then did as he'd advised himself.

Devorast waited until the little sparking flame following the length of twine dipped down into the deep shaft before holding his hands against his ears. Surero squinted, afraid of what ten pounds of—

The explosion was so loud it rattled his eardrums, regardless of his hands pressed to the sides of his head. He staggered back a few steps and closed his eyes. Bending at the waist he moved his hands from his ears to the back of his head, protecting it from the stinging rain of dirt and stones that pounded them both. The onlooking workers shifted back several paces like a school of fish fleeing a shark.

When it was safe to open his eyes again, Surero looked at Devorast. The Cormyrean stood there nodding, watching as the dust and smoke cleared to reveal a crater several times the depth and diameter of the first.

"We need more," he said.

Surero chuckled, nodded, and said, "I don't have a single grain of saltpeter left, and no one in Innarlith will sell it to me."

Devorast nodded, thinking, then said, "Phyrea's father harvests saltpeter at his country estate. I saw the lean-to when I worked there."

"That's interesting, but isn't Phyrea's father the master builder, and one of Rymüt's closest allies in the senate?" Devorast shrugged. "If Rymüt doesn't want us to have it—doesn't want *me* to have it since he's mage enough to know what I intend to use it for—he'll never sell it to us. I'm going to need a lot of it, too. Three quarters of every sack is sulfur, a tenth is saltpeter, and the rest charcoal. A young lady can't just hide it in her pockets and walk it out to us."

"She'll think of something," Devorast assured him, then turned and picked up his measuring stick again.

He walked down the hill, and Surero called after him, "Maybe she can steal us some of her father's wine, too. I can use it to mix the serpentine so it doesn't blow up in my face!" Devorast again made no indication he'd heard anything the alchemist had to say, so he added more quietly, "And if I drink enough of it maybe my hands will stop shaking all the time."

31

9 Alturiak, the Year of the Staff (1366 DR)
THE PALACE OF MANY SPIRES, INNARLITH

Salatis smiled and rubbed his hands together, gazing up at the jet black iron disk rimmed with purple-stained wood—the finishing touch to the shrine.

"Shar be praised," he whispered.

One of the men looked at him, his eyes wide. Salatis's blood ran cold, and the man looked away, sensing, perhaps, that he shouldn't have heard that name.

"Olin," Salatis said, still staring at the workman.

The black firedrake stepped up behind him with hardly a sound, and stood stiff and at the ready in his human guise. The workman and his partner wouldn't look them in the eye. Instead, they hurried to pack up their tools. They were such simple men, with their rough homespun clothes and dirty, calloused hands. They smelled of sweat and sawdust.

"Is there a problem, Ransar?" a stern, deep voice asked from behind him.

Salatis turned to see Insithryllax standing in the open doorway. The swarthy, intimidating man folded his arms and leaned against the doorjamb. He glanced at Olin with a smirk, but the black firedrake refused to look at him.

"No," Salatis said, "thank you, Insithryllax. What brings you here?"

"Just curious," Marek Rymüt's man replied, stepping into the room. Salatis could feel Olin move between them. "Back off, drake."

A sound like a creaking door rumbled out of Olin's throat—a bestial growl. Insithryllax laughed.

"Please, gentlemen," said Salatis. "Have some care with your behavior. You are in a holy place."

The too-curious workman glanced up at the symbol of

the Lady of Loss, and Salatis watched gooseflesh break out on his arms. He put a hammer into his toolbox, and Salatis sensed his reluctance to let go of the would-be weapon.

"My apologies, Ransar," Insithryllax sneered.

Salatis stifled a gasp and thought, Ransar. I am the ransar, aren't I?

"Not at all, Insithryllax," he said, watching the two workmen finish up their packing. "If you don't mind, though, I wonder if between the two of you, you might do me a favor and kill these two workmen."

The two men looked up at that, fear taking over their faces. They began to sweat profusely, and stood on shaking legs. One of them held up his hands, the other shook his head.

"Why?" Insithryllax asked.

"Because I am your ransar, and I wish it."

"Please, Ransar," one of the peasants blurted. "What—what have we done?"

"Pardon me," said Insithryllax, "but you are not *my* ransar."

The hair on Salatis's arms stood on end, and he suppressed a shudder. Olin, without a word, stepped closer to the two men, who backed away from him with their hands up to fend him off. He hefted his longaxe and smiled the leer of a killer—the toothy grin of the jackal.

The front of one of the workers' trousers bloomed with a dark shadow, and the stench of urine filled the dense air of the close space.

"Leave us alone," the man whimpered.

The other one sobbed, "Let us go home, my lord. Please let us go."

"You are excellent craftsmen and I'm sure your families are very proud of you," Salatis said, excitement making his heart race and his throat tighten.

"Please, Ransar," one of them begged.

"You will go to the Fugue Plane having done a great

service to the Dark Goddess. Perhaps there she will claim your souls and bring them with her to the Plane of Shadow where you will serve her as you served me."

Olin stepped forward, and set his longaxe on his shoulder.

"Oh, I see," Insithryllax said. "This little temple of yours is a secret."

"Careful," the ransar said, glancing back over his shoulder at Insithryllax.

The bolder of the two doomed men—the one who hadn't yet wet himself—took that as an opportunity to attempt to run past the three of them and out through the secret door to the ransar's hidden shrine—the hidden shrine they'd just finished building for him. Olin swung his heavy longaxe from his right shoulder, took the man's head off in the blink of an eye, and only stopped when the axe haft rested gently on his left shoulder.

Blood fountained from the decapitated man's neck as his body jerked to the floor. His partner was sprayed in the face, and yelped, trying his best to fend it off. He fell to his knees, then scrambled back until he fetched up against a wall. Babbling incoherent pleas for his miserable existence, he all but clawed the blood from his eyes.

Insithryllax chuckled in a mean-spirited way and said, "Collecting heads, are we?"

He tipped his head in the direction of the altar, behind which was a shelf. On the shelf was a big glass jar, tightly sealed with a waxed cork. Inside the jar was the grimacing, disembodied head of Osorkon.

"I hadn't actually thought of that, no," Salatis answered with a laugh. "Anyway, this new one isn't worth keeping."

The surviving workman groveled on the blood-soaked floor, crying. He retracted, staring up with pleading, animal's eyes, as Olin stepped up to tower over him.

"All this blood," Insithryllax said, "on your new floors."

"A small sacrifice," Salatis said, "for the favor of the Mistress of the Night."

"Weren't you a devoted follower of Malar just a tenday or so past?" Insithryllax asked.

Salatis stiffened and said, "I'll thank you not to mention that. Today, here in this place, I live for the dark secrets of Shar, divine daughter of Lord Ao." He paused and Insithryllax shrugged. "Captain Olin. . . ."

Olin brought the axe down again, and the man stopped crying all at once. When Olin tried to pull his axe out of the dead man's back, it stuck fast. The black firedrake vomited a black fluid over his axe blade and Salatis had to turn away. He could hear the workman's skin sizzle away, freeing the blade.

"Leave the mess," Salatis said as he stepped past Insithryllax, ignoring the strange man's grim smirk. "When Shar has had her fill of their souls, clean it up, and never come back in here again. Is that clear?"

Olin nodded, wiping the blood and acid from his longaxe onto the headless workman's back.

Insithryllax laughed again, which elicited a sharp look from the black firedrake. But Salatis left the shrine, confident that no more blood would be spilled there, until he ordered it spilled.

32

3 Ches, the Year of the Staff (1366 DR)
THE VILLAGE OF KURRSH

She couldn't see the man with the scar on his face, but he could hear him. It was as if he rode in the cart behind her, whispering in her ear the whole way.

You have no idea what he's using this for, the ghost told her. *You're helping him. Don't help him. What do you think is going to happen?*

Phyrea had no idea what was going to happen, but she didn't care. For the past two days she'd had enough to concern herself just handling the cart. She hadn't spent much time driving carts after all.

"Please," she whispered as she passed the first of the little cluster of waddle and daub buildings that comprised the village of Kurrsh, "just shut up."

She closed her eyes for a bit, letting the horse lead her, as the man with the scar on his face flooded her mind with a raw sense of righteous indignation.

"You're afraid of him," she whispered with a smile, and opened her eyes.

I can't be afraid of anything anymore, the man answered. *But I can see what you cannot see, and hear what you cannot hear. I know that he has no feelings at all—not for you, not for anyone. He cares only about this hole in the ground. He's manipulating you to help him when you know you should be fighting against him. Fight against him, Phyrea. Turn the cart around. Take us back to Berrywilde where we belong—where we all belong.*

Phyrea sighed and brought the cart to a stop. Four children wandered by, looking at her with unashamed curiosity. Her cart was loaded with plain burlap sacks. They couldn't know what the sacks contained, but whatever it was, it wasn't very interesting, so they kept going, speaking to each other in low voices. They smiled, giggled even, as they passed. From the way they walked and spoke, she could tell they were in no hurry, and they were happy.

Don't go in there, the man whispered. *If you go in there, I can't help you.*

"You don't appear to me when I'm with him," she whispered. "Why?"

The ghost didn't answer.

Phyrea climbed down off the cart, tied up the horse, and went into the squat little building. She took a deep breath, savoring the smell of ale and pipeweed. Though it was a warm afternoon for so early in the spring—the sun was shining even—a fire crackled in the hearth. She saw them right away—the place wasn't that big—but she stood just inside the door and watched them for a moment.

They sat at a table in the middle of the room, surrounded by the farmers and simple country folk of Kurrsh, and they blended right in. Even the dwarf didn't seem out of place. And Phyrea, the daughter of a senator, a bitter, resentful, petulant city girl, felt no less at home.

She smiled and walked to their table. The dwarf noticed her first and tapped the other two on their arms. When Devorast saw her, he smiled, and Phyrea's heart melted in her chest. She missed a step, almost stumbled, but slipped onto the chair next to him.

"I was afraid you weren't coming," Hrothgar said.

She nodded, her mouth dry, and looked at Devorast when she said, "I had some trouble with the cart. I felt like a peasant woman."

Devorast smiled again and said, "How did you like it?"

She made a show of sighing, and showed her teeth in a wide grin. "It wasn't so bad."

The third man looked at her in a way Phyrea was accustomed to being looked at by strange men. He tried his best to pretend he wasn't looking at her body, scanning her curves, sizing her up. She could tell his mouth was dry, his breathing just a little shallow, his heart maybe even racing a bit in his chest. She smiled at him, and he looked down at his mug of ale.

"You're the alchemist," she said.

"Surero," the man answered.

"A pleasure."

"And you brought what he needs?" asked the dwarf.

Phyrea nodded and said, "I have fifty fifty-pound sacks. I hope that will be enough."

Devorast and the dwarf looked to Surero, who shrugged and said, "It'll get us started, but there's a lot of earth to be moved. I'll always need more."

"I have to ask," she said. "Why saltpeter? I mean, I thought my father sold it to the army for some reason, and I don't know what else—is it spread on crops to make them grow better ... something like that?"

Surero glanced at Devorast, who shrugged. The young alchemist took his lead from Devorast, as did the dwarf, and as always, Devorast seemed on some fundamental level oblivious to it.

"What is it, anyway?" the dwarf asked.

"Horse manure," Surero explained, "mixed with wood ash and straw and left to compost."

"At Berrywilde, it's kept under a kind of shed, like a lean-to," Phyrea said.

"They water it with ... urine, too, don't they?" Surero asked. He looked embarrassed to say the word "urine" in front of Phyrea, and that made her smile. "It's formed into a powder."

"And that's what I have in the sacks," said Phyrea.

"I mix that with other elements to create a powder that, when touched by fire, explodes," Surero finished, making an expanding gesture with his hands.

"Is it difficult for you to get this for us?" Hrothgar asked her.

Phyrea started to answer, but didn't know what to say. Her father paid no attention to what was a tiny fraction of what was produced at Berrywilde. He wouldn't notice if she took it all. She could order more of the stuff made, even order another shelter built, and he wouldn't know or care. The people still working on the winery would do it if she told them to. She could have men deliver cart after cart of it to Kurrsh at least, where Devorast's men could haul it on to the canal site. It would be the easiest thing, but she would have to spend time at Berrywilde. The ghosts spoke more freely there. Their forms of light were brighter, more substantial there. And in the confines of the country estate, their words made more sense, and were more convincing. She never wanted to go back there again, but she had, for him.

She looked at Devorast, and he tipped his head, waiting for her to say something. She knew she must have looked as though she had something to say.

"So," she said, "aren't one of you big, strong men going to buy me an ale?"

33

21 Tarsakh, the Year of the Staff (1366 DR)
THE CANAL SITE

They had cut down trees, and arranged them over a hole that they'd dug in the ground. One man stood atop the cut trees, pushing and pulling on a long, straight saw. A fine wood powder clouded the air around him and fell into the pit like dirty snow. Svayyah had never seen that man before—he wasn't the man she'd come to find.

She'd cast certain spells on herself in preparation, and had come a long way across open land. The latter was something she didn't like to do, but she did it because of the message he'd sent her. She'd given him the means to contact her, but he'd never used it before. He'd told her that he'd let himself be lured north, and was sure that something was going to happen. She'd found the small copse of trees that they'd been cutting down, and turning into long, rectangular strips of wood using the pit-saw, and she saw three men, including the one on the top of the pit, but none of them were Ivar Devorast. She had the feeling Devorast was down in the pit, since she could see a man's hands rise above the lip of the hole when the saw was pulled up.

She slid out from behind the tree she'd been hiding behind, certain she'd startle the men who didn't know her—one or more of them might even have been the assassins Devorast feared, or at least suspected—but she didn't care. The other two men stood at the edge of the pit, stacking the freshly-cut lumber. Svayyah blinked in the bright daylight, her third and fourth eyelids keeping her eyes just barely damp enough. Bursts of brighter light burned her eyes and made her have to close them entirely. Because of that she couldn't quite see where the missiles had come from. There were two screams—loud and desperate, and both cut off in wet gurgles—and the sounds of three bodies falling to the ground, and the clatter of wood tumbling onto wood.

When she opened her eyes, she saw the men laying around the hole. The one who'd been standing atop the pitsaw rig was on the ground, and he was on fire. The bright light had been spheres of molten rock, burning orange and melting everything they touched—including human skin and bone.

She slithered faster toward the pit, and was still three nagalengths from it, when she saw the thing emerge from a thicker clump of trees. Her kind had always railed against the common mistake of calling the things "nagalike," or even considering them a species of the *naja'ssynsa*. What had killed the men with the conjured lava was no naga, but a banelar. Its spike-lined, heavily scaled body wasn't unlike a naga's. Its rigid purple back shone in the sun, and its yellow-green underbelly glistened with slime. Around its frowning, paper-thin lips writhed a dozen long, stringy tentacles. Two of the tentacles bore gold rings, and it wore a wide ribbon around its neck held closed with a shiny black brooch. Its pale green eyes squinted against the sunshine, and its heavy brows furrowed with a look that promised more violence.

Svayyah whispered a short incantation—a cantrip, really—and followed it with a whispered, "Devorast, if that's you, I'm here. It's a banelar."

The spell carried her voice from her lips to his ear without really crossing the intervening space.

The creature jumped. Svayyah had never heard of a banelar being able to jump that far, and there was something about it that just didn't look right. She'd cast similar spells herself, but couldn't know if it was a spell the thing had cast, or if it was an effect of one of the rings. The creature landed atop the pit-saw rig, sending up a cloud of sawdust. The logs creaked and popped under its weight. It slithered into a more comfortable position and looked down into the hole.

"Devorast," it hissed. "You are Devorast?"

Even before the thing had finished speaking, Svayyah had twisted her tongue through another, slightly more complex casting. She disappeared in mid-slither and instantly popped back into reality, but at the very edge of the hole. Not even bothering to see if it was indeed Devorast in the saw pit, she cast another spell as quickly as she could.

The banelar, startled by her sudden appearance, whirled on her and half-hissed, half-growled, then started muttering an incantation of its own.

Svayyah finished first.

She drew from the Weave a blast of air—like the sudden rapids in a narrow stretch of river—that smashed into the banelar and sent it sprawling off the pit-saw rig. It landed in a tangle with a still-smoldering corpse but was rolled off by the wind before it was burned. Its incantation was ruined by the sudden gust and the bruising impact. It rolled along the ground with an angry hiss.

Svayyah blinked again and she was inside the pit. She found herself in closer proximity to Ivar Devorast than she'd ever been. He was startled to see her appear out of the thin air, but just as quickly relieved. Inspired by the banelar itself, she gasped out a spell before he could speak, and he looked at her with a curious expression. She let her fine dry scales brush up against his hot, sweat-dampened skin, transferring the power of the spell to him.

"Jump," she told him.

He only had to think about it for less than one of his slow heartbeats, then a knowing smile crossed his lips. He bent his knees deep and launched himself into the air. Her spell enhanced the movement and sent him shooting into the blue sky like a bolt from a crossbow. While he was still in the air Svayyah blinked out of the pit and back up to the ground at the edge of the side closer to where the banelar had rolled off.

Something hit her—hard—the moment she materialized. She felt her snake's body come off the ground, and all she could do was tense, try to inhale with the wind knocked out of her worse than she'd ever experienced, and watch the pit pass beneath her. She hit the ground on the other side and as she rolled to an undignified stop among the tree stumps and one of the corpses of the woodsmen, she saw Devorast hit the ground and fare no better than she. Though she had been hit by something she could have sworn was a spectral ram, Devorast had simply failed to properly compensate for his increased ability to jump.

As Svayyah found her breath again and forced herself upright, gasping in huge lungfuls of the dry air, she watched Devorast jump again—and land on his feet. He pulled a woodsman's axe from a tree stump, and jumped again. His jump sufficed as a charge, taking him straight at the banelar.

"Your naga can't save you, human," the banelar shrieked.

Svayyah winced at the words, *"your* naga," and searched her mind for a spell.

Devorast took an aggressive swing with the axe, sending the banelar jumping several paces backward to avoid the axe head. Whatever magic allowed it to jump like that was obviously still in effect.

Svayyah tried to cast another spell, but coughed instead. She panted, but couldn't quite find her regular breathing rhythm.

The banelar had no such difficulties, and rattled off what sounded like a prayer. Devorast drew back his axe. The banelar's incantation came to an end, and so did Devorast's ability to move.

Svayyah spit venom to the hard, unforgiving ground and realized that Devorast was firmly held in place. Svayyah had sacrificed enough for Ivar Devorast and his canal that she simply couldn't watch Devorast fall to the poisoned fangs of a banelar.

"Away with you, *dista'ssara*," Svayyah shouted at the banelar. "This human is mine. You can owe me for the other three."

She cast a spell at the same time that sent bolts of solidified Weave energy hurtling unerringly at the banelar. The thing didn't even look up. The missiles raced through the intervening space, turning a little at the precise moment Svayyah assumed they'd bite into the banelar's greenish underbelly—but veered into the brooch and disappeared into the black design. The banelar stood, brushed itself off, and hissed so loud it started a dull pain throbbing in Svayyah's ears in time with her racing heart.

The banelar, having defeated her missiles without actually having to do anything, leaped at her. The spell effect was still active, and the banelar cartwheeled over first one then a second of the dead bodies. It brushed so close to Devorast that the fine hair right around his forehead rustled in the breeze. Devorast followed the thing's progress with his eyes, but otherwise stood stock still.

Svayyah blinked and disappeared again so that the banelar landed in what would have been the perfect offensive trap. Then she blinked again right away to move herself once more between the pit and the banelar.

The banelar stumbled to a stop, and Svayyah disappeared again—

—only to find that the banelar matched her spell-for-spell. She appeared just a little closer to the banelar. The creature uttered a word Svayyah recognized—Draconic for "horns"—and a ram's head made of blue-white mist charged through the air at her. Ready for it, her spell still active, Svayyah blinked out of its way and appeared a dozen feet off to one side to watch it rush past her, harmless, then disappear into the thin air.

Svayyah glanced at Devorast, who stood frozen in place still, and said to the banelar, "Are we supposed to be impressed with that? Holding that ape? You're out of your depth, banelar. We will not be so easily stymied."

The creature sneered at her and said, "I was paid to kill the monkey, but you I'll take for the meat."

Then it started casting another spell, and so did Svayyah. Though the banelar's spell had no visible effect, the naga conjured a trident shaped from shadowstuff in the air. The spectral weapon danced before her, and she smiled at the look of fear that flashed across the *dista'ssara's* eyes.

She blinked closer to the thing, whirled the trident around her in a full circle, anticipated the banelar's dodge, then stabbed in low and angled upward.

Though it appeared insubstantial the trident was solid enough when it touched the banelar. The creature jerked back and to the right, avoiding two of the three prongs, but the third dug a ragged furrow in its slimy underbelly.

The banelar hissed in pain, but looked at her with strangely renewed confidence, and cursed at her in what sounded like Orcish. Svayyah ignored the insult and blinked away before it had a chance to bite at her.

Svayyah materialized at the edge of the hole, her snake's body folding over the stack of lumber. She whipped the spectral trident around herself again and didn't hear the banelar speak the command word for its ring.

"How many cuts will it—" she started, then the breath was once more driven from her lungs by the ghost of a ram.

The force of the blow sent her sprawling like a limp, fallen vine, into the pit. She scraped against the dull edge of the saw blade that still hung from the rig. If she'd hit it at a slightly different angle the fall might have cut her—even killed her.

Svayyah wondered at the banelar's freshly attuned senses. She knew of any number of spells that might have helped, and knew it must have cast one. It was beginning to anticipate her blinks. It had sent the ram at her even before she'd appeared at the pit's edge.

And it can still jump, she thought.

She rattled off the words to a spell as fast as she could

and still be sure it would work, then blinked away before she had a chance to see its effect. But just the thousandth of a heartbeat before she altered her location she saw the banelar arc through the air, coming right down at her into the pit.

She was well away when the long steel saw blade shattered into thousands of twisted, razor-sharp shards.

Svayyah barked out a laugh and twisted her spectral trident in the air in front of her. As she expected, the banelar leaped from the pit. It was alive, but bleeding from dozens of cuts.

"That will cost you," it threatened.

"We have spent all we wish to already," Svayyah sneered. "Your miserable existence ends."

While she spoke the banelar stuttered out a ragged-edged incantation, swaying in time with it. Svayyah gathered the defenses she'd cast on herself close to her. She closed her eyes and slithered backward. The spell hit her in the eyes, making them water. Her vision blurred. She struggled to keep them open, battled to resist the magic that sought to blind her.

Not concentrating on any particular destination, she blinked away. She arrived somewhere nearby, but was momentarily disoriented. She saw a moving shape, blurred and indistinct, but knew it was the banelar.

"*Someone's* miserable existence ends now," the banelar hissed. "Of that I can assure you."

Devorast, she thought. It's going after Devorast.

She heard the banelar's voice chanting in Draconic. Svayyah recognized the words, even the cadence, and gasped. She blinked the last of the fog from her eyes and disappeared—once again knowing precisely where she'd end up.

The thing lunged at Devorast, whose eyes widened. He was helpless, and Svayyah could see from what parts of his face he could move that he didn't like it any more than she would have.

The naga appeared directly behind the banelar, her weapon made of shadowstuff held firm in the air above her head. She stabbed down hard, pushing the trident with the strength of her mind. It sank deep into the serpent creature's purple carapace, but she wasn't fast enough.

Devorast opened his mouth, but couldn't scream. The banelar bit into his shoulder so hard Svayyah heard its fangs scrape bone. The sizzling noise that accompanied that sound confirmed Svayyah's fears.

Svayyah twisted the spectral trident and pulled back with it, letting it slip past her body to drag the banelar off of Devorast. The banelar had a grip on Devorast's shoulder for the heartbeat or so it took to die, and the spell that held him rigid disappeared all at once. When the banelar's fangs came out, Devorast fell to his knees. With joints stiff and creaking, he put a palm to the wound, but hissed and pulled his hand away—burned by the already potent venom, made caustic by the banelar's spell.

The vile creature slumped to the ground, still and lifeless, so Svayyah let the spectral trident disappear.

She looked down at Devorast, who lay on the ground, writhing in agony, his jaw stiff and his eyes closed. Bright red fluid bubbled up through the punctures made by the banelar's fangs, as though his blood boiled.

Svayyah spoke the words of a spell and turned her head north, in the direction of the humans' keep on the banks of the Nagaflow. Not identifying herself, but being sure to mention Devorast by name, she whispered on the winds a message that would carry the half a dozen miles to the nearest human ear. She told them that Devorast was going to die, and die soon, and that he needed their help.

"We will stay with you until your people arrive," the naga told him, though she wasn't sure he could understand her.

Devorast was breathing—panting even—so he was still alive, but he'd lost consciousness.

Fortunate, Svayyah thought.

Knowing it would take time for the humans to cross the half a dozen miles from the keep—hopefully with one of their priests—and able only to hope that Devorast would still be alive when they got there, Svayyah turned her attention to the banelar. She used a spell to slip the rings off its still, limp tentacles, then stared at the brooch. It was a black triangle, its top rounded, the point on the bottom. In the center was a gold disk overlapped with an ebony symbol—the letter Z from the human alphabet—emblazoned above it. She didn't recognize the mark, didn't think it was the symbol of any god, but knew it had to have some significance. Banelars rarely if ever acted on their own. They were servant creatures. The brooch was a protective device, one that ate her magic missiles, but it was a sort of badge, too, that claimed the banelar in the name of—who? What?

Svayyah turned to the fitfully-sleeping Devorast and said, "I hope you live long enough to find out who sent this wretch, and exact your revenge." She sighed and studied the dying man. The muscles under his smooth skin quivered with strange tremors. "And now perhaps you will start to carry weapons—or at least a thrice-bedamned healing potion or two."

34

22 Tarsakh, the Year of the Staff (1366 DR)
SECOND QUARTER, INNARLITH

Anyone who understood the difference between beautiful and pretty could see that the girl was the latter. Her round face and big brown eyes were pleasing to the eye, but lacked definition. Her black hair was clean and combed, but she didn't bother doing too much more with it. Her simple white silk shift revealed enough of her body that customers knew what they were getting; not enough to appear crass.

"If there is anything I can get you while you—" she said.

"Nothing, thank you, girl," Marek interrupted, waving her away. "We aren't customers. We've come to see the lady of the house."

He could see the girl thinking, considering her response, sizing him up. She glanced at Salatis, and Marek could tell she recognized him. When her eyes passed Insithryllax and settled back on Marek, the Red Wizard could tell she'd never seen either of them before, and that concerned her.

"You can go, Cassiya," Nyla said. The girl couldn't help herself, she sighed in relief and scurried out. "I know she's not your type, Master Rymüt."

"She may be mine," Salatis cut in with a cheerful leer.

An annoyed grimace passed quickly across Nyla's face, then she smiled and turned to Salatis and said, "I can do better than that for the ransar."

Salatis dipped in a shallow bow and was about to speak when Marek said, "The ransar told me you had something to say to me?"

Nyla sighed and sat in one of the deep-cushioned easy chairs scattered around the tastefully-decorated parlor. A fire roared in a fireplace big enough to stand in, and the air smelled of wood smoke and rose oil. The woman put a hand to her forehead and traced around the edge of her eyepatch with the tip of a finger.

Marek gestured to Salatis to sit, and wondered briefly if the man would ever be used to his position enough to be offended when others sat while he stood.

When they had settled in Marek asked Nyla, "What can we do for you?"

"You know my business," she said, glancing between Marek and Salatis.

The ransar avoided her gaze, but Marek said, "It's an old profession."

Nyla might have wanted to laugh, but didn't. She said, "I have a hand in other things, and I have friends within the city and without."

"Do you require our assistance, Senator?" Salatis asked.

"No," she said, and Marek didn't believe her. "But it's occurred to me that I can help you."

"I'm all ears," Salatis replied with that same leer.

"This canal," she said.

The three men waited for her to go on, but instead she fingered her missing eye and appeared deep in thought.

"Go on, please," Marek prompted. He brought a spell to mind and cast it with a tap of his toes and a gesture he passed off as scratching an itch. It wasn't the best way, or the easiest way, to cast the spell, but it was worth it not to reveal himself. "Tell us what's on your mind. You're among friends."

Even before she spoke, Marek heard her voice in his head. She thought and spoke at the same time, his spell revealing her hidden intentions. Marek listened to both with great interest.

Tell them only what they need to know, she told herself.

"I understand you have reasons for not wanting Devorast to finish the canal," she said.

When Marek nodded, she thought, *The Black Network is angry enough with me. Keep it close.*

"And you have to be wondering why I would care when I've made my fortune in flesh, and that won't change— canal or no canal," she said.

"But you have friends," Salatis said, "and would like to keep them."

She glanced at the ransar, nodded, and thought, *You're not the friend I had in mind, fool.*

"I can help you," she said to Marek.

"What have you done?" he asked, staring deep into her eyes.

What does he know? she thought. Marek could feel the panic rising in her. *Does he know about the banelar?*

"I don't know what you mean," she said.

"Have you tried to help us already?" Marek asked. "You

haven't ... paid a visit to the Cormyrean, have you?"

He knows, she thought. *By the Dark One's divine corpse, he knows everything.*

"I want to help," she said, looking Marek in the eye.

"Well," the ransar broke in, "I'm sure your services will be of value to the city-state. But I haven't quite made up my mind in regards to the canal yet. There are arguments to be made both for and against."

Marek fought down the impulse to have Insithryllax melt Salatis in his seat. Instead, he concentrated on Nyla's thoughts.

I couldn't kill him, she told herself, *but the Thayan could.*

"I think we all want the same things," the Red Wizard said. "And I'm sure that all those we answer to ... within the city"—he glanced at Salatis—"and without ... will be happy as long as the result is a positive one."

Thank the Black Hand's memory, Nyla thought.

She smiled and said, "I just wanted you to know that I am your friend."

Marek returned her smile.

35

2 Mirtul, the Year of the Staff (1366 DR)
THE NAGAFLOW KEEP

Will he wake soon?" Hrothgar asked.

Surero shrugged in response, and the dwarf fought down the urge to punch the alchemist in the face. Instead, he sighed and looked down at Devorast. He lay in a narrow soldier's bed in a room near the very top of the imposing fortress. The room was cool, the spring air coming through the pair of arrow loops was fresh, and the sickroom stench that he'd been hit with when he'd first rushed to Devorast's bedside was gone.

"Or am I just used to it?" he muttered to himself.

"Pardon?" Surero asked, and Hrothgar shrugged him off.

The alchemist sat at a desk cluttered with glassware and iron pots. A little oil lamp burned under a glass bowl in which a strange yellow liquid boiled, sending orange steam into the air that smelled of deep earth—a welcoming sensation for the dwarf.

"Will he live?" Hrothgar asked.

"A tenday will tell," Surero answered, and Hrothgar could tell he was no more satisfied with that answer than the dwarf was.

"But it's been longer than that already."

"Twelve days since the naga brought him here," Surero replied. "And he's still alive, which is fortunate for him. This thing that bit him—the naga called it a banelar—did more than just poison him. Its venom had an acidic quality to it that burned him, and burned him badly—deep inside his blood vessels. It introduced a foul humor to his essential fluids."

"Everybody wants the son of a cow dead," Hrothgar said. "And all he wants is to dig a hole."

"Dig a hole and fill it with water," Surero replied. "And change the way trade moves across the Realms for centuries to come. A lot of people have killed a lot of other people for a lot less."

The dwarf could only stand there, looking at his friend who appeared already more dead than alive, and shake his head. Of course, Surero was right. The alchemist had also kept Devorast alive, his potions and ointments attacked the venom, neutralized the acid, and slowly started putting the man back together again from the inside out.

The door opened without a sound—Devorast had designed the hinges himself, years before—and Hrothgar turned to see Phyrea step into the room. She was pale. She didn't look well. When she saw Devorast laying on his back, the bedclothes pulled up to his chin, and the sickly bluish cast to his skin, a tear rolled from her eye, and she took a deep breath.

"There has been no change," Surero told her.

She nodded in response and moved to stand next to Hrothgar. The dwarf looked up at her, and she met his gaze and nodded, forcing a smile that Hrothgar was reluctant to return. Surero stood and joined them. For the longest time the three of them stood there, staring at their friend.

"I wasn't able . . ." Phyrea said at last. She shook her head, unable to finish.

"It's all right," Surero said. "I know someone in Saelmur."

Phyrea untied a small leather pouch from her belt and handed it to Surero. Hrothgar watched as the alchemist opened it, pulled out a silk handkerchief, and unfolded it to reveal two shining gold rings and a brooch of ebony and gold. One ring had a blue gemstone expertly cut in the shape of a ram's head. Hrothgar had marveled at the workmanship the first time he'd seen it. It was masterful, even for the finest dwarf gemcutters. The brooch bore the mark of the Zhentarim, and the mere thought of it made the dwarf grimace, though he wasn't surprised that they'd made that particular enemy.

The naga had left the items, saying they belonged to Devorast, though Hrothgar had never seen him wear any sort of jewelry. They all assumed they were worn by the would-be assassin. That they were imbued with magic was no question, but Surero had asked Phyrea to take them back to Innarlith to find out what, if anything, they could do, and how they were used. Also as they'd expected, her efforts had been hindered by not wanting to bring them to the attention of Marek Rymüt.

"He'll never wear them anyway," Hrothgar said.

"No, he won't, will he?" Phyrea replied. "He won't defend himself. He won't arm himself. He won't even recognize that there are people who want him dead. He does—"

She stopped herself, and Hrothgar was relieved. He didn't feel up to slapping her face.

"He fights when he has to," the dwarf said. "The rest of the time, he works."

36

8 Marpenoth, the Year of the Staff (1366 DR)
THE CANAL SITE

Even during the tendays that Devorast lay writhing in quiet agony, then slowly recovered, construction continued. At first many of the Innarlan diggers, woodcutters, and stonemasons had wandered back and forth from Innarlith, but work had become increasingly difficult to find in the city, so most eventually took up residence at the site. Word spread to neighboring cities, and men came from as far as Arrabar for the ransar's gold. When those coins diminished over time, increasingly replaced by excuses, Arrabar started to pay the Arrabarrans, Saelmur and Nimpeth supported their own people, and King Azoun sent gold by the trade bar.

They had dug for miles, a trench forty feet deep and three hundred feet wide. Parts of it had already been paved on the bottom and sides with stone blocks. All along the mile after mile the site stretched were scaffolds and rigs of all description—structures Phyrea had never seen before. Many of them *no one* had ever seen before, all of them drawn from the mind of one man.

When she compared in her mind the parts of the canal that she'd seen near completion and the drawings in the stacks and stacks of parchment in Devorast's little cabin, they were not merely similar, but perfectly identical.

It would be the greatest monument to one man Faerûn had ever known.

Phyrea stumbled on a loose rock, and Devorast took her hand to steady her. His fingers were rough and warm, his grip strong and reassuring. She shuddered at the feeling of his hand in hers, especially when he didn't let go. She could feel him smiling at her, but she didn't look at him.

"I can't come back here anymore," she said.

"Why not?" he asked, too quick for him.

She wriggled her hand free from his and felt the cold metal of a ring on his finger.

"What is that?" she asked him, then took his hand to examine the ring: a thin gold band traced with a line of engraved runes. "When did you start wearing this?"

Devorast shrugged, and pulled his hand away.

"It's been almost six months," she said. "Why would you start to wear that now? If it was anyone but you, I'd think you were wearing it for me."

He looked at her without speaking, but she knew what he was thinking. He wasn't wearing it for her.

"Curious?" she asked him. "Is that it?"

He smiled and started walking again. She didn't follow him.

"If you had died," she told his back, "I might have killed myself."

He stopped and turned, the cool autumn breeze pulling his long red hair away from his stern face. "That would have been stupid."

She shook her head, and tried not to start crying.

"I lived," he said, and turned around again but didn't walk away.

"Yes, you did," Phyrea replied. "You lived, and you went right back to work. And how many times since the spring have they tried to kill you?"

"If they truly wanted me dead," Devorast said, "they'd have killed me."

"That doesn't make sense."

"I think they have something else in mind for me," said Devorast. "They think they can frighten me, intimidate me."

"And when they finally realize they can't, if they haven't already, they will kill you," she said. "And when they do, I won't kill myself. I can't kill myself for you."

"Phyrea, I never asked you to—"

"I know," she cut in. "Of course you never asked that of me. You never asked anything of me. I got you saltpeter from my father's farm, but you paid me for it. You love me with your body but not with your heart—if you even have a heart. You live for this hole in the ground, even if it makes enemies of the whole of Toril, and you don't even bother fighting them."

"I fight—"

"For your life," she shouted. "When they attack you, you defend yourself. I know that. But you don't fight them, really. You know who it is. You know who's behind all of it, but will you go back to the city and find him? Will you confront him? Will you have it out—be done with it once and for all? No, you won't."

"I have no interest in—"

"Damn it, Ivar," she screamed at him, "they have an interest in *you!*"

He looked at her and shrugged. The gesture almost made Phyrea drop to her knees and tear her hair out in frustration. Her eyes blurred with tears.

"I know it's not cowardice," she told him, getting control of her voice. "But then what is it? I know how beneath you they are, but—"

She took a deep breath. She'd said it all before, been trapped by him too many times already. She'd given herself to him, and when she was with him, the ghosts that haunted her fell silent. But then days would pass—tendays, months—and she would realize once again that he gave her his body, but too little else—far, far too little of himself.

"Ivar, I can't—"

There was a flash of light, bright even in the midafternoon sun, and he rushed at her with his arms outstretched. He meant to embrace her, and Phyrea, startled, stepped back. His face was a stone mask—utterly unreadable. Her instincts told her to defend herself, but her reflexes failed her. He wrapped his arms around her and squeezed. She gasped when they left the ground.

The sound that followed close after the flash of light was a dull but deafening thud that stung her ears. She couldn't tell for sure but it seemed as though they hurtled through the air—easily a dozen feet off the ground—because Devorast had jumped, but how could that be? It must have been the explosion that launched them into the sky, but—

The ring, she thought.

As they rotated in the air she saw a massive orange and yellow fireball still expanding, showering the place where they'd been standing only half a heartbeat before with chunks of smoking rock as big around as her head. Men screamed, and the air hummed from the sound of the big rocks hitting the ground.

They landed hard enough to make her grunt, but Devorast landed on his feet and came to a stop with his body between Phyrea and the explosion. She pushed away from him and sprawled onto the ground on her back.

He didn't even spare you a glance, the voice of the sad woman whined in her head.

Phyrea closed her eyes.

I don't blame you, the old woman said—and Phyrea could see her burn-scarred face in her mind's eye. *I wouldn't want to see him running away from me again, either, if I were you.*

Forget him, the man with the scar on his face said.

Phyrea opened her eyes and looked over her shoulder. The man stood among the falling pebbles that rained down on her like warm, dry hail. The stones passed right through him.

"This is the last time," she promised the ghost.

The man shook his head, but Phyrea turned away from him, stood, and followed Devorast. She ran through a continuing rain of pebbles and specks of wood, and vegetation that the fireball had thrown into the air. By the time she reached the edge of the crater and stopped at Devorast's side, the rain of stones had stopped. Dust and smoke made her cough and stung her eyes.

"Who is she?" a workman asked.

She saw Devorast shake his head. On the ground at his feet was the mangled body of a girl. Devorast kneeled and turned her over. Her head rolled on a broken neck, and her dead eyes stared up at the sky.

"I know her," Phyrea said, then coughed again.

Devorast turned, surprised to find her right behind him.

"I went to finishing school with her," she explained. "Her father lost his seat on the senate and killed himself when the debts were called in. I lost track of her when she and her mother and sisters moved out of the Second Quarter."

"She ignited Surero's smokepowder casks," Devorast said. "Why?"

Phyrea rubbed the grit from her eyes with the back of her hand. "Why does anyone want to kill you?"

"What's her name?" the workman asked.

"Cassiya," Phyrea answered. "I think her name was Cassiya."

37

30 Marpenoth, the Year of the Staff (1366 DR)
THE THAYAN ENCLAVE, INNARLITH

Ransar," Marek Rymüt said with a flourish, "welcome to Thayan soil."

Salatis's eyes narrowed at that, though he'd agreed to it already. He stepped in and pasted a smile on his face. As he looked around at the glass cases filled with artifacts and unusual curios of the most exotic sort, he clasped a hand around a pendant that hung from a heavy gold chain around his neck.

"Azuth ..." Marek commented with a lift of one eyebrow. "Really?"

Salatis cleared his throat, took his hand away from the holy symbol, and said, "The High One's wisdom has entered my life of late, yes."

Marek smiled and stepped deeper into the showroom, making way for the ransar. Salatis followed, his expression alternating between fear, confusion, and longing as he went from case to case. He stopped at one, the echo of his footsteps pinging from the marble floor to the pounded lead ceiling.

"This . . ." Salatis said, looking down at a glass case that contained an ornately-crafted brass horn. "What is this?"

"Ah," Marek replied. "You have a good eye, Ransar. That is a horn of blasting."

"A horn of . . . ?"

"It's a wonderfully crafted piece, isn't it?" Marek said, stepping behind the ransar and laying a gentle hand on his shoulder. "Heavy, I suppose. Not . . . subtle . . . but beautiful in its own way."

"What does it do?"

Marek laughed, took his hand away from Salatis's shoulder, and set it on the glass. "There's someone I know of that would very much like to have this, I'm sure."

Salatis shook his head.

Marek sighed and continued, "People who hear its voice are laid low—not killed, mind you, but they don't like it too much. It has a tendency to loosen soil, as well, and even . . . dig holes."

Salatis nodded and let a grin spread across his face.

"But he'll never have it, will he?" Marek said.

"He's getting gold from the king of Cormyr, of all people," Salatis replied. "If indeed you mean to offer these things for sale, what's to stop him from buying it?"

"Me," said Marek.

"Well . . ." the ransar started, then finally figured out that Marek would decide who bought what, when, and for what reason. "And your superiors in Thay are comfortable with that? I mean, what if he came here with . . . five thousand gold pieces?"

"Well, first off," Marek replied, "he'd be seven thousand short." He gave the ransar a look that he hoped would tell him the rest, and by Salatis's response, it was enough. "I wonder to what extent King Azoun believes he can meddle in the affairs of an independent city-state."

The ransar's lips tightened, and his face paled. "He vexes me."

"He wants that canal built," the Red Wizard said as he crossed to another case. He looked down at the Wand of the Ten Mages—a one-of-a-kind piece there more for display than anything. Only one of the ten mages who'd collaborated in its creation could wield it, and they had all been dead for six centuries. "He wants his merchants to trade directly with Waterdeep, Baldur's Gate, and so on, without their caravans being picked apart by Zhents and orcs."

"He'll pay a hefty toll too," the ransar said trying to make himself believe it.

"Will he?" Marek asked. "For the use of a canal he paid to build? And will he pay you, or will he pay the nagas?"

Salatis frowned and said, "It's gotten out of control, hasn't it?"

"My dear, dear Ransar," said Marek as he moved to yet another case. He looked down at the weapon inside—a ghost touch halfspear that made him think of Phyrea. "This is your city now, and nothing to do with it is outside your control. At worst, all you have to do is rely on your friends, and you do have friends. The realms of the Old Empires, Tethyr, the Zhentarim, even the Emerald Enclave and my own homeland have made their opinions known. Cormyr and Arrabar, and even petty city-states like Raven's Bluff, are not to be taken lightly, to be sure, but neither are those aligned against it."

Salatis took a deep breath and said, "You know that I know that I owe my ascendancy to you, Master Rymüt. You know that I have agreed to this enclave of yours, agreed to your three laws, agreed to ... other things. But the canal will be good for Innarlith. It can be, anyway, and by all accounts he'll be able to do it. You've tried to kill him, so has Nyla, and others I don't even know of. I've sent black firedrakes against him myself, but nothing. If you tell me I must stop the canal from being built I will do my best to do that, but you should be warned that my best may not be entirely up to the task. There are other Realms involved now, all more powerful than our humble city-state. I could lose more than just the canal, but the city itself, should I push too hard in the wrong places."

It was Marek's turn to take a deep breath. Salatis could barely look at him.

"Well, then," said Marek, "let's put it out there then, shall we?"

"Please do."

"It would benefit me to sell the means to travel from here to the Sea of Fallen Stars through the use of magic, but it could also benefit me to finish the canal, also through magical means. The only reason the canal is still being dug is that Devorast refuses to be killed. But you ... all along you've had the power to stop it without killing him, or finish it without keeping him. Send the foreign workers away. Despite your fears, even Azoun won't march to war over this hole in the ground, especially if he's reassured that it will still be built. He can keep the trade bars flowing, for all that, but to me—with a generous return to my esteemed patron, of course"—and he winked at the ransar—"and not that arrogant bastard. Give it up, Salatis, or give it to me."

Salatis must have realized that his mouth had been hanging open in a most unflattering way, and he clacked his lips together.

38

Willem Korvan stared down at a blank sheet of parchment.

"Be seated, honored colleagues," Salatis said from the podium.

Willem sat with the rest of the senators, keeping his eyes on the blank page.

"I thank you all for allowing me to humble myself before you," the ransar went on, the greeting the same every time.

With a shaking hand Willem took the quill from its stand and dipped it into his ink well. He could tell from both the sound and the feel of it that the ink was dry.

"I will not take up too much of your precious time this evening," said Salatis, his voice echoing through the chamber. "Before I begin, I offer a prayer to Mask, the Lord of Shadows."

While the senate chamber echoed with the murmurs of the outraged or surprised members, Willem lifted the dry quill out and dragged it across the parchment anyway. Only the faintest smudge of gray-black marred the smooth surface.

"It is you, Lord of Shadows, that tells us the truth of what is most real: that which we can hold in our hands, lock in our coffers, or rule with the strength of our hands and hearts. We expect nothing from you, Honored Lord, but the truth of your words of warning. You have given us all you should and all you ever will, and for that we thank you."

The senators grumbled in response. Willem pressed harder and tore a small hole in the parchment sheet.

"The city-state of Innarlith is in possession ... no, I

apologize ... I should say that the city-state of Innarlith *was* in possession of a canal that will revolutionize trade in all Faerûn. Promises were made by my predecessor and his agent, but were those promises kept?"

Then Willem pressed harder still and scratched the surface of his desktop.

"This once promising endeavor became a drain on our precious but limited resources, but still we believed. Still we sent our gold and our workers out to the monster-haunted frontier and all of our gold and some of our workers didn't come back."

Hand still shaking—maybe shaking even worse—Willem replaced the quill and laid a hand flat on the sheet of parchment. Even there it trembled.

"But at least it was ours. At least it belonged to the city-state of Innarlith. But in the past months, even that has changed. But has it only been over the past few months? Or was it the intention all along, of the late Ransar Osorkon, to sell this city piece by piece to our neighbors? When we were told that others would share in our fortunes, that was fine. We hold the canal, but not the Vilhon Reach, not the Sword Coast—*but we hold the canal!*"

Willem tried to take a deep breath, but hiccupped instead.

"And now," Salatis went on, "here we are, months on, and not only our gold is being used to dig this hole, but Arrabarran gold, gold from Cormyr, gold from Aglarond, from Sembia even, and points all up and down the Sword Coast from Athkatla north to faraway Luskan. An army of men dig and saw and toil, and how many of them are Innarlan? How many are Cormyrean? How many Arrabarran? And if Mask's wisdom has taught us any-thing, it's that all you are is what you hold in your hand, and when Arrabarran hands hold our soil, our soil becomes Arrabarran soil."

Willem's vision blurred a little, and he started to blink so that the scene in front of him flickered—but what was it he was looking at? The new ransar babbling about something.

"But then what can we expect from this man, this foreign man, Ivar Devorast?"

That's right, Salatis was babbling about Ivar Devorast.

"He comes from Cormyr with his strange accent and high-handed manners. As arrogant as his king, he spits in the face of every member of this esteemed body, and every man, woman, and child who calls Innarlith home."

No matter where Willem went, how high he rose, or how many concessions he made to his patrons in the senate, the conversation always went to Devorast.

"This Ivar Devorast builds nothing for the city-state of Innarlith. So who does he build for? Azoun? The Simbul? Not me. Has he even come here? Has he even passed through our gates in months? He hides in my keep on the Nagaflow when his enemies strike at him—and he has attracted enemies, take my word for that—and he spends the lives of my soldiers to keep himself safe, but has he even once come before this body? We all know that he has not. Has he even once come to the Palace of Many Spires or the Chamber of Law and Civilityh, even just to report to his patrons on his progress? I can assure you, he has not."

Everyone always wanted to talk about Ivar godsbed-amned Devorast.

"So, who does Ivar Devorast work for?"

"Himself," Willem whispered, so softly even he could barely hear it.

"Does he work for King Azoun? I know I don't. And I know you don't."

Willem sighed and hiccupped again. He needed a drink.

"Senators," Salatis pronounced, his voice heavy with false drama, "I have come to you tonight to inform you that I have decided to call an immediate halt to all work on the canal. I have ordered the forces of the city-state, led by my own black firedrakes, to peacefully repatriate all foreign workers, and to seize all outstanding foreign gold, and I have ordered them to do this immediately."

Willem shook his head and almost laughed at that.

"When I am certain that things are well in hand—well in *Innarlan* hands—I will allow work to recommence. Until that time, the Cormyrean Ivar Devorast will no longer be welcome here."

Willem cringed. He closed his eyes and quivered as his face pinched up and his fingers curled into fists.

"Senators, I thank you for your time. Good night, and may the Lord of Shadows bless this body and the people of the great city-state of Innarlith. Praise be to Mask."

A deafening round of applause made Willem cover his ears with his hands, until he realized that Meykhati was clapping, so he clapped too. And he continued to clap as Salatis made his way slowly from the podium, clasping hands with a select group of senators—including Meykhati and Nyla—along the way.

Fools, he thought. He's not just going to go away.

Willem could never be that lucky.

39

4 Uktar, the Year of the Staff (1366 DR)
THE CANAL SITE

Tell him who you are, the old man demanded.

Anger flared through her, and through clenched teeth she said, "I am the daughter of Senator Inthelph, the Master Builder of Innarlith, and if you don't take two steps back from me this instant, there will be consequences."

Nicely done, girl, the old man murmured. *Well said.*

The man who stood before her with the wicked longaxe held in front of his chest seemed to stare right through her with his too-black eyes, but he did step back. With her best world-weary sigh, she stepped around him to the door of Devorast's little cabin. Before she could reach for the handle the door opened, and Surero stepped out. He looked surprised to see her, but smiled anyway.

"Is he here?" she asked.

Surero nodded and glanced back into the dim interior. Devorast appeared in the doorway and nodded in greeting.

Phyrea had expected him to be angry, or at least annoyed, and certainly offended that the ransar—one of the least visionary men she'd ever met—had shut him down entirely with a single proclamation.

Tell him, said the little boy. Phyrea could see him, one arm ending in a handless stump, at the edge of her vision. *Tell him you're happy it's over and that he's being sent away. Call him a bad name and tell him to go to a bad place.*

She shook her head and said, "It's wrong what's happening."

No, said the ghost of the burned old woman, *it's about time.*

"We knew it would happen eventually, though, didn't we?" Surero asked. His eyes darted from one to the other of the three black-haired guards with their longaxes and blank, emotionless expressions. "Maybe not like this, though."

"Have they hurt anyone?" Phyrea asked.

They should, said the man with the scar on his face. She could see him standing inside the cabin, next to Devorast.

Surero shook his head and stepped out of the doorway. "We should speak inside."

Phyrea stepped in, nodding, her eyes glued to the shimmering violet form of the man and the z-shaped scar that marred his otherwise handsome face. She felt her breathing grow faster and more shallow and did her best to control it. Her palms went slick with sweat. She'd never seen the ghosts and Devorast in the same place, had she? He used to—she thought—drive them away.

"Damn it all to the bottomless Abyss, Ivar," she said, a keen edge of near-panic in her voice. "I told you this would happen. I knew this would happen. I dreaded this day so much I did my best to make it happen sooner just to be through with it once and for all, but now that it's—"

The look on Surero's face made her stop. She couldn't look at the alchemist. Instead her eyes settled on the spirit-form of the man with the scar on his face.

It's over for him now, the ghost said without moving his lips. *Leave him behind you. He was destroying you anyway. He never loved you. Go back to Berrywilde.*

You belong with us, back at Berrywilde, the little girl whined. *She stood, an inch off the wood floor, in the corner next to Devorast's little cot.*

When she realized that Surero was trying to figure out what she was looking at, she closed her eyes and shook her head.

"Oh, gods of the Outer Planes, it is over," she said, and pressed her hands to her face.

"It looks that way," said the alchemist, "for now."

Devorast said nothing. Instead, he slid big sheets of parchment into a leather portfolio with his usual calm, slow demeanor.

Take us home, the little girl begged.

The door opened, and Phyrea jumped, startled by the noise and the light.

By the sound of his boots on the wood floor Phyrea would have guessed a stone giant had stepped in, but she knew before turning around that it was just Hrothgar.

"Say the word, Ivar," the dwarf grumbled, "and we'll fight 'em."

"Hrothgar—" Phyrea started.

"No," Devorast said.

The three of them waited for him to say more but he didn't.

"This is why ..." Phyrea said.

She held her breath, trying to think. She felt as though her brain was sunk in heavy, clinging mud.

Don't bother, the old woman, who she couldn't see, told her. *Just go, child.*

"This is why I've said the things I've said about you," she

said. Hrothgar stepped closer to her, but she kept her back to him and her eyes on Devorast. "This is what I've been telling you all this time would happen. I told you they would try to kill you, and if they couldn't kill you that they'd find some way, some excuse to take this away from you."

"Wait a moment, there," Surero said.

"They can chase us off today, girl," said the dwarf, "but not forever."

"Hrothgar's right," the alchemist concurred. "There's enough support in—"

"Oh, shut up, Surero," Phyrea snapped. "There's enough support to send gold, men, and goodwill, but not enough to go to war over. Who's going to send footmen here to fight the ransar for a strip of land that is Innarlith's whether you like it or not? Azoun? Will he go to war for your canal, Ivar?"

Devorast didn't look at her. He went about his packing.

"I told you they'd take it away and they have," Phyrea said. "But I hope you don't think the worst is over."

"That's about enough, girl," said the dwarf.

No, the man made of light said, *get it off your chest, then take us all back to Berrywilde with you.*

"No," Phyrea went on, "the worst is when they send someone here to finish it for you. And it'll be either my father or Willem Korvan, or both, and what will become of all this then? What mess will they make of it in the name of their two-copper ransar?"

Devorast looked at her, and the look on her face made gooseflesh ripple across the undersides of her arms.

He hates you now, the little girl said.

Yeah, said the little boy, *and that means it's all right to hate him back.*

He's almost destroyed you, the old woman said. Phyrea could see her sitting on Devorast's cot. *You're getting away just in time. He's wanted to destroy you all along—and not kill you, but destroy you—and there's a difference, believe me.*

Phyrea shook her head, turned, brushed past the dwarf who stared daggers at her, and burst out the door into sunlight that made her eyes close all on their own. She had to squint and stumble her way back to her horse.

Berrywilde, the old woman whispered in her ear.

She shook her head and whispered back, "No, I want to go back to Innarlith first."

40

5 Uktar, the Year of the Staff (1366 DR)
THIRD QUARTER, INNARLITH

Phyrea had no idea what made her stop, but was sure that if she hadn't, she'd have been killed.

She had no ability to cast spells, had never been trained in the Art, and had no ring or wand to help her see magical auras, emanations, or dweomers. All she had was instinct, or luck, or whatever it was that told her to stop. She took a deep breath and held it as she drew so close to the door her nose almost touched the lacquered wood. The keyhole was big—as big as the first two knuckles of her little finger—and set into a polished brass plate above the handle. She tried to look through the keyhole but saw only black. Either it didn't go all the way through the door, or the room beyond was unlit.

She unfolded her kit—a soft leather folio in which were arrayed a series of picks and other fine implements—but wasn't sure if she should even bother. Picking the lock would surely set off whatever trap it was she'd sensed on the door.

Why don't you just knock? the voice of the little girl echoed in her head.

Phyrea closed her eyes and slowly exhaled.

What is it? asked the sad woman, her thin voice on the edge of panic. *What's wrong?*

Phyrea let her exhale become a reedy hiss. Though she knew no one could hear the voices but her, she wanted them to be quiet anyway—she wanted them to let her think.

Is fire going to shoot out? asked the little girl. *If fire shoots out it will burn your face, and you won't be pretty anymore.*

Phyrea turned her head and saw the little girl standing behind her. At first it appeared as though she leaned against a wall, but in fact she stood so close to the wall that her right arm had disappeared into the wood paneling. Phyrea could see the outline of the shop's assortment of curios and decorative pottery through the wispy violet form of the spectral child.

The little girl who could walk through walls.

"Would you help me?" Phyrea asked, pitching her whispered words so low they barely registered in her own ears.

The little girl looked her in the eyes, and Phyrea's blood ran cold. Something about the way the girl looked at her made her want to scream.

You don't talk to us enough, the child whispered back, though her lips only moved once, parting just the slightest bit. *You should talk to us more. All we ever wanted was to be your friend, and for you to stay with us.*

Phyrea had to force herself to whisper, "Help me."

The little girl reached out to touch Phyrea's face— but she had been several steps away. The little girl had moved closer all at once, never stepping, not actually moving across the intervening space. Phyrea recoiled, lurching back away from those translucent fingertips, and bounced her head off the door. Squatting, she slid onto her backside.

The little girl looked hurt, offended, then she faded away.

Phyrea's head hurt, but worse, the blow had made a sound. She stiffened, spun, and rose to her feet in one motion, and brought her hand to the hilt of the short sword in its scabbard at her belt.

"Who's there?" asked a muffled voice from the other side of the heavy door.

Damn it all to the Nine bleeding Hells, Phyrea thought.

She'd wanted to sneak in. She'd planned on waking Wenefir from a deep sleep, unsettling him, starting off with him unbalanced so that she would have the upper hand. That was over.

"It's me," she said, her voice low but loud enough to carry through the door. "It's Phyrea."

You don't need to live like this anymore, the voice of the man with the scar on his face said. *Go back to Berrywilde.*

"The hells do you want?" the voice behind the door asked.

"Open the gods bedamned door, Wenefir," she demanded. "I need to talk."

"Have you come to kill me?" he asked.

"Did I say I came to kill you?"

"Yes or no."

Phyrea took a deep breath and let it all out at once to say the word, "No."

Wenefir paused, and Phyrea got the feeling he had some way of knowing whether or not she'd told the truth. The lock clanked open, and the hinge squeaked.

Revealed in the open doorway, Wenefir looked old and tired, chubby and soft. He looked her up and down and from the look on his face she could tell he thought she looked bad too, but in what way she wasn't entirely sure.

"I thought you were out of the business," he said, lifting an eyebrow.

"I am," she said. "I didn't come to fence something."

He stood there, staring at her, waiting, so she went on.

"You know why I'm here," she said.

Wenefir sighed and said, "I don't have time for this, Phyrea. What's happened to you?"

She shook her head, almost as though she were trying to shake off the look he gave her.

"I've been hearing the things you've been saying about the young senator from Cormyr, selling him around town like some piece of pilfered jewelry," he said. "I've also heard that you've been spending time with the other Cormyrean, the canal builder. Which is it, Phyrea? Which Cormyrean are you here to plead for?"

"I'm not here to plead for anyone," she lied. She was there to do exactly that.

And Wenefir knew it.

"You have friends in the senate," she said.

"So do you," he replied.

Phyrea shook her head.

"So, it's the canal builder," Wenefir concluded.

I don't like him, the little girl whispered.

Phyrea resisted the urge to look over her shoulder.

Neither do I, said the ghost of the little boy. *He doesn't have his man parts.*

"Is there anything that can be done?" she asked.

"Why?" Wenefir asked in return.

"What do you—?"

"What do I care about a canal, or about the Cormyrean nobody who's building it?" he asked.

"I could make it worth your while," she ventured, having no idea how she could, really.

He laughed.

"A favor then?" she tried. "A personal favor ... for an old friend."

He thought about it for a moment then said, "You steal things and bring them to me, and I give you gold. What makes you think, all of a sudden, that I can affect the whims and desires of the senate?"

"I know who you work for," she said, though she'd never wanted him to know she knew that, but he didn't look surprised.

"I've never meant to keep that a secret," he said, though she didn't believe him. "Anyone who mixes in your father's circles will have seen me with him."

"Is there something that can be done?" she asked.

Wenefir offered a weak smile and said, "Do you care that much? Really?"

She didn't answer, but looked him in the eye.

"Never come here again like this, in the middle of the night," he warned her. "Had you tried to pick that lock you would have been burned. You might have been killed."

Phyrea's breath caught in her throat. She looked over her shoulder, and the ghost of the little girl was behind her. The glowing violet child smiled. Gooseflesh broke out along the undersides of Phyrea's arms.

"Are you well?" Wenefir asked.

Phyrea nodded.

"If I have anything to tell you," he said even as he started to close the door, "I'll find you."

41

8 Alturiak, the Year of the Shield (1367 DR)
THE CHAMBER OF LAW AND CIVILITY

Willem Korvan wondered how long it had been.

How long had it been since he'd sat in the same room as Ivar Devorast?

His red hair as long and stringy, his simple peasant's clothes as unkempt, his eyes as cold and unintimidated as ever, Devorast sat quietly in a hard ladderback chair in the middle of the semicircular hearing chamber. Off in the east wing of the Chamber of Law and Civility, it was the largest of the hearing rooms, it's round outer wall lined with tall windows of cobalt blue glass. With the dull winter light coming in through the blue glass Willem thought everyone looked sick—worse than that, they looked dead. He felt as though he sat in a room full of ghosts.

Even Devorast looked spectral and sick, and Willem had never seen him look like that. As the people who didn't know him—didn't know the least thing about him—railed against him or heaped him with praise he just sat there, showing not even a trace of interest.

Willem sat in one of a row of chairs behind the senior

senators who had called the hearing at the request of the ransar. At times, Meykhati's back blocked his view of the assembly, but he could always see Devorast.

Having found out only the night before that he would be part of the hearing, Willem had gone out and gotten drunk, then had gone home and gotten more drunk. In the morning he drank a little more, and drank on his way to the hearing.

"Senator Korvan?" Salatis said, his voice booming, loud and angry.

Willem winced. His throat was tight and his mouth dry. Everyone was looking at him. He didn't try to stand.

"I've known Ivar Devorast," Willem said, "for a long, long, long, long, long time. A very long time longer than anyone else here." He cleared his throat and looked down at his hands, which he kept on his knees so they wouldn't shake so much. "That's how long I've known him."

"And?" the ransar prompted, irritated, his face turning red.

"And if that's what he said then that's what . . ." Not sure at all what he was trying to say, Willem stopped talking.

"Senator," Meykhati asked, "are you quite all right?"

Willem shook his head and replied, "I'm fine."

"With all due respect," someone Willem didn't know said, "is this man intoxicated?"

"Please, Ambassador," Salatis scolded. He stood from where he sat atop a raised dais—always a dais, Willem thought—and banged a gavel on the little desk in front of him. The blue windows were behind him and the whole room had the strange effect of a reverse amphitheater. The senators were arrayed in a semicircle with various witnesses seated in straight rows on the other side of the room, and Devorast seated in the center as though he were a scrap of territory over which two armies had gathered to fight. "We have certain rules of order here that I hope you will respect."

The man stood, bowed to the ransar, and said, "And are

there rules that concern whether or not a drunk can testify in a hearing like this?"

"This isn't Arrabar, Ambassador Verhenden," Salatis grumbled. "Until I decide otherwise, we will hear Senator Korvan."

"Verhenden," Willem said. "I've heard of you. Fael, right? Fael Verhenden, the ambassador from Arrabar. You're right, your excellency. You're entirely and completely and completely right about the fact that I'm completely drunk."

A disturbed murmur rattled through the room, and Willem laughed at them, the fools.

Salatis called the meeting to order again, and Willem said, "He'll build it if you let him, but he'll build it for himself. I can tell you that. This bastard ... this man doesn't care about Innarlith any more than he cared about Cormyr, and he sure as Tymora flips a coin doesn't give the south end of a northbound rat about the city of stinking Arrabar."

"I beg your pardon," the ambassador huffed.

"That's enough, Willem!" Meykhati hissed at him.

Willem shook his head and closed his eyes. The room spun. He couldn't focus on anything, so he just listened instead.

"Ransar," Meykhati said, "please accept my apology for Senator Korvan, who has suffered some at the careless hands of Ivar Devorast, apparently since they were both children."

Willem shook his head and asked in a loud voice, "Have I? I have suffered how at his hands? How did he suffer me? How ... ?"

"This is telling, Ransar," Meykhati went on. "Here is Devorast's countryman and friend, and under his influence, what has become of a young man with an outstanding career and by all accounts a fine, sophisticated mind?"

"Have you ever said the word 'forgiveness' and actually meant it, Ambassador?" Willem asked, his eyes still closed. "I drank when I knew I had to come here because he forgives me. I think he forgives me. Or maybe he just doesn't care. I think you have to care about someone to forgive him, don't you? Care just a little?"

"I'm sure you're quite right," said the ambassador from Arrabar.

Salatis banged his gavel in response.

"I'm not afraid of him," Willem said. "I'm afraid of what I am compared to him."

"Willem," Meykhati barked, "be still."

"Let him speak," a man who's voice Willem didn't recognize cut in.

"Sit down, alchemist," Salatis all but screamed. "You should still be in the dungeons, not out making these concoctions of yours that are perhaps the most dangerous part of this insane project."

"What I make is only dangerous when it's used by assassins sent by—"

"*Silence!*" Salatis screamed. "I will have order, or I will clear the room."

There was a moment of shifting chairs and scuffling feet, and Willem chuckled. His stomach turned, and his face flushed.

"We have heard from Warden Truesilver of Cormyr, Ambassador Verhenden of Arrabar, and Mistress Ran Ai Yu of Shou Lung," the ransar said. "The only other person here—the only one who was born and raised in Innarlith—who seems inclined to support Ivar Devorast is a failed alchemist and would-be assassin who should be marching this instant to the gallows but for the forgiveness of Master Rymüt. And then there was the testimony we've heard from our very own senators Meykhati, Nyla, and Djeserka; and Master Rymüt's man the esteemed wizard Kurtsson. Who am I to believe?"

Willem rubbed his eyes and opened them. He looked at Devorast, and his blurred vision made his old "friend" appear less hard, less intractable, softer.

"Answer me, Devorast," Salatis demanded.

"Believe what you will," Devorast replied. His voice made Willem's skin crawl.

There was a long silence that made the air in the room seem too heavy to breathe. Willem couldn't breathe, anyway. He scanned the room and his eyes fell on the face of Senator Pristoleph. Beside him stood his man, the soft and effeminate Wenefir. Willem was taken by the look on Pristoleph's face, the cold regard focused on Devorast.

"That's no answer," the ransar said to Devorast.

Pristoleph smiled as though he didn't agree with Salatis.

"I want to get on with my work," Devorast said. "Will you leave me alone to do that?"

The ransar stared him down for a long time while most of the people in the room squirmed in their seats. Devorast waited without barely taking a breath. Pristoleph turned and walked out of the room, Wenefir in tow. That made Willem smile, but he didn't know why. Then he was afraid he was about to vomit.

"No," the ransar said.

42

8 Alturiak, the Year of the Shield (1367 DR)
FIRST QUARTER, INNARLITH

You looking for something, squire?" the awful woman said. She spoke without ever closing her mouth all the way. Her brightly-painted, swollen lips never met. "Or you looking for some*one?*"

Willem looked at her, and his head and stomach spun in opposite directions. He staggered, his fine leather boots splashing in the greasy black puddles of the dockside street. The air stank of the Lake of Steam and the mildew that slowly ate away at the ramshackle buildings around him.

"Had a little of the grape, have we?" the woman said. She

laughed, and the sound made him sicker. "Need a hand?"

Willem shook his head and staggered again. She stepped toward him and all he could do was watch.

When she put her hand on him he found his last shred of strength. He stood up straighter and was about to tell her in no uncertain terms that she was mistaken if she thought he was the sort of man who might be taken in by her and her kind, but when he tried to speak he couldn't quite get his numb lips to form words.

Her dirty hand with its chubby sausagelike fingers prodded him. His head began to clear, and he stepped away from her and looked her in the face. She smiled wide enough that Willem could count her missing teeth.

"If I ain't your cup of tea, squire, just say so," she said with a suggestive leer.

Willem shook his head, but then his eyes found her hand. He saw a little length of string or twine dangling from her closed fist—a fist not quite closed enough. Her hand could easily have hidden his coin purse.

He drew his dagger and the woman backed away from him. The look in her eye was one part fear and one part resignation.

"You've had blades pulled on you before, haven't you?" Willem asked.

She forced a smile and said, "No worries, squire. No worries at all." Her eyes darted back and forth, up and down the long, dark, empty street. She couldn't keep the disappointment from reading in her eyes. They were all alone. "Just you be on your way, and we'll forget the whole th—"

He cut her face—not too deep, just with the very tip of the knife.

She gasped. "Don't you dare."

"Easy now," she whispered. She started to shake and backed away farther, until her back came to rest against the rough plaster wall of some dockside establishment closed for the night. "Easy does it, squire."

"Don't you dare," Willem repeated. The drink and the outrage made it hard for him to move his tongue, so his voice sounded alien in his own ears. "Don't you dare touch me."

She turned to run, and he kicked her feet out from under her. She fell sprawling onto her face with a grunt.

"Don't you dare try to take from me," he said, then kicked her hard in the side.

She squealed and coughed, a wet, phlegmy sound.

"Don't you dare try to get away," he growled, so low he wasn't sure she'd be able to hear him, but he didn't care.

She crawled to the end of a dark alley. Willem didn't understand why she thought she'd be safer in there. She drew in a breath to scream, so he kicked her hard again, forcing the air from her lungs.

"Don't you dare try to scream."

She reached for something in the folds of her grimy weathercloak. Willem watched her fumble out the knife. It was just an ordinary kitchen knife, but Willem wondered how many men she'd castrated with it.

"Don't you dare pull a knife on me," he said, and stomped down on her hand.

The bones made a crinkling sound, and the knife slid a few inches away. She grunted—not a very feminine sound.

"You lousy, Second Quarter son of a—" she snarled.

But she stopped when he kicked her in the face.

"Don't you dare," he said, kneeling down in the dark alley next to her, "call my mother a bitch."

She shook her head, which succeeded only in rubbing her face in the mud and muck on the alley floor. He cut her on the back of the neck while she was still lucid enough to feel the pain, to know what was happening to her.

"Don't you dare live," he whispered, then he took off his cloak and went to work on her.

The whole time he was killing her, he thought about that day in the hearing room. Had Salatis done the same thing to Devorast? Had they all done that to him? Had they killed him? Had they taken his life in that very room, one cut at a time?

The whore at least had the decency to defend herself. She'd tried to talk her way out of it. She'd tried to get away. She'd even tried to fight back. Devorast had done none of those things.

After washing the blood off his hands and face, he put his cloak back on, drawing it tight around his neck to hide the blood that had soaked into his tunic. He wiped the blood from his dagger and put it back in the sheath at his belt. The sound of footsteps alerted him to someone's approach, and he stood in the dark alley over the bloody corpse until she passed—another streetwalker—then he darted into the shadow of another alley across the street.

He went straight to the tavern he'd been on his way to when he was so rudely distracted. The building leaned a bit to one side and contained a permanent haze of pipeweed and wood smoke, and the lasting stench of stale beer and vomit. Over the past few months it had become one of his favorite places.

The sailors and dockhands who frequented the place never even looked at him twice. They all minded their own business.

He sat at a table in the corner, in the dark, and the woman who worked there—four hundred pounds if she was an ounce, and easily Willem's mother's age—brought him a flagon of ale and a tin cup with some kind of distilled spirit they made out back. He didn't have to ask for it anymore.

He lifted the tin cup and held it out to the empty chair across from him.

"Halina, my love," he whispered to the shadows.

He downed the fiery liquid and grimaced. A tear came to his eye.

Would you still love me, he thought, if you knew who I really was?

He turned the tin cup over and set it down on the table.

Would Phyrea love me, he asked himself, if she knew who I really was?

43

9 Alturiak, the Year of the Shield (1367 DR)
SECOND QUARTER, INNARLITH

You may want to shield your eyes," Pristoleph said.

He looked up at Wenefir with a relaxed smile, and his friend turned away, a hand over his eyes. Looking back at the fire, Pristoleph smiled wider and sighed. He concentrated on the flames that danced in the big round brazier. The copper bowl was ten feet around and dominated his private chamber. The room was warmer than most humans would find comfortable. Surrounding it was a collection of cushions made from different fabrics imported from all over Toril, from Shou silk to Zakharan wool to something called "cotton" from distant Maztica. Each of the pillows cost more than his mother had made in a year of selling her body. Every one of them was a symbol of how far he'd come. The room, sealed away with just him, and his most trusted companion, and the fire, was a symbol too.

He let his mind go blank, banishing all worries of politics and ambition, and let his thoughts surround the orange tongues of flame. He could feel the heat not only on his face, but in his mind as well.

"Yes," he whispered, then opened his eyes.

The flames burst into a brilliant white flare that would have temporarily blinded a human. Pristoleph's eyes drank the brilliance in with a greed all their own.

He let the flame burn brighter for a moment longer than normal, until he noticed that Wenefir had begun to sink to the floor. He cut his connection with the flames, and the light returned to its normal dull, warm orange glow.

Wenefir shook his head and rubbed his eyes, and said,

"How can you stand that, let alone enjoy it?"

Pristoleph shrugged and replied, "My mother always told me I had my father's eyes."

The only other living soul who knew what he meant nodded, smiled, and said, "Well, now that you've gotten it out of your system, there are things we should discuss."

Pristoleph nodded back and gestured to one of the floor cushions. Wenefir took a long time to lower himself to the floor, but soon found a comfortable position on a lamb's wool cushion from Aglarond.

"First tell me," Pristoleph asked, "how fare the coffers?"

"You know full well that coin is pouring in from the docks," Wenefir replied.

"The Guild of Stevedores . . ." the genasi said with a grin. "And all because of that Thayan pig's ridiculous speeches."

"He may be a pig, but I hope he never hears you call him that." Pristoleph shrugged and Wenefir continued, "He's been a good ally."

"He had his own reasons for shutting down the harbor, I'm sure," said Pristoleph. "Someday I hope to know precisely what they were. But in the meantime, I'll enjoy the gold that his rabble rousing has made for me."

"For all intents and purposes you control the flow of trade in and out of the city," Wenefir said. "That's quite a gift from someone not necessarily known for his selfless generosity."

"No one is truly selfless," Pristoleph reminded his friend.

"That's what I mean. I don't trust him."

"And why would you?" Pristoleph replied. "I don't either, but then I don't trust anyone, do I? At any rate, as long as he can be counted a friend, we avoid a powerful enemy."

"It's not like you to avoid enemies."

The two men exchanged smiles.

"You did not contribute to the hearing regarding the canal," Wenefir said. "Why not?"

"Did you expect me to?"

Wenefir wiped sweat from his brow. He wasn't nervous—he had nothing to be nervous about—the room was hot.

"The canal will surely increase shipping traffic, which will increase my income from the docks," said Pristoleph. "I'm inclined to think that's a good idea, but at the same time I understand why Marek Rymüt is opposed to it. It made sense to simply stand mute."

"I wonder, though," Wenefir said, a thoughtful cast to his features. "Which is the most damaging addition to the city-state of Innarlith? Ivar Devorast's canal, or Marek Rymüt's enclave?"

Pristoleph thought it over for a moment then said, "Both, or neither. The Thayan thinks he can pull coin into Innarlith by sending people and goods to the Vilhon Reach by means of the Weave. The Cormyrean's going to do the same with a big hole in the ground. As long as those goods move through our docks, well...."

"And in order to send them by magical means, does Rymüt even need our docks?"

"Point taken," Pristoleph said, the thought sticking in his head like a bur.

"The Thayan Enclave draws coin for Thay," Wenefir went on. "It fills their coffers, not ours, and puts a foreigner in a position of inestimable power."

"A cogent argument against it," Pristoleph replied. "but...?"

"But," Wenefir said with a mischievous smile, "he's already driven out every other mage, or made a partner of them, and we need magic too from time to time. Not everything is worthy of the spells necessary to disappear it from place to place."

"There will still be ships," Pristoleph said, picking up the train of thought, "and if they go through a portal to the Vilhon or a canal, either way they load and unload here."

"And there are other sources of magic besides the

Thayan," Wenefir said. He had that look in his eye that Pristoleph had been seeing more and more, and liking less and less.

"You know how I feel about that," said Pristoleph.

"Cyric's network is growing stronger and stronger by the month," Wenefir said. "I have made strong ties with many of the most powerful priests in the region. Show them that you're open to their help, and they could make you ransar."

"Like the Red Wizard made Salatis ransar?" Pristoleph asked. "Is that what it takes? A source of dark magic?"

"Apparently, yes," Wenefir said. His voice had grown thinner and higher, betraying his unfortunate deformity. "In any event, it doesn't hurt."

"Don't be so sure."

"I am sure about Cyric," said Wenefir.

"It's not the god that worries me," Pristoleph replied, "but his servants in Faerûn. Still, a new ally is always better than a new enemy."

"Then I'll leave it at that for now."

Pristoleph smiled and tossed a flask of warm water to his sweating friend.

"Thank you," Wenefir said, and he drank all that was left in the flask but still appeared thirsty.

"This canal," Pristoleph said, changing the subject in as unsubtle a way possible, "will cause chaos, though. Either way—if they build it or abandon it—there will be confusion for some time. The city-state—the whole region from Calimshan up through the Vilhon Reach—will be off balance. If they eventually decide again on the former, it will be very off balance, and for a very long time."

"And you're wondering how you might benefit from the chaos?" asked Wenefir.

"If you can find a way to benefit from it," Pristoleph told him, "it isn't chaos."

44

It's all right, Kurtsson," Marek said, though he wasn't the least bit certain that was true. "That will be all for the night."

The Thayan didn't look at Kurtsson, didn't want to exchange any sort of nervous or knowing glance. He listened to the other wizard stand, pause—hesitate—then finally leave. Marek had every reason to believe that the Vaasan would be listening in on what happened next—he had any number of ways of doing that—but it wouldn't matter.

"Good evening, Wenefir," Marek said. He didn't bother trying to smile. He didn't even stand. "It's late for a visit."

"Not quite middark," Wenefir replied. "But my apologies just the same."

Marek put his hands on the table in front of him, palms flat down.

"Everything is well, I hope," the Red Wizard said.

"That remains to be seen."

Marek cleared his throat and finally managed to smile. A sense of relief washed over him, though he wasn't sure exactly why.

"May I offer you a drink?" Marek asked, and Wenefir shook his head. "Please sit."

"I didn't come here to kill you," Wenefir said.

"Of course not," Marek replied. "If anything I said or did gave you the impression that that thought had crossed my mind, please excuse me."

"I will have a brandy after all."

Marek didn't have to stand to reach the bottle or a glass. He kept a tray at hand when he worked late. He poured the drink, and leaning forward in his chair, handed it to Wenefir.

"Please, sit," he said again.

Wenefir took a sip of the brandy—a very small sip. Maybe he didn't even drink any at all really, but just touched it to his lips. He sat on a stool, his wide, soft body almost seemed to drape itself around the little seat. He set the glass down on the table.

"That's pretty," Wenefir said, nodding at the flambergé that sat on a swatch of black velvet in the middle of the table.

"Isn't it?" Marek replied, wondering if that could be what Wenefir had come for—but why? That sort of thing wasn't really his style, or Pristoleph's.

"Tell me you didn't make it," said Wenefir.

"Oh, no," Marek replied with a chuckle. "No, that one's old—how old I'm still trying to determine—but old. It belongs to a friend, truth be told."

"Truth be told. . . ." Wenefir repeated, a wistful look further smoothing his already soft features. "It must be a very good friend, to allow you to hold onto something of such obvious value."

"It's what I do."

"It's enchanted?"

"Of course," Marek said. "Why else would I have it?"

Wenefir shrugged, and a little smile crossed his face. They sat for a moment in silence.

"I had a conversation, earlier this evening," Wenefir said at last, "with Senator Pristoleph."

"I hope he's well."

Wenefir nodded and said, "He appreciates your help in regards to the situation on the quayside, and elsewhere, and he understands your position in regards to the canal."

"But. . . . ?"

Wenefir smiled, seemed relieved, and said, "There will be ships, either way."

"Either way?" Marek stalled, though he'd sorted it out easily enough.

"He's prepared to align himself openly with whatever

eventuality you have in mind for the canal," Wenefir said. "Of course, it would help if he knew your intentions."

"Either way . . ." Marek whispered.

Wenefir smiled, so did Marek, and they both laughed.

"He is a man after my own heart," said Marek.

"I'm sure he would be both delighted and horrified to hear that."

Marek closed his mouth. His tongue felt dry all of a sudden.

"So?" Wenefir asked.

"Well," Marek said, taking a deep breath. "My first impulse is to close the whole thing down, but I'm not sure that's entirely possible."

"No?"

"There is an expression, I think from Cormyr—or is it Sembia?" Marek said. "They say, 'The cat is out of the bag.'"

"Meaning?"

"Meaning that the idea has been expressed that a canal could be dug to connect the Sea of Fallen Stars with the western oceans. More than that the idea has been expressed that this little bit of empty land to the north-west of Innarlith is the best place to do it. And it is the best place, you know. I've consulted maps."

"Have you?"

Marek let a breath hiss out of his nose and said, "I have."

"So you'll let him finish it?"

"Bane's bloody corpse, no," Marek said. "Not him."

Wenefir tipped his chin up, smiled a little again, then nodded and said, "Ah. You'll finish it yourself."

"After a fashion," Marek replied. "I will have it finished, but I won't be using shovels and sweaty backs."

"No?"

"Well," the Thayan said with a wink, "if you can't beat them, profit from them."

"Another Cormyrean expression?"

"No, no, I'm quite sure that one's Sembian."

They shared another laugh.

"There might come a day," Wenefir said, "that Senator Pristoleph will desire an upward change in station."

Marek felt his face flush. He forced a smile and said, "I was led to believe—"

"Calm yourself, Master Rymüt," Wenefir interrupted. "Just something to keep in the back of your mind. For the nonce, let's say that Senator Pristoleph looks forward to the increase in shipping traffic the canal will provide, and he trusts in your ability to build it, using the many wondrous means at your disposal."

Marek bent forward a little in a bow as Wenefir stood.

"Middark has come and gone, I should think," Wenefir said. "I will thank you for your hospitality, and be on my way."

Marek stood, bowed again, and watched Wenefir leave. When the door closed, he sat again and sighed.

The door opened a few moments later, and Kurtsson stepped into the room.

"Should I be concerned?" the Vaasan asked.

"Of course, dear," Marek said, then paused to down the rest of Wenefir's brandy. "A wise man is always concerned."

"But if Pristoleph is—"

"Pristoleph," Marek finished for him, "is doing what we always knew he would. And we'll either survive him or not."

45

10 Alturiak, the Year of the Shield (1367 DR)
SECOND QUARTER, INNARLITH

You look awful."

Willem, startled, gasped and stepped backward into a nightstand. The touch of something on his leg startled him again, then he jumped at the thought that if he knocked it over it would make a loud noise. He hissed a curse when he whirled to catch it.

"Graceful," Phyrea whispered.

Willem winced at both her tone and the pain that seemed to drop onto his head from above. His eyes burned. He took a deep breath and closed his eyes. He could feel her behind him, just standing there. He heard something drop to the floor and turned. The nightstand teetered a little but settled on its legs. From his peripheral vision he saw her cloak in a pool around her feet.

"What are you doing here?" he whispered.

"I—" she started, her voice booming in his ears.

He shushed her and she stopped. His head throbbed.

"You look awful," she whispered.

"You said that," he whispered back. "I believe you."

He turned to face her but rubbed his eyes, trying to get some feeling back into his face along with anything but sandpaper under his eyelids. It wasn't working.

"Why are we whispering?" she asked, whispering.

"I don't live alone," he replied, taking his hands from his eyes and blinking in the dim candlelight of his bedchamber.

Phyrea worked at the laces of her leather bodice and said, "That's right . . . your mother."

He nodded and asked, "What are you doing here?"

She didn't answer, but continued to unlace her top.

"It's late, isn't it?" he asked, still blinking.

"It's early," she replied.

"I thought you hated me," he said.

She dropped the bodice to the floor with her cloak. The sight of her took Willem's breath away.

"You've been drinking," she whispered.

He opened his mouth and shook his head, which hurt. She unlaced her leather breeches, then seemed to suddenly realize she was still wearing her boots.

"You don't smell good," she whispered. "I can smell you from here."

She took off one boot and placed it next to her cloak.

"I'm sorry," he said.

"You certainly are."

She took off her other boot.

"Why did you come here?" he asked her.

"Well," she replied as she slipped out of her breeches, "I'd have thought that would be obvious by now."

She wore nothing underneath.

"I don't understand," he admitted.

She stood there, naked, looking at him with such an expression of utter contempt that Willem had to look away from her.

"I don't please you?" she asked.

"You're the most beautiful woman I've ever seen," he said. "You're the most beautiful woman in all of Faerûn."

"Thank you."

"You should go," he said. "You don't have to—"

"What?" she asked.

He didn't know what to say.

Phyrea smiled at him the way people smile at other people's misbehaving children. She stepped out of the clothing at her feet and crossed the room to Willem's unmade bed. She slipped under the covers, but kicked them away, presumably so he could see her.

"I don't feel well," he said.

"Take your clothes off."

He shook his head, but started to unbutton his shirt. His fingers were numb, and he had trouble.

"Everyone wants us to marry," he said.

"Who's everyone?"

"Your father," he told her, "Marek Rymüt . . . other people."

"Well then I guess we had better marry," she said.

"Each other," he said.

A look crossed her face—plain as day—that told him in no uncertain terms that the very thought of that was a fate worse than death for her. She couldn't bear the very idea of it.

"I'm tired," he said, and took off his shirt.

"You're drunk."

He shook his head again and winced at the dull agony.

"Not anymore," he said.

"There's no reason for you to feel sorry for yourself, Willem."

"Isn't there?"

Her expression changed again. She pitied him. He hated that.

"I'll kill you," he said, "if you ever look at me like that again."

She took a short, shallow breath, and the look of pity disappeared, replaced in an instant with confusion.

"Are you trying to scare me?" she asked.

He slid out of his trousers and said, "No."

"Then why would you say something like that?" she asked as he walked to the bed.

He sat down and said, "I'm tired of people not thinking much of me."

"Then you should do something worthwhile."

He reached out to touch her face, and she flinched away, so he did too. She smiled in an apologetic way he found confusing.

"May I touch you?" he asked.

"I came here so you could touch me," she whispered.

He touched her face. Her skin was soft—not warm but hot.

"What do you want from me?" he asked.

"Do you need to know that, really?" she asked. He could feel her jaw working under the flesh of her cheek. "How long has it been since you asked my father for my hand in marriage?"

Willem's face went hot, and he tried to stand, but she held his arm. He didn't struggle against her weak grip.

"Other people have been straightforward with me," he said. "I've been told what to do, and what to expect in return. But it seems as though every time I do what I'm sure people want me to do, they return that with ever greater contempt."

"You're not from here," she whispered. "Innarlith can be an unambiguous place."

He leaned in to kiss her, but not all the way.

"That's not true at all," he whispered.

She leaned in the rest of the way, and their lips met. The kiss took the pain from his head, the stiffness from his joints. With the briefest flick of her tongue she pulled back.

"Everyone wants gold," she whispered. He could feel her breath hot on his face with every syllable. "They all have different ways of—"

He kissed her, and their tongues met. He pulled away when he thought for a moment that he might pass out.

"—trying to get it," she went on, "but that's all anyone here wants."

"That's true everywhere," he said, moving his hands from her face, down her long neck to her shoulder. He traced the edge of her shoulder blade with a finger and she put a hand on his chest.

"You were a pretty boy," she said as if trying to convince herself that that had any significance.

"I'm no boy," he said, and moved his hand down to wrap around one perfect breast.

"No," she whispered, her flesh responding to his touch even if her voice didn't.

"I will love you," he whispered, "if that's what you want."

She shook her head and replied, "That's the last thing I want."

She leaned in and let her lips play along the side of his neck. He closed his eyes.

"Tell me what you want," he said.

"No," she replied.

A tear came to Willem's eye, and he wrapped his hands around her neck, but didn't squeeze.

"Are you going to kill me?" she whispered. "Are you going to strangle me in your bed, with your mother in the next room?"

He clenched his jaw closed so tightly he thought his teeth might shatter.

"If I thought for a moment you could do that," she breathed. "I never would have come."

He kept his hands on her throat, and took a deep, steadying breath.

"If that's where you want to touch me, suit yourself," she said. "I want you inside me, Willem."

He took his hands away from her throat.

"That's a good boy," she whispered.

Halina, he thought. I'm sorry.

46

18 Alturiak, the Year of the Shield (1367 DR)
The Sisterhood of Pastorals, Innarlith

Marek Rymüt couldn't believe they'd allowed him entry. He'd seen the building from a distance a few times. One part temple, one part convent, the Sisterhood of the Pastorals seemed cut from glass. He'd never seen so many windows, or uninterrupted panes of glass quite so enormous. His off-hand comment to the dour old woman who'd shown him in, that the clerics and lay-worshipers who called the place home "should surely think twice before throwing stones," was utterly lost on her.

She took him to a hothouse of sorts where Halina knelt on a flagstone floor, digging with her hands in a pot of dirt. Dressed in a simple peasant's smock, no shoes on her feet, her hair a tangled mass pinned up out of her face, she looked twice her true age. She didn't notice him standing there, looking down at her, for what felt like a terribly long time. The dour sister shuffled off, and Marek ignored her stern, warning glance.

"Has your dirt goddess made you deaf, girl?" he said.

Halina was so startled, she tipped the pot over, spilling dirt into her lap and burying the little plant that sat on the floor in front of her.

"Uncle?" she said, looking up and blinking.

"One and the same."

"How did you . . . ?" she muttered, still blinking.

"I presented myself at the door and asked for you," he said. "That will be the last time, I should add, that I will answer a partial question. You may be surprised to see me, but let us take that as a sign of your own shortsightedness and move on from the shock and awe of it so that we can speak in complete sentences."

Halina looked down at the floor and said, "If you've come here to take me ho—to take me to your house, I'm afraid I will not be going with you."

"I'll do nothing of the kind," he said. "I made promises to your mother, my younger sister, that I would see to your care after her death. Surely I can't allow you to just wander off without explanation."

"I'm sorry, Uncle," she muttered, still not looking at him.

Marek stepped back from her and let his attention drift to the many potted plants that lined the glass room. He touched the petal of a large red flower.

"I can't say I've ever been to this part of the Third Quarter before," he said. "It doesn't smell as vile right here as it does in the rest of the quarter."

The Sisterhood of Pastorals sat only one major thoroughfare east of the Golden Road, barely more than a stone's throw from the north gate. Across the street to the east was the impoverished and crime-ridden Fourth Quarter.

"The sisterhood is a beacon for the people who call this part of the city home," Halina recited. "It reminds them of the beauty of nature and the loving embrace of the Great Mother."

"Yes," Marek drawled, "I'm sure the beggars and drunkards of the Fourth Quarter are delighted to accept the Great Mother's loving embrace in lieu of food."

"Please," Halina whispered, and her voice had a desperate sound to it that grated on Marek. "Please don't say things like that. Not in here."

The Red Wizards looked around and smiled. He was in Chauntea's temple after all—enemy territory in some ways. He made a show of shrugging and moved to another potted plant that he pretended to examine.

"If you intend to stay here," said Marek, "I will be happy to be rid of you."

Halina let go a long, hissing breath then said, "I'm just trying to lead a good life."

That perked Marek's interest. "A good life?" he asked. "And what is a good life? Planting flowers in pots at the command of a pack of—" He stopped before saying "nature witches" aloud. He was, after all, surrounded by nature witches. "Well, there now. I've done it myself. Perhaps there's something in the air here that makes it difficult for one to finish a thought."

He smiled down at her, and Halina looked up at him. She returned his smile, but it was half-hearted at best. Brushing the dirt from her gown, she stood and faced him.

"I don't know what a good life is," she said.

"No?"

She shook her head and told him, "Maybe it's a life spent crying less than I do. I would like that life, good or evil."

"Indeed," Marek said with a sneer. "Crying, Halina, is not a legitimate form of expression. It's a sign of weakness—of a loss of control. You know I forbid it in my house. Are you telling me you've cried under my roof?"

She couldn't look at him anymore, but to her credit at least she didn't back away.

"Every day," she whispered.

"You're forgiven," he said, speaking quickly so as to keep her off balance.

"No," she said. "No, I'm not. I'm sorry."

"Do you think *I've* led a good life?" he asked.

He waited for longer than he should have for her to answer and was about to go on when she said, "No."

"Really?" he replied, glancing at her only briefly before returning his attention to the plant.

"I don't know. I don't know if you've led a good life, or even if I've led a good life. I just know I want to lead a good life."

"That Cormyrean did things to you, didn't he?"

He could feel her vibrate from a distance, she squirmed so terribly. Marek resisted the urge to laugh, and instead made himself wait for her answer.

"He did nothing I didn't want him to do," she whispered. "Don't make me talk about that."

"He seemed happier after he'd been with you," Marek said. And he wasn't simply torturing her—though he was doing that, too—it was something he'd actually noticed. Willem Korvan was in love with her.

"Did he?" she asked. "I could never tell."

"Did he throw you out?" he asked. "Is that why you came here to dig in the dirt?"

"No," she replied, "he didn't throw me out."

"But he didn't marry you."

She sighed and shook her head.

"What are you doing here, really?" he asked, and looked her in the eye.

She met his gaze for only a heartbeat before turning away and saying, "I'm helping people."

"How?"

"The Sisterhood of Pastorals teaches people how to tend to the soil and harvest the bounty of the Great Mother. We teach people how to feed themselves, and if we can't do that, we feed them. We help people to live."

"Do 'we'?" he asked. She seemed quick to include herself among Chauntea's Pastorals. "You've only been here a few days, Halina. How many people have you helped?"

"No one, yet, I suppose," she replied. "But if I stay, if I work hard, I could help hundreds, maybe thousands."

He laughed, but just a little.

"You shouldn't laugh at that," she said. "That's not funny here."

"The idea that by planting flowers in pots you're going to help thousands of people is funny anywhere, Halina," he said, risking Chauntea's wrath. "But leaving that aside, are you telling me that altruism alone guides your actions now? If you can't satisfy one eager young Cormyrean, why not feed the masses?"

"That's cruel to say it like that."

"Is it cruel to say it, or cruel to do it?"

"I don't understand," she admitted.

"No," he teased. "No, I guess you wouldn't."

"It's not altruism that brought me here," Halina admitted. "And no, I don't think that I'm going to single-handedly feed thousands of starving people."

"Then what do you want, girl?" he pushed. "Say it."

"Happiness."

"And what makes you think you deserve that which has eluded so many?"

"I said I want it; I don't think I deserve it," she whispered. "And that's why I'm here."

"You don't know why you're here."

"I'm here because he wouldn't marry me," she said.

"And that's what you wanted?" he asked. "That's what would give you this elusive 'happiness'?"

She nodded and sighed again. She sounded as tired as she looked—as beaten.

"I've told you before, Halina, that your happiness, your needs, are of no consequence," the Red Wizard said. "You are not some goddess, or some lone creature inhabiting a plane of her own. You are a young woman who is a part of two societies. You are a part of the community of the city-state of Innarlith, and you are a citizen of Thay. Those communities require your service, not your happiness. They require your obedience, not your opinion. They require that you do as you're told. At times, I'm afraid, they require that you don't run off to some convent to wallow in self-pity, digging in the dirt while you cry over a lost love."

A tear rolled down her cheek, and he grimaced at the sight of it.

"Halina," he said, "I want you to listen to me very carefully while I tell you precisely how you will live every day of your miserable existence from this day forward. When I am finished, you will have the choice of doing what is required of you or—"

"Pardon me," Willem Korvan said.

Marek almost gasped.

"Master Rymüt," Willem said, "please excuse me, but may I ask that you step out for a moment and allow your niece and I a moment to speak with each other?"

Rymüt was less surprised to see Willem Korvan standing there than he was by the young man's appearance. If the homespun clothing and dirty hands aged Halina, Willem appeared even older, and his clothing was as fresh and clean as his hands. The Cormyrean's eyes had sunk deep into his face, rimmed underneath with dark bags that made him look as though he'd been punched in both eyes.

"Senator Korvan," Marek said with an over-wrought bow.

He glanced at Halina, who didn't notice him. She stared at Willem with her mouth hanging open and tears in her eyes. The young senator stared back, and appeared as surprised by her appearance as she was by his.

Marek walked out of the greenhouse, past Willem. When he was out of earshot he muttered a quick incantation that would allow him to listen in on them. He walked at a brisk pace, under the watchful eye of more than one priestess, but was not prevented from sitting on a low stone bench under a strange sort of tree he'd never seen before, which grew in the central rotunda of the sisterhood's glass house.

". . . awful, Willem," Halina said. Her voice was clear to Marek, though he knew no one else around him could hear her. "You've been drinking. Have you been drinking?"

"Yes," Willem replied.

"Why are you here?" she asked.

"Why am I here?" Willem replied. "Why are *you* here? You disappeared. I couldn't find you. I had to call in favors before I was told where you were."

"I'm sorry," she said. "I didn't think you'd—"

"Halina—" Willem grunted.

Marek sighed. It was going to be a long conversation if they both insisted on stopping midsentence, and his spell wouldn't last forever.

"I came here when I finally realized I had nowhere else to go," Halina said.

Her voice sounded different to Marek, and it wasn't just the spell's occasional distortion. She spoke differently with Willem than she did with Marek. She was more relaxed.

"You're looking at me," she went on, "as though you don't understand what I mean."

"I don't," Willem admitted. "I didn't drive you away, did I?"

"No, you didn't," she agreed. "But you didn't take me in, either."

"I—"

"Loved me?" she finished for him.

"Yes," he said with much eagerness.

Marek heard footsteps, a sound of some small disturbance, and Halina said, "No, please don't."

More shuffling feet then Willem replied, "You won't let me touch you? Have you taken some vow of chastity here?"

"Don't be vulgar," she scolded, and Marek lifted an eyebrow at her tone. "I am not a priestess here. I've come to help, and to think, and the sisters ask nothing more of me."

"And that's it, then?" he asked.

"Willem, you just said you loved me." There was a pause during which Willem might have nodded. *"Loved* me. Past tense."

"No, Halina," Willem whined. "I love you. I love you in the present tense."

"Then why won't you marry me?" she asked and Marek was relieved that she'd finally come to the point.

"I will," the Cormyrean replied.

"Why?" she asked. "And when?"

"Halina," said Willem, "I will marry you now, this precise moment, if that's what you wish."

"What do you wish?" she pressed him.

"I want you," he said. "I want you now, and forever. If I have you, maybe I won't have to drink to keep from shaking. If I had you to come home to at the end of the day, I would come home. If I knew that you loved me and would love me forever, I would never again ki—"

He stopped short, and Marek held his breath. Was he going to say "kill"?

"Willem?" Halina said.

"I love you," he replied. "I love you with my whole heart. I'm only happy when I'm with you. I'm a better man, with a brighter future. I smile only when I am with you."

"Willem..."

"Forgive me," he said, his voice low and quiet. "Halina, please forgive me for everything I've done and will ever do. Forgive me, and love me, and save me."

"Save you?" she asked.

"Save us both," he begged.

"And my uncle?" she asked.

Marek's ears perked up at that, of course.

"What of him?" Willem answered, and his voice was so dismissive, Marek's blood almost began to boil.

"If he doesn't approve?" she asked.

"We don't need his approval," Willem said, though Marek thought quite differently. "I am a senator, and you are a grown woman. We can do as we please."

"At the risk of an ally as powerful and important to you as my uncle?"

Ah, Marek thought, good question, girl.

"I don't know that your uncle is an ally of mine as it is, Halina," Willem said—a point that Marek found surprisingly perceptive. "He is friends with several of my friends, and more than one of my patrons. I don't think he'll risk those relationships to stop ours."

And there you are entirely wrong, my dear boy, Marek thought. Should I decide to, I will grind you into gravel.

"Marry me today," he said.

"That can't be possible, Willem," she replied.

"Tomorrow then."

Marek smiled again at Willem's eagerness and thought, So much a boy still, this one.

"Tomorrow," she said.

"Yes?"

"Yes, Willem," Halina replied.

"I love you," he told her.

"I love you too," she said.

Marek rolled his eyes.

"Come with me now," Willem said.

"I can't," replied Halina. "I'll need to speak with the sisters."

"If I come tomorrow to collect you . . . ?"

"I'll be ready," she said.

"Tomorrow, then," he said.

"Tomorrow, my love," she replied.

There were more sounds of shuffling feet, then the unmistakable echo of a kiss, and Marek cut the spell off with a scoffing grunt. The sound drew the further attention of the sisters, and he smiled and nodded at a few of them before rising and crossing to the door out of the temple of Chauntea. He left laughing.

47

19 Alturiak, the Year of the Shield (1367 DR)
SECOND QUARTER, INNARLITH

He couldn't remember buying most of the clothes in his closet. They all looked the same, and none of them looked good. People often complimented him on his taste in clothing, on the cut and material, and so on, but looking at the contents of his closet, he couldn't believe that. He didn't let himself think about what he'd spent—thousands of gold pieces—on those pointless rags.

"Really, my dear," his mother said. "Whatever are you doing?"

He ignored her. He didn't have much time, and accommodations had to be made.

"You can at least answer me," she pressed. "Willem?"

He stood back and looked at the closet. It wasn't quite half empty, but it would have to do.

"Just like that, then?" his mother went on. "And you refuse even to discuss it? We aren't a family anymore. Is that it? I'm no longer welcome here? My opinion is of no consequence to you? You have no care at all for—"

"Please, Mother," Willem finally said.

"Did I raise you to interrupt people?" she asked, her eyebrows arched, and the eyes underneath them cold and angry.

"I'm sorry, Mother," said Willem, "but I am a grown man, and I have to ask you to respect—"

"Your mother," Phyrea said. Willem jumped, his heart skipping a beat, and Thurene gasped. "You should respect your mother, Willem dear."

"My goodness," Thurene gasped, a hand on her chest.

"Phyrea?" Willem asked. "What are you doing here?"

"Well," Thurene cut in, "I for one am delighted to see you, Phyrea dear. I'm sure you'll be able to talk some sense into my lovesick son."

"Lovesick?" the master builder's daughter teased, winking at Willem and leaning against the doorjamb. "Do tell, Senator."

"It's that Thayan girl," Thurene sneered.

Phyrea glanced off to one side as though she'd heard a sound from somewhere downstairs. The gesture made the hair on the back of Willem's neck stand on end.

"Is something wrong?" he asked.

Phyrea tried to smile, and she shook her head, but still it appeared as though she heard someone downstairs.

"Is someone with you?" asked Willem.

"No," she answered, but he didn't believe her. When she said, "Of course not," she seemed sincere.

"Don't be silly, my dear," his mother said. She seemed confused by the whole exchange—and truth be told, so was Willem. "Now, Phyrea, please help me convince my son that he's opening his home, his life, and his family, to the wrong young woman."

Phyrea smiled and said, "Willem, you're opening your home, your life, and your family, to the wrong woman."

Willem rubbed his eyes and sighed.

"Besides," Phyrea added, "we both know you're going to marry me."

Thurene gasped again, and Willem's blood ran cold.

"I need to sit down," he said, but didn't sit down.

"My stars!" his mother exclaimed, again with her hand on her chest.

"Halina is waiting . . ." Willem started.

"She'll get over it," Phyrea said, then she looked back behind her again and sort of shook her head.

"Someone's down there," said Willem, crossing to the door.

Phyrea held out a hand to stop him, and they ended up in an uncomfortable embrace.

"Did you hear something?" Thurene asked.

"Hello?" Willem called down the stairs. "Is someone there?"

Phyrea stood with her eyes closed and her head down while Willem listened for a response, or any sound at all. There was nothing. When he relaxed Phyrea sighed and pressed herself into him. All he wanted was to hold her, to touch her, and for a moment he forgot that his mother was a pace and a half behind him.

"Come with me," Phyrea whispered in his ear, her breath hot on the side of his face.

She took him by the hand and started to lead him into the hall and to the stairs.

"Should I come with you, my dear?" Thurene asked.

"No," Phyrea told her.

"Oh . . ." his mother breathed. "Well, I . . . I'll wait for you here, then. Willem?"

Willem couldn't look back at his mother. All he could see was Phyrea. Her perfect beauty eclipsed everything.

"Don't worry, Madam Korvan," Phyrea said. "I'll take him from here."

His mother was left at the top of the stairs, blustering and confused.

Phyrea led him out of his house. A coach waited in the street, and she all but pushed him into it. Phyrea rapped on the wall of the coach, and the driver whipped the horses out into traffic. Willem brushed his fingers through his hair and was surprised that it was wet.

"It's raining," he muttered, not having noticed before.

Phyrea nodded and leaned in toward him. Her lips met his, and he drank her in. Her hands were on the side of his face, and he put his on her shoulders. When he moved them down to her breasts she didn't flinch or pull away.

Her lips came away from his, and she whispered, "You knew this would happen, Willem. It had to. It had to be us, after all."

Willem shook his head and tried to think of Halina, waiting for him at that awful temple, waiting for him to come and get her so that they could live happily ever after. But he couldn't get a picture of her to form in his mind, and the thought of her waiting, and waiting, and waiting for a husband who would never come didn't make him feel anything at all.

She drew away from him, but gently, and took his hands in hers. She squeezed his hands a little in a calming, reassuring way, and a hiss passed her lips as though she was shushing him, but he hadn't made a sound.

Willem sat still, listening to the sound of the coach's wheels clatter over the cobblestones, and the rain patter against the roof. A little wisp of steam escaped his lips when he exhaled. It was chilly and damp—winter in Innarlith. Outside the coach the Second Quarter streets went by in a blur, not because they were moving particularly fast, but because Willem's eyes refused to focus on distant objects. The rain kept most of the people off the streets, and the dull gray air was lit by the warm glow of candlelight and hearthfires in the passing windows.

They'd gone south away from his house and at the end of the street turned left to head east toward the Third Quarter. He wanted to ask where they were going, but he liked the quiet better.

"I know what I'm doing," Phyrea whispered to herself, though it sounded as if she was talking to someone else.

Willem looked at her, but she avoided making eye contact and squeezed his hands again.

He hoped she was right. He hoped she knew what she was doing. He certainly didn't.

At the next major thoroughfare the coach turned right to lead them back south, along the very edge of the line between the Second and Third Quarters.

"Why me?" he asked, not sure where the question came from, or why all of a sudden he wanted to talk. Part of him hoped she wouldn't answer.

"My father wants it," she said, sounding unconvinced.

"I love you," he said.

To her credit she didn't wince. He felt her hands grow warmer, though, and begin to sweat.

They rode in silence for a while longer, and the coach turned right onto the wide avenue of Ransar's Ride, what some people called Sunset Boulevard because it lined up almost perfectly with the Midsummer sunset. They headed back into the heart of the Second Quarter and Willem noted a few of the shops where he'd bought the clothes he'd moved from his closet to accommodate—

Phyrea.

He'd made the space for Phyrea to move in with him, so they could be together as man and wife.

They turned left again, near the Peacock Resplendent, heading south once more. Though Willem couldn't see out of the front of the coach he knew that the Chamber of Law and Civility was only a few blocks ahead of them. Could it be she was taking him there? Wedding ceremonies had been held there, according to common law. Phyrea's father would likely wish the blessing of Waukeen, but Phyrea might have talked him into a civil ceremony.

When the coach passed by the ornate edifice without a moment's pause, he grew only more confused.

"Of course I won't," Phyrea whispered, so low he could just barely hear her.

He wanted to ask her who she was talking to, but he couldn't bring himself to speak. He gently squeezed her hands, which felt slick with sweat, and sat in silence as the coach continued south. The wide avenue curved to the west, leading them to the First Quarter and the docks beyond, but they turned left at a fork in the road and were heading south again. They'd nearly crossed the entire length of the city from north to south. They could have been headed to the Cascade of Coins—the temple of Waukeen—after all.

He looked at Phyrea and his breath caught. Her beauty overwhelmed him. He took a hand away from hers and touched her cheek. She leaned in to his touch and frowned. She looked sad—as if she might even cry—then she smiled.

The coach pulled to a stop, the horses clomping to the side of the street.

Willem looked around. He knew the neighborhood—not well, but he knew it. They hadn't come to the Cascade of Coins.

"Master Rymüt's house?" he asked, recognizing the large manor home with its walled grounds.

Phyrea nodded, making no move at first to exit the coach, and said, "He wants people to call it the 'Thayan Enclave' now. I don't know why. Maybe he thinks he's some kind of ambassador now."

"He is, I suppose," Willem replied, "an ambassador of sorts."

Phyrea sighed, and the coachman opened the door and stepped aside. She stepped out onto the street not quite as if she were being marched to the gallows, but close. Willem shared that feeling when his boots touched the cobblestones.

Marek Rymüt appeared at the gate, a huge grin plastered on his round face. The tattoos on his head looked even stranger, uglier than normal with the rain spattering off them. He waved them both toward the gate, and Phyrea hesitated for just a fraction of a heartbeat, so Willem did too. Marek only grinned wider.

Willem followed Phyrea through the gate. He avoided looking the Thayan in the eye. Marek looked at him with undisguised lust that made Willem squirm. He wanted to reach out and hold Phyrea's hand, but he didn't. He wondered, though, as they walked across the rain-drenched grounds to the main house, what he would have done if he had taken her hand. Would he have pulled her back into the coach, away from there and whatever was going to happen? Or would he just have felt better knowing she was pulling him toward that unknown, unavoidable fate?

"Ah," Marek said from behind him, "young love. . . ."

They went into the house and paused, dripping wet. Marek stepped in front of them, and still smiling ear to ear, said, "Ah, what a wonderful afternoon this is. Welcome to the Thayan Enclave, and let me say how pleased I am that you have chosen our—"

"Please, Master Rymüt," Phyrea interrupted. "Can we get on with it?"

Marek seemed disappointed, but didn't argue, he bowed and motioned to a velvet curtain the color or rich red wine. Without hesitating, Phyrea stepped through the curtain. Willem looked at Marek, who leered at him. If for no other reason than to get away from the Thayan, he followed her through the curtain, and what he saw in there stopped him cold.

A freezing cold sweat broke out on the back of Willem's neck, and he stopped breathing. He looked around at what was once a comfortable, ordinary sitting room. But it had been transformed into what could only be described as a temple. Candles burned on virtually every surface. The walls were draped in black velvet. An apothecary's cabinet had been made into an altar, and the floors were covered by canvas tarps. Behind the altar stood a man Willem recognized, but in his current state, he couldn't recall the man's name. He was as rotund as Marek, but softer, more feminine somehow, clad in a hooded black robe of some homespun, rough fabric.

Phyrea took his hand, and Willem jumped. Marek giggled from behind them.

"Step forward," the man in the robe said.

Phyrea did as she was told, dragging Willem forward by the hand.

"Good afternoon, Wenefir," Phyrea said with a coy smile that didn't suffice to cover the dread that quivered in her eyes.

Willem remembered: Pristoleph's man.

"In the name of the Dark Sun, I bless this union," Wenefir said. "For the glory of the Prince of Lies, I bind you."

Cyric, Willem thought. Cyric?

"Willem Korvan," said Wenefir, "you must state your intentions."

"My in—?"

"Say you want to marry the girl," Marek explained.

"I want to marry her," he said before he could think it through, then he closed his eyes.

He didn't want to see the rest of it. He heard Phyrea tell Wenefir that she wanted to join her life to his. When Wenefir gave him a metal cup he drank from it and tried to pretend that it wasn't blood he was drinking. When the Cyricist tied his wrist to Phyrea's with a length of silk cord Willem didn't pull away. When he was told to repeat one bit of disconnected madness after another, he repeated it. He did all of it, said all of it, with his eyes closed.

Finally, Wenefir cut their wrists loose and stepped very close, so close that Willem could smell his sour breath. Still, Willem didn't open his eyes.

"You are man and wife, now," Wenefir said. "Seal it with a kiss, or not, as you wish."

Willem heard footsteps and opened his eyes. Wenefir and Marek left the room. He looked down at Phyrea. Her whole body shook. He'd never seen her so pale. She seemed on the verge of bursting, or shaking apart. She turned on him and looked at him with the wild eyes of a panicked animal.

"Phyrea," he said, and reached out for her.

"No," she shrieked, her voice loud and out of control.

Willem didn't know what to say. She glanced at him one more time, then ran from the room. He followed her, but only saw her disappear through the door. Marek stepped up next to him and wrapped an arm around his shoulders. Willem tried to pull away, but the Thayan held on tight.

"Might not be a proper wedding night tonight, my boy," Marek said with a toothy grin, "but she'll be back."

Willem blinked, fighting back the tears that came to his eyes. He looked down at Marek, who grinned at him as if he knew something Willem didn't.

But then that was always the case with Marek Rymüt. He always knew more than anyone else, and Willem always knew less. All Willem knew at that moment was that he had betrayed Halina, betrayed his own spirit, perhaps, in taking part in a ceremonial vow to the mad god Cyric. And his only prize was Phyrea, who had done what he should have done the second she'd appeared in his bedchamber: run.

He pushed away from the laughing Thayan and walked out of the house, and he had no idea where to go.

48

19 Alturiak, the Year of the Shield (1367 DR)
THIRD QUARTER, INNARLITH

Phyrea ran up the stairs to her flat, making for the door as though she were being chased. And in a way, she was.

Don't go in there, the man with the scar on his face insisted. She could feel his anger building. *He'll destroy you.*

She stumbled and had to stop to keep from falling. She leaned against the wall and did her best to dry her eyes with the palm of her hand.

Please, please listen to us, Phyrea, the woman with the quiver in her voice begged. *I don't understand what you're doing. Why would you go to this man, who hates you? He will kill you, and if he kills you here in this stinking hovel, you'll be destroyed. He really will destroy you. Don't lose yourself. Don't make me lose you. I can't lose you, Phyrea. Not you too.*

"Shut up," she said. "Just shut up."

Take us back, and stay with us, the little girl moaned. *I want to go home.*

Phyrea climbed the last few stairs and all but fell through the door into her dismal flat.

Run! the little boy screamed into her mind so loudly she couldn't help but clasp her hands over her ears.

"What's wrong?" Devorast asked.

She took her hands away from her ears and closed the door behind her.

We're trying to help you, the man with the scar said. Phyrea could feel his searing disappointment.

"Phyrea?"

She leaned against the wall and tried to wipe the tears away again, but couldn't. She blinked at Devorast, who stood on the other side of the room. Knowing she wasn't going to need it, that at least for a short time she would have to stay with Willem, she'd told him he could stay there. With the canal site deserted, the workers gone home, he had nowhere to go.

"Touch me," she whispered. Then louder: "Hold me."

He walked to her, and she met him in the middle of the room, collapsing into his arms. He started out holding her, but within a few heartbeats, he was holding her up.

"What's happened?" he asked.

"I gave myself to Willem Korvan," she sobbed.

"Why?" he asked, and in only that one word she could detect no trace of how he actually felt about what she'd said.

"Because you wouldn't let me give myself to you," she said. He stepped away from her, and she almost fell to the floor. "I love you."

"And I love you," he said.

She couldn't tell what he was thinking, but she could tell he was thinking.

"Tell me," she pleaded.

He can't, the old woman told her. *He can't tell you, because he doesn't know.*

He can't give you what you want, the sad woman added.

"There's nothing more to tell," he said. "I'm happier when you are with me than when you aren't. I don't know what else you want me to say."

She went to him, and he took her in his arms again. She kissed his neck.

"What do you want from me, Lady Korvan?" he said.

She stepped back and slapped him across the face so hard it stung her fingers and left her numb up to her elbow. A welt raised on his cheek, and a brief flash of rage crossed his face, but in an instant he was back to his normal emotionless mask.

You see? the old woman's voiced echoed in her head. *All you'll ever get from him is a passing rage, then nothing. He'll give you nothing.*

And we can offer you eternity, the man with the scar said.

"What's keeping you in Innarlith now?" she asked Devorast. He shrugged and shook his head. "Can't we go away, then? Can we just get on a ship and go? The Shou woman, your friend, if she's in port can she take us to Shou Lung? Can we go to Calimport or Marsember? Raven's Bluff, maybe, or even Waterdeep?"

She went to the door and threw it open.

Go, the man in her head told her, *but not with him.*

"Walk through this door with me," she said. "Come away with me, and we'll never smell this rotten city again."

He shook his head and replied, "I've started something here."

"And they won't let you finish it."

Can we go home now? the little girl asked.

"You know I'll finish it anyway," he said, "eventually."

"Eventually?" Phyrea almost screamed. "What does that mean? I have no idea what that means. Eventually?"

"What of your husband?" he asked.

She had to look away from him for a moment and she said, "To the Nine Hells with him. To the Abyss with him."

Damn it, just go! the little boy screamed in her head.

"If we could just go, we could be happy," she said.

Devorast shook his head, and the gesture made Phyrea feel as though she was going to pass out.

"I'm exhausted," she whispered. "I'm just so tired."

Go back to Berrywilde, the sad woman whimpered. *Go back there and rest, with us. We'll let you rest.*

"Stay here," Devorast said. "Sleep here tonight, and in the morning, do whatever you want to do, and go wherever you want to go."

"But not with you."

He didn't answer, but she shut the door anyway.

He can never give you what you want, Phyrea, the old woman told her.

"I know," she whispered, and still she stayed the night.

49

20 Alturiak, the Year of the Shield (1367 DR)
SECOND QUARTER, INNARLITH

The office of the master builder had acquired a smell to it that made Willem's stomach turn. The first time he'd been there, he'd been impressed with its opulence, drawn to the power of the position that could command such a space. In time, though, it had come to smell like decay, it had withered like the old man who inhabited it. The space itself seemed to have shrunk.

"It's extraordinary," the master builder said, shuffling through a huge stack of parchment sheets. "With a little work, this could actually be done."

"A little work?" Willem couldn't help but say.

The parchment sheets held Devorast's designs for the canal, seized by Salatis's men. Willem didn't even want to look at them. He knew what the pages contained. And he knew that no work on the part of Inthelph could possibly improve on them.

The master builder nodded and pushed the sheets aside. He sighed, and his teeth began to chatter, though the room was warm. He stared down at the floor, at nothing.

"I've news," Willem said.

The master builder didn't seem to have heard him. He just stared down, his teeth clicking.

"It concerns Phyrea," said Willem.

Inthelph looked up at that, the beginnings of a smile on his face. He blinked and rubbed his eyes with weak hands.

"She and I have been married," Willem said. "It all happened very fast. I can't begin to apologize for your not being there, not having the opportunity to send her off with a proper ceremony, and so on, but . . ."

Inthelph grinned from ear to ear and stood on legs that seemed to creak under his meager weight. He stepped to Willem, reached up, and put his dry hands on either side of the younger man's face.

"My boy," the old man said. "My dear, dear son. I could not possibly be happier to hear this news. This is the sort of thing I've been waiting for, you see."

Willem took a step back and Inthelph flinched away. A look of passing terror showed in his eyes and something about that petty weakness made Willem angry. The anger must have showed on his face because Inthelph stepped even farther away, moving into the corner of the room like a caged animal.

"What have you been waiting for?" Willem asked.

Inthelph swallowed and said, "For you."

"For me?"

The master builder nodded and said, "You have no idea how much I worried about Phyrea. She's my only child, my only heir. Bad enough she was a girl, but then she insisted on rejecting everything I tried to give her. She would steal things, break things . . . she had no respect for me, for her betters, or for herself. Until you came along, that is."

Willem shook his head, speechless at how wrong the master builder was.

"I knew you were the one, Willem. I knew you would be the steadying influence that both my daughter and my city needed."

Willem closed his eyes, amazed at the master builder's upside down interpretation of everything. Willem wasn't even a steadying influence on himself.

"I've felt like a father to you, my boy," Inthelph went on. "I hope you've felt like a son to me. And now that's true under the law and not just in the way we see each other. You are my son now."

Willem sighed, no longer caring that the master builder would mistake it as—what? Willem being overwhelmed by the emotion of the moment? How could a man so old be so crushingly naïve?

"I am prepared to step aside," Inthelph said. "I am old, and have worked hard for too many years. I have an interest in wine, you see, and well . . ."

"Master Builder, I—"

Inthelph waved him off, smiled, and said, "Please don't refuse me, Willem, I won't know what else to do. I can't bear the thought that you might turn your back on me the way Phyrea has. I wanted you in her life to bring her back into mine, not so that she could take you with her."

Willem sighed again and cast about for a chair. He found one and sat, elbows on his knees, his head in his hands. He couldn't help thinking of Devorast and his perfect, calm self-assurance. And Willem had surrounded himself with just the opposite. Phyrea seemed to be an entirely different person every time he saw her. The master builder was a scared, insecure fool.

Maybe I belong in this family after all, Willem thought.

50

20 Alturiak, the Year of the Shield (1367 DR)
SECOND QUARTER, INNARLITH

Of course," his fat mother said, "in Cormyr, it's all but impossible for anyone to rise above his station the way my Willem has. To think, he's been here only—oh, my stars, has it been nine years?—nine years, and he's a member of the ruling body."

Phyrea smiled and tipped her head graciously to one side while the ghost of the old woman said, *And all he had to do was sell himself on the cheap to a bunch of crusty old men who've raised him like a pig.*

"You must be very proud," Phyrea said.

Thurene grinned so that Phyrea thought her head would split in two and everything above her upper lip would fall to the floor behind her. She put her teacup down on the saucer in front of her with a faint click. Something about the sound made Phyrea's skin crawl.

Why are you wasting your time? the man's voice said.

He stood directly behind Willem's fat mother, staring down at her as though he was about to strangle her. Phyrea, startled by the ghost's sudden appearance, almost dropped her own teacup. The hot brown liquid sloshed over the side and burned her hand, leaving it red and sore.

"Oh, my," Thurene gasped.

"It's all right," Phyrea said, and placed her cup on her own saucer. She wiped the still-hot tea off her hand with her other palm, ignoring the linen napkin that sat on her lap. She saw Thurene eye the movement, and the old woman's gaze lingered on the hem of her dress, which Phyrea was sure she found too short—scandalously so. "I've had worse injuries."

"I can't imagine," the old woman said, confused. She didn't believe her. "Can I get you anything?"

"Of course not," Phyrea answered.

The ghost continued to stare down at her. Phyrea looked him in the eye. He smiled back at her, his face as cold as stone. She could see the painting on the wall behind him: a badly-rendered portrait of Thurene herself. The artist didn't add the blotchy liver spots and the wispy patches of hair at her temples that made her look more like a man than a woman. He was kind to her chins as well. The translucent violet apparition glanced over his shoulder at what Phyrea was looking at, and his smile became an annoyed scowl.

Thurene turned, stiff and slow, in her chair, also curious as to what Phyrea was looking at. She didn't see the ghost standing behind her, and when she turned back to Phyrea she was smiling.

"Willem commissioned that, of course," she said, brimming with pride in her son.

Phyrea had to swallow the bile that rose in her throat.

"And you're quite certain you're well," Thurene said.

"No," Phyrea replied, all falseness gone from her tone. "I'm not the slightest bit certain of that. I'm not. You know what I used to do, before I met a certain man?"

Thurene shook her head, nervous, scared even, but drawn to Phyrea's intensity as much as her words.

Phyrea picked up a paring knife from the silver tea tray on the low table between them. Thurene's eyes fastened to the little silver blade and followed it. With her other hand Phyrea lifted her skirt, showing even more of one firm thigh. She knew that Thurene could see at least the first few in the row of little scars, some still not entirely healed, that marked her otherwise perfect skin. She held the blade to her thigh, but didn't cut, at least not right away.

"Oh, my, no," Thurene breathed, but Phyrea could tell she really wanted her to do it. The old woman wanted to see it. "Phyrea . . ."

Do it, the ghost of the man said.

Phyrea looked up at him, ignoring her mother-in-law. She let her eyes linger on the scar on his face, the scar in the shape of a **Z**. He sneered at her.

"You want me to," she whispered.

I want you to, yes, the ghost said.

At the same time Thurene gasped, "Goodness, no!"

But if you cut, the man said, his lips moving but not in time with the words that echoed in Phyrea's head, *keep cutting. Cut and cut and cut until you're one with us at last.*

But not here, the voice of the old woman intruded.

"Phyrea . . ."

Phyrea looked around the dull, dimly-lit sitting room for the old woman, but the apparition was nowhere to be seen. All there was to see was expensive but unremarkable furniture, art that showed an utter lack of taste, and all the little things that made the house more Thurene's than Willem's. It was an old woman's house.

"It makes me feel something," Phyrea said, turning back to Thurene.

"Phyrea, please, I—"

Phyrea pressed down on the knife and the hot wetness of the blood was the first sensation, followed only after Thurene's shocked gasp by the pain.

"It isn't bad, but it hurts," Phyrea whispered.

Yes, the ghost of the man whispered, *it hurts.*

Phyrea watched as the man faded away, drifting into nothingness like a wisp of steam.

"For at least the space of a heartbeat," Phyrea said, her eyes closed, "all you think about is the little stab of pain and not the horrible, bloated beast of a woman that's sitting across from you, the pretty but frivolous man you've sold yourself to like a whore's whore, and the sad, pathetic ruin of your own life."

She opened her eyes again and laughed in Thurene's horrified face.

"Wouldn't you prefer it back in Cormyr?" Phyrea asked. She held up the pairing knife and a few drops of blood clung to the blade. "If you went back there, you might live out the rest of your life like a sow in a pen, spared the slaughter by a farmer gone sentimental."

Thurene swallowed, which caused her chins to waggle in a ridiculous way. Her skin was so heavily powdered it was impossible for Phyrea to be sure, but it appeared as though she'd gone pale.

"Willem doesn't know I do that to myself," Phyrea said then licked her own blood from the blade, reached down, and cut a sliver of pear. Thurene gagged, a hand at her throat, her eyes wide. "Pear?" Phyrea offered.

She held the slice of ripe fruit out to her mother-in-law, who shook her head and shrank away.

"You s-said," Thurene sputtered, "you said ... you said that you did that ... before you met my Will—"

"I said nothing of the kind," Phyrea interrupted. "It's not your pathetic son who's very presence makes me feel as though there may be some hope for our miserable, porcine existences."

Phyrea placed the slice of pear on her tongue and held it in her mouth, sucking the juices from it until it sizzled. With the tip of her finger she drew up the little smear of blood that oozed from the cut, and licked it off with the tip of her tongue. Thurene gagged again, but Phyrea enjoyed the salty tang of her own blood as it mixed with the tart sweetness of the pear. As she chewed, she pulled the hem of her dress down until it almost touched her knee.

"Phyrea, I—" Thurene started, but choked to a stop when the door opened and Willem walked in.

What are you doing here? the voice of the sad woman murmured.

Phyrea looked to the door, ignoring Thurene's struggles to stand and her blustered, shrill greetings. The woman stood next to the door, not sparing Willem a glance as he stepped in. Made of pale violet light, she looked as though she was about to cry, the same as always. There was something both comforting and terrifying about that particular undead creature.

Phyrea didn't stand, even when Willem walked into the room. He looked back and forth between his new bride and his mother with crippling uncertainty. Phyrea imagined she could hear crickets chirping in the still expanse of emptiness inside his handsome head. He drew in a deep, shuddering breath and slipped his rain-soaked weather-cloak from around his shoulders.

"Willem, my dear," Thurene all but screamed.

"Really, Mother," he said, "are you all right? What have you two been talking about?"

He eyed Phyrea with a look that surprised her. Maybe he wasn't so stupid after all.

"Oh," Phyrea said, her voice light, almost girlish, "we've been having a wonderful time, just us girls."

"Really. . . ." Willem said, not believing her. He looked at his mother and raised an eyebrow.

"We've been having tea," Phyrea cut in before Thurene could speak. "Would you like some?"

"Everything is fine," Thurene said, but her face was pleading and desperate.

"Or would you rather just turn in?" Phyrea asked, and had his full attention.

Phyrea stared at Willem, keeping his eyes away from his mother, but she could sense Thurene sagging, almost falling to the floor.

Willem swallowed and said, "I'd love a cup of tea, thank you."

He handed his weathercloak to his mother, who almost dropped it and looked at it as though it was some alien creature from a foul outer plane. Phyrea smiled at both of them and turned back to the tray. She picked up the knife, ignored both Thurene's series of little gasps and the laugh that echoed in her head from the man with the z-shaped scar, and cut another slice of pear. She held it up to Willem, who took it out of her hand without a second thought. She looked at Thurene with fire in her eyes, and the old woman was smart enough to swallow whatever it was she wanted to say. Willem ate the slice of pear with a smile.

"I . . ." Thurene said, "I'm feeling . . . tired."

"Mother?" Willem said, turning to look at her.

Thurene turned her eyes to the floor and started for the stairs.

"I'll leave you alone," she muttered. "Good night."

"Good night, Mother," Willem called after her. "Sleep well."

When he turned back to Phyrea, she patted the seat next to her and smiled.

51

It had been some time since Marek Rymüt had been at sea. It wasn't exactly his preferred method of travel. The deck rose and fell at irregular intervals, but the motion was smooth, almost comforting, without any violent lurches to challenge the stomach. Though it wasn't yet spring, the air was warm with only a light wind. The smell of the lake had numbed his nose so he hadn't been able to smell it since only a little while after they'd shoved off from Innarlith. The sail on the single mast fluttered above him. He found the noise irritating.

"It is a lovely day, isn't it, Master Rymüt?" the young woman standing next to him said. He glanced at her and smiled. "And the ransar's yacht is most impressive," she added.

"Well," Marek said with a sigh, "one does have the responsibility to keep up appearances."

"Of course," said the young woman. "And I would also like to tell you again how delighted I am to—"

"Please, Senator Aikiko," Marek said with a wave of one hand. "You may not want to thank me once you've seen this hole in the ground."

The senator giggled in a way that some men might find alluring, but made Marek cringe. He spared her another glance, noting the clothes she wore. She'd dressed for an expedition, in tan tunic and trousers. Though the sky was a gray overcast, the sunlight dim and diffuse, she wore a hat with a brim. Overall she looked like a petty aristocrat on her way to a masque dressed up as a laborer.

"I can't wait, Master Rymüt," she said, her smile never wavering. "I can't wait."

She smiled. Aikiko was a pretty woman, small and

delicate with features that had a subtle hint of elf to them. She might have been a half-elf, but Marek knew she was in fact entirely human. Her father, himself a senator before his untimely death a decade past at the hands of a bitter political rival, was from Innarlith, but her mother was Kozakuran.

"Do the others know why we're here?' she asked.

Marek shrugged and shook his head. One of the reasons he'd thought of Aikiko was as a way to get rid of her. She'd become a fixture at his regular meetings for the junior senators, and her voice and cloying mannerisms irritated him.

Kurtsson emerged from below, his pale skin and bored expression somehow reassuring. When he spotted Marek and Aikiko he approached with the minimum of greetings. Any further conversation was cut short by the approach of the last two of Marek's guests.

"Ah, Senators Djeserka and Korvan," said Marek, "so good of you to join us."

Willem appeared sheepish, embarrassed, though he wasn't necessarily late. Djeserka's look was as vacant as usual.

"Djeserka," Marek said, "is it true that you once apprenticed to the man who built this vessel?"

Djeserka seemed surprised by the question, but gathered himself quickly and nodded.

Marek smiled, stomped a foot on the polished mahogany deck, and said, "Fine workmanship. Do you know its name?"

"She," Djeserka answered, "is *Heart of the Heavens.*"

Marek laughed and said, "A strange custom that, referring to boats and ships as 'she' and 'her.' I'll never understand why that is." He looked at Kurtsson and winked. "We should start calling wands 'she.' " The Vaasan chuckled. " 'She's as good a wand of fire as any created in the workshops of forgotten Siluvanede.' "

Aikiko laughed along though Marek could tell she

didn't really understand the joke. Willem looked out at the water with an unpleasant grimace. He didn't seem to enjoy being out in the water, or could it be that he didn't enjoy the reason. Marek didn't care either way.

"Well," the Red Wizard said, "on to the matter at hand, yes? We're on our way to the site of the canal that we're certain will one day link the Lake of Steam and the Nagaflow and on and on, talk, talk, talk. It's an undertaking that I argued strenuously against when it was first presented to me. It's something that I felt would have a profoundly negative overall effect on the city-state."

He paused and smiled. Kurtsson at least knew that Marek had no interest in the overall effect that anything but his own trade in magic items might have on the city-state, but the others seemed to accept his words well enough.

Of the four of them, Willem looked the least interested. He appeared unwell, his skin was pale and deep, dark bags hung under his eyes. Somehow he was no less handsome. His eyes darted around, never focusing on anything for long. Marek couldn't tell if he was drunk, frightened, or both.

"This whole thing was the work of one man," Marek continued. "For all intents and purposes he's a renegade from Cormyr who came to Innarlith with selfish designs. He had his way with our fine city-state for longer than he should have been allowed, indulging in his own desires without care for the greater good."

Marek paused again, happy to see that Willem, Aikiko, and Djeserka seemed to be caught up in his disingenuous oratory. Kurtsson was more concerned with an errant cuticle, but then he was the smartest of the four.

"I'm happy to say that as time went on I changed my opinion of the canal itself," Marek said. "I'm now of the mind that it will be a crucial part of the future of trade not only in the fair city-state of Innarlith but throughout the coastal regions of Faerûn. What has changed is who will build it, and how it will be built."

Aikiko smiled and clapped her hands in front of her mouth like a schoolgirl. Kurtsson raised a disapproving eyebrow at the gesture. Djeserka stared at Marek with a blank expression, waiting patiently to hear the rest of it. Willem grew more and more upset with each passing breath.

"You will build it," Marek said. "You four—not one man alone, but a group of political-minded individuals who can bring different skills and various strengths to the endeavor. This is too big, and too important a job to be left to one man and his costly hubris."

He watched Willem squirm at that.

"How it will be done," the Red Wizard went on, "is through the careful and liberal use of the Art. Where once there was a small city of men employed to sweat and dig, there will still be some men, but alongside them will be workers of a less fragile nature. Where previously there was employed a dangerous mix of rare earth elements that but for Tymora's gracious whimsy would surely have killed hundreds of innocent laborers, there will be predictable spells cast by responsible and experienced mages supervised by Kurtsson and supplied by the Thayan Enclave."

Marek paused one last time to take a breath and gauge their reactions. Nothing had changed, Aikiko was still the happiest, Kurtsson the most prepared and stoic, Djeserka the least intelligent, and Willem the most terrified.

"You will finish this," Marek said, "by the command of Ransar Salatis, and with the aid of the Thayan Enclave, for the good of the people of Innarlith. Don't bother to tell me you accept the responsibility. I know you do."

He smiled, fended off Aikiko, who tried to embrace him, and watched Willem run to the rail and vomit over the side.

52

Warm today, isn't it?" Surero said to the girl who ladled soup into his bowl.

She glanced up at him, and he smiled as wide and as brightly as he could. The expression caught her eye, but she didn't return his smile.

"Thank you, Sister," he said.

"I'm not a sister," she replied. She spoke with a thick accent that the alchemist couldn't immediately place. "Not a proper sister, anyway."

"Your accent," he said. "You're not Innarlan."

She shifted her eyes as if ashamed, at least for a fleeting moment, and said, "I am Thayan."

"Have we met before?" he asked, before he'd even thought to say it. She didn't really look familiar, but there was something about her....

She shook her head, her blue eyes narrowed, and she seemed to try to place him but couldn't.

"My name is—" he started, but was interrupted by a nudge to his shoulder.

The man behind him in line, a rough-looking middle-aged sailor with skin like centuries-old leather was impatient for his soup.

The girl handed Surero his bowl and said, "Please accept this with the prayers of the Pastorals that you will find your way under the blessed eyes of the Earth Mother."

He'd heard her say precisely the same words to the men in line in front of him.

Surero took the soup and said, "May I have one more, for my friend?"

"Aye, missy," the old sailor grumbled, "and I'll be needin' a dozen fer me crew."

The old man broke out in gales of toothless laughter, and Surero laughed a little with him. The girl appeared embarrassed.

"I'm sorry," Surero said, "but it really is—"

She silenced him with a wave of her hand and poured another bowl of soup for him. When she handed it to him she smiled.

"Thank you, Si—" he stopped himself—"sorry."

"Halina," she said. "Please accept this for your friend with the prayers of the Pastorals that he will find his way under the blessed eyes of the Earth Mother."

"Halina," he replied, "thank you."

"Aye," the old sailor cut in again, "thanks be to ye an' yers, and now maybe the rest o' us can sup a bit, eh?"

Surero shared another smile with the pretty Thayan girl, took the two bowls of soup, and made way for the rest of the hungry men. As he walked back to the table he tried to imagine that she was watching him go, but in truth he couldn't feel her eyes on him. The exchange had lifted his spirits some, and he was still smiling when he set the soup bowls down on the table.

"Thank you," Devorast said as Surero sat. "I could have gotten my own."

"Think nothing of it," the alchemist replied. "I thought I'd spare you the blessing. I know how you feel about gods, priests, and prayers."

"Why the smile?" asked Devorast.

Surero blinked. Though it would have been a perfectly normal question from just about anyone else in Faerûn, from Devorast it made Surero's head spin.

"Why the smile, he asks me," Surero said. "All right, then, Ivar, it was a girl."

Devorast began to eat his soup, giving no indication that he was listening at all.

"You know, like people, only female?" Surero said.

"I'm familiar with the species," Devorast replied between bites.

Surero wanted to laugh, but it caught in his chest. He took a deep breath as a wave of anguish washed over him. Sweat broke out in strange places on his body. When he looked down at the soup, his stomach quivered, and he couldn't imagine eating it.

"This is it, then," he said.

He paused, hoping Devorast would say something, but he didn't.

Surero looked around himself at row upon row of crude tables that had been cobbled together, perhaps by the sisters themselves, from scraps of salvaged lumber. The tables were scattered with dented tin bowls and spoons of one sort or another. The men who sat at the tables were the same: dented, old, salvaged, scattered.

"The fact that they've beaten me is easy enough to believe," Surero said. "I expected it all along. But they didn't really beat me, though, did they? Who was I? All I did was mix a few common elements together to help you dig faster. It's you they've defeated, and that just ... I really didn't think it was possible."

"All you've talked about for months is how 'they' will eventually win," Devorast reminded him.

"In the name of every god in the steaming Astral, Ivar, I didn't really think it would happen. I mean, honestly. Marek Rymüt is dangerous—but he's dangerous to people like me, not to people like you. And Willem Korvan?"

Devorast shrugged at that.

"I should thank you, still," Surero said. "You've been very kind to me, in your own way. I won't forget that you've supported me all this time since the ... since we came back to the city. I can never forget that. If I'm alive today it's because of you."

"Why did the Thayan have you released?"

Surero almost gasped, he was so startled by the question, but he answered, "I have no idea. And don't think that question hasn't plagued me."

"He would have done it for some reason," Devorast went

on. "You think you've been beaten now, but what of then? He had you in the ransar's dungeon. All he had to do was say one word in the Chamber of Law and Civility, and they would have hanged you."

Surero rubbed his eyes with the palms of his hands, heaved a great sigh, and said, "No, they would have beheaded me."

"In Cormyr, you would have been hanged."

Surero laughed and said, "Six of one . . ."

Devorast went back to his soup, and Surero picked up his own spoon, thinking he might give it a try, but he just didn't want it.

"I can't even feed myself," the alchemist said, his voice quiet, his heart heavy. "I have no means to keep myself alive but the mercy of others."

"Your smokepowder is unrivaled," Devorast said. "I've never heard of anything like it."

"I wonder how far away I will have to go before someone will be willing to risk buying it from me."

"Marek Rymüt's power doesn't extend beyond this city," Devorast told him.

"So at the very least he's driven us out."

"Leave if you want to," Devorast said, then paused to finish his soup. "I still have work to do."

"No, Ivar, it's over. The canal is theirs."

"No," Devorast said, and Surero almost fell out of his chair, driven back by the weight of Devorast's self-confidence. "That canal has never been anyone's but mine, and it always will be."

PART III

53

29 Eleint, the Year of the Banner (1368 DR)
THE NAGAFLOW

Though the water in the wide river was muddy and brown, from a thousand feet in the air, details were revealed. Insithryllax soared on a warm updraft, his huge wings unfurled. The warm air rushed along their surface, and the great wyrm reveled in the sensation of flight. It had been too long since he'd allowed himself to truly fly—too much time spent in the form of a human, contained in their claustrophobic buildings, or in the sharply delineated confines of Marek Rymüt's pocket dimension.

He dipped down to avoid disappearing into a low cloud where he wouldn't be able to see the river below him. He would be easier to see from the ground, but no one was expecting him, so there was a good chance they wouldn't be looking up. Even then, there was little anyone could do from still nearly a thousand feet—not to a creature as powerful as he.

As much as Insithryllax enjoyed the freedom of the air, he longed for the thrill of the hunt as well, and it was that longing that kept his attention on the river. He saw a promising shape, but quickly realized it wasn't slithering the way it should—it was just a log. The outline of a boat revealed itself from under half a dozen feet of water near the eastern bank. It had been there for at least a year.

He beat his mighty wings once as the cloud passed overhead, and he gained altitude. He'd come almost to the northern end of the river where it widened into the long, narrow lake, and so he tipped his right wing down to make a gentle turn in that direction. He kept his eyes on the river, and before he was able to turn all the way back around to the south he saw it.

From over a thousand feet it just looked like a snake. The thing slithered through the water, twisting and dipping in pursuit of something he couldn't see from so high up—a school of fish, most likely.

The dragon moved his wings in subtle ways and turned in a series of ever-narrowing spirals. Flapping his wings again would have helped him align himself in the air better, but it would have made a lot of noise—maybe even enough noise to be heard from the river below. To avoid that he continued to soar, changing the shape of his wings to move in the air.

When he was properly aligned, his lips curled up into a great toothy grin. Eyes still on his prey, he angled his head down at the swimming creature, then tucked his wings to his side. He fell, and fell fast.

The air whistled in his ears. His fifth eyelid slipped over his eyes to protect them, but the transparent membrane still allowed him to see. He arrowed at his target, coming at it from behind. The creature didn't turn to look at him. It continued on its way, not diving deeper, or trying to avoid the enormous black dragon in any way.

Insithryllax opened his mouth and worked up a full volume of acid in the glands on either side of his lower jaw, under his tongue. It felt as though his face was swelling—and it was an unpleasant sensation. It made him want to empty the acid, spray it over his prey in a deadly black rain, but he resisted the temptation. From so high up and into the water, the acid would be far less effective than it would be when he was closer to his prey.

He was nearly there when he caught motion out of the corner of his eye: another naga swimming toward the one he dived at. The second of the two snake-creatures looked up and over at him. They didn't quite make eye contact, but the naga's eyes widened in surprise—it saw him.

It was too late for Insithryllax to change direction, so he smashed into the river water with a spectacular splash. The naga he should have bitten in half the second after he hit the water had been warned by its companion, and it squirmed out of the black dragon's path.

Insithryllax arched his back so that he was almost bent in half, and he swooped through the cold water. He broke the surface with the naga—which one of the two he wasn't sure, but didn't much care—only a few feet to the side of him. He twisted his neck and bit, but the huge snake-creature slithered out of harm's way fast, and the black dragon's jaws came together on nothing but dirty river water.

Though frustrated by the failure to make quick work of the naga, Insithryllax drank in the smell of the river water, which was so like the swamp back in Thay where he'd spent the first ninety-six years of his life—before Marek Rymüt found, charmed, then befriended him.

The dragon's next instinct was to flood the water in front of him with his caustic acid, but he stopped himself. He had to make it look as though—

Pain flared in his side, and the dragon clawed out with both left legs. He twisted his great neck around and saw the shimmering after-effects of some sort of Weave energy sparking along the ebon scales on his left side.

Movement from the corner of his eye, and he whipped his head at an approaching naga. The thing growled out an incantation as it slithered toward him, and against his better judgment Insithryllax let loose his acid breath. A cloud of what looked like black smoke clouded the water and rolled over the naga. Its words sputtered to a halt and turned into a reedy squeal as the caustic liquid, diluted as it may have been, began to eat at its face.

The flesh fell away from the naga's skull, and its eyes dissolved into the water. Its long, snake's body spasmed, cramping and twitching in a ghastly death-dance that kicked up soot and floating debris—including strips of the naga's own burned flesh and bone.

Though the naga was dead, in an effort to salvage it for his own purposes, Insithryllax turned in the water and sliced the top quarter of the serpent-creature clean off with one swordlike claw. The body drifted on the river current, and the dragon started to reach for it, but changed direction again—fast—when the second naga passed close enough to be seen in the murky water.

"What do you want here, wyrm?" the naga asked in Draconic.

Insithryllax found her voice pleasing somehow—maybe it was just because she spoke his native language, and it had been so long. . . .

He turned, floating, still submerged in the cold, murky water. He drew in a great lungful and relished it. It had been a long time, too, since he'd spent any time underwater.

Facing the naga, he bared his great fangs in a sneer. The naga twitched in the water and backed off. She began to rattle off a spell, and Insithryllax snapped at her, his long neck closing the distance between them with a single pulse of coiled muscles. The naga managed to slither backward in the water so that the dragon's jaws came together only inches from her.

She finished her spell, and the water pounded against Insithryllax's face so hard it curled his lips off his teeth. He had to slam all of his eyelids shut, and still it felt as though the water moved so fast it might scoop them from his skull. Water was forced up his nose, and he coughed out a spray of bubbles—but the bubbles instantly popped. The water pushed his head back and to the side, and it took all of the great black wyrm's considerable strength to keep his neck from snapping.

He unfurled his wings in the water and brought them down and forward once, pushing as hard as he could.

Though he didn't quite manage to counteract the fast-moving current, magically generated by the naga, he did lift himself up and out of the focus of its effect. He was at least able to open his eyes.

Insithryllax's head lay just a few inches beneath the surface. He twisted his head around first right then left, and saw the naga floating, her lips moving, her eyes burning at him.

He pulled together the energy for a spell of his own, feeling the power coalesce in his throat.

The naga finished her spell first, and she shot up out of the water like an arrow loosed from a bow. Insithryllax had only to lift his head above the water to trace her path—straight up, trailing water beneath her like a wake in the sky.

She arced over the surface of the river, slithering in the air as though struggling with the sensation of flight. Insithryllax drew in a breath and roared.

The spell he'd cast augmented the already deafening sound into a physical force. The naga cringed at the sound and dipped in the air. Her tail splashed in the water then she curved back up and away, skillfully avoiding the hammerlike effect of his enhanced roar.

Insithryllax's spell effect faded as quickly as it had manifested, and the naga slithered and twisted until she stood almost perpendicular to the surface. She shot straight up again, then turned for the far bank.

Insithryllax beat his wings once, generating great waves that crashed against the riverbank, swamping the thick vegetation.

He watched the naga fade from sight as she flew away by the power of a spell. The naga was smart enough, then, not to face him. But she was a witness. Insithryllax wondered if that would matter—and if it was worth chasing her down.

With his version of a shrug the wyrm sank back into the water and followed his nose to the three-quarters of a

dead naga he'd left floating in the current. When he found
the body he wrapped a huge, handlike claw around it, beat
his wings over and over again until they not only broke
the surface but had shed most of the water that clung to
them. He took to the air, shook himself dry—or dry enough.
His scales still glistened with river water when he turned
south toward Innarlith carrying the dead naga. He cast a
spell that rendered him invisible so the poor little people
of that petty city-state wouldn't come to a complete halt
while they watched a dragon land in their midst.

54

1 Marpenoth, the Year of the Banner (1368 DR)
THIRD QUARTER, INNARLITH

Marek wondered at the feeling of familiarity, being in a
temple where he knew he was unwelcome. Not that he was
particularly unwelcome at the Cascade of Coins. Maybe it
was the location, in the Third Quarter among the tradesmen and workshops. . . .

"It could be that I'm uncomfortable with temples in
general," he said.

Pristoleph nodded, and Marek could detect at least a
trace of sincere camaraderie. It was a strange sensation.

"I never had a religious upbringing," Marek went on,
"and a life of study in the Art has taught me not to rely on
the whims of gods and goddesses, but to force power from
the eternal Weave."

"Careful," Pristoleph said, pausing to sip wine from a
gleaming gold cup, "that kind of talk might attract thun-
derbolts in a place like this."

Marek winked and said, "I've risked worse."

"Why come then?"

"It is the sort of social gathering one needs to attend,"
the Thayan replied, "whether one likes it or not. I'd like to
think I'm not the only one here under false pretenses."

"Waukeen seems the type to forgive and forget," Pristoleph said. "For the right price, anyway."

"You're circling him," the Red Wizard risked.

"Excuse me?"

"Salatis."

Pristoleph smiled, and declined to answer directly.

"So, who will you honor tonight?" Marek asked. "Wenefir?"

"Marthoon is a festival honoring guards," Pristoleph said.

"And isn't he—?"

"Wenefir is my friend," Pristoleph cut in, his gaze cooling rapidly.

"Of course," Marek replied with a curt bow. "I apologize if I suggested otherwise. I meant only that it's well known in the city that he ... looks after you."

"As I look after him."

"Of course," said Marek. "Is it true that they have a dozen of these?"

Pristoleph nodded and said, "But not all in honor of guards. And you?"

"I beg your pardon?"

"Who are you here to honor?" Pristoleph asked. "Surely not Salatis."

"I suppose one could say that I'm here to honor guards in general."

"A fine answer," said Pristoleph. "I wonder why you feel I'm circling him."

"The priests here are calling themselves 'Waukeenar,'" Marek said. "I could have sworn they were 'Waukeenites.'"

"No, I think it's always been 'Waukeenar,' but I could be wrong," said Pristoleph. "Apparently I've been too busy circling the ransar to study church protocol."

Marek smiled and said, "We're all very busy, aren't we?"

"It's always good to have one's day full."

"I wonder how much more full a ransar's day is," Marek said. "Of course, should he find he was able to trust his friends, a certain amount of pressure could be set aside."

"Trust?" Pristoleph asked. "Really?"

"I know it can be difficult to imagine, but let's say that if he should decide that a new aqueduct is required, say," Marek explained, "perhaps the ransar would trust his closest allies to make sure that the right people are allowed to supervise its construction."

"Speaking of construction," Pristoleph replied, his eyes roaming the space above them, "what do you call this?"

Marek followed the senator's eyes up the length of a tall marble column. The column, and seven more just like it, supported a triangular roof that protected the wide front doors of the temple. The festivities had spilled out into the street in front of the building, and the doors had been left open and unguarded—the guards were being honored within, showered with gold and silver coins, with like sums being thrown into a deep well that served as the centerpiece of the temple proper.

"That would be a portico," Marek replied.

"Portico..." Pristoleph repeated, as though he'd never heard the word. "I suppose it's important to have an entrance that conveys a sense of power."

"Indeed."

"Why Salatis?" the senator asked.

Marek blinked at the question, and took a step backward. Pristoleph raised an eyebrow and stared at him, waiting for an answer. In order to simply have something to do while he thought, Marek laughed. Pristoleph smiled, but didn't join him in laughing.

"It's terrible in there, isn't it?" Marek asked. "All the colors ... it confuses the eye."

Pristoleph glanced through the open doors at the garish decorations, rugs with intricate designs, everything gilded and overly decorated.

"I keep trying to focus on one thing," the Thayan said.

"I think if I can pay most of my attention to one thing among many, I might be able to put up with the confusion around me."

"But when there is so much detail," Pristoleph said, "so many colors, and all this embarrassment of riches, it can be difficult to choose one thing worthy of attention. Certainly it's not something that should be selected at random."

"I will admit, though with some reluctance," said Marek, "that I too often act with some impetuosity. But then one always hopes he'll think through every decision with care, but time and circumstances don't always allow that luxury."

Pristoleph smiled and tipped his chin down in the tiniest bow. His bright red hair moved in a way that seemed unnatural, as though it had a life of its own. Marek couldn't look away from it.

"Perhaps," the Red Wizard said, his voice low and coming from deep in his throat, "a little impetuosity might do me well tonight."

"Risking a thunderbolt," Pristoleph said, looking Marek in the eye and slowly, infinitesimally shaking his head, "I wonder what you think of the persistent rumor that the Merchant's Friend has actually fled her worshipers."

"I have heard that," Marek replied, forcing his face to mask his disappointment.

"That she was killed, or fled Toril's sphere, a decade ago?"

"During the Time of Troubles," Marek said. "But then, here we are."

"Could the Waukeenar simply be putting up a brave front?" asked Pristoleph.

"Everything is possible," Marek said, "but to answer that with any accuracy one would have to ask the very people who would be most intent on keeping the secret."

"And I suppose it doesn't matter anyway."

A bell rang, and one of the younger Waukeenar called

the faithful—and those just visiting—into the temple's central hall for some formal rite or another. Pristoleph gave Marek a smile and started to move off into the crowd. The Thayan stopped him with a hand on his shoulder. The genasi glanced down at the touch with a face so stern it seemed carved from stone. Marek took his hand away and reached into a pocket. Pristoleph watched his every move, and Marek had no doubt that the senator was ready for anything—including an assassination attempt.

Marek withdrew a polished silver box from his pocket, two inches by six inches, and hinged on one side. He offered the box to Pristoleph with a shallow bow.

"What is this?" the senator asked.

"A gift," Marek replied. "Consider it a token of good will from the Thayan Enclave."

Pristoleph took the silver box and looked Marek in the eye. He'd been taken off guard, and Marek made a note of that.

"Please don't try them on," Marek said when Pristoleph opened the box to reveal a pair of pince-nez spectacles with lenses of opaque magenta, "until you are in a private place."

Pristoleph closed the box and smiled. Marek could see that he had intrigued the genasi, and worried him at least a little.

55

2 Marpenoth, the Year of the Banner (1368 DR)
THE GOLDEN ROAD

Insithryllax, in the form of a human, stepped out into the middle of the road and crossed his arms in front of his chest. The rider pulled his horse to a stop and regarded the dark man with a soldier's critical, suspicious eye, but didn't draw his sword.

"Let me guess," the rider said. " 'Stand and deliver,' is it?"

Insithryllax laughed, hiding an incantation in the stuttering chuckle. The power gathered inside him, tingling first the tips of his fingers, then making his forearms almost sizzle. The sensation made him stop laughing and just smile.

"I am a rider in the service of the League of Lightning Mercenary Company and House Wianar of Arrabar," the soldier said. "Think twice, bandit."

"Ah," the disguised dragon replied, "good. You're the ambassador's escort."

The soldier's eyes narrowed, and his cheeks flushed. Insithryllax let the gathered Weave energy loose, thrusting his arm up and out to point at the rider. The soldier got a hand almost to his sword before the blinding blue-white flash of lightning arced from the dragon's outstretched palm and slammed into him.

The soldier jerked forward, not back, in his saddle. The horse screamed, but the man made no sound at all. It was if he screamed in reverse. He lungs seized, drew in air, but kept it lodged in his collapsed chest. The skin stretched tight over cramping muscles, and his eyes popped in his skull.

The warhorse bucked, trying to dislodge its rider. The man's armor had begun to glow red from heat, and Insithryllax could smell the stench of smoldering horseflesh. The lightning bolt disappeared, and finally the horse was able to dislodge its rider. Insithryllax fought down the urge to transform into his true form and make a meal of the animal, and he let it run westward up the Golden Road in a blind, agonized panic.

The soldier lay motionless in the middle of the road, slowly broiling inside his own armor.

A bloodcurdling scream ripped through the air from the east, and Insithryllax broke into a run, casting a spell as he went.

"Remember what I told you, children," he whispered into the wind, "no acid, and no survivors."

He ran half a mile down the middle of the road, uphill most of the way, and when he came to the hillcrest, he skidded to a stop, sending a little splash of standing water into the still, cool air. Rain began to patter on the muddy road around him. A black shape passed over his head with a flutter of leathery wings, but Insithryllax didn't flinch. He followed the black firedrake's swooping dive. It went for another of the riders, a man so like the one he'd just killed they could have been twins. The rider got his sword out of his scabbard before the firedrake tore his face off as it passed. He screamed and fell from his mount. Another black firedrake perched on him and started eating him while he died.

His horse reared and shrieked, confused, until it was taken down by a firedrake's crocodilian fangs. As it went down, it kicked the side of the carriage, popping it up on two wheels. The firedrake, its mouth still on the horse's neck, pushed out with one wing and tipped the carriage the rest of the way over. The driver ran, heading perpendicular to the road and downhill.

Insithryllax cast a spell as he walked toward the overturned carriage. When he was done, he sent five slivers of green light speeding after the fleeing driver. The missiles twisted around each other in the air, dipping up and down as though avoiding a series of invisible obstacles in the air, but they hit the running man in a cluster in the middle of his back, and dropped him. He slid in the mud for half a dozen yards on his face, his arms limp at his sides.

The rear outrider thundered up, a lance held firmly at his side. He growled out a long, guttural battle cry that made Insithryllax laugh, but then the dragon's attention was drawn to the carriage. A hand appeared in the open window, smeared with blood.

A black firedrake roared, and Insithryllax broke into a run, casting another spell as he did so. A crackling sizzle cut the air. The approaching rider let loose a shriek of agony, and before Insithryllax even turned to look he knew the source of the sizzle. The smell hit him next, and he redirected the spell away from the carriage and to his errant child.

The gust of wind knocked the black firedrake on its face and caught in its wing. The veiny black membrane ballooned up, and the force of the magic-driven air twisted its wing back and up so hard the bones snapped like twigs.

The firedrake shrieked in concert with the melting rider. The other firedrake turned on Insithryllax with an angry hiss, but backed off when the dragon merely tipped his head to one side.

He stood next to the carriage and muttered another spell, allowing himself the luxury of using the human gestures. The exercise gave the man time to crawl through the window and on to the side—which had become the top—of the carriage.

Insithryllax reached up, grabbed the man around the wrist, and pulled. With a yelp the man tumbled to the mud at the dragon's feet.

"What—?" the man demanded, struggling to get to his feet. "What in the name of Toril do you think you're doing?" He got to his feet, but staggered. Stepping back from Insithryllax, he steadied himself with a hand on the carriage. "Have you any idea who I am?"

"Ambassador Fael Verhenden of Arrabar," Insithryllax said.

The ambassador looked up at him, blood trickling down the side of his face from a cut in his scalp. He studied the dragon's dark face as though trying to place him. A black firedrake reared up behind Insithryllax and the man screamed and fell back against the underside of the carriage. He put his arms up to fend the creature off.

Insithryllax knelt down in front of the man and grabbed him by his bloody jacket. Drawing him close, he looked the terrified ambassador in the eye. The spell he'd cast worked on the man's mind, opening it like a sack into which the dragon could toss whatever he pleased. He could see the spell working in the way Verhenden's pupils dilated.

"It was nagas," Insithryllax said. "You were beset by nagas. Your men managed to kill one, but they overwhelmed you with spells."

The ambassador quivered, whimpered a little, and nodded.

Insithryllax drew the dagger out of the sheath at the ambassador's belt. He held it up close to the man's bulging, accepting eyes.

"You fought as best you could, but were armed only with this dagger. One of the nagas used some kind of magic to take it from you. It danced in the air of its own accord"—Insithryllax bounced the dagger up and down in front of his face—"then it slit your throat."

With a flick of his wrist Insithryllax dragged the sharp edge along the side of the ambassador's throat, pressing it in deep. Blood poured out, the Arrabarran gasped for air and managed only to begin drowning in his own blood. Insithryllax watched him die then stood up, turned, and went to stand over the firedrake that still writhed in the mud with its wind-shattered wing twitching at its side.

"You," he said. "I told you no acid."

The wounded firedrake cringed beneath him as Insithryllax shed his human guise. His body trembled then convulsed, and as the black firedrakes watched, he grew to many times his human size. Finally he stood in his true form, his long, lithe body protected by scales the color of the sky at middark. Horns curved forward from each side of his head, and his eyes blazed with crimson light.

The wounded firedrake looked away.

Insithryllax opened his enormous jaws over the crippled monster and bit it in half. With only a few bone-splintering chews, he swallowed the first bite, then took the rest. That done, he ate the acid-burned rider, armor and all.

When he'd swallowed the last bite, made bitter by the black firedrake's acid, he turned on the other firedrake.

The creature shrank back from him a little but stood his ground before his gigantic father.

"You," the great wyrm rumbled, "get the dead naga and leave it here."

The black firedrake bowed and went off in the direction of the place where Insithryllax had hidden the water naga's remains. He looked around at the carnage and checked for any other signs of acid, or any evidence that the black firedrakes might have been involved, but saw none. Even if they brought the ambassador back from the dead, or questioned his corpse, he would insist that it was water nagas who'd killed them all.

56

23 Marpenoth, the Year of the Banner (1368 DR)
THIRD QUARTER, INNARLITH

Pristoleph held a little fire in his hand. Yellow-orange tongues of flame lapped at the chip of black wood at its heart. The heat felt good against his palm. It would have scorched a human, blistered him, but Pristoleph wasn't quite human. He stared at the fire's dance, kept small and contained by the power of his will. The movement mesmerized him, and he let it make his mind go blank.

Outside the window of the tall turret in Pristal Towers—his overly large manor home—the city of Innarlith slept. When he started to think again, he thought of the city. It had started out as his enemy. The city tried to kill him when he was a baby, and over and over again through his childhood, but he'd never let it. He beat it, and by the time he'd seen his thirtieth year, the city was his to do with as he pleased. He'd bought a seat on the senate, but kept largely to his own ways and his own circles. He'd never sought, or had been particularly interested in, the Palace of Many Spires, preferring to act at least a bit from the shadows, but . . .

"But things change," he whispered to himself.

He closed his palm around the fire. The coal sizzled and popped in his hand. The feeling made him smile.

When it settled, he tossed it into the brazier with the other coals and sighed. Tired, he rubbed his eyes and thought of going to bed. He looked at it, wide and comfortable, and richly appointed in silk, but it had no appeal.

Pristoleph considered going for a walk. It had been a long time since he'd done that. For the longest time he would wander the streets of the Fourth Quarter, visiting the avenues as a senator that he used to haunt as a street urchin. He would mark the passage of time by the houses that had collapsed or burned, the shanties that had been erected, the dead dogs in the midden. But he hadn't done that in a long time.

He'd stopped going to the docks as well. Since he'd started to "employ" undead dockworkers supplied by Marek Rymüt, he had to pretend, like the rest of the senate, that he was opposed to the very idea. He had to blame it on the guild he'd helped create. He had to make sure that the workers who'd played so easily into his hands and Marek's were blamed for their own obsolescence.

He didn't go to the docks because of the smell, and because it made him feel tired to be there. He couldn't tell anyone, even Wenefir, how tired he felt. Most of he time, he couldn't even tell himself. Thinking about it just made him more tired.

His eyes settled on the little silver box.

He took a deep breath and blinked. He'd forgotten about it, and there it sat on the side table where he'd left it, next to an oil lamp he hardly ever lit. Pristoleph reached out and picked it up, opened it, and stared down at its contents.

The spectacles didn't make any sense. The lenses were opaque. He knew they were enchanted in some way—considering the source that was a certainty—but the Thayan had never said how. For all Pristoleph knew, they'd blind him the second he put them on his nose. They'd either blind him, or show him something.

He thought of a dozen things that Marek Rymüt might want him to see, and that was in the first few heartbeats, before he let his imagination wander. None of the possibilities particularly interested him, but still he lifted the pince-nez from the box, and turned them over in his hand.

He sighed again and stood. Still holding the spectacles, he crossed to his writing desk, pulled a sheet of parchment from a drawer, and wrote a brief note:

"Wenefir, if the pince-nez have harmed me in any way, kill Marek Rymüt."

He signed it with a certain sigil that would prove to Wenefir that he'd written it himself. He replaced the quill and sat back in his chair.

With a little shrug, he placed the pince-nez on his nose with his eyes closed. There was no sensation of anything out of the ordinary at first, and certainly no pain. After a moment he finally opened his eyes.

When it appeared as though he'd been transported to a strange room he closed his eyes and took the pince-nez off his nose. He blinked his eyes open and was happy, though not entirely surprised to be in his own bedchamber.

Pristoleph looked down at the pince-nez again and thought about what he'd seen. It was another bedchamber, someone else's. He'd never been there before, but when he had the spectacles on, it was as though he was actually there.

He put them on again, sat back, and studied his new surroundings in more detail. He seemed to be sitting on the edge of a bed. His head turned, but he didn't feel the muscles in his neck working, and he hadn't wanted to turn his head. A man or a woman—he couldn't tell under the down and linen bedclothes—slept in the bed. He could see the rise and fall of the figure's breathing.

His head turned again and his vision scanned over the room. It was a cramped space, at least compared to what Pristoleph had grown accustomed to, and decorated in what he found to be an overly garish fashion.

He reached out with his right hand, but couldn't see it, even when he was sure he held his palm a scant few inches from the tip of his nose.

A man stood in the open door of the bedchamber, and Pristoleph had the uneasy sensation that they had made eye contact. Something was wrong with the pince-nez, though. The man appeared transparent, as though made of deep violet light. He didn't seem to entirely belong in the scene, and Pristoleph realized maybe he wasn't in the scene at all, but—

He flipped the pince-nez off his nose, stood, and whipped his head from side to side. He'd thought perhaps the man was in fact standing in his own bedchamber, and Pristoleph saw him filtered through the magenta lenses.

But Pristoleph was alone.

"Whose eyes am I seeing through, Marek," Pristoleph whispered, "and why?"

Seeking the answer in the item itself, he put the glasses back on. His host had moved from the bed to sit in front of the dressing table. He saw a woman's delicate hand where he thought his own should be. She took a silver brush from the dressing table and looked up into a mirror.

Pristoleph gasped.

She was beautiful.

As she brushed her long, straight black hair, Pristoleph found that he could hardly breathe. He watched her, fixated by her deep blue eyes that were so sad and so troubled and so full of promise.

No woman had ever had that effect on him. No woman had ever stopped him cold.

A tear fell from one eye and she let it trickle down her smooth, flawless cheek without wiping it away. He felt uncomfortable watching her cry, but it was as though he'd fallen under the influence of some spell—and perhaps he had done just that, but he didn't care. He not only couldn't, but didn't want to look away.

Still looking deeply into her own eyes, she picked up a little cuticle knife from the dressing table and ran the sharp blade along the inside of her arm. He couldn't feel any pain, but he could see her wince in the mirror. The little line of red sat among scars and still-healing cuts on the same patch of skin.

When she looked at herself in the mirror again, she was smiling.

Pristoleph grabbed the pince-nez off his face and threw them to the floor. He stood, nearly falling back over his chair, but stayed on his feet.

The door opened, and the guard posted outside stuck his head in, looking around.

"Senator?" he said, seeing nothing amiss.

"It's all right," Pristoleph told him, and waved him away.

The guard nodded and closed the door.

With a deep breath to calm himself, Pristoleph knelt and picked up the spectacles. One of the lenses had broken into tiny shards that were no longer magenta, but ordinary clear, colorless glass.

"Why?" he whispered, though the man he was asking—Marek Rymüt—couldn't hear him. "Why show me her?"

Hours later, Pristoleph finally collapsed into bed without an answer to that question.

57

24 Marpenoth, the Year of the Banner (1368 DR)
SECOND QUARTER, INNARLITH

The meat had not been cooked at all. Willem stared down at it, trying to find it in himself to be disgusted, but he couldn't quite muster it. He kept his hands in his lap.

"I told you, no," Phyrea whispered.

She sat at the other end of the dining table, and had no place setting in front of her, just a crystal tallglass of red wine that she wasn't drinking. She looked off through the arched doorway to the sitting room, staring at empty space as though someone stood next to the *sava* board between the two wingback leather chairs.

"I beg your pardon?" he asked. His voice, pitched no louder than normal, seemed to boom in the still, heavy air of his dining room.

Phyrea shook her head, still looking at nothing, then turned toward him. Her eyes blazed with what Willem could have sworn was fear—but what could she possibly have to be afraid of?

"Were you speaking to me?" he asked.

In an instant the fear turned to contempt, and she said, "No. You aren't hungry?"

He glanced down at the raw meat and said, "No, thank you. Are you sure you don't want me to recall the cook, or perhaps you would feel more comfortable hiring someone else—someone of your choosing?"

"I told you I don't like people buzzing around me," she said.

"Then tell her to stay in the kitchen."

"I might want to go into the kitchen," Phyrea replied. She put a hand on her wine glass but didn't pick it up. "I suppose you miss the maids and cooks and little girls you can take to your bed whenever you choose, but things have changed, and it's time for you to grow up."

Willem blinked, both at the accusation, and at the sudden turns her temper took.

"I never . . ." he started, but trailed off when he realized she wasn't listening, and wouldn't care either way. "It's good to be home," he lied instead.

They'd been married for twenty months, and in that time she'd fired his household staff and scared his mother all the way back to Cormyr. He'd spent fewer than one night in twenty at home, having been overwhelmed by the process of restarting Devorast's project with the aid of two people even less competent than himself. In most ways that mattered he and Phyrea were still strangers, but Willem remained unable to look at her without reeling at her perfect beauty. Even as tired as she looked, even when she twitched and glanced away at nothing, startled by silence, Phyrea was the most beautiful woman in the world.

"The fresh air agrees with you," she said. "You're a very handsome man."

He nodded in thanks, but couldn't keep the suspicion from his eyes.

"Eat your dinner, now, before it gets cold," she said. Phyrea, leering, glanced at the bloody red meat on the plate in front of him. "Be a good boy now. If you eat it, I'll let you touch me. I'll take you to bed, but you have to eat it all."

He looked down at the raw meat again, and swallowed.

She shushed him, though he hadn't said anything, then she whispered, "He will."

"Will I?" Willem asked her.

"I wasn't talking to you."

He picked up his knife and fork, and she laughed at him.

"Go on, now," she said. "I'll make it worth your while."

He cut a little square off the side of the meat and held it up. Blood the consistency of water ran down the tines of his fork and dripped off the meat onto his plate.

She looked at him with wide eyes, and her open mouth was turned up in a trace of a smile.

"I will have to leave again tomorrow," he said.

She shrugged.

"I'm not entirely certain when I'll be back."

Phyrea looked to her left and nodded to no one.

Willem put the raw meat in his mouth and started to chew. It wasn't bad.

58

Willem had no idea what the man's name was, but he assumed he was some kind of foreman. Anyway, he was the one who talked to Willem most often, told him what was happening and asked for things. He was a short man, barely taller than a dwarf, but stocky and solid. He had a face like worn leather and dull eyes the color of mud. His greasy hair was always ragged and unkept, even falling out in patches. His clothes were spattered with holes and crusted with dried mud. He smelled of sweat and freshly-turned soil.

"Please come quickly, Senator," the little man said, his voice shaking in time with his panic-stricken eyes. "Please . . . there's been a terrible accident."

Willem sighed. He'd lost track of the number of terrible accidents that had befallen the workers since he'd taken over the construction of the canal. Men died, were injured, fell to disease, and simply walked home in such numbers it frankly amazed him that there was anyone left to dig at all.

"Senator?" the little man prompted.

Willem scowled at him, and he backed away a few steps, but still seemed determined to have Willem follow him. Willem stood and the man started off, apparently in the direction of the accident. Willem stretched and looked up into the overcast sky.

"At least it isn't raining," he whispered to himself, then yawned.

"Senator?" the little man asked.

"Oh, for the sake of every god in the Outer Planes, man," Willem huffed, "what do you expect me to do?"

"Senator?" the man asked with a look of disappointed confusion.

"Honestly...." Willem went on. "What is it this time? Another trench collapse? Someone hacked his hand off with an axe? Someone blinded by a flying splinter? Do I look like a priest to you?"

"But, Senator, I thought ..."

Willem waited for him to go on, but he didn't. Perhaps the grubby little man had finally realized that he hadn't thought anything at all. He looked down at the ground at his feet, and Willem almost felt sorry for him.

Willem stepped out of the protection of his tent, and his foot sank half an inch in the mud. He sighed and looked down at his expensive boots, which had long since been ruined.

"Damn this mud to the Barrens of Doom and Despair," he muttered. "Aren't you sick of the constant damp?"

The foreman shook his head, confused, simple.

"Did someone die?" asked Willem. "Is that what you're all in a fluster over?"

The foreman nodded.

Willem sighed and said, "Are they buried?"

The foreman nodded again.

"Loose soil, or mud?"

"Mud," the man replied.

"Mud ..." Willem sighed. "Don't you hate mud? I hate mud. I know people use that word too lightly, too often, 'hate.' But I hate this mud. I'm tired of being wet and cold. I'm tired of living outside like an orc. This is a life for savages, sitting in the rain, living in your own bathroom, for Waukeen's sake."

"Yes, Senator," the foreman agreed—or pretended to.

Willem saw a trace of annoyance pass through the man's features, and he fought down the impulse to draw his sword and gut the man where he stood. There were too many others around to see it, and even Salatis might consider that overstepping his bounds.

"What caused these men to be buried in the mud?" Willem asked. "Was it a naga?"

"A naga?"

"Yes, fool, a naga. You know, the giant snake things with human faces that eat slow-witted fools like you just to spite me. Was it a thrice-bedamned naga, or not?"

"No, Senator," the foreman replied. "I mean ... no one saw any naga."

"Just because you couldn't see it, doesn't mean it wasn't there," Willem said. "They've turned on us, you know."

"They have killed men to the north, I hear," the foreman said. "But that's miles away, Senator."

"They traveled for miles inland to kill the ambassador from Arrabar," Willem said. He stepped back into his tent and did his best to wipe the mud from his boots, but all he did was make the dryer, brown grass inside a little bit muddier. "So what happened, then?"

"It was just a mudslide, Senator. On account of all the rain we've been having."

"Really?" Willem asked, a growl to his voice that might have been due more to the fact that the cold and damp had settled in his chest than out of anger. "Could it really have been on account of all the rain we've been having?"

The foreman, sheepish, looked down at his feet.

"How many?" Willem asked.

"Senator?"

"How many men, damn it?"

The foreman nodded and said, "Fourteen souls. Tragic, ain't it, Senator? A human tragedy, this."

Willem rolled his eyes and sighed.

"Senator?"

"Are you sure they're dead?" Willem asked.

"Well, they've been under there a long time."

"Have you started digging them out?"

"I think some of the men went at it while I ran for you, yes."

Willem rubbed his eyes and blinked, looking past the grubby foreman, and down a steep hill to the edge of the enormous trench. Most of the length of it that he could see was deserted, not near finished. Men walked here and there, sometimes alongside ox carts with various tools and supplies. He couldn't draw a sense of urgency out of the scene no matter how hard he tried.

"There's so slim a chance that I will live to see this done, it's impossible to measure with the mathematics known to me," Willem said.

"I wouldn't know anything about that," the foreman replied, even though Willem hadn't asked him anything.

"Do you like it here?" Willem asked the man.

"Yes, Senator," the foreman lied.

"Are we paying you?"

"Yes, Senator."

"What for?"

"Senator?"

Willem looked the man in the eye and said, "What are we paying you for?"

"To help build the Grand Canal," he said, and Willem could hear the capital letters in the little man's prideful voice.

"What do you mean 'Grand Canal'?" Willem asked.

"That's what it's called, isn't it?"

"No."

The foreman looked surprised, and remained confused. He blinked at Willem then glanced off in the direction of the day's terribly tragic mudslide.

"No one has named it," Willem said. "Stop calling it that. Did Devorast call it that?"

"I never met that man, Senator," the foreman said. "I started after he was ... after I took over for that helf-elf chap."

"So there are now fourteen fewer men working," Willem said.

"Senator?"

"Get back to it, then," Willem said.

"Yes, Senator," the foreman replied, disappointment plain on his leathery face. "We'll have the bodies dug out by nightfall."

"No, you won't," Willem said, and the foreman had the nerve to looked surprised, even offended. "I want you to continue with your day's tasks. Light torches to work past nightfall if you have to, but finish. Then you can dig up your dead if you like."

The man stared at him, speechless.

"Wrap the bodies, but don't send them back to Innarlith," Willem said.

He'd nearly forgotten something Marek Rymüt had told him some tendays before.

"But their families—" the foreman started.

"Leave that to me," Willem said. His skin crawled, and he had to look away from the foreman's confused, puppy-dog eyes. "On your way, now."

59

6 Uktar, the Year of the Banner (1368 DR)
THE CANAL SITE

Willem looked at the line of canvas bundles and frowned. Stained with dried mud, the dull, bone-colored material bore the muddy brown handprints of the men who'd wrapped them and carried them to the open stretch of ground near the shore of the Lake of Steam. The sulfur smell of the water drove away the ripe stench of the dead bodies in the canvas bundles.

The short, squat foreman stared at Willem as though awaiting orders. When Willem shooed him away with a wave, the man started to turn but hesitated.

"Oh, what is it?" Willem demanded of him, all patience fled.

"Shouldn't I have a few men ready, Senator?"

"Whatever for?"

"To load the bodies on the boat?"

"What boat?" Willem asked.

The foreman inhaled, was about to answer, then let the

breath out in a gasp. He stared, wide-eyed, at something over Willem's shoulder.

Willem put a hand to his sword hilt and turned as a strange sound—sort of a mixture of hissing and tinkling—flittered from the air behind him.

Marek Rymüt stood in the muddy grass and blinked up at the sky. The sparse, scudding rain dampened his bald head and made him grimace. His strange tattoos glimmered under a sheen of rain water.

"Master Rymüt," Willem said, taking his hand away from his sword.

Marek tried to shake the wet from his voluminous robes and nodded in response. He took a couple of steps forward and finally glanced over the scene.

"Send your man away," the Thayan commanded.

Willem turned to the foreman, but the grubby little man was already walking away at a brisk pace, his short legs bouncing him down a little hill. Willem smiled when the foreman lost his footing and slid the rest of the way down the hill on his backside. When he stood, covered in wet mud, he broke into a run and disappeared among a gang of workers loading lumber onto ox carts.

"Difficult finding good people these days, isn't it?" Marek said.

Willem turned and traded smiles with the Thayan, who gestured to the canvas bundles.

The two of them stepped closer to the line of corpses, and Marek said, "I do wish you'd put them in a tent or something. This incessant rain goes straight to my joints."

"I apologize, Master Rymüt," Willem replied, "but we used all the canvas we had left to wrap the bodies."

Marek sighed and said, "Well, that was unnecessary, wasn't it?"

Willem looked over at the wizard, watched him wiggle his fingers as if stretching them, warming them up for—what? He'd seen musicians do the same thing.

"The men were more comfortable wrapping them in

something," Willem said, leaving out the fact that he'd ordered it himself. He was uncomfortable with dead bodies just laying out in the open. He wondered why that could be. What did he care, really? "I can have them—"

"No, no," Marek interrupted. "No, it's better we do it ourselves. If it's true the men felt uncomfortable with the sight of their dead comrades, I suppose they'll be even less comfortable with what's about to become of them. If we compel them to help, you could have a mutiny on your hands before they have a chance to think twice."

"Mutiny . . . ?"

The Red Wizard laughed and said, "Really, Willem, my dear, you didn't expect your rabble to *like* that their dead comrades are being put back to work alongside them."

Willem took a deep breath and said, "I hadn't thought about it."

Truth be told, Willem didn't actually care. When he thought about it, he couldn't help feeling as though there was a time, long ago, when the thought of employing zombies, of having a hand in the desecration of the dead, when any sort of a hint of the use of slave labor, would have turned his stomach. Where he'd come from, in Cormyr, it simply wasn't done.

"I'm not in Cormyr anymore," he said aloud, though he hadn't intended to speak.

Marek laughed again and said, "You've been out in the cold and wet too long, my boy. Or is it your young bride who's causing you to talk to yourself? They say that after a time, married couples begin to resemble one another."

Willem shook his head.

"Pardon?" the wizard prompted, and Willem winced at his irritated mien.

"Shall we unwrap them?" Willem asked.

Not waiting for an answer, he squatted next to one of the bundles, drew his dagger, and cut the twine that held it closed. Marek stood watching him as he pulled back the heavy, wet material to reveal the still features of a young man barely out of his teens. Though the men had washed his face, mud still clogged his nostrils and crusted in his eyelashes, holding his eyelids closed.

"Sad, isn't it?" Marek said.

Willem didn't look up at him. He could hear the sarcasm in the Red Wizard's voice. Willem thought that if he turned and saw that Marek was smiling, he might become offended, and he just didn't have the energy for that.

"You look tired," the wizard said. "You should get back to the city more often."

"I'm needed here," Willem lied.

"Of course you are," Marek said, playing along.

Willem went to the next bundle, and the next, as Marek Rymüt stood watching in silence. By the time he had removed the canvas from all fourteen of the men, he was soaking wet and covered with mud. The smell of the dead bodies mixed with the lake's stench made him gag several times while he worked. After the first one, he stopped looking at their faces.

When he was done, he stood and brushed the mud off his hands as best he could.

"Come here, Willem," Marek said.

Willem walked over to the Thayan, who stood with his hand in a velvet sack he must have produced from a pocket while the senator was busy unwrapping the corpses.

"Take these," the Red Wizard said, pulling from the sack a handful of little black stones, "and place two in each of their mouths." He nodded at the bodies, and Willem took the stones. He shifted them in his cupped hands. "Onyx," Marek explained. "Two in each mouth."

Willem turned to go, but Marek reached out and grabbed him by the forearm. Willem flinched at his cold, clammy touch, and almost dropped the gemstones. Before he could speak, Marek's other hand came up, and Willem didn't quite have time to register the dagger before the blade bit—not too deeply—into the flesh of both his wrists.

Willem hissed and again almost dropped the gems, but

Marek let fall the dagger and held both his hands over Willem's, squeezing them together. Pain made Willem's breath catch in his throat, and he could feel the hot blood mixing with the scudding precipitation, which was cold enough to help soothe the pain. Marek stared down at his hands and began to babble in a language that made Willem's ears ring. Willem started to shake, and though he could breathe again, he couldn't speak.

Marek let go of him all at once, and Willem stepped away.

"Don't drop them, my boy," Marek said.

"What on—what are you . . . ?" Willem blustered.

Marek glanced down, and Willem followed his gaze to his own hands. The cuts on his wrists had already healed, the pain had been replaced with an uneasy nettling, and the black gemstones were traced with delicate slivers of deep crimson—blood red.

"My apologies, Willem," Marek said. "It works better somehow if you don't know it's coming."

Willem got the distinct impression that was a lie. "*What* works better?"

"Place the stones in the corpses' mouths now," said the Thayan. "Two in each mouth."

Willem hesitated.

"I've infused them with your blood," Marek explained, though it appeared to tire him to have to do so. "When they animate, they will look to you for instruction, not me."

A chill ran through Willem's body, and his knees went weak. He blinked, but gathered himself quickly. He wasn't sure he—

"Go on, now," Marek said, irritated. "I'd like to return to the warmth of my hearthfire before dark, if you don't mind."

Willem turned and squatted next to the first corpse. Though it wasn't easy, he shifted all of the little stones to his left hand. After a few tries he finally figured out how to hold the stones with one hand and force the corpse's mouth open with his right. He dropped two of the blood-infused onyx chips into the dead man's mouth and pushed it closed.

"Good boy," Marek said.

Willem grimaced at that, but moved on to the next body, and so on down the line of dead workers. When he was finished he stood, and almost fell to the ground when his head spun. His head felt heavy and his eyesight dimmed. Blinking, breathing deeply, he began to feel normal again after a moment.

"You should eat better," the Thayan told him with a wink.

Willem shook his head and stepped away from the bodies.

Marek began chanting meaningless words and waving his hands in front of him. His face was set and determined, cold and inhuman, and though he might have looked or sounded ridiculous if it was indeed meaningless gibberish and waving about, Willem knew there was nothing random about it. Willem's hair began to stand on end, and he itched his scalp. He shivered and had to clench his teeth together to keep them from chattering.

One of the bodies moved.

Willem stepped back, almost skipped in the mud, and drew in a sharp breath.

A second corpse twitched, and the arm of a third reached up to the sky then fell back down. Within a few heartbeats all fourteen of them jerked where they lay on their backs.

Bile rose in Willem's throat, and he choked it back.

One of the dead men rolled over onto all fours. Mud dripped from its nose, and it opened its mouth wide, its dead lips falling away from teeth caked with dried mud. The two stones fell out of its mouth and splashed onto the wet ground. The thing, its mouth still open, staggered to its feet. Still clothed in its simple homespun peasant's blouse and breeches, at first it looked almost normal. But the pale, gray cast of its skin and its yellowed, jaundiced eyes betrayed it. Its arms hung limp at its side, and it staggered. When its boot—and it only wore one, the other was likely still buried in the mud where it had died—stepped on the onyx chips, Willem heard a quiet crumbling sound. When it moved its foot again the two gemstones were gone, replaced with a black powder.

Two or three at a time, the other corpses awakened, rolled over, and expelled the gemstones. They stood, shifting on uncertain feet, staring blankly in whatever direction they happened to be facing when they first stood.

Marek approached them, and the creatures didn't seem to notice him at all. He bent and retrieved one of the stones. He came to Willem and held it out to him. Willem took the gemstone in his hand before he realized it had just been spat out by a zombie. The thought made him flinch and squeeze the stone, which crumbled to black dust in his hand.

"It's like a piece of charcoal," Willem said, brushing the dust from his hand.

"More than twenty-five gold pieces each," Marek said. "Worry not, though, I'll bill the ransar."

Willem looked at the black dust that still coated his fingertips. There was no trace of red. His stomach turned at the thought that his blood had somehow been ingested by those hideous abominations.

"They're all yours, my boy," the Thayan told him. "Keep your commands simple. They're not quite as quick-witted as they were in life, though by the look of these peasants and the nature of the work they were content to do, I doubt it was a long way down for any of them."

Willem nodded, but avoided looking at the zombies.

"Really, Willem," Marek said, putting a hand on his shoulder, "why so squeamish? They're better workers now by half. All they lack is the ability to understand how little they matter in the world. Think of it that way, and it's really a blessing for them."

Willem couldn't look at the Thayan's leering smile. And the wizard's hand lingered too long on his shoulder.

"Let me know when you have another five and ten of them," said Marek, "and I'll come back, or send Kurtsson, to make more for you. In time, you'll have more undead than living workers, toiling away at all hours without a drop to drink or a bite to eat, oblivious to the weather, and so on. You'll want to wear something over your mouth and nose in the summer months, believe me, but I'm guessing that was true when they still breathed, eh?" Willem nodded and shook his head at the same time. The zombies had all turned to look at him, awaiting his command.

60

11 Uktar, the Year of the Banner (1368 DR)
PRISTAL TOWERS, INNARLITH

I don't remember the last time I was in the Fourth Quarter," Phyrea said, swallowing the breathless awe that threatened to overwhelm her.

Her host smiled graciously, but she hardly took notice. The opulence around her made her legs shake.

"If you have any questions about anything you see," said Pristoleph, "please don't hesitate to ask."

Ask him why he lives in such luxury, surrounded by starvation and want, the old woman said.

Phyrea shook her head at the apparition, checking out of the corner of her eye to see if he had noticed. If he had, he was too much of a gentleman to comment.

"It's not the . . ." she started. "You have impeccable taste."

He looked at her—really looked at her, in a way that only one man had before.

Get out of here, the man with the scar on his face said. *This one is not to be trifled with.*

"It's quite something that we haven't met before," Pristoleph said.

Phyrea stopped at a burled wood side table to admire a tea set that looked to have been cast from platinum traced with gold and accented with diamonds. She couldn't have begun to guess at its value.

Do you like that? the little girl asked. Phyrea looked over at her. She stood on the other side of the hall next to an identical side table. She had her hand on a cup from a similar tea set, but one made of the most delicate porcelain. *Is it better than this one?*

Phyrea didn't respond. She tried not to respond to the ghosts when people were able to hear her, but she desperately wanted to tell the little girl to stop.

The ghost picked up the teacup.

Phyrea gasped.

"Is something wrong?" Pristoleph asked.

The teacup shattered on the floor. The little girl smiled and faded away.

"What—?" the senator said, crossing the hall in a few long strides. "How did that happen?"

Phyrea didn't follow him. She couldn't move.

Well, the man with the scar on his face said—she saw him standing at the foot of the wide, sweeping stairs, *that's never happened before. How did she learn to do that?*

Phyrea shook her head and closed her eyes.

"Was that you?" he said.

"What?" Phyrea gasped. "No."

It was me, the little girl said into her mind.

"Is there someone with you?" Pristoleph asked.

"What?" Phyrea muttered. "No."

"The man with the scar in the shape of the letter Z?" the senator asked.

Phyrea stared across the hall at Pristoleph and when he approached her she backed away, fending him off with her hands. He stopped a few paces from her. She looked around herself but couldn't see any of the apparitions.

None of them spoke to her.

"How do you know about him?" she asked, not sure she wanted to hear the answer.

"The pince-nez," he replied. She squinted at him, and he explained, "Spectacles ... lenses that you wear over your eyes. Marek Rymüt gave them to me. When I put them on I could see through your eyes—it was as though I were you. That's when I saw you for the first time, eighteen days ago, in your own mirror."

"And you saw ... him?"

"It looked as though he was there, but not entirely. It was as though he was somehow added onto what I was seeing."

"Made of purple light," she whispered, and he nodded.

"Do you see him now?" he asked.

She shook her head.

"Do you see him often?"

"Most of the time," she replied. "They appear to me everywhere, any time they wish, except when I was with—"

She almost choked on his name. The ghosts were gone, then, just like they used to stay away when she was with Devorast.

"Used to," she whispered.

"What did you say?" Pristoleph asked. "Are you talking to him now?"

"No," she said, and felt the almost forgotten sensation of a smile on her face.

He smiled back at her, and for the first time she noticed his hair, red like Devorast's, but different—not human, somehow. It appeared to move as though blown by a wind from below.

"Why did he give you those lenses?" she asked. "Why would Marek Rymüt want you to see through my eyes? Why would he arrange for us to meet tonight?"

Pristoleph said, "He arranged this meeting because I asked him to. As for the pince-nez, I have no idea, but I'm happy that he did."

Phyrea smiled, still, even when she began to cry.

61

Even the place setting was intimidating. Willem placed his hand on the handle of the fork without picking it up, and ran his fingertip over the row of tiny ruby berries that accented the engraving of twisting vines. He blinked at a sparkling rainbow that beamed from a crystal decanter. The empty plate before him was made of a material he couldn't identify with any certainty. It appeared to be ivory, but somehow hewn from a single piece. It couldn't be, and he was afraid to ask.

Phyrea sat across from him and as hard as it was to tear his eyes from the magnificent opulence around him, he couldn't keep himself from looking at her. He'd never seen her look more beautiful, and for the thousandth time at least he wondered if she were truly human at all, and not some Astral being, some creature of the outer heavens. But as she listened to Pristoleph's perfunctory small talk, there was something else about her, something he'd never seen in her before. She seemed almost at peace, and peace was something he'd stopped trying to imagine for her.

"I'm curious, Senator," Pristoleph said. "How goes your canal?"

Willem bristled and had to clear his throat before he could answer, "It's an honor to be asked to work on something so monumental, but of course it's the ransar's canal, not mine."

He felt Phyrea's burning stare then, but wouldn't look at her. He knew what she was about to say—or maybe she would leave it unsaid: It was Ivar Devorast's canal.

"I'd go you one more, Willem—if I may call you Willem?" said Pristoleph.

There was no sense that any other answer but "yes"

would ever be acceptable. It was the senior senator's way of informing him that henceforth he would call Willem by his first name. Willem nodded without hesitation.

"I'd say the canal belongs to the people of the city-state of Innarlith," Pristoleph went on.

"If not all the people of Faerûn," Phyrea cut in.

Willem's skin crawled, and he looked at everything but Pristoleph and Phyrea.

"All the people of Toril, even," Pristoleph said with a heaviness to his voice that brought out the beginnings of a simmering rage in Willem, though he didn't understand in any concrete terms why he would feel that way. "It will spark a revolution in trade."

Willem nodded and cleared his throat again.

"Don't you think so, Willem?" Phyrea prompted.

She seemed legitimately interested in what he had to say, and it was so unexpected, all he could do was clear his throat again.

"Are you quite all right?" Pristoleph asked.

"Yes," Willem said around a deep breath. "I'm fine, thank you. It's just ... difficult for me, sometimes, to remember what it's like to sit at a proper table and have a proper conversation with proper people."

"Conditions at the canal site are rather primitive," Phyrea explained.

"I can imagine," said Pristoleph.

"I'm not sure you could, Senator," Willem said, plunging forward despite his best intentions. "It's awful. The cold, the rain, the mud ... the mud gets everywhere. It's all over you in the space of the first afternoon. None of your clothes are ever dry. Fires provide warmth—everything. You live your life around an open fire like orcs—worse, goblins. It's not a life fit for humans to live."

"I'm sure there are humans living in worse conditions," Pristoleph said.

"I can't imagine," Willem replied.

There was a short silence that commanded Willem's

attention. Almost against his will, he turned to face the senior senator, whose hair seemed to dance more quickly, as though agitated.

"I don't have to imagine," Pristoleph said, and his eyes allowed no argument. "I have but to remember. You see, I was born to the streets of the Fourth Quarter. From the day I could walk I started to fight to survive. I had no family to speak of, and in parts of this city, one doesn't have to actually do anything to attract enemies."

Willem nodded, his neck stiff, and sweat began to pool under his arms. He wanted a sip of water but was afraid to pick up the goblet for fear of revealing how badly his hands were shaking. He kept his hands in his lap.

"It was a difficult life," Pristoleph went on, "but not without rewards. Growing up that way, being that sort of a child, made me the man that I am today."

Willem nodded again and glanced around the cavernous dining room—a space so large Willem's entire house could easily have been constructed inside it. Part of him wanted to ask Pristoleph if he was, in fact, the richest man in Innarlith, but then he didn't have to. He was sitting in all the proof of that anyone would ever need.

But then Willem wondered: Wouldn't he be more important than he is? Wouldn't he be ransar, if that were true? Instead he seemed to be the senator that everyone deferred to when they had to, but rarely even spoke with. His appearances at social affairs both private and public were rare occurrences.

"I am a man who doesn't trust easily, Willem," Pristoleph continued. "I keep my own counsel, and I do what I think is best. Often, that is also what's best for Innarlith. Rarer still, it's what's best for other people."

"We should always consider others," Willem muttered. His face flushed, and he cleared his throat again, feeling like a child speaking out of turn.

Pristoleph laughed—laughed at him—and the blood drained from Willem's face.

"Wherever possible, yes, I suppose so," the strange man with fiery hair replied. "But not always, and so here we come to the reason I asked you and your lovely young bride to join me for dinner."

"I'll admit, Senator," Willem said, "that I've been curious..."

"Three days ago I met Phyrea for the first time," Pristoleph said. "For the first time in person, at least"—the two of them traded a conspiratorial smile that almost made Willem whimper in fear—"and very quickly afterward I decided to make her my wife."

Willem blinked, choked back the impulse to chuckle, and shook his head.

"My deepest apologies, Senator Pristoleph," he said, "but for a moment I thought you said..."

The look on Phyrea's face made it impossible for him to continue.

"You will step away," Pristoleph said. "Phyrea and I will leave on the morrow for a long sea journey. When we return, we will be wed."

"But..." Willem blustered. "But that's..."

He looked to Phyrea, who smiled at him in a freakishly maternal way that made Willem's skin crawl anew.

"You will go back to the canal," Pristoleph went on. "Go back and finish it. Make a name for yourself. From what I understand you don't deserve it, but Phyrea has asked—by the Nine Hells, she's *demanded*—that you be allowed to finish it. It will be your monument, your greatest achievement, and Phyrea will be mine."

Phyrea smiled and looked down.

Willem's jaw opened and closed, but no words came out.

"You can, of course, choose to be difficult," Pristoleph said, and again, Willem's attention was dragged kicking and screaming to the man's eyes. A spark blazed in them that Willem didn't think matched the candlelight, as though his eyes were lit from within. "Will you be difficult about this?"

Willem swallowed, mesmerized by the strange man, and well aware of the otherworldly woman that had attracted his attention. Willem didn't think either of them were human, certainly not human like he was, not flawed, afraid, incompetent, and—

"Willem?" Phyrea asked.

"I won't be," he said. It was so difficult to get the words out he practically barked. "I won't stand in anyone's way."

"Very well, then," Pristoleph said, his voice as light and as casual as though they'd just come to agreement to get together later for a game of *sava*, not that he'd just appropriated a man's wife. "Let's eat, shall we?"

Willem sat through the meal desperately trying not to throw up.

62

21 Uktar, the Year of the Banner (1368 DR)
THE CANAL SITE

Fifteen more dead men awoke, choked out a dusty black coal, and staggered to their feet.

"I'm beginning to think," Willem said with a sigh, "that for every one you bring back from the dead, two or three living workers flee back to the city."

Marek Rymüt chuckled and said, "Let them go. We've made arrangements to collect bodies from the Fourth Quarter mass graves, so they'll come back from the city in due course anyway."

Willem shuddered at the thought of it. He rubbed his wrists where he'd been cut and healed again. His body shook, his nose ran, and his head throbbed. He wondered if he had any more blood to lose.

"I hate the winter here," he muttered. "It's so cold. Every day it's so dark and cold."

"But isn't it colder in Cormyr?" Marek asked. "It's likely snowing there, no?"

Willem shook his head, but replied, "Yes, I suppose it is. Still, this damp—not damp but incessant soaking rain—sucks the warmth from your body. It's killing me. Its absolutely killing me."

"This?" said Kurtsson, who'd finish creating a handful of zombies himself. "This is warm. It's warm here."

"Ah," Marek said with a jovial laugh, "the Vaasan perspective. Surely even you can take heart in that, Willem."

"No, I can't," said Willem.

"Really, my boy," Marek said, "perhaps you need to spend more than a night or two with that lovely wife of yours. I've been encouraging you to get back to the city more often and for longer stretches."

"My lovely wife isn't there," Willem said, surprised that Marek, who always seemed to know everything, didn't know that. "She's gone off with another man."

Kurtsson laughed at him, and Willem spun on the Vaasan, which only made him laugh harder.

"Kurtsson," Marek said in a stern tone, "perhaps you could be of use with spells for the cause?"

The Vaasan wizard quieted a bit, but didn't stop laughing. He wandered off into the work camp, playfully passing between shambling rows of undead workers. Willem watched him go, not keen to see the look on Marek Rymüt's face, one way or another.

"I have to admit that I'm a bit disappointed you're only now telling me this," the Thayan said. "I knew, of course, but I was hoping that by now I'd gained your confidence."

Willem choked back a sob and wiped snot from his nose onto the back of his sleeve. His clothes were ruined from the wet and mud anyway, so what was the difference?

"Do you know where they've gone?" Marek asked.

"Do you?" Willem shot back—too fast, too forcefully—and fear that he'd offended the Thayan actually staggered him. "My apologies, Master Rymüt. I'm not myself."

"I should say you aren't," the Red Wizard replied, his voice devoid of anger. "You look terrible—worse every time

I see you. You're not wearing that item I provided you."

"It stopped working."

"I can find you an—"

"I'm dying out here," Willem said. "This thing is killing me."

"That was no one's intent, Willem. If you'd prefer to come back to the city, no one will fault you."

"But we both know that they will," Willem said. "They will fault me, they will blame me, they will shun me, they will punish me, and as sure as the mud and rain will kill me, they will just as fast."

"People will speak and act on your behalf," Marek promised without sincerity.

Willem gasped out something like an exhausted laugh and said, "I'm sure they will. Maybe one of the other senior senators will decide to move into my house. Meykhati, maybe? Or what if Salatis covets my eyes? He'll have them dug from my screaming skull as easily as Pristoleph took my—"

Willem stopped. His throat closed over anymore words. Tears streamed down to mix with the rain on his face.

"You've put yourself in the dragon's lair, my boy," Marek said. "This little city on the edge of the world has its own rules, and chief among those rules is the strong survive. Gold is what they all covet, gold and the power it brings. You've gone after power, Willem, and I'm surprised to find you naive enough to believe that there would be no consequences."

"This place has no honor," Willem said.

That made Marek laugh, and laugh long and loud.

When the Thayan finally got hold of himself he said, "Please, Willem. The same is true in your precious Cormyr, as it is in my own beloved Thay. The thing is, you see, that as the son of a boarding house wife, you simply weren't prepared for it."

Willem shook his head, though he knew that Marek spoke the truth.

"So, what now, then?" the Thayan asked.

"I will stay here and die desecrating the dream of a better man," Willem said.

"My, Willem, you do have a sense of the dramatic at times. I'll grant you that."

"Look at them," Willem said, ignoring the wizard's last comment. "I know you created them, but have you really ever looked at them?"

"The zombies, you mean."

"The walking dead," Willem replied, "yes. Don't you sometimes wish you could be like that?"

"No," Marek said. "No, I don't."

"They haven't a care in the world," Willem went on. "They aren't happy, but they aren't unhappy, either, and do you know why?"

"Because what little brains they had in the first place are rapidly rotting in their skulls?"

"No," Willem replied. "I mean, yes, of course, but no. They're neither happy nor unhappy because they don't seek happiness. They don't know what happiness is—or at least they don't imagine they might someday know what happiness is. They exist, and that's enough for them. They do as they're told, and are left to do it. They aren't teased with gold, comfort, women, power.... No one leads them on."

"Perhaps the cold and damp have gotten to your thinking worse that I thought, my boy," Marek said. "Healthy men do not envy the undead—at least not this sort of shambling, mindless walking corpse. It almost sounds as though you'd like to be one."

"Perhaps I would," said Willem.

"Well," the Red Wizard replied, his voice dense and full of meaning, "that could be arranged."

Willem looked at the Thayan and almost screamed at the look he saw in the man's eyes.

But he didn't scream. Instead, he shook his head and excused himself. He walked back to his tent, leaving the

Thayan to disappear, sending himself back to Innarlith by means of his own magic.

In his tent, Willem sat on his canvas chair, opened a new bottle of brandy, and drank it.

All of it.

63

22 Nightal, the Year of the Banner (1368 DR)
THE SHINING SEA, SEVENTY MILES NORTH OF
LUSHPOOL

They had been at sea for twenty-nine days, and in all that time Phyrea had not heard a single word uttered by anyone who wasn't physically present—and alive. She spoke almost exclusively with Pristoleph. The crew went about their duties, rarely if ever seen from the sections of the ship reserved for she and the vessel's master. She'd only ever been on one ship she thought was nearly a match to Pristoleph's impressive *Determined,* and that was the strange ship that Devorast had made for the woman from Shou Lung.

They were impressive because they were unlike anything she'd seen before, and were reflections of the geniuses behind them, but that was where any comparison ended.

Determined was one of the biggest ship's she'd ever seen, and she was dedicated to only one purpose: the recreation of her master. Friends of Phyrea's father owned sailboats and yachts of all sorts, but none of them approached *Determined* in sheer size and luxury. It was as though a wing of Pristal Towers, gilded appointments and all, had been set afloat.

Phyrea climbed the stairs to the sun deck, as had become her habit after a light lunch in the salon with Pristoleph. High above the main deck, the sun deck was hidden from the sight of the crew. Though open to the tropical sun and fragrant breezes of the Shining Sea, it was entirely private.

Her favorite chaise had already been turned to face the sun by a butler she rarely saw, but who's effect she felt throughout the day—every day. She dropped her silk robe to the deck planks and stretched, naked, basking in the warmth of the sun. She brushed a hand slowly down her flat stomach and could already feel the sun heating her skin. She'd taken on a deep, rich color, and when she looked at herself in the mirror, she couldn't believe the change. Gone were the bags under her eyes, the haunted, faraway look, the exhausted, defeated droop of her shoulders.

She heard footsteps climbing the stairs and was so confident that it was Pristoleph that she didn't cover herself, or even turn around. She sat, stretching, on the padded chaise and closed her eyes, tipping her face up to the warm sun. She imagined she could feel the perfect blue sky, unmarred by even the tiniest wisp of a cloud, soaking into her pores to nourish her in a way no food ever could.

"You are the most beautiful woman on the face of Toril," Pristoleph said.

He sat in a deck chair next to her, and she looked at him and smiled.

"Thank you," she said.

They had repeated the same words every day for the past twenty, and it had become another in a parade of simple comforts.

"Are we really on our way back?" she asked.

"We'll be at harbor in Innarlith as soon as three or four days from now."

Phyrea sighed.

"Are you disappointed?" Pristoleph asked.

"No," she replied. "I knew that eventually we would have to go home. All this last month, though, I've wondered why I've traveled so little in my life. My father's coin could have carried me to Waterdeep and back a hundred times, but I never really went any farther than our country estate."

She took a deep breath and sighed. She didn't want to

think about Berrywilde, and the ghosts she seemed to have finally left behind.

"I take *Determined* out at least one month in every twelve," Pristoleph said, though he'd told her the same many times before. "It never ceases to amaze me what getting away from the city can do for me, especially this time of year when the rain, the dark clouds, are so oppressive."

"Oppressive . . ." she repeated, carefully considering the word. "It is. It is oppressive. I wonder if people there . . . if people would be better, would treat each other better, if the sun shined more often, and the Lake of Steam smelled like this sea and not the stinking innards of the Underdark."

"You know what I think about that," he replied. "People are people, and the weather might make you tired, or affect your mood, but ultimately what ails Innarlith goes deeper than too many rainy days."

"But people there hate each other," she said. "I know. I'm one of them. I've done hateful things, over and over—things to degrade myself and others. Here, under this perfect sky, I can't imagine what made me such a misanthrope."

"Everyone is an altruist on a tropical afternoon," he said. "When you have to fight for a piece of a pie that can only be cut into so many pieces, you do what has to be done."

She sighed and said, "I wish I'd stopped at what I had to do, sometimes."

He shrugged that off, but still she could tell he thought about it.

"Still, I can't help thinking people would be better to each other if they all had a month like this every year," Phyrea thought aloud.

"I have a month like this every year," Pristoleph said, "and I'm an unconscionable bastard."

Phyrea laughed, and Pristoleph joined her. She kept laughing until tears streamed from her eyes. Eventually they both took deep breaths, and finally sat, smiling, in silence for a while.

"Well," Phyrea said at last, "I'll try to overlook that side of you."

"That's the best any man can ask from a woman," Pristoleph replied.

"Is it?"

"No," he answered without pause. "The best a man can ask is love—true love, if there is such a thing."

"There is," she whispered.

"And if I thought you felt that way about me I wouldn't be a bastard anymore."

"Oh," she joked, "I doubt that one thing has anything to do with the other."

She did love him, but not the same way she loved Ivar Devorast. To Phyrea, Pristoleph and she were like old friends who hadn't seen each other in twenty years, but who fit back into a familiar, comforting groove the second they'd reacquainted.

"When we return," she said. "I'll bring my things and stay with you?"

"Of course," he said.

"I can't imagine living in such a beautiful place, surrounded by all that . . . beauty."

"Your father is no pauper, Phyrea," he reminded her.

"Of course not, but . . ."

"It's important, I think, to surround yourself with the best of everything."

"Why?" she asked. "To impress?"

"No," he replied. "To remind me that the works of man are superior to the works of nature."

Phyrea smiled at that and nodded.

"Do you hear that?" he asked.

She listened, but all she could hear was the crack and pop of the wind in the sails, the creak of the rigging, and the gentle sound of the shallow waves against the hull—the sounds of the sea.

"Do you?" Pristoleph asked again.

She shook her head.

"The whisper of waves. . . ." he said.

Phyrea nodded and was about to ask him what he meant, but instead she listened again. She could hear it, but only because she didn't hear the voices telling her to do things, asking her to murder herself. She wondered what else she'd missed under the weight of those voices.

"I do," she said, wiping a tear from her eye with one finger.

"What does it say to you?"

"Nothing at all," she said, "and that's fine with me. I'd rather hear the waves whisper of nothing, than suffer through the lies of light."

64

26 Nightal, the Year of the Banner (1368 DR)
SECOND QUARTER, INNARLITH

I just can't understand why it is that you hate me so, Phyrea," Willem said. "What have I done to make you see me with such contempt?"

Phyrea didn't want to answer him. She opened a drawer in the bureau and shifted through the scant few pieces of clothing she'd left before she went away with Pristoleph.

"There isn't really anything here I want anymore," she said.

"So you're going to leave it?" he asked. "What am I going to do with it?"

She bit her lip, cutting off the sarcastic, hurtful reply that came to mind. Instead, she scooped up the lace undergarments and stuffed them into the bag she had open on the bed.

"I can have the rest sent to you, if you can't stand to be here," he said, "or if you don't want to go through them. I can imagine how awful this little hovel must seem to you now."

"Your house is fine, Willem," she said. "That's not it."

"Then what is 'it'?" he pressed. "You ran my mother back to Cormyr and dismissed my staff. I wasn't even here most of the time, so if you found my presence so distasteful, at least you didn't have to suffer me much."

"Is that the life you wanted?" she asked him, though when all was said and done she didn't care to hear his answer. It didn't matter. "Were you really content with simply avoiding my distaste?"

He exhaled—not really a sigh—and leaned against the wall of his bedchamber.

Phyrea picked up the bag and walked past him, tense and uncertain of what he might do, but he did nothing to stop her. She stepped into the hall, leaving him silently leaning on the wall in the room behind her. The little girl stood at the top of the stairs, her eyebrows drawn into a V that twisted her eyes into smoldering pinpoints. Her purple-black lips pulled away from her teeth, which were needle fangs that glistened with a vile light of their own.

Phyrea screamed and dropped her bag. She recoiled back so fast and so out of control she nearly fell.

"No," she whispered.

You left us, the little girl's voice shrieked in Phyrea's head. *You went away and you left us, you bitch.*

"No," Phyrea whimpered, horrified by how weak her own voice sounded.

We knew you would come back, the man with the scar said.

Phyrea closed her eyes so she couldn't see him.

"What happened?" Willem asked. He'd come out of the bedchamber. "Phyrea?"

She shook her head and pushed him away, but not hard. He stopped and didn't try to come any closer.

"What's wrong with you?" he asked.

Tell him, the man demanded. *Tell him we're here. Tell him we've been waiting here for all this time.*

We have been, the little boy said.

"No, Willem...." Phyrea gasped.

We've stood over him while he tried to sleep but couldn't, the old woman said.

We watched him drown his sorrows in drink, the sad woman told her.

"Let me go," she said.

Go, yes, the little girl said. *Go back to Berrywilde.*

"I'm not stopping you," Willem said.

Phyrea opened her eyes and stormed forward, grabbing her bag as she passed it. She went past a violet-glowing form that she didn't look at. She ran down the stairs, leaving Willem behind, but the ghosts followed her. They tormented her out into the street. The little girl sat across from her in the coach and sneered at her.

"Home, Miss Phyrea?" the driver—Pristoleph's driver—asked.

She almost said yes, but at the last minute she said, "The Green Phoenix. In the Third Quarter."

The coach jerked to a start, and Phyrea closed her eyes and clasped her hands over her ears. Though she couldn't see them, they never spoke to her through her ears anyway, so she suffered, occasionally sobbing, with their incessant barrage of threats and demands until the coach finally pulled up in front of the sprawling brick building that housed the Green Phoenix.

"Shall I accompany you, Miss?" the driver, who Phyrea knew was also a more-than-capable fighter armed with magic and his master's protection, asked.

Without stopping or looking behind her, she said, "I'll be fine. No."

She burst into the common room of the dark, smoke-filled tavern and all but ran to the bar.

"Orerus," she demanded, slapping her palm on the bar. "Where is he?"

The skinny old woman behind the bar blinked at her.

"Now!" Phyrea screamed. "Where?"

The old woman pointed to a curtained doorway behind her and stepped aside.

Phyrea leaped the bar and tore though the curtain. She ignored the powerful aroma of the brewing vats, and the screaming tirade of the incorporeal girl.

"Surero," she whispered, wiping tears from her eyes and abandoning the alchemist's assumed name. "Where are you?"

"Phyrea?" he called from the back of the large room.

Pristoleph had helped her keep track of him, and she'd been surprised, but delighted to hear that he had taken a position as brewmaster for the Green Phoenix—an honorable enough use for his peculiar skills—under the name Orerus, Surero reversed.

He stepped out from behind one of the big copper kettles and greeted her with a smile that quickly faded to a scowl of concern.

"How did you find me?" he asked. "What's happened?"

"Do you know where he is?" Phyrea asked.

"Yes," Surero replied, not having to ask who she meant by "he."

Phyrea felt her knees give, and she lowered herself to the dirty floor, ignoring the sticky residue of the ale vats that coated every surface.

"Gods," Surero whispered. "What's happened to you?"

She took a deep breath and laughed a little while she cried.

Kill him, the man with the scar said. *He'll deliver you back to Devorast if you don't kill him now. You know that man will destroy you.*

"I just need to know that he's alive, and that you know where he is—that someone knows where he is," she said. "I don't know why. I'll never see him again, but I had to know that."

Good girl, the old woman whispered into her reeling mind. *Never see him again.*

"Phyrea," Surero said, "what is it?"

She struggled to her feet and said, "Where is he?"

"Ormpetarr."

She nodded and mouthed a "thank you," then turned to leave.

"Phyrea?" he called after her, but she didn't stop, turn, or answer.

65

28 Nightal, the Year of the Banner (1368 DR)
THE THAYAN ENCLAVE, INNARLITH

You've disappointed so many people, Willem," Marek Rymüt said.

Willem squirmed in his seat, and Marek had to force himself not to grin. When he really looked at Willem, it was easier not to smile. He looked worse. His eyes had sunk into his face and were rimmed with dark circles. His teeth were yellow, and his lips dry and cracked.

"You realize that, don't you?" he pressed.

Willem sighed and a tear rolled down from his right eye.

"I do, yes," Willem said. "Is that why I'm here? Did you send for me because you wanted to tell me I've disappointed you?"

"Among other things, yes."

Willem's head drooped on his shoulders, and he looked at the floor.

"Are you having work done?" Willem asked, his voice dull and faraway.

"Oh," replied the Thayan, "the canvas . . . no."

Willem nodded as though the answer he'd gotten could have been anything but unsatisfying. Marek had had the floor covered with thick canvas, and most of the furniture had been moved out too. It did appear as though he was having the room painted.

"Can I offer you a drink?" Marek asked.

Willem looked up at him with wide, wet eyes, like a lost puppy. Marek had never had a puppy, though he had occasionally used them to practice spells on, and to test potions, but that was back home in Thay.

"I'll take that as a 'yes,'" said Marek.

He poured brandy from a crystal decanter and handed the glass to Willem, who took it in a grip so weak Marek grimaced at the possibility he might drop it and spill it. He glanced down at the decanter—he hadn't prepared much, but there was still enough left in case Willem dropped the first one.

"You aren't having one?" Willem asked.

Marek shook his head and watched the younger man down the brandy in one swallow, grimacing against the burn of it.

"Tell me you at least tried to stop them, Willem," said the Thayan. "I want to hear from you that you did everything you could to keep her—to keep her away from him."

Willem shook his head, refusing to look Marek in the eye. The Red Wizard had a sudden impulse to kick him hard in the chin, to force his miserable face up.

"You just let another man walk into your home and leave with your wife?" Marek said.

"No," Willem muttered. "No, we went to his house, and I left her there."

"That's pathetic," Marek said. "That's quite simply the most pathetic thing I've ever heard."

He picked up the crystal decanter and poured more of the brandy into Willem's glass. The young man sat there, slumped down, and stared at the umber liquid.

"Speak, Willem," Marek demanded. "Explain yourself."

"What's there to explain?" Willem asked, then swallowed half the brandy in his glass. He coughed, not bothering to put a hand up to cover his mouth. "What could I have done?"

Marek smiled down at Willem and said, "What could you have done? Hmm ... let me think. To begin with, you could have poisoned his drink."

Willem shook his head. Spittle dropped in a long,

stringy line from his lower lip. He put the glass to his mouth and drank some, but poured the rest of the brandy on the floor.

"You could have rendered him helpless," Marek went on. "And once he was unable to move, the poison making his muscles go rigid and unresponsive, you could have done anything you wanted to him. He would have been entirely under your power, yours to do with as you wished."

Willem slumped forward and fell onto the floor without changing from the hunched, sitting position he was in. His head bounced and scraped along the canvas tarp.

"I expected so much from you," Marek said.

Willem looked up at him, blinked, his eyes confused at first. His lips twitched, but he couldn't speak.

Marek took a deep, rattling breath and smiled. His face flushed, and his heart began to race.

"Oh," he breathed. "Oh, Willem. That must be awful—terrible. I can only imagine. . . ."

Willem blinked at him again and fear replaced the confusion in a wave that made his pupils dilate.

Marek, reluctant to turn away, stepped back to a side table and opened a long, hinged wooden box. Inside was the sword Phyrea had brought him. The wavy blade glimmered in the candlelight. Marek bit his bottom lip and held his breath as he lifted the flambergé out of the velvet-lined box with all the reverence the exquisite weapon deserved.

When he went back to look down at Willem, the sword in his hand with the blade tipped down until it almost touched the floor, Marek thought he saw Willem shake his head. But the poison wouldn't allow him even that scant gesture. Marek thought perhaps he sensed so strongly Willem's powerful desire to make at least that tiny, futile gesture that he simply imagined the movement. Willem's eyes pleaded for mercy.

Marek dropped to his knee, one creaking, popping joint at a time. His generously-proportioned body was unaccustomed to sitting on the floor and when his full weight settled onto his knees, they burned in response.

He looked Willem in the eyes, and with his free hand he brushed the hair from the younger man's forehead.

"Pretty Willem," he whispered in a mocking rendition of what he thought "soothing" might sound like. "Everything will be all right. You wanted this, didn't you? You told me you did. You told me you envied them. You said you wanted to be one of them."

Marek shifted his weight to hover closer and closer over Willem's face. The younger man's mouth hung open, and the tip of his tongue protruded just the tiniest fraction of an inch

"Willem, my dear, dear, sweet boy," Marek whispered, "please believe me that if I thought there was any way to avoid this...."

Willem's eyes widened as Marek moved closer still, then the Thayan couldn't see his eyes anymore. His lips met Willem's and closed around them. The tip of his tongue darted in, and though Willem was unable to return the kiss, at least he couldn't back away. The poison made him appear dead—stiff and unresponsive—but Willem was still very much alive, warm and breathing.

Marek took his lips away from Willem's and punctured the helpless Cormyrean's skin with the tip of the sword.

Only his eyes responded at first. Marek knew that Willem could feel every inch of the flambergé's cruel blade winding its way ever so slowly from just to the right of his belly button, up under his ribs. Then Willem's breaths started to come faster, and ever more shallow. Marek guided the blade to the middle of Willem's chest in hope of avoiding either lung. Willem panted—a rapid succession of gasps that were almost all exhale, and no inhale. Tears streamed from his twitching eyes.

Marek shushed him and pressed harder with the sword. It took all his strength and skill to slide the long blade into Willem's fast-beating heart. He could feel the firm resistance of the thick muscle, and the blade jerked in his grip in time with its beating.

When it finally did pierce his heart, blood poured freely down the length of the blade and oozed out of the wound in his stomach. His eyes bulged, and for a moment Marek thought they might pop. Instead they relaxed, but they didn't close. He let go of the sword hilt, leaving the flambergé sheathed in Willem's body.

Marek let out a long, slow breath in time with Willem Korvan's last exhale. He smiled down into the face of the dead man and smiled.

"Shhh," he hissed. "That's a good boy."

66

29 Nightal, the Year of the Banner (1368 DR)
THE TEMPLE OF THE DELICATE CHAOS, INNARLITH

Marek stepped out of the dimension door onto a rough flagstone floor that shifted under his weight. He staggered, his hands out to his sides, and almost fell. The stone bobbed on something that might have been water, but was too thick. The effect was the same as floating, but the movement was slower.

As the spell effect dissipated behind him his eyes began to adjust to the dim light from torches set in iron sconces on the tiled walls. The tiles had apparently been salvaged from wherever tiles could be salvaged from. Few were the same size, and almost none of them were of matching colors. The effect might have been pleasing had they been arranged with the care and vision of an artist, but it was no mosaic, just a random jumble of shapes and colors.

Marek stepped to another flagstone, riding the slow undulation under his feet, growing more secure with the uncertain footing. The flagstones did indeed float in some thick, gelatinous medium. Marek swallowed to settle his stomach. His first few steps had disturbed many of the stones around him so that the floor rose and fell in waves throughout the chamber.

The room itself was a circle that Marek judged to be a hundred feet in diameter. The torches were not set at even intervals around the circumference so there were bright spots, and places where the shadows were deep as night. He got the distinct feeling that something—more than one something—watched him from the shadows, so he quickly ran through a spell.

Blinking, he refocused his eyes, and a bluish cast descended over the room. The shadows were peeled back when he set his attention on them, and indeed strange creatures that might have been insects or lizards stared at him, following his every move with twitching antennae, darting forked tongues, and bulging compound eyes.

Another spell, and blue-green fire flickered over his body, covering his robes in a glowing sheen that would give the creatures a painful surprise should they choose to attempt to do him harm.

"That won't be necessary," Wenefir said from behind him.

Marek knew better than to try to turn around too fast on the undulating floor, so instead he took his time, planting his feet with care.

"Well, better safe than breakfast," Marek said, stalling.

Wenefir laughed a little and stood with his hands clasped in front of him. He wore breeches of billowing purple silk but was naked from the waist up. Folds of hairless fat drooped off him, and Marek was reminded of why he so rarely went shirtless himself. His smile was cautious, suspicious, and set to turn at the slightest provocation.

"I was surprised to see you step into this place so easily," Wenefir said. "Well done, Master Rymüt."

"I can show you how to ward against dimensional intrusion," Marek replied.

"For a price, of course?"

"I'm sure we can come to a mutually satisfactory arrangement," said Marek.

"And yet I'm sure that you had a very different purpose in mind when you made the decision to invade the sanctity of Cyric's holy shrine this morning."

Marek dipped into as deep a bow as his girth and the floating floor would allow, and said, "Indeed, my good friend. I suppose it would be safe to consider this a social call."

"This is not a salon, Master Rymüt, but a holy place," said Wenefir, but Marek could tell the man was curious to hear what he'd come to say.

"Then I will dispense with further niceties and bring us to the meat of the issue," the Thayan said. "Your mas— excuse me . . . your *friend* Pristoleph has made a very bad decision of late and I've come in the hopes that between the two of us we can either show him the error of his ways, or at the very least mitigate the damage his impetuosity might cause."

"Whatever do you mean?"

"The girl," Marek said, and left it at that.

Wenefir wore his thoughts clearly on his face. Marek didn't need a spell to see that the Cyricist was no friend of Phyrea's. Marek smiled, trying to defuse the expression with as much sympathy as possible. If he had guessed right about how Wenefir would feel about Pristoleph's sudden and acute obsession with Innarlith's most beautiful prize, the rest would be easy.

Remembering where he was, and that Wenefir was likely capable of mind-intruding magic gifted him by his mad god, Marek tried to keep his surface thoughts clear.

"It's a matter of the heart," Wenefir said, though his eyes pleaded for argument. "I can't imagine what we might be able to do to make him feel differently."

"All that in due course," said Marek. "For now, though, can we agree that the relationship is an unhealthy one?"

"Perhaps, but I'd be curious to hear your reasons for thinking so."

Marek nodded and replied, "She is married to another senator. You know that well enough, having performed the ceremony yourself."

"Cyric smiles upon those who change their minds," Wenefir said, almost showing his disappointment over that bit of scripture. "No marriage in his name is ought but temporary."

"Be that as it may, among the city's social circles it will be frowned upon."

Wenefir nodded, happy enough to concede the point. "Has there been talk?" he asked.

"Oh, there's always talk," said Marek. "Had it simply been a matter of divorce and remarriage tongues would wag among the wives and servants, but ultimately the city-state would have gone on about its business, but that, I'm afraid, is not the worst of it."

"Oh?"

"There's the matter of Senator Willem Korvan," Marek said.

Wenefir raised an eyebrow and asked, "What of him? He's been drinking, but don't we all? I understand he's been mostly away, at the canal site. I can't imagine he'd be stupid enough to publicly resist Pristoleph."

"Oh, and he isn't," Marek assured him. "In fact he's done just the opposite. Instead of crying on the shoulders of his fellow senators and making a sticky social situation any worse, he's disappeared."

"I'm sorry?"

"He's gone, and no one knows where," Marek said, though he knew precisely where Willem Korvan—or what was left of him—was.

"A young senator on the rise like that, with influential friends. . . ." Wenefir thought aloud.

"Why, even if he was humiliated by Pristoleph's appropriation of his cheeky young bride," Marek said, leading

Wenefir in a disturbing direction, "why would a rising star like Willem simply walk away from all he's worked so hard to build? In some ways he's the heir apparent to Innarlith."

"I can assure you that neither Pristoleph nor myself had anything to do with his disappearance," Wenefir said. "I was told that he had acquiesced—surrendered, as it were, of his own free will."

"Such as a boy like Willem has free will, yes," Marek said. "Please believe me that I did not come here to make that accusation."

"So you believe he's gone to ground?" Wenefir asked, dire thoughts clouding his eyes. "Is he holed up somewhere planning some reprisal, or gathering allies against Pristoleph?"

"And Pristoleph," Marek said, "like all of us, has enemies to spare."

Wenefir nodded, and his eyes played over the shadows along one unlit section of the curved wall. Marek followed his gaze and saw the strange creature there take a tentative step forward, looking to Wenefir for instructions. The Cyrist held up a hand—a subtle gesture—and the creature slinked back into the deeper darkness.

"He was one of your boys," Wenefir said. "What has he told you?"

Marek brushed aside the implication that weighed heavily in Wenefir's eyes and said, "I have not heard from him, nor seen him, in days. But there is more to consider than Willem Korvan. There's the master builder. Phyrea is his daughter, after all, and he fought for the marriage with Willem. And he isn't necessarily counted among Pristoleph's allies. And the master builder has the ear of the ransar."

"And you have the mind of the ransar," Wenefir retorted. "What have you told Salatis to think?"

"You overestimate me."

"No, Marek, I don't think I do," Wenefir said. "You were right to come to me. This relationship has implications, and those implications will have to be more carefully considered."

"Carefully considered," Marek suggested, "by someone with a clearer view, unfiltered by love, lust, and so on."

Wenefir's eyes went cold, and a tickle of fear played along the edges of Marek's consciousness.

"I'll show you the way out," Wenefir said.

Turn on each other, Marek thought as he followed the soft, strange man to a hidden door. Turn on each other over a girl.

He tried not to laugh as he climbed the spiral stairs that would take him a hundred feet up to the street.

67

30 Nightal, the Year of the Banner (1368 DR)
THE CITY OF ORMPETARR

*P*lease, please, can't you let us go home? the little girl begged. Don't look at him.

He has replaced you, said the old woman. *He's replaced you in his heart. There are other women. He didn't wait for you.*

Surely you didn't expect him to wait for you, said the man with the scar on his face.

He should have, the younger woman sobbed. *Why didn't he?*

Phyrea stood at the foot of the skeletal pier that stretched out into the calm expanse of the Nagawater. The ghost of the old woman stood in front of her, and most of what she saw of the pier was filtered through her insubstantial violet form. Phyrea hugged herself and shivered. Even her heavy wool weathercloak didn't keep the chill away from her bones. When she caught the ghostly woman's eye she shivered worse. The spirit's freezing gaze cut her like a dagger, and her head ached.

"He won't kill me," Phyrea whispered.

Yes, he will, the little girl replied.

"You will," she whispered.

The woman sneered at her, her eyes flickering orange. Phyrea put her hands over her eyes. The old woman's shriek rattled her skull, and beneath her the planks shuddered.

"Go away," she whispered, and opened her eyes.

The old woman was gone, and before her stood Ivar Devorast.

Phyrea took a step backward.

"I can't go away," he said. "I have work to do."

He wore the same simple tunic and breeches he always wore, and though it was cold, he didn't have any sort of cloak or coat. He held a carpenter's hammer in one hand, loose and comfortable at his side.

"Not you," she said, shaking her head.

Phyrea expected one of the ghosts to say something, but they remained silent. She looked around but couldn't see any of them. She smiled.

"You're not surprised to see me," she said.

He shook his head, but said nothing. His red hair whipped around his face in the steady wind.

"What are you doing here?" she asked.

"Helping to build a pier," he said.

"But why?" she asked.

"They want to start building ships," he replied.

She waited for him to say more—then smiled. It had been a long time since she'd had to do that, to wait for him to say more. She couldn't believe how much she'd missed it.

"Will you build ships, then?" she asked.

"I'll build the pier," he told her.

"And you won't think of the canal?"

"I think of the canal every day," he said, and a darkness descended over his face that made Phyrea shiver.

"Will you come back?"

He just looked at her. He didn't shrug or nod or shake his head.

"I have something I wanted to tell you," she said.

He waited for her to go on, and that made her smile again.

"I'm going to be married again," she said.

"Again?" he asked.

"I left Willem over a month ago."

"Why did you feel you had to tell me that?"

"I don't know," she said. "No, yes I do. I had to give you a chance to stop me."

"If you don't want to marry this man," he said, "then don't. If you want to be here with me, then stay."

"And there's nothing you want to say to influence me one way or the other?"

He stood there and stared at her again, and she sobbed and laughed at the same time.

"You just can't . . ." she started. "Can't you just tell me if you want me or not?"

He shook his head, and Phyrea thought he looked sad, but wasn't sure.

"I shouldn't have come here," she admitted.

"No, you shouldn't have," he said, "if you don't know what you want."

She sighed and looked down. Her hair flew around her face, and she hooked it behind her ear. Some of the other men who were working on the pier walked past them. They looked at her, glanced at Devorast, but kept going.

"I do know what I want," she said, her eyes darting at the passing men. "I *did* know what I want. I wanted you. I wanted you to love me. I wanted you to protect . . ."

She couldn't keep talking, but didn't cry. Devorast didn't say anything.

"I wanted to give you the chance to fight for me," she told him.

He shook his head.

"I know," she said, wiping a tear from her eye. The wind caught her hair again and made her blink. "Maybe I came to tell you that I found someone like you—so like you—in ways I thought were impossible. And he loves me enough to take me away from someone else."

"Did you come to say good-bye?" he asked.

"I'll never say that to you, Ivar."

He looked over his shoulder at the skeletal pier.

"I'm keeping you from your work," she said, and turned to go.

"Stay," he said.

She stopped, waiting for more, but he didn't say anything.

"Why?" she asked.

"For all the reasons that brought you here in the first place," he said.

Phyrea shook her head and replied, "No. I won't stay here to be a laborer's wife. But if you take me back to Innarlith and reclaim what's yours, I'd be happy to be a canal builder's slave."

The boards under her feet rattled and the sound of the hammer hitting them made her jump.

"Damn it, Phyrea," he said. "I don't want a slave."

She sighed, didn't turn around, and said, "I can't be anything for you but a slave. I can't do anything for you but surrender myself, body and soul. If you won't take that from me, there's another man who will."

"Go to him then," he said.

Tears fell from her eyes, but she refused to let him see her sob. She walked away, leaving him standing there watching her go.

68

30 Nightal, the Year of the Banner (1368 DR)
THE LAND OF ONE HUNDRED AND THIRTEEN

Lightning flashed across the sharply delineated skies of Marek Rymüt's private dimension. No thunder followed, and no rain fell.

He took a deep breath and enjoyed the pure silence of the chamber high atop the tall tower that had finally been completed for him. Its twisted, needle-like architecture had come to him in a dream—a dream of the future of Thay that a part of him hoped he would never see.

On the floor in front of him lay the motionless form of Willem Korvan. The body was stiff with rigor mortis, and held straight by the long-bladed flambergé still sheathed in him from his stomach to the base of his neck.

Marek sighed at the sight of the handsome face made ugly in death. Not only was his mouth twisted into a grimace, lips pulled back from yellowed teeth and gums turning black, but his cheeks had sunk in so far they almost appeared to have been tucked up under his cheekbones.

He turned to the side table against the inside wall and tapped the hardwood top in front of each of the items that had been laid out there. A tiny scrap of raw meat—he'd asked for it to be human flesh, though it didn't necessarily have to be—lay on a fine porcelain plate as big around as Marek's hand. On an identical plate next to it was a shard of bone, jagged on one end, and rounded on the other. It looked like a finger bone. On a square of red velvet sat a loose black onyx gem he'd paid three hundred gold pieces for. A clay pot filled with brackish water sat next to another that contained a handful of dark brown soil traced with gray dust that had been scooped by Marek's own hand from a freshly-turned grave. The last item was a glass vial, corked and sealed with wax.

He picked up the vial first and held it up to one of the whale oil lamps that lit the room. Inside the vial was a clove of garlic that he'd stolen from a rival wizard. That wizard had written, in a delicate and minute hand, an odd little poem on the tiny clove. It was written in Draconic and held power that Marek had waited more than four years to bring to bear.

"I don't think he really knew exactly what it would do," Marek said in a quiet, calm voice, directed at the dead body of Willem Korvan. "Thadat...." He spoke the dead wizard's name with venomous contempt. "They never know what they have until I take it from them."

He looked down at Willem and thought about that.

"You never knew what you had," he said.

Marek frowned and drew a fingernail around the wax seal, breaking it. He pulled out the cork and placed it on the table, then tipped the vial so the garlic clove dropped onto his palm.

"You'll thank me for this later, my boy," Marek whispered, then he bit the clove in half and swallowed what was in his mouth without chewing it. The little nugget of garlic would stay in his stomach, lodged there to soak its power into him for years, even decades. "And this one is for you."

Marek sank to one knee, enduring the pain in his hip and ignoring the popping of his joints. He dropped the remaining half of the garlic clove into Willem's open mouth. With a deep breath, he climbed back to his feet.

"What next?" he breathed.

In answer to his own question, Marek picked up the onyx gem and turned back to the corpse. Once again he struggled down to one knee. He had to force the stone into Willem's mouth, sliding it up under his teeth and forcing it past his bloated, dry tongue.

"A special stone, for a special boy," the Thayan whispered.

He looked up at the table and sighed, smiling. He should have had the black firedrake—the runt he'd kept for himself as a personal servant—place the material components on the floor next to the body, so he wouldn't have to keep kneeling and standing.

He stood, and retrieved the two bowls. Kneeling again, he dipped two fingers into the grave dirt and drew a short line on Willem's bare chest. He went back for more dirt, then more and more as he drew vile sigils across the corpse's pale flesh. When he was done, he poured the water over the dusty symbols. The water soaked into the grave dirt, adding just the touch of chaos necessary to bend the evil runes into their most potent configuration.

Marek stood and looked down at the body—it was just right. Everything was perfect.

He began one of two simultaneous spells, the incantations wrapped together in a way that tested even his experienced tongue. He paused only as long as it took to swallow the sliver of raw meat. His fingers traced intricate patterns in the air, the shard of bone pressed against his left palm with his middle finger. When the bone dissolved into dust, he dropped both hands to his sides.

Still chanting the interwoven necromancies, Marek bent at the waist and wrapped a hand around the hilt of the flambergé. With one swift motion, he pulled it free. The precise moment that the tip of the blade left Willem's cold flesh, his body jerked and his bulging, vacant eyes rolled around in their sockets.

Still holding the extraordinary sword, Marek stepped back, and let Willem—or to be more precise, the creature that Willem had become—roll onto its belly and vomit out the desiccated black gemstone.

"Stand, thrall," Marek ordered.

The creature struggled to its feet, its whole body shaking. It looked down at itself, naked and pale, the lightning that flashed in the window playing over the sword wound that no longer bled. Marek could see its eyes focus, and a dim beginning of sentience returned to its gaze.

"That's right," Marek said, letting a wide grin spread across his face. "You're no zombie to be made to dig and claw at mud, my boy."

The creature looked at its creator, its smoldering eyes running up the wavy length of the blade and stopping on Marek's grinning face.

"Yes," the Thayan said, taking a step closer to the hunched, naked undead wretch. "You know me. You know your master."

Recognition flooded into the creature's eyes all at once, to be replaced a moment later with impotent rage, then a desperate realization of what had become of it.

"Good morning, my boy," Marek Rymüt said, then he started to laugh.

The creature grunted, its lips still pulled away from its teeth in a terrible grimace. It lifted its sunken face, skin stretched tight and so pale it was almost green, up to the ceiling, to the lightning outside.

Marek laughed.

The thing that had once been Willem Korvan screamed.

Marek didn't stop laughing, and his creation didn't stop screaming, for a very long time.

To be concluded in
Scream of Stone
June 2007

THE WATERCOURSE TRILOGY

THE NEW YORK TIMES *BEST-SELLING AUTHOR*
PHILIP ATHANS

A MAN CONSUMED BY OBSESSION...
DRIVEN BY AN OVERWHELMING VISION OF
WHAT MIGHT BE.

THE WIZARD
Pledged to the Red Wizards of Thay from boyhood, he will do anything
for anyone who can give him more power.

THE SENATOR
A genasi, he has fought his way up from the gutter and will never go back.

THE MAN
A master builder, he walks the coast of Faerûn, and the waves whisper to
him of a mighty work, a task worthy of his talents.

WHISPER OF WAVES
November 2005

LIES OF LIGHT
September 2006

SCREAM OF STONE
June 2007

For more information visit **www.wizards.com**

R.A. SALVATORE'S WAR OF THE SPIDER QUEEN

THE NEW YORK TIMES BEST-SELLING SAGA OF THE DARK ELVES

DISSOLUTION BOOK I

RICHARD LEE BYERS

While their whole world is changing around them, four dark elves struggle against different enemies. Yet their paths will lead them all to the most terrifying discovery in the long history of the drow.

INSURRECTION BOOK II

THOMAS M. REID

A hand-picked team of drow adventurers begin a journey through the treacherous Underdark, all the while surrounded by the chaos of war. Their path will take them through the heart of darkness and shake the Underdark to its core.

CONDEMNATION BOOK III

RICHARD BAKER

The search for answers to Lloth's silence uncovers only more complex questions, allowing doubt and frustration to test the boundaries of already tenuous relationships.

EXTINCTION BOOK IV

LISA SMEDMAN

For even a small group of drow, trust is the rarest commodity of all. When the expedition prepares for a return to the Abyss, what little trust there is crumbles under a rival goddess's hand.

ANNIHILATION BOOK V

PHILIP ATHANS

Old alliances have been broken and new bonds have been formed. While some finally embark for the Abyss itself, others stay behind to serve a new mistress – a goddess with plans of her own.

RESURRECTION BOOK VI

PAUL S. KEMP

The Spider Queen has been asleep for a long time, leaving the Underdark to suffer war and ruin. But if she finally returns, will things get better... or worse?

For more information visit **www.wizards.com**